FINCH

JEFF VANDERMEER

CORVUS

First published in the United States of America in 2009 by Underland Press.

This paperback edition first published in Great Britain in 2011
by Corvus, an imprint of Atlantic Books Ltd.

Copyright © Jeff VanderMeer, 2009

The moral right of Jeff VanderMeer to be identified as the author
of this work has been asserted in accordance with the
Copyright, Designs and Patents act of 1988.

All quotes in *Finch* from *Shriek: An Afterword* are copyright © Tor Books, 2006
and are used by permission.

All rights reserved. No part of this publication may be
reproduced, stored in a retrieval system, or transmitted in any form
or by any means, electronic, mechanical, photocopying, recording,
or otherwise, without the prior permission of both the copyright
owner and the above publisher of this book.

GREENWICH LIBRARIES

~~WO~~ EL

3 8028 02028492 0

Askews & Holts	06-Jul-2011
AF	£7.99
3239543	

This is a work of fiction. All characters, organizations, and events
portrayed in this novel are either products of the author's imagination
or are used fictitiously.

1 3 5 7 9 [illegible] 2

A CIP catalogue record for this book is available from
the British Library.

ISBN: 978 1 84887 478 7

Printed in Great Britain by CPI Bookmarque, Croydon

Corvus
An imprint of Atlantic Books Ltd
Ormond House
26-27 Boswell Street
London WC1N 3JZ

www.corvus-books.co.uk

ROYAL BOROUGH OF GREENWICH

Follow us on twitter  @greenwichlibs

ELTHAM
CENTRE
LIBRARY
0203 915 4347

Please return by the last date shown

EL 3/2020

12 NOV 2021

Thank you! To renew, please contact any
Royal Greenwich library or renew online or by phone
www.better.org.uk/greenwichlibraries
24hr renewal line 01527 852385

Heavy with shadows
and dark as sin.'
JOE R. LANSDALE

GREENWICH LIBRARIES
3 8028 02028492 0

JEFF VANDERMEER is the winner of two World Fantasy Awards and has been shortlisted for the Hugo Award, the Bram Stoker Award and the Philip K. Dick Award. *Finch* was nominated for the World Fantasy Award, the Nebula Award and the Locus Award.

FOR ANN & FOR THE REBEL ANGELS:

Victoria Blake

John Coulthart

John Klima

Tessa Kum

Dave Larsen

Michael Moorcock

Michael Phillips

Cat Rambo

Matt Staggs

*"When they give you things ask yourself why.
When you're grateful to them for giving you the things
you should have anyway, ask yourself why."*

—Lady in Blue, rebel broadcast

MONDAY

Interrogator: What did you see then?

Finch: Nothing. I couldn't see anything.

I: Wrong answer.

[howls and screams and sobbing]

I: Had you ever met the Lady in Blue before?

F: No, but I'd heard her before.

I: Heard her where?

F: On the fucking radio station, that's where.

[garbled comment, not picked up]

F: It's her voice. Coming up from the underground. People say.

I: So what did you see, Finch?

F: Just the stars. Stars. It was night.

I: I can ask you this same question for hours, Finch.

F: You wanted me to say I saw her. I said I saw her! I said it, damn you.

I: There is no Lady in Blue. She's just a propaganda myth from the rebels.

F: I saw her. On the hill. Under the stars.

I: What did this apparition say to you, Finch? What did this vision *say*?

1

Finch, at the apartment door, breathing heavy from five flights of stairs, taken fast. The message that'd brought him from the station was already dying in his hand. Red smear on a limp circle of green fungal paper that had minutes before squirmed clammy. Now he had only the door to pass through, marked with the gray caps' symbol.

239 Manzikert Avenue, apartment 525.

An act of will, crossing that divide. Always. Reached for his gun, then changed his mind. Some days were worse than others.

A sudden flash of his partner Wyte, telling him he was compromised, him replying, "I don't have an opinion on that." Written on a wall at a crime scene: *Everyone's a collaborator. Everyone's a rebel.* The truth in the weight of each.

The doorknob cold but grainy. The left side rough with light green fungus.

Sweating under his jacket, through his shirt. Boots heavy on his feet.

Always a point of no return, and yet he kept returning.

I am not a detective. I am not a detective.

Inside, a tall, pale man dressed in black stood halfway down the hall, staring into a doorway. Beyond him, a dark room. A worn bed. White sheets dull in the shadow. Didn't look like anyone had slept there in months. Dusty floor. Even before he'd started seeing Sintra, his place hadn't looked this bad.

The Partial turned and saw Finch. "Nothing in that room, Finch. It's all in here." He pointed into the doorway. Light shone out, caught the dark glitter of the Partial's skin where tiny fruiting bodies had taken hold. Uncanny left eye in a gaunt face. Always twitching.

Moving at odd angles. Pupil a glimmer of blue light at the bottom of a dark well. Fungal.

"Who are you?" Finch asked.

The Partial frowned. "I'm—"

Finch brushed by the man without listening, got pleasure out of the push of his shoulder into the Partial's chest. The Partial, smelling like sweet rotting meat, walked in behind him.

Everything was golden, calm, unknowable.

Then Finch's eyes adjusted to the light from the large window and he saw: living room, kitchen. A sofa. Two wooden chairs. A small table, an empty vase with a rose design. Two bodies lying on the pull rug next to the sofa. One man, one gray cap without legs.

Finch's boss Heretic stood framed by the window. Wearing his familiar gray robes and gray hat. Finch had never learned the creature's real name. The series of clicks and whistles sounded like "heclereticalic" so Finch called him "Heretic." Highly unusual to see Heretic during the day.

"Finch," Heretic said. "Where's Wyte?" The wetness of its moist glottal attempt at speech made most humans uncomfortable. Finch tried hard to pretend the ends of all the words were there. A skill hard learned.

"Wyte couldn't come. He's busy."

Heretic stared at Finch. A question in his eyes. Finch looked to the side. Away from the liquid green pupils and yellow where there should be white. Wyte had been sick off and on for a long time. Finch knew from what, but didn't want to. Didn't want to get into it with Heretic.

"What's the situation?" Finch asked.

Heretic smiled: rows and rows of needle lines set into a face a little like a squished-in shark's snout. Finch couldn't tell if the lines were gills or teeth, but they seemed to flutter and breathe a little. Wyte said he'd seen tiny creatures in there, once. *Each time, a new nightmare.* Another encounter to haunt Finch's sleep.

"Two dead bodies," Heretic said.

"Two bodies?"

"One and a half, technically," the Partial said, from behind Finch.

Heretic laughed. A sound like dogs being strangled.

"Did the victims live in the apartment?" Finch asked, knowing the answer already.

"No," the Partial said. "They didn't."

Finch turned briefly toward the Partial, then back to Heretic.

Heretic stared at the Partial and he shut up, began to creep around the living room taking pictures with his eye.

"No one lived here," Heretic said. "According to our records no one has lived here for over a year."

"Interesting," Finch said. Didn't interest him. Nothing interested him. It bothered him. Especially that the Partial felt comfortable enough to answer a question meant for Heretic.

The curtains had faded from the sun. Tears in the sofa like knife wounds. The vase looked like someone had started a small fire inside it. Stage props for two deaths.

Was it significant that the window was open? For some reason he didn't want to ask if one of them had opened it. Fresh air, with just a hint of the salt smell from the bay.

"Who reported this?" Finch asked.

"An energy surge came from this location," Heretic said. "We felt it. Then spore cameras confirmed it."

Energy surge? What kind of energy?

Finch tried to imagine the rows and rows of living receivers underground, miles of them if rumor held true. Trying to process trillions of images from all over the city. *How could they possibly keep up?* The hope of every citizen.

"Do you know the . . . source?" Finch asked. Didn't know if he understood what Heretic was telling him.

"There is no trace of it now. The apartment is cold. There are just these bodies."

"How does that help me?" he wanted to say.

Finch usually dealt with theft, domestic abuse, illegal gatherings. Flirted with investigating rebel activity, but turned that over to the Partials if necessary. Tried to make sure it wasn't necessary. For everyone's sake.

Murder only if it was the usual. Crimes of passion. Revenge. This didn't look like either. If it was murder.

"Anyone live in the apartments next door?"

"Not any more," the Partial replied. "They all left, oddly enough, soon after these two . . . arrived."

"Which means they made a sound." *Or sounds.*

"I'll interrogate anyone left in the building after we finish here," the Partial said.

What a pleasure that'll be for them.

Still, Finch didn't volunteer to do it. Not yet. Maybe after. Not much worse than door-to-door interviews in unfriendly places. Many didn't believe his job should exist.

"What do you think, Finch?" Heretic asked. Just a hint of mischief in that voice. Laced with it. Just enough to catch the nuance.

I think I just walked in the door a few minutes ago.

The bodies lay next to each other, beside the sofa.

Finch frowned. "I've never seen anything quite like it."

The man lay on his side, left hand stretched out toward the gray cap's hand. The gray cap lay facedown, arms flopped out at right angles.

"Might be a foreigner. From the clothes."

The man could've been forty-five or fifty, with dark brown hair, dark eyebrows, and a beard that appeared to be made from tendrils of fungus. That wasn't unusual. But his clothes were. He wore a blue shirt long out of fashion. Strange, tight-fitting long pants. Dirty black boots.

"He's not from the city," Heretic said. Again, an inflection that bothered Finch. A statement or a question?

What's on his mind?

Finch squatted beside the bodies. Took out his useless pen and his useless pad of paper. Above him, the Partial leaned over to take a picture.

The dead gray cap looked like every other gray cap. Except for the one glaring lack.

"I don't know what caused the injury to the other one, sir."

I don't know what caused the leg situation.

"When we find out," Heretic said, "we will be just as understated."

The exposed cross section, cut almost precisely at the waist, fascinated Finch. He almost forgot himself, poked at the tissue with his pen.

The cut had been so clean, so precise, that there was no tearing. No hemorrhaging. Finch could see layers. Gray. Yellow. Green. A core of dark red. (A question he was too cautious to ask: *Was it always that dark, or only in death?*) Within the core, Finch saw a hint of organs.

"Is this . . . normal?" Finch asked Heretic.

"Normal?"

"The lack of blood, I mean, sir," Finch said.

Gray caps bled. Finch knew that. Not like a stream or a gout, even when you cut them deep, but a steady drip from a leaky faucet. Puncture wounds healed almost immediately. It took a long time and a lot of patience to kill a gray cap.

"No, it's not normal." The humid weight of Heretic was at his side now. A smell like garbage and burnt glass. Made him nauseous.

"None of this is normal," the Partial ventured. Ignored.

Finch looked up at Heretic. From that angle: the pale wattled skin of Heretic's long throat.

"Do you know who . . ." Finch hesitated. Gray caps didn't like being called "gray caps," but Finch couldn't pronounce the word they did use. *Farseneeni* or *fanaarcensitii*? The Partial circled them, blinking pictures through his fungal eye.

"Do you know who that is?" Finch said finally, pointing at the dead gray cap.

Heretic made a sound like something popping. "No. Not familiar to us. We cannot *see* him," and Finch understood he meant something other than just looking out a window.

"Have you . . . ?" Couldn't say the whole sentence. Too ridiculous. Terrifying. At the same time. *Have you eaten some of his flesh and picked clean the memories?*

But Heretic had been around humans long enough to know what he meant. "We tried it. Nothing that made sense."

For a second, Finch relaxed. Forgot Heretic could send him, Sintra, anybody he knew, to the work camps.

"If you couldn't decipher it, how will I?"

Then went stiff. Richard Dorn, a good detective, had questioned Heretic too closely. Nine months to die.

A bullet to the head. In that case.

But the gray cap said only, "With your fresh eyes, maybe you will have better luck."

Heretic pulled a pouch out of his robes, opened it. Finch rose, stood to the side as Heretic sprinkled a fine green powder over both bodies. Could've done it using his own supply, but Heretic enjoyed doing it. For some reason.

"You know what to do," Heretic said.

In time, a memory bulb would emerge from both corpses' heads. Did the *fanaarcensitii* rely too much on what made them comfortable? No autopsies, just mushrooms. But also hardly any experts left to perform them.

Nausea crept back into Finch's throat. "But I've never. Not a gray cap. I mean, not one of your people."

"We don't bite." The grin on that impossible face grew wide and wider. The laughter again, worse.

Finch laughed back, weakly.

"Write down whatever you encounter, whether you understand it or not."

Mercifully, Heretic looked away. "A gray cap and a man. Dead in such a manner. We need to know *everything*."

"Yessir," Finch said. He couldn't keep the grimace off his face.

Heretic seemed to take it for a smile. As he walked past on his way to the door, he patted Finch's elbow. Finch shivered. A touch like wet, dead leaves sewn together and stuffed with meat.

"Report in the morning," Heretic said. "Report and report and report, Finch." The laughter again.

Then Heretic was gone. The hallway shadows ate him up, the apartment door opening and closing.

Finch could hear his own breathing. Shallow. The sudden panicked drumming of his heart. The butterfly blinks of the Partial, still snapping photographs.

Took a breath. A second. Closed his eyes.

A sunny day by the river. A picnic lunch. A tree with shade. Long, cool grass. With Sintra.

2

No obvious bullet or stab wounds. No tattoos or other marks. Grunting with the effort, Finch turned the man over for a second. He seemed heavier than he should be. Skin warm, the flesh solid. From the position of the arms, Finch thought they might be broken. A discoloration at the edge of the man's mouth. Dried blood? When Finch was done, the man settled back into position as if he'd been there a hundred years.

No point checking the gray cap. Their skin didn't retain marks or burns or stab wounds. Anything like that sealed over. Besides, the cause of the gray cap's death was obvious. Wasn't it? Still, he didn't want to assume murder. Yet.

Out of the four "murders" in his sector over the past year, two had been suicides and one had been natural causes. The fourth solved in a day.

Disappearances were another subject altogether.

He stood. Looked down at the tableau formed by the dead. Something about it. Almost posed. Almost staged. But also: the man's neck, half-hidden by the shirt collar. Was it . . . twisted? Who could tell with the gray cap. Impossibly long, smooth, gray neck. (*Did that mean Heretic was old, this one young?*) But also torqued.

Finch glanced up at the tired, sagging ceiling. About ten feet.

"They look like," Finch said. "They look like they both *fell*."

Could that be the sound the neighbors heard?

"The spore camera's first shot is of them on the floor," the Partial said.

Finch had forgotten him.

Turned, stared at the Partial. The Partial stared back. Taking Finch's photo with each blink.

"I could . . ."

"What?" the Partial said. "You could what?"

I could tear out your eye with my bare hands. Not a thought he'd seen coming.

"You know what I think?" the Partial said.

Finch tamped down on his irritation. Tried to remember that, in a way, none of the Partials were more than six years old. Disaffected youths no matter what their age. All pale. Or made pale. Humans who'd gotten fungal infections and liked it, Truff help them. Got an adrenaline rush from heightened powers of sight. Enhanced by fungal drugs autogenerated inside the eye. Pumped into the brain. In a sense, their eye was always looking back at them.

I'll never know what you think. Not in a million years.

"You *volunteered* for that," Finch said. Pointed at the Partial's eye. "That makes you crazy. So I don't need to know what you think."

The Partial snickered. "I've heard it all before. And you'll never know what you're missing . . . But here's what I think, whether you want it or not. That man's not really human. Not really. I should know, right? And something went wrong. And maybe they didn't die here but were, I don't know, moved."

Finch gave the Partial a long glance. Turned to kneel again by the man's body. The second half of what the Partial had said made less sense than the first.

"Just do your job." *I'll do mine.*

The Partial fell silent. Hurt? Seduced by something new to click?

Finch really didn't care. Something had caught his attention. Two fingers of the man's left hand. Curled tight into the palm. Grit or sand under the fingernails. Finch got to his knees, leaned forward, took the man's hand in his. The warmth of it surprised him, the green spores already ghosting into the flesh. He pried the fingers back. Revealed a ragged piece of paper. A pulse-pounding moment of excitement.

Then he pulled it out. Released the fingers. Let the arm fall. Shielding the paper from the Partial with his body.

Normal paper, not fungal. Old and stained. Torn from a book? He unfolded it. Two words, written hurriedly, in black ink: *Never Lost.* And below that some gibberish that looked something like *bellum omnium contra omnes.* Self-contained, or once part of a longer message?

Definitely torn from a book. On the back a printed sentence fragment, "the future can hold when the past holds ambiguity such as this," and a symbol. Somehow familiar to Finch. Although he didn't know from where.

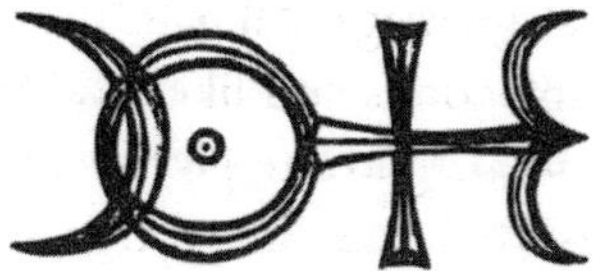

Stuck the paper in his boot before the Partial could blink that he'd found something. Got up. Pulled gloves from his jacket pocket and put them on. Opened the pouch at his belt.

Heretic had forgotten the preservatives, but would blame Finch if it wasn't done. Corpses didn't last long otherwise. Within forty-eight hours, you'd be breathing them, as the spores did their work.

Carefully, he sprinkled a blue powder across both corpses. Not spores this time, but tiny fruiting bodies. The powder smelled like smoke from the camps to the south. Or the camps smelled like the powder. Pointless to wear the gloves after the hundreds of fungal toxins and experiments that had been released into the air. The millions of floating spore-eyes. Yet still he did it.

Blue mingled with green. The green disappeared as he watched, colonized by the blue. The two bodies would not decay now. They would linger, suspended, until Finch returned to collect their memories.

". . . and know you don't want to eat the memories," the Partial said to Finch's back. Sounding triumphant.

Finch's thoughts had been so far away he'd missed the first part.

"Is that all?" Wanted to laugh.

Did they talk this way together in the barracks near the camps where the gray caps housed them like weapons? Spewing out each day and night like black ants. Foraging on the flesh of the city. Observers and security both.

"You're afraid of change," the Partial said. "Of being changed. That's why you hate me."

Swiveled abruptly in his crouch, hand on his gun. Met the Partial's corrupted gaze.

"Is that all?" Finch repeated. "I mean, are you done with your picture-taking?"

No skill when every blink was an image. No honor in a perpetual voyeurism. A kind of treason against your own kind. "It warps the privacy of your own life," Wyte had said once, as if he knew. "Permanent occupation. I wouldn't want to live that way." Yet now Wyte did. And so did Finch. In a sense.

"I'm never done," the Partial said. "And if you've got a past, you should be worried. They'll work through all the records some day. Maybe they'll find you."

Funny thing is, Partial, Heretic already knows my past. Most of it. And he doesn't give a fuck. That's not who I'm worried about.

Wanted to say it but didn't. Unsnapped the clasp on his holster. The fungal gun trembled there like a live thing. Wet. Dripping. Useless against a gray cap. Very useful against a Partial. *Still human, no matter how much you pretend.*

"Get the fuck out of here."

"I see everything," the Partial said. "*Everything.*"

"Yes," Finch said, "but that's unavoidable, isn't it?"

The Partial stared at Finch. Seemed about to say something. Bit down on it, hard. Walked out into the hall. Slammed the door behind him.

Leaving Finch alone with the bodies.

* * *

Now Finch can see the frailty death has lent them. Now Finch can see the vulnerability. The way the light uses them in the same way it uses him. He walks to the window. Looks out across the damaged face of Ambergris.

Six years and I can't recognize a goddamn thing from before.

Harsh blue sprawl of the bay, bled from the River Moth. Carved from nothing. The first thing the gray caps did when they Rose, flooding Ambergris and killing thousands. Now the city, riddled through with canals, is like a body that was once drowned. Parts bleached, parts bloated. Metal and stone for flesh. Places that stick out and places that barely touch the surface.

In the foreground of the bay stands the scaffolding for the two tall towers still being built by the gray caps. A rough pontoon bridge reaches out to them, an artificial island surrounding the base. The scaffolding rises twenty feet above the highest tower. Hard to know if they are almost complete or will take a hundred years more. Great masses of green fungus cling to the tops. It makes the towers look shaggy, almost as if they had fur, were flesh and blood. *A smell like oil and sawdust and frying meat.* At dusk each day the gray caps lead a work force from the camps south of the city. All night, the sounds of hammering and construction. Emerald lights moving like slow stars. Screams of injury or punishment. To what purpose? No one knows. While along the lip of the bay, monstrous fungal cathedrals rise under cover of darkness, replacing the old, familiar architecture. Skyline like a jagged wound.

Twenty years of civil war. Six years of the gray caps.

To Finch's left, southwest: smudges of smoke, greasy and gray, above the distant mottled spectacle of the Spit, an island made of lashed-together boats. A den for spies. A sanctuary for the desperate and the lawless.

Beyond the Spit, the silhouette of the two living domes covering the detention camps. Broken by the smoke, hidden by debris. Built over a valley of homes. Built atop the remains of the military factories that had allowed the two great mercantile companies, House Hoegbotton and the invading House Frankwrithe & Lewden, to dream of empire, to destroy each other. And the city with them. Finch had fought for Hoegbotton. *Once upon a time.*

Between the domes, the fiery green glitter and minarets of the Religious Quarter, occupied by the remnants of native tribes. Adapting. Struggling. Destined someday to be wiped out. He can see the exposed crater at the top of the Truffidian Cathedral. *Cracked. All the prayers let out. Nothing left.*

To Finch's right, on the north shore: the Hoegbotton & Frankwrithe Zone. Huge tendrils of reddish-orange fungus vein into the rocks lining the water. A green haze obscures any view of what might be left on the north shore. Six years ago, the HFZ had just been northern Ambergris: wild, yes, but not infected. Then, under sustained attack by the gray caps, the rebel army had retreated there. So much heavy armor, munitions, and ordnance had gone in, along with twenty thousand soldiers, that it is hard for Finch to believe all of it could just vanish or molder. Yet, apparently, it had. They'd gone in and the gray caps had created the Zone around them. Only the rebel commander they called the Lady in Blue and some of her soldiers had escaped the trap.

Once, the HFZ had grown in size every day. Now, it has stopped, covers about ten square miles. Almost every citizen can see it. For all the good that did. *Will the rebels return?* is the question everyone asks, even now. When the wind is strange—gusting this way and that without purpose—great glittering particles from the north drift orange and purple and blue across the bay into Ambergris. Even the gray caps don't enter the HFZ except by proxy. Content to let the remnants of the rebels wander through a toxic fungal stew, goes the theory. Almost like another camp, without fences or guards.

Except, no one comes out of the HFZ.

Beyond the towers, beyond the bay, the far shore of the River Moth. Distant. Unattainable. Beyond that, although Finch can't see it, just feels it: the eastern-most edge of the Kalif's empire, the Stockton Commonwealth to the south, the Morrow Protectorate to the north. Between them and Finch: security zones. Blockades. Set up by the surrounding countries. All three as determined as the gray caps that no one gets out of Ambergris. Even as they send in their spies to steal the city's secrets.

Finch turns away from the window. It leaves him sad and cold and frightened. The towers especially. What will happen when the gray caps have finished them?

A view like that could drive a person mad.

3

"*When the time comes, right, Finch?*"

Back at the station, which used to be Hoegbotton & Sons' headquarters. High ceilings. Hints of gold leaf and mosaic. Dull light from tiny round windows set in rows across both side walls. A tortured light that never gave any hint of the weather outside. Sometimes in the early morning and late afternoon they had to use old lanterns. The chandeliers had been ripped out long ago.

Back at his desk with the other detectives. The must of fungal rot from the green strip of carpet running from the front door down the middle. The whole back of the room hidden by a curtain. Smell of bad coffee from the table that also housed their only typewriter. Shoved up against the far wall. Next to the holding cell.

Ten desks. Seven detectives. Skinner, Gustat, Blakely, Dapple, Albin, and Wyte furiously scritching away on their notepads with sharp pencils. Some on the phone. All of them like schoolboys in an incomprehensible class. None of them likely to ask questions of the teacher.

Only a weak hello when Finch had walked in. Too much effort. Not yet over the paranoid morning jitters. Ever more difficult to know what to say. How to act. They all assumed the gray caps spied on them. Difficult to remember all day long. Especially when strange things happened with just enough irregularity to make them think *that was the last time*. The air pungent with old and new sweat. Laced with some underlying funk that was almost sweet.

Albin, just off the phone, out of the corner of his mouth: "I'm not risking my life for a lost dog. Too many Partials there. Besides, it's an old Hoegbotton neighborhood." Albin, the Frankwrithe & Lewden man. Finch might've shot at him back during the war.

Former scientist. One of the few not killed by the gray caps or snatched by foreign powers in the chaos of the Rising.

Finch's mood had soured on the way back to the station. A tortuous route. The gray caps had banned bicycles and motored vehicles four years ago. Too many suicide bombings by rebel sympathizers. Not much fuel anyway, and no one outside the city willing to resupply, even on the black market. Too dangerous. And few alternatives since the horses had been eaten long ago.

Instead, makeshift bridges over the canals. Through a sector where a lot of gray cap buildings had gone up, scrambling the landscape. Changes didn't correspond to any map. Sliced through existing apartment complexes, divided or blocked streets. Displayed an arrogance about the way things had been and were now that angered Finch.

Then a mob to avoid at the corner of Albumuth and Lake, when he'd almost made it back. One of the huge blood-red drug mushrooms hadn't yet released the morning ration. Not Finch's problem. But the addicts were mad. They wanted their fix. *Wanted out.* They stood beneath the slow-breathing dead-white gills waiting for the purple nodules that also fed them. *Wanted oblivion. A nice trip into waves of light and a past that didn't include dead bodies and nightmares.*

Maybe someday he'd join them. Instead, another rickety bridge over another canal. Had looked down at his frowning reflection in the silver-gray water and hadn't recognized it. Broad shoulders. Still muscular but losing some of it. Too much alcohol. Not enough nutrients in the gray caps' food. The man lingering in the water seemed at least forty-five, not forty. The hooded eyes. The paleness of the face. Wavery. Indistinct. Never in focus.

"When the time comes, right, Finch?"

"Sure, Wyte," Finch said. "When the time comes."

"You'll know what to do." The voice, once so deep and gravelly, had changed since Finch had first met Wyte. Become soft and liquid, lighter yet thicker.

"I'll know what to do."

The ritual conversation.

Ritual had a purpose. Ritual cordoned off fear. Ritual made the abnormal ordinary. The memory hole beside each of the desks. The deep green vein running the length of Wyte's arm. Pushing up ridge-like against the fabric of Wyte's long sleeve. Like the green carpet leading back to the curtains and what lay beyond.

Finch took his gun from its holster. Recoiled from the touch of the grip.

"For Truff's sake," Finch said. Laid it on his desk with a squelch.

The gun had been issued by the gray caps. Dark green exoskeleton, soft interior. Its guts stained his hand. Reloading didn't seem like an option. It had been seeping a lot lately.

"I wonder if it's dying on me," Finch said. To Wyte, who sat at the desk to his left.

Should I have been feeding it?

Wyte grunted. Reflexively writing up reports on nothing in particular. Lost husbands. Unidentifiable corpses. Vandalism. Finch had cases, too, but nothing that couldn't wait.

"Hate these things," he said, again to Wyte. Again, to indifference.

Heard Blakely muttering to Gustat: ". . . they're saying that we're addicted to a special mushroom that grows out of our brains." Gustat chuckled but it wasn't funny. Rumors could get a detective killed by some desperate citizen. *Any excuse that didn't slip through the fingers.*

Finch rummaged in a drawer. Found a worn handkerchief. It predated the war. He'd gotten it from an expensive clothing store further up the boulevard. Didn't know why he kept it. Luck? Grimacing, he picked up the gun with the handkerchief. Shoved the thing into a space under his desk. Next to the box with the ceremonial sword his father had given him. Brought back from the Kalif's empire twenty years before. Wrapped in cloth. Finch could always get to it in a pinch. Made him feel perversely safer knowing it was there. In its gleaming scabbard.

"I'd rather get shot than use that gun," Finch said, too loud. Not sure if he meant it.

Gustat and Blakely, joined at the hip, looked up, glared. Both had a flushed look. Like they'd been drinking.

"Shut up, Finch," Blakely said.

"Yeah, shut up," Gustat echoed. Fiercely.

This caused Dapple to bring a case file so close to his eyes it hid his face. Dapple was the worst of them. He'd been an artist once. Landscape painter. Watercolors. Popular with the tourists. No market for that now. No landscapes to speak of that you could spend hours painting without taking a bullet for your troubles. Sure to become a druggie, or a creature of the gray caps in his cringing way. At least Gustat and Blakely, even though they annoyed Finch, still had their wits about them.

Almost as if to cover for Finch, Wyte asked, "So, Finchy, just how bad was it?" "Finchy" sounded closer to his real last name, so Wyte often called him that. To avoid slipping up.

Finch turned toward Wyte. Hadn't wanted to. No telling what he looked like.

Wyte: a tall man, late forties, with a handsome face, powerful shoulders and chest. Tattered olive suit. Eyes gray. A spark of green colonizing the brown of each pupil. Right temple: a purple birthmark that hadn't been there yesterday. Smelled of cigarette smoke to cover the stench of mushrooms. Even though cigs were hard to come by. Once, he could have entered a crowded bar and all the women would have found a way to stare at him.

"A double," Finch said. "In an abandoned apartment. One gray cap. One male human." Then told Wyte the rest.

"Dancing lessons gone terribly wrong," Wyte said. His grin only manifested on the left side of his mouth.

Skinner, next to Wyte, hazarded a snicker. But Skinner snickered at everything. Finch didn't find it funny. He was still seeing the bodies. Skinner expressed too much zeal pursuing cases that involved the rebels. Why hadn't Skinner become a Partial?

"This is nothing good, Wyte." *Good* equaled *will go away quickly*. This could linger.

Wyte, as if realizing his mistake: "Do you want me to take the memory bulbs?"

"No thanks."

Who knew what a memory bulb would do to Wyte in his state? Finch didn't want to find out. The late Richard Dorn had sat at his desk for nine months after the gray caps had forced him to eat a memory bulb despite his wasting disease. Dead. Turning into a tower of emerald mold. The desk sat in a corner now, abandoned, a smudge on the seat of the chair.

Worse for suspects kept in the holding cell. Bring in a thief, do the paperwork, then the gray caps decided. Attempted murder? Might be disappeared by morning. Or sent to the camps. Or let off with a fine. The guy Blakely had brought in the other day was still there. Slumped in a corner. Clearly thought his life was over.

Never bring anyone in unless you have to. Unless you're certain.

"Are we in trouble on this one?" Wyte asked. Black patch on his neck, slowly moving. Nails a faint green. A whiff of something toxic.

Not the same kind of trouble.

Finch shrugged. "Who knows?" A routine call could turn into disaster. A disaster could go away overnight.

Wyte leaned back in his chair, hands behind his head. Red stains on the shirt's underarms.

Finch had known Wyte for more than twenty years. They'd fought in the wars together. Known the same people before the Rising. Played darts at the pub. Had drinks. Sudden gut-punching vision: of his girlfriend back then, a slender brunette who'd worked as a nurse. Laughing at some joke Wyte had made one night, the days of Comedian Wyte now long past except for the occasional flare-up that just made it worse.

Some cosmic mistake or cruelty, to work cases together when Finch had once worked for Wyte as a courier for Hoegbotton. Each a reminder to the other of better times. Since then, Wyte's wife Emily had left him. He'd taken up in a crappy apartment just north of the station. Never saw his two daughters. They'd been smuggled out to relatives in Stockton before the Rising. Finch couldn't work out how old they might be now.

Someday Wyte will be a silhouette on the horizon. Someone familiar made distant.

And Wyte sensed it.

"You can help with the fieldwork going forward, Wyte," Finch said. *If you don't become the fieldwork.*

"No problem. Be happy to."

"I'll put my notes in order," Finch said, "and after I use the memory bulbs, we'll start in on it. Tomorrow."

Wyte wasn't listening anymore. Gaze far away. Disengaged. Apocalyptic thoughts? Or maybe he was just registering the inside of the building.

They all conducted an unspoken war against the station. It tried to make them forget its strangeness. They tried not to forget.

Finch turned back to his desk and started sorting through the mess. Hadn't organized it in a week. Hadn't had the energy.

Mirror. Pills to protect against infection. Spore mask for purified breathing. Writing pad. Pencils. Telephone. Broken telephone. Folders on open crimes. Folders on closed crimes. Paper clips across the bottom of drawers. A list he'd made of complaints from people who had called him, thinking he could help. Usually he couldn't.

Maybe once, early on, he had convinced himself he could do some good, sometimes even imagined he was a mole, getting close so he could strike a blow. Imagined he was in it to defend Ambergris from the enemies that surrounded it. Imagined he was protecting ordinary citizens.

But the truth was he'd been tired, had stopped caring. Broken down from too much fighting, too many things connected to his past. And when that spark, that impulse, had returned, it was too late: he was trapped.

"I'm not a detective."

Heretic: "You're whatever we want you to be, now."

If he just left one day, what would happen to Wyte? To his other friends? To Sintra?

And: Did they know about Sintra?

Nothing seemed missing from his desk. Still, a good idea to take stock. Lots of things disappeared during the night, or were replaced by mimics. More than one detective had screamed, picking up a pencil that was not a pencil. Finch took out the piece of paper he'd found in the dead man's hands. Placed it in front of him. What could the words mean? Finch took out a writing pad, scrawled

> *Never Lost.*
> *Bellum omnium contra omnes*

across the top. Stared at the strange symbol. It looked oddly like a baby bird to him.

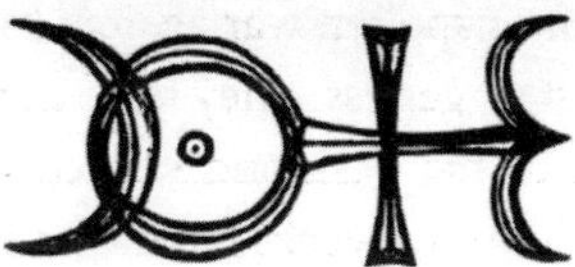

Randomly ripped from a book to write on? Or something more? Abandoned the question. Wrote:

two bodies
fell

Thought about the Partial, daring to contradict Heretic. Heretic's secret amusement. What did that mean? At least he knew what Heretic on the scene meant: the gray cap must suspect the case had some connection to the rebels and their elusive commander, the Lady in Blue. She who was now larger than the city and yet not of the city. Most saw her hand in any act that seemed to cause the gray caps grief. Although such acts of resistance seemed rarer and rarer. Some thought she didn't exist. Or was dead.

The trapped rebel soldiers. The Lady in Blue.

Was the fate of either better or worse than his?

* * *

Finch sees again, back across six long years, the columns of tanks and infantry in retreat, traveling through the city toward the north. Recognizes with hindsight that the path they took had been chosen by the gray caps. Forced by the rising water.

Distant explosions had split the air as the gray caps attacked stragglers at the end of the column. Even then, small-arms fire no longer registered with Finch unless it was close by.

Despite the risk, many people had come out to watch the rebels. From the roadside. From balconies. Peering out of windows reinforced with metal bars. To bear witness to the rumbling tread of the tanks. To remember the faces of the troops: pale and dark, old and young and middle-aged. Beneath green helmets with the intertwined H&S/F&L insignia that rankled so many. Armed with automatic weapons, bayonets, knives. Most in uniform. Many damaged. A welter of bandages on heads, legs, arms, that hid evidence of strange fungal wounds.

One man's face held Finch's attention. Salt-and-pepper beard, creases in his forehead, wrinkles that made him look as if he were squinting. A red patch on his cheek. Body slumped, then tensed, against the lurching of the tank. A gaunt hand clutching his Lewden rifle, knuckles prominent. Gaze turned forward, as if unwilling to acknowledge the present.

Which had made Finch realize again that these men and women leaving, they were the same ones who had fought one another during more than three decades of the War of the Houses, broken only by armistices, cease-fires, and the dream of empire. The ones who had brought ruination upon Ambergris in so many ways before the Rising.

Yet they were still from Ambergris, of Ambergris, and even Finch felt it in his chest, Wyte standing there beside him with his Emily. Almost as if Ambergris itself was retreating, leaving behind only ghosts and children. But also leaving a perverse giddiness. A sense of celebration at seeing such a mighty force. The retreat portrayed as a new beginning. The lull before the launching of a great offensive.

Even the tanks were part of Ambergris. They'd come out of the eighty-year-old metal deposits found in eastern Ambergris that had catapulted the city out of the past but not yet into the future.

Rebel tanks had two turrets: one pointed ahead, one unseen beneath that pointed at the ground. Specially built to open up and deliver bombs to underground gray cap enclaves. Once, their rough syncopated song had been heard all over the city. Juddered through the ground into the walls of buildings and tunnels alike. Like a kind of defiant echoing growl.

In retreat, though, it was the singing of the troops as they left that Finch heard, their voices ragged over the rumble of the tanks. Patriotic songs composed long centuries before. A refrain that had started as a prayer by the Truffidian monks.

Holy city, majestic, banish your fears.
Arise, emerge from your sleeping years.
Too long have you dwelt in the valley of tears.
We shall restore you with mercy and grace.

City of wounds. City of wounding. For a moment, Finch had felt the urge to climb up onto one of the tanks, to join them in what was then the wilderness of North Ambergris. But Finch wasn't one of them. He'd had no officer to report to. Had bought his own weapon. Off the books, off the record. An Irregular, fighting alongside other Irregulars in his neighborhood. Defending their sisters, brothers, parents, and neighbors against the invaders.

After the last tank had rumbled past, Finch had gone back with Wyte and Emily. To await the next thing. No matter what it might be. *The need to work. To eat. To have shelter.* People were already telling themselves things might still be better under the gray caps than during the War of the Houses, at least. Joked about it. Like you might about a passing storm.

Waiting it out at Wyte's house. By candlelight. Drinking. Laughing nervously. Trying to forget. Finch's father dead almost two years.

Just after midnight: a sound like a giant flame opening up and then winking out. A devastating *whump,* as of something hitting the ground or rising from it. When they looked outside, they'd seen a dome-like haze above the north part of the bay. Green-orange discharge like sunspots. They'd just watched it. Watched it and not known what to say. What to do. Barricaded the house. Spent the rest of the night with weapons within reach.

In the morning, a paralyzing horror. Across the bay, when they slipped out through back alleys to get a clear view: the seething area that became known as the HFZ, and no sign of anyone alive. No sign of the tanks. No messages from the rebel leadership.

Thought but not said: *Abandoned. Gone. On our own.*

Then the realization, as the gray caps began to appear in numbers in the streets, and as their surrogates the Partials began to help occupy the city, that the war was over for now. That each citizen of Ambergris would need to make some kind of peace with the enemy.

Always with the hope sent out across the water toward the HFZ: that the tanks, the men, might come back. Might re-emerge. That the rebels were not dead. Destroyed.

Lost.

4

Mid-afternoon. A soft, wet, sucking sound came from the memory hole beside his desk. Finch shuddered, put aside his notes. A message had arrived.

Some detectives positioned their desks so they could see their memory holes. Finch positioned his desk so he couldn't see it without leaning over. Tried never to look at it when he walked into the station in the morning. Still, the memory hole was better than the dead cat reanimated on Skinner's doorstep, message delivered in screeched rhyming couplets. Or the mushroom that walked onto Dapple's desk, turning itself inside out. To reveal the message.

Exhaled sharply. Peered around the left edge of the desk. Glanced down at the glistening hole. It was about twice the size of a man's fist. Lamprey-like teeth. Gasping, pink-tinged maw. Foul. The green tendrils lining the gullet had pushed up the dirty black spherical pod until it lay atop the mouth.

Finch sat up. Couldn't see it. Just heard its breathing. Which was worse.

The gray caps always called them "message tubes," but the term "memory hole" had stuck. Memory holes allowed the detectives to communicate during the day with their gray cap superiors. Finch had no idea if the memory holes were living creatures or only seemed alive. Fluid leaked out of them sometimes.

Once, impulsive, Finch had crumpled up the wrapper around the remains of his lunch and shoved it down the hole. Lived in fear the rest of the day. But nothing had happened. When he'd thought about it since, it had made him laugh. Heretic, down there, hit in the head with a piece of garbage. Maybe cursing Finch's name.

Now Heretic's message vibrated atop writhing tendrils.

Finch leaned over. Grabbed the pod. Slimy feel. *Sticky.*

Tossed the pod onto his desk. Pulled out a hammer from the same drawer where he kept his limited supply of dormant pods. Split Heretic's pod wide open. Spraying slime.

Beside Finch, Wyte winced, got up for some coffee.

Disgusted, or was it too close to home?

"There's no pretty way to do it, my friends," Finch called out. "Just look away." No one acknowledged him this time. Too usual. Even Finch's refrain.

In amongst the fragments: a few copies of a photograph of the dead man, compliments of the Partial.

And a message.

Pulsing yellow. An egg of living paper. He pulled the egg out of the shattered pod. Began to massage it until it spread out flat. Kept spreading, to Finch's surprise. Then began to unspool. Like a long, wide tongue. And kept on growing.

That was unusual enough for the other detectives to gather round.

"What in the hell is that?" Blakely asked, Gustat beside him. Dapple shyly peeked over Blakely's shoulder. Albin and Skinner were out on a call or they'd have been right there too. Anything to waste time.

"Looks like Heretic's given you a long to-do list," Gustat said. Too young to have known anything but war and the Rising.

Finch said nothing. By now, the pliant paper had grown to drape itself over both sides of Finch's desk, sliding into his lap. Clutched at it. Saw the rows of information in the reed-thin, spidery print common to gray cap documents. He let out a long, deep breath.

"It's the records of everyone who ever lived in the apartment of the double murder I was at this morning. Going back . . ." He checked as the paper finished unspooling. "Going back over a century. More."

Pulse quickening. *How am I supposed to investigate* that?

> MORDEN, JONATHAN, OCCUPANCY 3 MONTHS, 2 DAYS, 11 MINUTES, 5 SECONDS—WORKED IN FOOD DISTRIBUTION IN THE CAMPS . . .

> WILDEN, SARAH, OCCUPANCY 8 MONTHS, 3 DAYS, 2 MINUTES, 45 SECONDS—NEVER LEFT THE APARTMENT EXCEPT FOR GETTING FOOD. HAD THREE CATS. LIKED TO READ . . .

* * *

A sudden panic. Smothered by the past. Lost in it.

Tried to get a grip. Wadded the paper up, pocketed the photographs. While the other detectives gave out nervous laughs. Returned to their desks. Frightened again.

No one wanted this kind of case.

A sudden anger rose in Finch. *Did Heretic really think that this list would be helpful?* It was scaring the shit out of him.

Wyte had been standing behind the others, holding his coffee mug. Loomed now like an actor from backstage, suddenly revealed.

"A lot of information," Wyte said.

Finch glared at him. Hands splattered with yellow and green. "Find me a towel."

Wyte put down his coffee, rummaged in a desk drawer.

> SILVAN, JAMES, OCCUPANCY 15 MONTHS, 3 DAYS, 1 HOUR, 50 MINUTES, 2 SECONDS—COLLABORATOR WITH A SPLINTER REBEL FACTION . . .

> HUGHES, SHANNA, OCCUPANCY 1 MONTH, 2 WEEKS, 3 DAYS, 10 MINUTES, 35 SECONDS—KILLED BY A FUNGAL BOMB . . .

"Maybe they got it from the old bureaucratic quarter?" Wyte whispered out of the side of his mouth as he leaned over to give Finch the towel. Smell of sweat mixed with something sweeter. "Maybe they just copied it down?" Returning to his desk, receding into the background.

"It's half-encrypted with their symbols, Wyte," Finch said. Tried to correct for the disdain in his voice. "It contains surveillance information. They collected it themselves."

From underground. Using a million spore-eye cameras. Somewhere, he knew, in one of a series of images captured by the gray caps: evidence of his past that Heretic didn't know about. *Finch as a Hoegbotton Irregular fighting against Frankwrithe & Lewden in the War of the Houses. Finch standing side by side with F&L soldiers against the gray caps before they Rose.* What he'd done.

Except the gray caps didn't have the time to pore over that many images unless given a good reason. And Finch hadn't. Only Wyte knew the truth.

> GILRISH, MEGHAN, OCCUPANCY 10 MONTHS, 3 WEEKS, 6 DAYS, 14 HOURS, 15 MINUTES, 6 SECONDS—OWNER OF A GROCERY STORE . . .

> BARRAN, GEORGE, OCCUPANCY 2 YEARS, 1 WEEK, 5 DAYS, 7 MINUTES, 18 SECONDS—DIED OF OLD AGE . . .

Finch stared at the first rows of names on the paper. The sheer density of information defeated him.

Kept thinking about the bodies. Saw them lying there on the floor of the apartment. *They dropped in out of thin air.*

Why there?

A riddle wrapped in a puzzle. Perversely comforting, that the memory bulbs might hold the answers.

Never lost.

Bellum omnium contra omnes.

Never lost.

Said it three times under his breath. Wondering if Wyte was staring at him. Still didn't dislodge an answer.

"Well," Finch said, out of the corner of his mouth, "do you know what those words mean? *Bellum omnium contra omnes*?"

But Wyte was done talking to him about the case.

Sometimes the overlay of reality seemed a sham. One day, he would turn a corner on a rubble-strewn street. Pass through an archway into a courtyard. Be back in that other, simpler world. When he worked in the same building but as a Hoegbotton courier. Not as a detective. When he worked for Wyte, not with him.

Am I dead? he thought sometimes, walking down that green carpet he remembered from a different city, a different time. *Am I a ghost?*

Six in the afternoon. Time to leave. He packed Heretic's list in a satchel and holstered his miserable gun. Watched Blakely and Gustat put on spore gas masks "just in case." *Just in case of what?*

Just in case there's one fungus in the whole damn city you haven't been exposed to yet?

A nod. A handshake or two. Muttered goodbyes to Wyte. Then they dispersed. The night shift would arrive soon. Partial patrols outside started in only two hours. Curfew. Gray caps lurking. You rarely saw more than one, but that was one too many. A detective's badge might help or it might not.

The others headed north, up Albumuth. Wyte was a hulking shadow hanging back at the rear. Finch went south, but not home. Not yet. First, he had to pick up the memory bulbs from the crime scene. But he also had decided not to trust the Partial. Wanted to interview some of the residents of 239 Manzikert Avenue himself.

A different route than that morning. Late-afternoon sun like dark gold against brick walls. The street sloped on an incline before following a gentle curve downward. Tight high walls of shoved-together tenements and lofts. Hoegbotton territory, before the Rising. Finch brushed by a man or woman covered up in robes. Another person ducked into a doorway, face made a question mark by an old gas mask that might or might not keep spores out. Stain of blue-green lichen in the gutter. A rancid quality to the air.

Faintest hint of the bay from the cross street. Mostly obscured by mansards and rubble. Glimpse of the two towers. Did the sky match? Or was it darker between the towers? Had a bet going with the other detectives about the purpose of the towers. To dull the fear.

A hint of shadow moved behind him as he rounded a tight corner. It made him cautious. It made him paranoid. He stopped a minute later. Pretended to tie his shoe. Managed a backward glance. Nothing.

Imagined it?

Wouldn't put it past Heretic to have him followed. Or maybe it was just some ragged kid hoping to mug a passerby. As he rose, Finch made sure to pull his jacket back. To show his gun. Such as it was.

239 Manzikert Avenue was a dark vertical slab of stone and wood with blackened filigree balcony railings crawling up the front. Trees

left black leaves and rotting yellow berries on the steps. If the berries had been edible, the steps would've been clean.

Ornate double doors stripped of the metal that had once served as inlay. Steps guarded by a three-legged cat that hissed. Then hopped away. Beyond the doors, a hallway studded with lights so dim it would've been hard to read by them. Finch stepped inside. The feeling of being followed shut off. Like it'd been attached to a timer inside of him.

The floor squeaked. Freshly waxed. It hadn't been waxed in the morning. Finch smiled. Old Hoegbotton trick. Cheap security. *Bell the cat.* He went squeaking to the stairwell. Already knew the elevator didn't work.

The outside light couldn't seem to push through the tiny windows set into the walls. The stairwell got darker the further up he went. But, gradually, more evidence of people. A dog howling. The flushing of a shared toilet. A screaming child. A mother's raised voice. The smell of something spicy being cooked for dinner. Filtered through the exhausted, stale funk of a place in which too many had lived in close quarters for too many years.

Finch knew not to start on the first couple of floors. No one liked to live that low if they had a choice. *Ambergris Rules.* Better to live next to a corpse than one floor above the gray caps' underground realm. His father had taught him that.

Stopped at the fourth floor. Just to be safe. Fourth or sixth. Anyone on the fifth was long gone. Either after the corpse arrived and before the Partial came to talk to them. Or after the Partial came to talk.

Finch had a simple formula. A polite knock. Short questions, in a friendly tone. Didn't like to go in like Blakely, guns blazing. Or like Gustat, using threats to coerce. They got information, sure. But not always the right information.

He worked the long line of closed doors to either side of the discolored, torn carpet. At the fifth door, a mother answered, holding her son. Maybe five or six, born around the time of the Rising. The mother looked worn. Pale and thin. Probably starving herself to feed the child. Probably thought that holding the kid would make Finch play nice. The kid's open, eager face confounded Finch. Almost like seeing another species. Parents kept their children hidden. Went out to forage for them. Finch's father had done the same for him. During the wars.

"What do you want?" she asked.

Finch decided he wanted nothing. Asked a couple of easy questions. Showed her the photo of the dead man. The woman didn't recognize him.

Tried a couple more doors. A middle-aged man in a tank top and shorts answered holding a frying pan. For defense? For dinner? Either way, he didn't know anything, hadn't seen anything.

Neither did the old married couple who might've lived there for forty, fifty years. Might even have recalled when 239 Manzikert Avenue hadn't been a dump. The man stood behind the woman, peering out with the kind of distant stare Finch associated with the camps. The wife had a blotch of purple on her forehead that might've been a birthmark or might've been fungus.

The next interview went better. A man of about sixty answered. Slight build. Large blue eyes, accentuated by the wrinkles in his forehead. A cultured voice. He wore a too-tight dinner jacket. The points of the collars on the white shirt beneath stabbed the flesh of his neck. His wrists showed from the dark ends of his cuffs. He looked like a child in a straitjacket.

As Finch questioned him, he slowly realized the man had dressed up for the interrogation. Had heard him at other doors down the hall. Soon, the man was asking him to come in for tea. Polite in a way that hadn't been common in Ambergris for years. Finch guessed violinist or theater owner. Either that or he'd once been the doorman.

He didn't know anything about the murders. (Finch couldn't recall when he'd started calling them *murders,* but the word felt right.) Thought the man in the photograph looked familiar, but couldn't place him. In the way people do when they're trying to help.

Then the man asked if the people living there had been of use.

"People living there?" Finch echoed.

"Yes. There were people living there. A man. A woman."

"Really?"

"Yes. I don't know their names."

Didn't know anything else, either.

Who was lying to him then? Heretic? The Partial?

Remembered Heretic's strange mood as he headed up to the fifth floor.

* * *

In the apartment, the bodies lay much as before. Except that each had sprouted a thick, emerald-green stalk topped by a nodule. The detectives called them memory bulbs. No one could pronounce what the gray caps called them. Sounded like a word between *loam* and *leer*. An aqua-colored nodule for the man. Bright orange for the gray cap. Which meant Finch had learned something new.

The bodies still looked peaceful. Even with the dull light streaming through the open window. The man looked better preserved than when Finch had seen him that morning. Sometimes death did that. For a time.

A figure stepped out of the back room. The Partial, grinning.

"Shit." Finch's gun appeared in his hand. Heart pounding.

"I'd aim that somewhere else if I were you," the Partial said. Fungal eye blinking and blinking. *Recording.*

Finch transferred his gun to his left hand. Shook his right. Green liquid hit the floor. *Goddamn gun.* Wiped his hand on the side of the couch.

"Did you follow me here?" Finch demanded.

One eyebrow arched. "Getting paranoid? Afraid you'll be found out?"

Snarled, "Why do you keep saying that?"

The Partial smiled. Triumphant. "Everyone has something to hide."

"Why didn't you tell me two people lived here?" he asked the Partial. "A man and a woman. Did you question them? And where are they?"

A preternatural calm to the Partial as he countered with, "Tell me what was in the dead man's hand."

Finch stepped back. Took in the narrow face, all slab of tongue and uncanny black-green left eye. Right eye atrophied from the repurposing. Dull orange lichen lived there now. The tongue moved like Finch's pet lizard's tongue. Tasting the air. The amount of energy that went into the eye meant they had to suck on gray cap-provided mushroom juice seven or eight times a day. *Looked like green pus.*

What was their name for themselves? A gray cap word. Sounded like *grineeknsenz* or something just as ugly. Rumor had it they'd made a pact with the gray caps. That soon they'd be made more like the gray caps, in return for their service.

"Nothing important," Finch managed finally.

"Isn't that for me to decide?"

"It's for Heretic to decide. It'll be in my report."

"I hope it is." The Partial's gaze was cold and dark. "We notice more than the gray caps, Finch. And we're more prepared to use what we find than they are."

That surprised Finch. Was the Partial criticizing Heretic? *Safer to ignore it.*

"What did the people who lived here tell you?"

"Nobody lived here."

Finch chewed on that for a moment. Was the Partial *hiding* something from Heretic? He patted his satchel. "I've got the entire list from Heretic of anyone who lived here." *Idiot.* "You're saying it won't include the two who lived here?"

"They don't live here," the Partial said, a hint of warning in his voice. "They don't live anywhere anymore. They didn't know anything important."

Dead, then. Disappeared into the abyss of history.

Appalled, Finch said, "Heretic knows this?"

The Partial nodded, folding his arms. "Don't take anything from the bodies this time except for the memory bulbs. I'm supposed to guard them. I've been here all day. Someone will always be here."

The way the Partial said this made Finch think the man, the abomination, was applying for martyrdom. Did the Partial think Finch was weak just because he hadn't allowed the gray caps to take his eye? Part of Finch wanted to hit the Partial in the mouth for that. Instead, he squatted next to the man's body. Looked so peaceful.

Was he alive for a time? In the room? Was he fighting the gray cap? Fleeing him?

The Partial, from in front and above him: "I'll watch. Just to make sure."

Make sure of what?

"Stay where I can see you."

"Such distrust," the Partial murmured.

Finch knelt beside the man's body. Pushed aside the matted hair on the man's head to get a good grip on the stalk. Held the bulb in his hand. *Sticky, porous, rubbery.* Gently twisted it off the stalk. A *pock* sound as he detached it. He put the bulb in his pocket. Pulled the stalk out at the root. Left behind a round indentation about a half inch deep. Blood began to fill the small wound.

That'll leave a scar.

Let loose a yip of nervous laughter. Shut it down.

But the Partial still noticed it. "I knew you didn't want to eat their memories."

Finch ignored the Partial. Repeated the process for the gray cap. *No blood, no pock sound.*

"You might be the first person to ever eat a gray cap's memory bulb. Aren't you the lucky one."

Finch rose to face the Partial. "Pathetic idea of security, by the way. One Partial. First thing any intruder will want to do is shoot out or cut out your eye. Followed by cutting off your head to make absolutely sure." Said each word slowly. Savored each.

The Partial wasn't smiling now. The eye twitched. He advanced on Finch until he stood inches away. Finch looked into that ruin of a face and tried not to turn away in disgust.

"Finch. Finchy. Whoever you are. You're not as smart as you think. I'm not the only one here. We've got this whole building staked out. If anyone comes here, we'll see them. The spores will see them."

Bellum omnium contra omnes. "Never lost" in a dead man's hand.

"Who would come here? And why?"

"Followers of the Blue." The Partial seemed on the verge of saying more. Caught himself.

But Finch had heard enough. A grin broke across his face. *Didn't turn back soon enough.* He gave the Partial a last poisonous stare.

"What? Nothing more to say?" the Partial called after him as he headed down the stairs. "I'm disappointed, Finchy . . . Someday, though, Finchy, someday . . ."

Out onto the street, amid the black leaves. The rotten fruit. A memory bulb in each pocket. Looking now for the signature of the rebels in every figure that he passed.

Followers of the Blue . . . The Lady in Blue.

A thousand tales told about her by now. Told by old men to young men. Told by mothers to sons and daughters. Most are about her voice. No one agrees on where the Lady in Blue came from, but everyone agrees that during the worst of the War of the Houses her voice was heard coming from courtyards, buildings, even underground. Or seemed to. Some thought she was an opera singer transformed by grief over a slain lover. That she was in some way the voice of the city, coming up from the earth. Believed this even though it could not be true. None of it could be true.

Then her voice started coming to the people on the radio stations of House Hoegbotton and House Frankwrithe, before the Rising. In those interim years when the Houses combined forces to confront the true insurgents. The enemy hidden in the ground.

Finch remembers some of those broadcasts. Listened to them with his father. Near the end.

The Lady in Blue would begin in a low, slow voice. Almost the murmurs of a lover. Her voice would build in volume and strength. Until she was exhorting the people of Ambergris to stand firm against not only the "underground invader," but also against the avarice and selfishness of its own leaders.

That her voice came from everywhere was reinforced by background noises in her broadcasts. Many different settings. Sometimes the sounds of the River Moth behind her. Sometimes a windy tower. Sometimes a water-clogged basement that she would claim was actually an underground gray cap stronghold. Often, she sounded weary. So incredibly tired. And other times strong, defiant.

Then the gray caps Rose, and Hoegbotton and Frankwrithe alike became the rebels. Dead. Dispersed. Fled. Lost. But the Lady in Blue survived, and by surviving she seemed to have again become greater than herself. Neither the green of the Hoegbottons nor the red of the Frankwrithe & Lewdens, but all the colors mixed together. People clung to the hope that she would return in force to save them. Even though she'd never been more than a voice on the radio to most of them.

Finch has seen the gray caps' files on the Lady in Blue, of course. Knows that she was born Alessandra Lewden in the Southern Isles. Received her education from various private schools in Morrow and Stockton. Then became Alessandra Hoegbotton in a politically advantageous marriage arranged during a brief truce between the Houses. Wife to the opera singer Joseph Hoegbotton, who was shot dead by an insane rival after a performance. After which Alessandra disappeared for several years. Until House Hoegbotton needed her for their latest propaganda tool: radio broadcasts. Across enemy lines. The disembodied voice of the self-described "Lady in Blue" coming out of houses and the back rooms of cafés.

Unclear from the files if Alessandra had given herself over entirely to Cause Hoegbotton. But it didn't matter when Cause Hoegbotton and Cause Frankwrithe–Lewden came together. The Lady in Blue just became more powerful. Sometimes, she was the only thing connecting the two factions.

But fascinating to Finch: her voice coming over the radio had driven the gray caps insane with anger. At first, they did not understand this new invention, brought to Ambergris by the busy scientists of the Kalif's empire. So for a time her voice seemed to come from everywhere and nowhere. Magically. Or a magic that was beyond them, unaffected by spores or fruiting bodies. You could not re-create radio using fungi. You could not spy on it from within.

The gray caps, the files revealed, had spent at least as much time trying to track her down as preparing for the Rising. But they could not locate her. They flooded tunnels. Sent spore armies rushing down remote streets. Blocked off passageways. Still, they couldn't find her. Which made Finch, even conflicted, admire her, reading the files. Understanding the cost of being constantly on the move. Constantly in flux.

Sometimes that cost came through over the radio. A mad howling. As if the city were a creature gone insane. Capturing the sounds of warfare. Of demolition. Of fighting with the gray caps or the Partials.

But for the last several months Finch knows there have been no radio broadcasts from the Lady in Blue. From Alessandra Lewden. Little or no organized rebel activity anywhere in the city. Meanwhile, the towers continue to rise in the bay. People grow more and more used to their situation. Becoming cynical about the Lady in Blue. Distrust reborn between former Hoegbottons and former Frankwrithes. Even Wyte's noticed it.

The fact is she hasn't saved Wyte, him, or anyone from six years of living under gray cap rule.

5

Home is an apartment in a twelve-story rundown hotel. He'd moved there six years ago, three months after the Rising, two years after his father's death. In its day, during the worst of the fighting between House Hoegbotton and House Frankwrithe, it had become famous as a kind of sanctuary. Far enough away from the battles to be neutral. Near enough to the merchant quarter to be profitable. Everybody trying to make money on the war.

But those days are gone. Outside the hotel, a statue of a dead composer stands guard beyond the crumbling steps that lead to the gaping front door. Powder-burned, nose shot off, one raised arm just a stone stump. A raving madman lives near the statue. Finch has no idea how he survives the gray caps' patrols at night.

Inside, the lobby is dank and dim and molding. An old crooked photograph on the wall captures a few signs of the hotel's lost luxury in a scene from some long-ago party. A strain of pale green lichen has infiltrated the faded burgundy of the carpet. Gives the floor a spongy feel and sheds a disconcerting, ghostly glow that leads Finch through the entrance after dark.

Elsewhere, bulbs burn fierce or dull, like mismatched cousins. Always, a ghastly yellow haze. A curling faded wallpaper that sometimes *isn't.* Smells that change by the hour, dictated by the currents in the basement. Walls knocked out. Old furniture piled high. A courtyard through the middle of the hotel. The basement is awash in water, an intrusion from the River Moth.

Finch knows many of the people in the building by name. A kind of survival strategy. *Strangers mean danger*. Like a leftover slogan from the old days when Hoegbotton gangs purified their neighborhoods of the "F&L scourge," and F&L gangs returned the favor. He doesn't know how safe his presence makes those around him, but he does his best. Tries to notice what's going on. Likes to believe he is doing what his father would've done.

The crumbling sign on the roof still reads " otel Mur t." Crows nest in it.

Sometimes Finch hides behind the sign.

Peers out across the skyline, toward the bay, from its shelter.

His apartment was on the seventh floor, but Finch ignored the dirty marble stairs and the stubborn elevator. Followed the wormy carpet into a darkened courtyard instead. A snarl of bushes and long grass along the path. At the center, a ragged vegetable garden of tomatoes, carrots, squash. Didn't know who tended to it. He turned left, pushed open the first door, took familiar steps down into the dark two at a time.

Bottom of the stairs. Finch turned right, faced a door at the end of a stub of hallway.

Rebecca Rathven lived there. He could hear the sounds of water, the slap of fish surfacing, coming through the air ducts. Mixed, sometimes, with Rathven's cackling laugh as she read something funny in her books. On a quiet night, the odd sounds traveled as far up as Finch's floor. Finch liked the sounds. And he liked Rathven. Found her useful. Found her interesting. Sometimes in a sinister way.

Who takes a flooded basement as an apartment in a hotel full of empty rooms?

Finch knocked. Heard footsteps. A pause. An appraisal through the peephole.

She was used to visitors, but still cautious. People came to Rathven for information from the past. They came to her if they'd lost the thread. They came to her to talk. Why? Finch, like most people, had books, but Rathven had a *library*.

That library changed with every visit. Rathven kept shifting the stacks against the inroads of the river. People who owed her favors helped her create barricades of wooden beams and homemade sandbags. He'd told her to move, to go higher. But the effort, *all of those books* . . . she said she would, but she hadn't yet. Might never.

The door opened wide enough for Finch to smell soggy pulp. *Trying to save the unsalvageable.* A wavery yellow light crept into the hall. Rathven's long face appeared, tilted up at him. Startling white skin, almost translucent. Looked at times like something broken. Then like something strong. Dark hair shot through with lighter strands. Thick black eyebrows, hazel eyes, high cheekbones, thin lips curled in a smile. Blue dress and brown sandals. Finch could never tell her age. Somewhere between twenty-five and thirty-five. Had never found a way to ask.

"Finch." The word invested with some secret amusement. "Come in?"

Smiled, shook his head. "But I do have something for you. A list. A long list."

"A list of what? Laundry list? Shopping list? Enemies? Friends?"

Finch laughed. "You should've been a detective."

"I *am* a detective," she said. The ritual refrain.

"List of names," he said. "People who lived in an apartment where two murders took place. And you'll love this: it's more than a century of names."

Not quite a frown, but a kind of quiver to the lips. A caution entering the eyes. She'd guessed the source. Not hard, really.

Rathven had been in the work camps for three years. Had the brands on the bottoms of her feet, the red-gold marking of fungus she could hide but never forget. There was a pulsing sensation sometimes, she'd told him. A restlessness. He'd never asked what else had happened to her there. Didn't really want to know.

She helped him because he'd gotten her brother Blaine, who went by the name "the Photographer," out of the camps and into the hotel. Dozens of old cameras in the Photographer's fifth-floor apartment. The man used the cameras to take thousands of photographs of water. Funded that obsession by running a black market for goods. Finch bought or traded with him like everyone else. Using gray cap vouchers, food pods, or salvaged items.

If the Photographer ever cut him off, or Rathven ever stopped helping him, Finch knew it would feel like a punch to the kidneys. *Friendship or need?*

He leaned over, pulled the list from his satchel. Felt tired suddenly, like he'd stolen something from her but realized it too late. "Could you read it? Tell me if any names are familiar. Maybe from your books." Would pay her in information and fungal antidotes, like usual.

Rathven took the paper gingerly. Prodded the spongy edges with one finger. "Only if you tell me why."

"Recent murders."

The color went out of her face.

"Got a piece of paper?" he asked.

She nodded, reached behind her. Handed him an old envelope. Return address from somewhere in the Southern Isles. *Might as well be some imaginary place now.*

Drew the symbol. Handed the paper back to her. "Do you know what this is?"

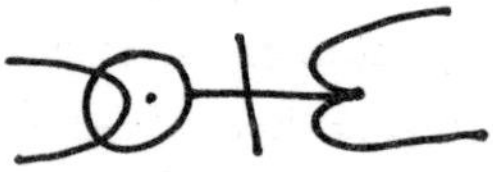

A disdainful glance. "It's a gray cap symbol, of course. Very poorly drawn."

"Can you check it out? I've seen it before. But I don't know what it means."

"Sure. I don't know how long it will take."

"That's fine . . ." Lingered, unsure how to ask for more. Then just said it: "Another favor. Memory bulbs tonight. Can you check on me? Call, or knock on the door if the phones are out? In an hour or two?" No idea when Sintra would get there. No point taking chances.

Now came the frown, as he knew it would. But she nodded. "I will. I will, Finch. Don't worry." Reached out to squeeze his arm. Then withdrew her hand quickly. As if she'd shown weakness.

He stared at her now. Smiled. Sometimes he felt a closeness with her he shared with no one else, not even Sintra. She'd never fought the Rising. She'd just read her books, preserved them. Protected them. Shared them. Eked out a living making crafts. At least, this was the story she'd told him. A small part of him still wondered why she'd been taken to the camps. Or why she'd been let go. *"I was too sick to work,"* she'd told him. But she'd never looked sick to him.

"The gray caps like to confuse randomness with purpose," Wyte had said once. But Finch didn't believe that. Just believed they kept the purpose buried deep.

"Thank you," he said. The words came out a little ragged. "Long day. I'll call when I take them. If the phones work."

"I'll come up and knock if I don't hear," she said. In return, he knew he'd have to help push back the encroaching river one more time. Each task had its own price with Rathven.

She shut the door, taking the light with her.

Finch's apartment was near the end of the hall. Had to negotiate a hothouse wetness to get there. Tendrils and caps of red-and-green fungus sprouted from the walls. Gray caps only cared about keeping the streets clean. No help from his next-door neighbors, either. Almost like they thought it gave them camouflage.

No one around, except his cat Feral, a big brute of a tabby, crying to be let in. Bumping up against his legs while Finch made shushing sounds. Feral was loud, always trying to trip Finch and bring him down to eye level.

Sometimes the little old man in the apartment opposite heard Finch and came out, but not tonight. A former accountant, the man liked to sit in a shaft of sunlight from the hall window. Smile and talk to himself and nod, and read from the same ragged book.

Two minutes to unlock and then relock. Only Sintra knew the sequence. Still not comfortable with that idea. Had thought about changing the key.

Flash of another dark room. A worn bed. White sheets dull in the shadow. Didn't look like anyone had slept in it in months. Dusty floor. Two corpses.

Flipped a switch. Relief when the lights actually came on. Faded floral print wallpaper. Root-like edges to the frayed beige carpet. Worn-out furniture.

Relief at being able to hang up the role of detective in the closet, along with his jacket. To let the tough exterior come off like a mask worn for a festival.

"Hold on for Truff's sake," Finch said to Feral as the cat ran to the kitchen through the living room.

Feral had wide round eyes. They gave his owlish face a perpetual look of surprise. Finch had rescued him as a kitten from a fungus that had wound tendrils around the animal while he slept. Still had purple patches on his flanks, sometimes growing, sometimes not.

No sign of Sidle, his windowsill lizard. Never really knew if it was the same lizard anyway. Felt compelled to pretend for some reason.

After feeding Feral, Finch put the two memory bulbs on the kitchen counter. Poured himself a glass of Trillian's Premium Whisky, aged eighteen years. An F&L brand trading off a famous name. Something no self-respecting H&S man would've drunk before the Rising. He had six bottles left in the closet. Next to the boxes of cigars. These had been his father's habits, his legacy. Nothing better had replaced them. The smell of cigar smoke made him feel like his father was right there, beside him.

Cigars. Whisky. Both working as a kind of peculiar clock or timer. When they ran out, would his life as Finch run out, too?

Heretic's touch like wet, dead leaves sewn together and stuffed with meat.

Dinnertime, but he wasn't hungry.

A long, shuddering sigh as he sat in the old leather chair next to the couch in the living room. Under the light of an old glass lamp shaped like an umbrella that he'd taken from the lobby. Watched the dusk dissolve into night.

On the far wall hung three of the hotel's original tourist scenes of Albumuth Boulevard. A far better view than the one from the small balcony abutting the kitchen. All the balcony could show him was more of the night sky, a sliver of the two towers, and the alley below. *A view saved for emergencies.* A second view could be had from the bathroom by opening the small latched window and standing on the toilet. Finch could look down into the courtyard whenever he wanted. Between the two sight lines, he had as much forewarning as he could expect. If what came after him was human.

Not a bad place. At least he had a separate office next to the kitchen and extra bookcases, overflowing, on the wall closest to the door. He'd made them from planks torn up from the rotting eleventh floor.

Even before the Rising, Finch had enjoyed reading. So many nights at the old house in the valley he and his father had sat reading in silence, separate yet together. To block out the night. The wars. Now the gray caps' camps lay so close that a crushed foundation under a heap of garbage was all that remained of the house. Nothing left but the books and other things he'd rescued.

Some books had been bought during cease-fires. Before the Rising destroyed the idea of bookstores. A few had come from his grandparents, who had returned to the Southern Isles when he was ten. Memories of them were like spent matches dull against a sudden darkness. He leafed through the books for signs of them sometimes. *A folded letter. A note that never dropped to the floor.*

But most of the books had been his father's, rescued from the old home. About a dozen Finch knew from long repetition, part of his father's home-schooling when it was too dangerous to go to class.

His father had started out as a brilliant engineer. In his youth, he had served in the Ambergris military in that brief, bright window when they'd taken on the Kalif's empire. He was with the troops as they advanced into a desert strewn with oases and hunched trees with gnarled black branches. As they took the Kalif's lands, and contemplated their own vision of conquest. As they were pushed back.

With Finch's mother dead in childbirth, his father had raised him after the war. A strange life, seesawing between wealth and poverty. Father's many important yet strange friends. His connections with Hoegbotton & Sons. And yet sometimes things had been bad enough Finch's father had supported them doing odd jobs and trading books for food. Or burning books for fuel.

Back at the old house, there had been many photographs of his father. The broad-chested muscular form of the man, tight in that characteristic Ambergrisian uniform of olive green. Wedge of a hat tilted to the side as was the fashion. On a hill or in a city or atop a tank. Surrounded by fellow soldiers or alone. Always smiling. Eyes dark dots looking into the camera. Seeming aware of future fame, but not of how it would come. Nor of how far he would fall.

Finch had chosen "John" for his new identity because it was his father's name. "Finch" was just a common bird, a creature no one would ever notice. He'd burned all photographs except one the night he'd changed his name. Displayed on the mantel, it showed his grandparents just arrived from the Southern Isles. At the docks with their suitcases beside them. Looking faded, remote, and confused. Grandpa had been a carpenter. Grandma a homemaker. There were no relatives on his mother's side. His father was four years old in the photo. This image was all Finch was willing to risk.

Once, Sintra had asked about the people in the photo. He'd said he didn't know them. That he'd found the photo on the street and liked it. True, to a point. Hadn't known the four-year-old. Never really knew his grandparents. Just another nonmemory from a lost life, and most days he didn't regret that.

On the back of the photograph, his father had scrawled a few lines: "Sometimes a man will see in his own image a desert, and it is the need to make that desert bloom which drives him again and again to action, as hopelessness compels us to our end. Sometimes, too, a man will flee in the enemy's direction, eager to weather any punishment—physical or mental—that proves he is still alive. Or, he does so from a pride that lies to him, tells him he can change what seems unchangeable." From a book? His own thoughts? Finch would never know.

Feral jumped up on his lap. Began to purr as Finch petted him.

The rough-smooth taste of the whisky scratched and soothed his throat. He sank further into his chair. Maybe Sintra would come by tonight.

Never lost.

"Yes, I know, fat boy," Finch murmured. Could sit there all night. Forget what he had to do and pull out a book that he'd read three or four times already. Pretend he lived in a better world.

Turned on the small radio on the table next to him. Feral stopped purring for a second. Only one station across the dial: the gray caps' station. Gone any cacophony of voices and music. Usually just a single signal, filled with cryptic clicks and whistles. Punctuated by propaganda delivered in flat tones by human readers. *". . . A spy is caught and killed just outside the Zone . . . Sector*

509 has been scheduled for renovation. Anyone living there should relocate immediately."

But, tonight, nothing. That made thirty-seven days of static. What did it mean? Was it just another slackening of attention? Or something more serious? Finch had noticed a pattern. The new dislodged the old. A puppet government in place for six months dissolved when the gray caps turned to building the camps. Electricity no longer reliable since they'd started in on the two towers. These failings brought a twisted optimism. *Maybe they can't do everything at once.* Or maybe there was a purpose to all of it that he just couldn't see.

He pushed a complaining Feral off his lap. Walked back into the kitchen.

The memory bulbs lay on the counter. Vaguely round. Pitted and whorled. Smelling of both salt and offal. Already rotting?

Finch looked down at the cat, which had followed him expecting a treat. Wondered what would happen if he fed a bulb to Feral.

"You want to eat one of these and I'll eat the other?" he asked Feral.

The cat walked back into the living room. Finch laughed. "Smart choice." Picked up the phone receiver, dialed Rathven's number. A crackling interference. *At least it's working.*

Through the static: "I'm taking one now. Give it an hour. If I don't call back, check on me."

"I will. Be safe."

"Thanks."

Finch put the receiver down. *Be safe.* Don't slip on the carpet. Don't fall out the window.

Which poison first? Finch picked up the orange one. *Get the worst over with first.*

Each time he ate a memory bulb, he became someone else. *Different* when he returned.

These would be his fourth and fifth. The first had belonged to a girl of ten and had given him nightmares for a year. Montages of a ragged doll. Soup made with dog bones. A bleak apartment without even wallpaper. Turned out there'd been no foul play. Her parents dead, she'd starved to death. The second had been a young man, the third a young woman. A double suicide unspooled in his head. Left him with longings he didn't know he had. Regrets that weren't his. Memories of people he didn't know. Or want to know.

Finch had never eaten two in one night.

How many would change him by just a little too much?

Fuck it.

Opened his mouth wide. Placed the bulb on his tongue. The taste of the gray cap bulb was dry. Like dirt and sand. The worst part was you had to eat them whole. Crunch down on the ridiculous size of it until your jaw ached. No good cutting them up, grinding them down to paste, adding them to food or water. Ruined the effect. His skin prickled as his mouth took in the strange texture, the taste. An odd, sickening blend of cinnamon-pepper-lime. Sour breath.

Dread, and yet also a thin layer of anticipation. To be taken out of his own life. If only for a little while.

He stumbled into the chair. Feral butted his head up against his slack arm.

Memories didn't come out the way one might expect. Nothing logical or ordered about them. Almost as if you were standing on a street corner as a motored vehicle raced by. As it passed you, a thousand pieces of confetti flew up. You had to try to catch as many of them as you could before they hit the ground.

Finch closed his eyes.

Leaned back.

Let it hit him all at once.

Come to:

At the bottom of a well. Layers of rough stone spiraled up to a distant pale light. A wriggling mass of worms or insects or something thick and strange pushing down through the light, extinguishing it. Sudden image of a monstrous City, balanced atop a single building greater than anything ever built in Ambergris, and it all housed in a cavern so huge that the ceiling is lost in blue-tinged darkness.

Come to (faster now):

A stumbling, jerky run through a tunnel. A surrounding mob of gray caps click and whistle with insane speed. A glimpse of blue sky, winking out. A burning motored vehicle, ancient model. A parade with a huge black cat caged and orange-yellow-green lights spread out along the route. Superimposed: an enormous grub drowning in a sack of its own liquid skin. A dark-green frond of fungus five stories high. Blood, lots of blood, pooling out across the ground. A man's face, in extreme agony, suddenly gone black in silhouette, turning into a huge door made half of volcanic rock and half charred book cover. And on top of the door a smaller door, and a small door set into that one. Hand on the doorknob. Opening . . .

Come to (slower now):

A stone fortress in a desert. Spinning out into open space—falling, falling, falling. And then a face Finch recognizes, the dead man's, smiling. Beatifically. More mud and dirt and the smell-sound of a river nearby. Side view of water flowing, ear to the grass. Something licks the moisture from his eyes before huffing and going on its way. Falling again, through black fabric studded with stars. The dead man falling, too, staring right at Finch, expression oddly calm. Words from the man's mouth in the clicks and whistles of the gray caps' language. And then, a sudden and monstrous clarity that can never be put into words.

Come to:

Moving slowly among a thousand swaying fungal trees in a thousand vision-shattering shades of green. Nearby, a rotting tank with the insignia of the Houses on its side, asleep under the fruiting bodies. The sound of footsteps. A hint of movement other than spores, strained through the heavy sky. Hunting for something. But what? A man. Moving in front of them. Night. Strange numbers and words spilling out emerald against a field of darkness. Shadowing the man. The orange sky dominated by the shambling hulks of floating fungal fortresses. *Things* crawl and fly and swim between the fortresses. Running now, just yards behind the man. But the man was turning to face them. The man was looking right at him when he disappeared. Winked out. Leaving only the smile. And that only for an instant. An intense feeling of confusion and surprise. Then: falling through cold air and couldn't feel his legs.

Returned whining. Keening. A low, animal sound from deep in his throat. Lay curled up on the chair. Sweating. Things crawled around inside his skull. Didn't know how much time had passed.

An enormous grub drowning in a sack of its own liquid skin.

Coughed. Sat up.

A rotting tank with the insignia of the Houses on its side, asleep under the fruiting bodies.

Feral rubbed up against his extended arm. Finch got up, made it to the phone, dialed Rathven, said "One done, one to go" when she answered, and hung up. Grabbed the second memory bulb. Collapsed back to the chair.

A monstrous City, balanced atop a single building.

Started laughing. Didn't know what was so funny or why he couldn't stop.

Falling through cold air and couldn't feel his legs.

Wondered how much this would mess him up.

6

The night half over. *Something important slipping away?*

Drank more whisky, and let it swirl around his mouth. Held the burn in the back of his throat. Followed by numbness.

The sounds out in the dark beyond the window hadn't made him shudder or start for a long time. Skitterings. Moanings. A cut-off shout of alarm.

A spotlight of lavender and crimson painted itself across the far wall of his apartment, then leapt away. Once, Finch had seen a shoal of spores take the form of a huge, bloated green monster. Spiraling red eyes. It had bellowed and dived into a neighborhood to the north. Smashed itself into motes against the ground.

A child might see that and cry out in delight.

Sidle, quick-shadow, scuttled up the side of the wall near the window. Pursuing moths that had flown into the apartment. Sidle was a happy little predator with bright black eyes. Didn't care about anything but his next meal. Finch could put him in a cage with a branch and water, and Sidle would be content his entire life. So long as he got fed.

"I guess we'll soon find out what kind of bastard he was," Finch said to an oblivious Feral. Feral was looking up at the wall. Mesmerized by Sidle's stalking of the spiraling moth. Finch wondered how many Sidles Feral had caught over the years.

Finch forced the second bulb into his mouth. Chewed it into a dull paste as he moved from the chair to the couch. Lay down. Swallowed.

The room spun a little. Righted itself.

The ceiling had a few odd discolorations but nothing to suggest infiltration. *Invisible spies.* Who lived upstairs, anyway? Sometimes lately he had heard a person pacing across the floorboards in the middle of the night.

After a minute or two, Finch sat up. Nothing seemed to be happening. Nothing at all.

The dead man sat in the chair next to him, smiling.

"Uhhh!" Finch leapt to his feet.

The man was flanked by a Feral grown large as a pony. A Sidle grown as large as a Feral. They both looked at him the way Sidle had been looking at the moths.

"Sit down," the man said. An order, not a suggestion. In a strange accent. The man looked much younger than he had on the floor of the apartment. Had lost the fungal beard.

Finch sat down slowly. Didn't take his eyes off the man. Left hand groping across the cushions. Where was his gun?

"I've been waiting for someone like you," the man said. "You won't understand it, but I'm going to give you what I know. Just in case."

The window behind the man no longer showed the city. What it did show was so impossible and disturbing Finch had to look away. And yet the image entered into him.

The man said Finch's name. Except he didn't say "John Finch." He used Finch's real name. The one buried for eight long years.

Finch tried to slow his breathing. Failed. Chest felt like something was going to explode.

He must be *inside* the man's memories.

Then why is the man sitting across from you?

"Who are you?" An obvious question. But it kept pounding against the inside of his skull. So he had to let it out.

The man laughed.

"I didn't say anything funny."

"More to the point," the man said, "who are *you*? And who are you with?"

"Shut up. This is just one of your memories. Manifesting in me. It isn't real."

Blindingly, unbelievably bright, a light like the sun shot through the window. The night sky torn apart by it. Through the tear: a turquoise sea roiling with ever-changing patterns.

"You don't have to understand it. Not now," the man said.

Didn't know if he was inside a mushroom or outside the universe. Glimpses of the city from on high: each street, each canal, an artery filled with blood. Hadn't known there could be so many shades of red. Spiking into his eyes.

"Be careful," the man said, echoing Rathven, and took Finch's hand. The man's hand was warm. Calloused. *Real.* "Don't lose your self, no matter what happens."

The man and Feral and Sidle disappeared. The window became a huge mouth, and they were all nothing more or less than memory bulbs within it. Finch fell through the same skein of stars he had seen in the gray cap's memory.

Woke up:

Teetering on the battlements of an ancient fortress, looking out over a desert, the sand flaring out for miles under the seethe of dusk. Moments from someone else's childhood. A parent's death. Sitting in a blind. Crawling through tunnels.

Woke up:

A cavern glittering with veins of some blue metal, huge mushrooms slowly breathing in and out. Seen in a flash of light that faded and kept fading but never went out: more caverns, an old woman's face, framed by white hair; another woman, in her twenties, her thirties, her forties. A shadowy figure hobbling down a street.

Woke up:

The insane jungle of the HFZ, almost floating above it, through it, coming out into a clearing ringed by twelve green men planted in the ground, arms at their sides, their mouths opening and closing soundlessly. And the jungle was made of fungus, not trees, poured over trucks and tanks and other heavy machinery junked and rusted out and infested with mushrooms, some of it still slowly, slowly moving. And back to the fortress, at the edge of a man-made cliff, many hundreds of feet above the desert floor, and out in the desert a thousand green lights held by a thousand shadows motionless, watching. A sound of metal locking into place. A kind of mirror. An eye. Pulling back to see a figure that seemed oddly familiar, and then a name: *Ethan Bliss*. Then a circle of stone, a door, covered with gray cap symbols. And, finally, jumping out into the desert air, toward a door hovering in the middle of the sky, pursued by the gray cap, before the world went dark.

Wake up . . . Came out of it seconds, centuries, later. To find Feral and Sidle watching him. Feral on the floor near the couch. Sidle on the windowsill, a large black moth trapped between his clockwork jaws.

The phone was ringing and ringing. Reached out for it. Put it to his ear.

"Are you okay?" Rath's voice.

"I'm going to be fine. I think."

Hung up.

Closed his eyes.

TUESDAY

I: The *fanaarcensitii*. You said he had fallen from a great height. Did anything you saw in the memory bulbs support that idea?

F: Instinct. I didn't trust what I saw.

I: Why not?

F: Because I haven't felt the same since I ate them. Because they were scenes out of a nightmare. I don't know.

I: There's one strange thing in all of this.

F: Just one?

I: A mention of a fortress. In a desert. Do you know the name of this place?

F: No.

I: I think you do.

F: I don't even know if it was real or not.

I: Is this real?

[screams]

1

Woke to a weight on the bed next to him. Went rigid. Sucked in his breath. Reached for his gun. Then relaxed. Recognized the smell of her sweat, some subtle perfume behind it. Sintra Caraval. The woman who had been part of his life for the last two years. She smelled good.

He could feel her staring at the back of his head. Her breath on his back. He smiled. Didn't open his eyes. She kissed his neck.

She was naked. Smooth, soft feel of her breasts against his shoulders. He was instantly hard. Opened his eyes. Turned over on his back. Sintra turned with him so she was nestled under his left arm. A surge of happiness startled him. Through the window: dim light creating shadows out of the darkness. Her brown skin somehow luminous against it. She'd told him she was half nimblytod, half dogghe. Tribes that had lived in Ambergris since before settlement. Before the gray caps.

Even in the darkness, Finch knew her face. Thick, expressive eyebrows. Green eyes. Full lips. A thin scar across the left cheek he'd never gotten her to talk about. A nose a little too long for her face, which gave her a questioning look.

An exotic lilt to the ends of her sentences as she whispered in his ear: "I let myself in. I wasn't trying to startle you."

He started to get up, to lock the door. She pushed him back down.

"I locked the door behind me. No one else can get in."

Finch stopped resisting her. The key was the greatest act of trust between them. Was that good or bad?

"Sintra," he said sleepily, bringing his right arm around to cup one warm breast. "I could get used to you. I really could." Not really listening to what he was saying. Still waking up. Reduced to the kind of meaningless words he'd mouthed at fifteen. Having sex in his room with the neighbor's daughter while his father was out.

"You could *get used to me*?" she said.

When mock-angry with him, she raised her eyebrows in a way he loved.

"A bad joke," he said. Hugged her closer. "I'm already used to you." Kissed the top of her head. Relaxed against her, the shudder that had been building up overtaking him. Then gone.

Then, more awake: "Let's escape. Tonight."

He'd worked it out in his head hundreds of times. Along the shore of the HFZ at dusk. A rowboat. Not a motorboat. To the end of the bay. Then either west to the Kalif's empire or south to Stockton. West because it was easier to get through the security zones in the desert. He knew places there. Places his father had shown him on maps.

Escape. Now.

Imagined she was grimacing, there, in the dark. The way she always did when he mentioned it.

"Bad night?" she asked.

"Just don't betray me," the man said, and took Finch's hand.

"Confusing night."

"Tell me later."

Then she was kissing him and he was kissing her. Tongue curled against tongue. The salt of her in his mouth. A hunger. A need. His hand between her muscular thighs. His cock in her hand. A pulse. A current that made him want to touch, to kiss, every part of her. Warmth and softness at his fingertips. Burning in her hand. An intake of breath. A little sighing cry. He turned and turned until he was above her, his forearms brushing her shoulders. Moaned as he slid into her and kept kissing her. Dissolving his poisoned thoughts. Not thinking at all. Becoming someone else.

She felt so good that he had to stop for a moment. Locked his elbows to hold himself up over her, looked into her eyes, her hands on his chest.

"I love your neck," he said, and kissed it. "And your eyes." Kissed her eyelids. He could see her better now, light colonizing shadows.

She wasn't smiling back. Wasn't responding.

"John," she said, looking worried. "John, you're crying blood."

She wiped a too-dark tear away with her finger.

"Am I?" he said, trying to smile, and came with a long shuddering groan before the thought could hit him.

Occupational hazard.

Later. Lying in bed together. Feral pushing his head against a bedpost, already wanting breakfast. The blood tears had stopped almost as soon as they'd started. Remembered Wyte had told him it could be an after-effect of eating memory bulbs. It hadn't hurt. It had just surprised him. He'd daubed his eyes clean with a bathroom towel. Had stared for a moment at the worn face of the stranger trapped in the cracked mirror.

A desert fortress. An army of silent gray caps. And Ethan Bliss, Frankwrithe & Lewden's top man for so many years.

Pushed the thoughts aside. Sintra would have to leave soon. *The place on the back of her neck where she liked to be kissed. Soft brown hairs. Crisp salt taste.*

"How was your work yesterday?" he asked her, holding her tightly to him. Skin so warm against his body.

"The same as always."

What did that mean?

"The same as always," Finch echoed. "That's good."

"I guess," she said. She sounded distracted.

Still didn't know what Sintra did, or even where she lived. Remnants of the dogghe and nimblytod had carved out a defiant kingdom for themselves in the ruined Religious Quarter. But Sintra might not even think of herself as one of them, integrated into the city. He'd never asked. Sometimes he daydreamed of her being a rebel agent. Comforting. Utterly unreal. But that didn't matter.

"I'm lonely. Even with you."

"Someday, it will be different . . ."

That she preferred him not knowing hurt him. Even though he understood the sense of it. Even though they made a game out of it.

"Where do you work?"

"In the city."

"And what do you do?"

"Answer questions. Apparently."

He'd known everything about his past girlfriends. But even in their lovemaking Sintra seemed to change from week to week.

Exhausting. Exciting. Dangerous.

Still missed the normalcy of the one time she'd stayed long enough to make breakfast. A surreal, sublime morning. They'd met at a black market party the night before. Taken off his detective's badge, gone as a civilian wanting some fun. Bumped into each other on the makeshift dance floor. In someone's basement. Everyone there expecting the gray caps to blast up through the tiles and send them to the work camps.

"Your day wasn't as good, I can tell," she said now. Bringing him back.

"I have a difficult case."

"How difficult?"

He sat on the chair and talked to me. The cat was as big as a pony and the lizard was as big as a cat. And me, I was as tiny as a reflection in Feral's eye. A perverse nursery rhyme.

"Difficult enough. A gray cap cut in half. A dead man. In an apartment. But they seem to have fallen from the sky . . ."

Sintra sat up, looked at him. "Where were they found?"

Finch stared back at her. Surprised by her sudden interest. Sometimes he shared details as an act of faith. But not on something that might pull her down with him.

"Down by the bay," he said. Waited.

Sintra considered him as he'd considered her. Then changed the subject. "Is that why you were crying? Because of what the memory bulbs showed you?"

"Yes." Propped himself up on an elbow. Shuddered, winced. An aftershock? Pressure in his head. Like his brain had outgrown his skull.

Sintra hugged him. Kissed him. He laid his head against her chest. She scared him sometimes. Both from her presence and her absence.

"Maybe it was a bad reaction to a drug," she said. "Maybe you inhaled a bad spore."

Back before the Rising, Sintra said she had been a doctor's aide.

"Unlikely." He and his fellow detectives got fed antidotes every few months. One perk of working for the gray caps. He stole extras for Sintra and Rathven. Sintra always took them with her. Never used them in the apartment.

"But it's over now."

"Yes. It's over."

He broke off the embrace. Feral was cleaning himself in a shaft of light by the window. Sidle was motionless on the windowsill. Drunk on the new sun.

Sintra wrapped the sheets around her and stood up, walked toward the window. Leaving Finch naked and exposed on the bed. Watching her as he put his underwear back on. Remembering the first time they had made love. How he'd checked the sheets, the pillows after she'd left. Wanting to breathe in more of the smell of her. How there had seemed to be no trace of their sex. Only his memory of the act. As if he had entered a ghost.

She turned to stare at him, framed by the window.

"I'll come back in a night or two," Sintra said. "That's not long."

"No, it's not long," Finch said. Thinking of the station. The other detectives. Work fatigue washed over him.

Memory holes and Wyte and Heretic and wanting to scream, to just start shooting.

"Maybe I'll even spend the night. If I can," she said. A curious look on her face, like she was testing him. She held her hands behind her back, one leg slightly bent, her body bronzed and perfect to him. "What do you think of that?"

Must have been obvious what he thought, because she couldn't take the weight of his gaze. Looked away. Leaned down to pick up her knapsack, retrieve her clothes.

Not that he doubted she felt the same. He knew why she kept her distance. The same reason he did.

Except, it's not working for me.

A long kiss. A final hug.

And she was gone.

All he could feel was the ache in his thighs. The damp spot on the front of his underwear, colder now than before.

* * *

Just once, Sintra left something behind. Finch keeps it hidden in a desk drawer. No reason for him to keep it. But no reason to get rid of it.

Written in longhand, Sintra's concise notes are about mushrooms, which no longer come with any field guide. Ignorance can lead to death, even though since the Rising the gray caps have kept the streets clear. Personal curiosity? Something to do with the black market? Has she helped someone she shouldn't help? Given aid to some group the gray caps are hunting down?

Does it make her a spy to have this information, or just pragmatic? Does it make him complicit to keep it, or just sentimental?

> *This incomplete list doesn't include fungal weapons. These mushrooms all perform certain tasks or "work" within the city. If any have a secondary or tertiary purpose it is unknown at this time.*
>
> *(1) Tiny white mushrooms almost like star-shaped flowers—found most often around surfaces where dead bodies have recently lain or where some conflict has occurred. Like the chalk outlines used by detectives pre-Rising to mark bodies? Warnings, or . . . ?*
>
> *(2) Green "spear" mushrooms with sharp, narrow hoods and long, slender stems—four or five will be found around a building targeted for transformation. Three days after the appearance of these green spear mushrooms, the building in question will begin to look moist or spongy, due to infiltration from below. By the fourth or fifth day, it will begin to crumble. By the sixth day, the building has blown away in the wind. On the seventh day, a new structure has usually blossomed, overnight. This new structure may take any of a number of forms, all fungal-based.*
>
> *(3) Red "tree" mushrooms with huge caps and strong, thick "trunks" or stems—these can grow up to eighty feet high and are*

much more resistant to storms and high winds than other kinds of mushrooms. They appear to have a filtration system that gives them stability by letting air pass through millions of "pores." In a sense, they float. An examination of distribution patterns from any height reveals that they have been "planted" in regular patterns forming rough "spokes" radiating out from the bay, interrupted only by the HFZ and the Religious Quarter. They regularly expel from their gills a smaller, purple mushroom with a strong euphoric effect and high levels of digestible protein.

(4) Purple "drug" mushrooms with ball caps and almost no stems—dispensed from the red "tree" mushrooms, these purple mushrooms are clearly meant to serve as "crowd control" by giving the people of the city sustenance and making them dependent. These mushrooms create a strong addiction by affecting the pleasure centers of the brain. They also create hallucinations intended to pacify, most drawn from happy memories.

Definitely her handwriting. She's slipped more than one message under his door while he's out. Tells himself: *I'll throw it away when I know more about her.* But nine months have passed since he found the note. She hasn't told him anything more than what he knew before.

Yet caution loses out when she walks through the door. Remembering how, on days when he's expecting her and she's late, the fear creeps aching into his muscles. Finds himself gulping air like water. Thick and heavy. Lost. *Never lost.*

2

After Sintra had left, Finch fed the cat, grabbed a quick bite, and cleaned off with a couple of pails of once-used bathwater. Fresh shirt, same pants, same jacket. Kicked Feral out to explore on his own while he went down the stairs to the courtyard, then the basement.

Rath's pale, angular face peered out from behind the door. Evaluating him. Looking for something.

She let Finch in without a word. Through a hallway brightened by walls painted light green. Probably to conceal rot. Then into a larger area with a few chairs, her strange library to either side. Beyond, where Finch had never gone: the start of entropy. The bruises of gray and blue stains spread across the ceiling. Disappeared into the darkness of a tunnel.

"Nothing new, I see," Finch said.

Rath laughed. "Not that you'd notice."

Finch brushed by her to sit in an armchair on a blue throw rug. Rising above him, water-damaged paperbacks and hardcovers had been stacked unevenly on warped shelves. The shelves perched on stilts to fend off any sudden rise in the water level. The weighted smell of moisture seemed both fresh and claustrophobic.

"Coffee?" she asked. The usual.

Hesitated, said, "No. Tea, please." Didn't know why.

Rath disappeared into the tunnel. Did she have a kitchen back there? Maybe a bedroom. Maybe more books. A whole troupe of clowns. The thought made him smile.

Stray pages saved from long-drowned books caught his attention as he waited for her. Red eye peering from monstrous face. Lines of scrawl in an unknown language. Diagrams of buildings or plants or motored vehicles. A black-and-white photograph of a gaunt five-year-old girl in a ragged dress standing in the muddy track of a tank.

Truff knew who had lived here before, collected the books originally. Or how long it had taken Rath to organize it all. Or how much she had added to it, scavenging across the city. The collection was an ever-changing scene of preservation and dissolution. So many things saved only to be destroyed by time. Always with the water gurgling its way along the floor. Sometimes fish would get trapped, their fins brushing against pipes or grillwork and making a sound like quills over skulls.

She came out with a teapot and two cups on a tray. Set it down on the table between them. Poured him a cup.

"You sure you want this?" she asked. Skeptical.

"Yes." Took the tea gladly. His head still hurt. The tea tasted different. Better. Drove out the lingering taste of the memory bulb.

"I haven't looked at the lists," she said, sitting opposite him in a low wooden chair with a green blanket atop it.

"Didn't expect you to yet," Finch replied. "What about the symbol?"

"Now, *that* I did get around to," she said. "If only because it was easy."

"I've seen it, I've just never known what it meant."

"You're not alone. We know more about what the symbol is associated with than what it means."

A broken version was scrawled by the gray caps as a warning, Rathven told him. At the beginning of the city's history, when the gray caps sent back the eyes of Ambergris's founder, the whaling captain John Manzikert, on the old altar now drowned by the bay. Manzikert, who had slaughtered so many gray caps and driven them underground.

"It looked like this," she said, drawing it for him:

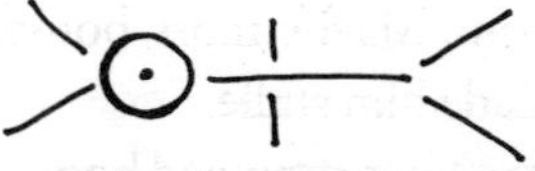

It had figured prominently in the recovered journals of the monk Samuel Tonsure, Manzikert's fellow traveler underground. Had appeared in unbroken forms at various times since, at crucial moments in history.

"Give me an example," Finch said.

"The Silence," Rathven said. "That symbol, according to the accounts I have, appeared everywhere, all across the city."

Finch gave her a sharp look. "I never heard that." But an intense feeling overtook him, telling him that he *had* known. Just forgotten.

Rathven shrugged. "I'm just telling you what's in the histories. Half the books down here mention the Silence, so it's not hard to track down."

The Silence. Seven hundred years ago, twenty-five thousand people had vanished from the city. The only survivors had been aboard the ruler's vast fleet of fishing ships, fifty miles downriver at the time. Many a horror story had been written about the Silence. It had shaped Ambergrisian life ever since. Especially attitudes toward the gray caps. Everyone had believed the gray caps had done it. When they'd Risen, some people said it was because of Manzikert's genocide against them, and because of something they hadn't finished during the Silence. Revenge, after waiting patiently for centuries. Of course, who could confirm that? The gray caps said less now that they were aboveground than when they'd been below.

"A broken symbol means a broken pact, some believe," Rathven said.

"I found it on the back of a scrap of paper used to scribble a note. Torn from a book. It probably isn't connected to the case." Wanted to move on for reasons he couldn't identify.

"Probably." In a tone that said, *Why waste my time asking me to research it then?*

Took the photo out of his pocket. "I want you to have this while you research the list."

Rathven took it. Winced.

"What?"

"He's dead, Finch."

"Of course he's dead. It's the murder case. I need to know who he is. It's very strange. I can't get my head around it. I need your help."

And there's no one in the station I trust to thoroughly check out that list.

"Are you sure you *want* to tell me more?" Rathven said.

People came to Rathven who the gray caps would count as enemies. Seeking information from her library. Information from *her*. Finch turned a blind eye. But someday somebody was going to test Rath's neutrality, her ability to put it all in a locked box.

A sound distracted him. A sudden retreat of water somewhere in the darkness behind him. He'd seen fish "walk" up out of that darkness. Watched them gasping as they tried to be something other than fish. Once, Finch had heard a splashing like oars, from deep in the tunnel. Had asked Rath, half-serious, "Is there something you want to tell me?" She'd ignored him.

Finch put down his tea. Leaned back in the chair. *Do I trust Rathven more or less than Sintra?*

"A dead man and a dead gray cap. In the same apartment. The gray cap is just a torso with arms and a head. No blood. True, it's a gray cap. But maybe they weren't even murdered. Maybe murdered, but not in the apartment. I didn't get much out of the memory bulbs." *Not much I can share.*

It felt good to talk. Drew the tension out of him. Got rid of a strange echo in his head.

Rathven nodded, looking serious. "Didn't get much? So you got *something*." She waited, expectant.

"I haven't given you enough?" he asked with mock shock. "No. That's not all. They seem to have fallen from a great height. Maybe from the walls of a desert fortress. I have to file a report today."

Do I sound crazy?

"What other clues?" Rathven asked.

Suddenly irritable: "Jumbled memories. Including a conversation with the dead man. Must have imagined that."

"What?"

"Just what I said! Are you deaf?" *The man laughed again. Blindingly, unbelievably bright, a light like the sun shot through the window. The night sky torn apart by it.*

Realized he'd shouted at her. "Sorry."

Rath gave him a look he could not interpret. "You're not the same today," she said.

"Do you think I can do what I do and not be changed?" Spitting out the words. "Take memory bulbs? Work in the station?"

"I don't care," Rathven said. "If you change too much, I won't let you back in here." An intensity behind her gaze. Seeing someone or something other than Finch. *Couldn't even imagine . . .*

"Sorry," Finch said. The words took an effort. Gritted his teeth. Said it again. *Fuck!*

Rathven looked down. Took a sip of tea. Said, "So the dead man was talking to you?"

Fair enough. Move on. Realized that he needed to take more care with her. *She's not one of the detectives at the station.*

"It must have been," he said. "Imaginary, I mean."

"What else?"

"Nothing else. Just the piece of paper that symbol was on the back of. Some words. *Never Lost.* And then *bellum omnium contra omnes.* Ever heard those words before?"

"No," she said. Still, Finch sensed interest.

"You don't know what it means?"

"How would I know what it means if I've never heard it before?"

Couldn't bring himself to say "sorry" again, so he said nothing. "Maybe you're asking the wrong question. *Bellum omnium contra omnes.*" Rathven said it like an echo from another world. As if it had no meaning at all.

"How do you mean?"

"I *mean,* does it matter what it means? Why did he have words on a scrap of paper when he died? Pretend for a second that it's any word. Any word you know: city, cow, apartment, saucepan, book, paragraph."

"A code? A password?" Felt foolish for not seeing it before. "Might not mean anything at all."

She pointed at him. "And that's what makes it valuable."

"But why? Why have part of it in gibberish?"

She shrugged, gave him an impish look. "I'm not the detective."

I'm not a detective either.

"We should be detectives together." Relaxing into their time-worn call and response.

* * *

"They're here and then they're there, and sometimes they don't know the difference, and if you let them, they'll keep making that the whole point of everything they're doing to the city. They'll break you down by not telling you what you already know, should already know, because that's the way they operate. Knowledge is the lack they seek in us, and when they find it, they turn the key, open a window, and it's all back to where we started."

Finch endured the rant from the madman outside the hotel, then made his way back to the station.

The suspect from yesterday wasn't in the cage. Instead, an old woman with light blue eyes staring from a face crisscrossed with wrinkles. As if from behind a fence of her own making. She could've been a thousand miles away for all the help Finch could give her. Ignored her as a casualty. Ignored Albin quietly feeding her questions like he was at a zoo. Continued on to his desk.

More of the same from the detectives around him. Indifference, absence, fear, boredom. Blakely and Gustat as always inseparable, whether in agreement or argument. Skinner out on a call, about to tell a man his missing wife was probably dead. Dapple drawing something on a piece of paper. Lost in another world.

Wyte had turned away from him for once and was hunched over as if Finch were trying to cheat from him on a test. He looked bulky, blotchy.

Finch leaned over. "Don't let your pencil burn up."

Wyte grimaced, said, "I'm busy, Finchy. Really. I am." And kept writing. It looked incomprehensible to Finch.

"Last will and testament?" Wished he hadn't said it.

"Shut up, Finchy," Wyte said. Still scribbling.

"I'm not pathologically reporting on evidence I haven't gathered yet," Finch said, "and they haven't come to cart me away."

"You're just lucky," Wyte mumbled.

A light green stain began to spread across the back of Wyte's blue shirt.

Finch cleared space on his desk. Brought the typewriter over. One of the best models Hoegbotton had ever made. A hulking twenty-pound monster that reminded Finch of just what Ambergris could accomplish back in the day. Hundreds of thousands had been shipped out to cities up and down the River Moth. "Combat-ready" went the slogan, and it wasn't a joke.

Looked at his notes. Didn't want to tell Heretic about everything he'd found. Not until he knew more about what the words meant. Discounted the symbol entirely. Even though it had burned its way into his head. *"Focus on what you can control. The rest is just distraction."* Something his father used to say.

What could he report that was *solid*? A few moments gazing into space. Then he started to type. Stopped when he got to a part that bothered him.

Both memories contained images of a desert fortress. Both memories contained images of falling.

From a great height? Maybe.

Finch took a sip of his coffee. He'd washed the cup beforehand to make sure no fungus, visible or invisible, had taken root. Sometimes the gray caps did strange things with the mugs during the night.

Both memories contained images from the HFZ.

I think. How would I know, never having been there?

From analyzing

"My memory of . . ."

both memories it seems certain that the gray cap

Fanaarcessitti? Fanarcesittee? Always typos in these reports.

that the fannarcessitti was in pursuit of the man. But I don't know why.

Then Sintra was kissing him and he was kissing her. Tongue curled against tongue. The salt of her in his mouth. His hand between her muscular thighs. A hunger. A need. Something that didn't exist outside the sanctuary of his apartment.

Recognized the strength of that need, the danger of it, on the way to the station.

He exhaled sharply. *That way lies madness.*

More to the point, he shouldn't even have been on this case. Not many people made the distinction between what detectives did and what Partials or gray caps did. Never do police work anywhere near your own area. Never let the people where you lived know your job. And yet, 239 Manzikert Avenue was only a mile from the hotel. Why had Heretic put him in charge? Didn't trust Wyte anymore? Or was there some other reason? Leaned forward in his chair. Had to make some progress. *Just dive into it.*

The man's memories had more coherence than the fannarcessitti's memories. I could not tell if this was because the fanarcesitti's mind had been more confused and disjointed at the time of death or because, as a human, I could more easily read the man's memories.

Nothing during the experience brought me any closer to knowing the identity of the man.

I wish the memory bulbs had been more useful.

But he had seen *one* person he recognized. He leaned back and thought about Ethan Bliss. What he knew. What he didn't know.

First, the impersonal. Bliss had fought for Frankwrithe & Lewden during the War of the Houses. Behind the scenes. No one seemed to know for sure what he did for F&L. Secret ops? Bliss had joined the political wing. Risen quickly to become F&L's number one man in Ambergris. Had been instrumental in forging the alliance between the F&L and the Lady in Blue. Then, right before the gray caps took over, he dropped out of sight. Probably returned to his native Morrow, only to reappear a couple of years ago. Because of how Morrow had suffered from the gray caps having cut off the flow of water? Ships suddenly resting on a dry riverbed. Trade disrupted. Drinking water scarce.

This new Bliss had reverted to spying. Had connections to the Spit. But hadn't made common cause with the rebels, according to Finch's informants.

Although, when you paid informants in food and clothing, how valuable could your information be? More valuable? Less?

All of this made Bliss of special interest to any detective who hated foreigners messing around in Ambergris business. Finch could've used Bliss as a snitch, perhaps, but hadn't. He was wary of who Bliss might be working for now. If he worked for anyone other than himself.

Second, the personal. Bliss had been at his father's house a couple of times when Finch was maybe twelve, thirteen. He could recall looking through the kitchen window to see Bliss and his father in the garden. The smaller man compact, unmoving. His father unruly, animated, throwing his arms about, pointing at Bliss and demanding something. And yet, seeing the two figures there like that, Bliss had seemed in his silence and self-possession to be the one in charge.

Thought, too, that Bliss might've been in one of the photographs he'd burned before becoming Finch. But Bliss was one of many visitors. During the few peaceful years, there had been lots of parties at their house, with people from both sides.

Finch had seen Bliss give speeches, too. One, in front of the Voss Bender Memorial Opera House, to a crowd of almost ten thousand. He'd looked striking in an evening coat and tails. A chestful of honorary medals that made you notice the glitter more than the man. Urging *cooperation* and *common cause* in that silky voice when, just a year or two before, behind the scenes, he'd caused House Hoegbotton so much grief. Bombings. House-to-house battles to clear insurgents. Fighting in narrow streets where tanks were no help, but where F&L fungal bullets worked just fine.

Third, whatever the gray caps knew about Bliss, if they knew about Bliss. Finch couldn't remember pulling the file on him. He'd have to put in a request. Which he hated doing. Couldn't know what Heretic would "request" in return.

Took out the form anyway. Wrote in what he needed. Under "subject," he filled in Ethan Bliss's name and a few others. For cover. If Finch put in his report that he'd seen Bliss in the dead man's memories, Bliss was as good as dead. Or would want to be. And Finch couldn't be sure what it all meant until he questioned Bliss. Which wouldn't happen if Heretic got hold of him first.

Why the hell was Ethan Bliss in the memories of the dead man?

Typed:

Perhaps a fannarcesitti would be more useful in reading the man's memories?

What would a gray cap see? Baiting Heretic gave Finch a grim satisfaction. Gray caps hated eating human memories. Almost as if there were a taste, a smell, that repulsed them. Finch couldn't recall Heretic ever eating one. Could human memories harm a gray cap?

It is not entirely clear that these deaths are murders, rather than accidental. The two may have died somewhere else and been brought to the apartment. Residents of the apartment building have no additional information. Rumors that two people lived in apartment 525 cannot be confirmed.

Just covering himself in case whatever game the Partial was playing went south. Yet, stubbornly, couldn't bring himself to mention the scrap of paper. Despite the fact the Partial knew about it. Had the Partial told Heretic? Maybe. Maybe not.

Finch pushed his chair away from the typewriter, hands behind his head. The report made no sense. Composed of smoke and shadows. Doubted Heretic would find it convincing. What did it mean that the dead man had *spoken* to him? Another thing he hadn't put in the report. Some instinct had warned him against it.

Ripped the paper out of the typewriter carriage. A mechanical tearing sound loud enough to make all the other detectives turn toward him in one motion that seemed choreographed.

What the hell are you looking at?

Realized he'd said it out loud.

Jammed his report into a pod, along with the request for files. Shoved that down the memory hole gullet. *Choke on it.*

A minute later: a sound coming from the damn thing. *Incoming.*

The pod. The tendrils. Hammer. Egg. Extraction. A message from Heretic.

STAY LATE TONIGHT TO MEET

"Fuck," Finch said.

"Is it bad?" Wyte asked.

"Why do you always ask that question?"

"Why is the answer always yes."

"Then you shouldn't ask it."

Staying late always unnerved him.

Have to get out of here.

"Come on," he said to Wyte. It would do Wyte some good, too. "We're going to go talk to Ethan Bliss."

If they could find him.

* * *

On a table near the desk in his apartment, Finch has a map of Ambergris from before the Rising. It covers the whole table, renders the city in perfect detail. He has no idea what it's made of. Never tears. Never wrinkles. His father had given it to him when he was thirteen. "You'll never need another." Made a mark on it with a green pen every time he sent his son on an errand to a new location.

Insisted Finch take the map with him everywhere. Even though it was heavy. Even if Finch had been to a place before. "The streets are shifty. I want to make sure you don't get lost."

The errands? Collect letters. Drop off packages. Say a single word or phrase. *"Shipping lanes." "The weather is too cold for this time of year." "Mr. Green says you are a lucky man."* Never to the same people. Old, young, male, female, each one with secrets behind their eyes. He played it like a game. Delighted in the mystery of not really knowing the rules. Then he'd return, a human homing pigeon, to their house.

"Official business," his father said. He held an important position for H&S because he was a war hero. Anyone could tell that from all of the photographs of him fighting against the Kalif, and from the people who came over to visit. Some of them wearing funny hats and uniforms.

But by the time Finch was seventeen, his father had stopped sending him on these errands. He'd felt discarded. Hadn't understood then that his father had turned to others when Finch began to ask questions. When he began to have a sense of the secrecy behind his missions. *A tallish, dark-haired, serious boy with few close friends his age, taught at home by his father.* Those journeys across the city had meant a lot to him.

But he'd kept the map, used it for his new job, which his father had gotten for him. Courier for Hoegbotton business interests. Running invoices and shipping inventories between the main offices and the warehouses at the docks. Sometimes, if the conflict heated up, if F&L cut off certain roads, he had to find alternate routes.

Trade "has to keep on an even keel, no matter what," his boss Wyte liked to say. Wyte, seven years his senior, with an office in the brick building on Albumuth they'd both work at after the Rising. Even then Wyte had seemed too large for the world around him. Desk too small. Him too clumsy. But to Finch he'd been the height of authority.

The map shows that brick building, with a green mark by it. It also has detailed views of the Bureaucratic Quarter, the Religious Quarter, and what had unofficially been known as the merchant district before the wars. Albumuth Boulevard, the great snake wending its way through almost every part of the city. The valley that had been the home of so many citizens. The docks. The swampland to the north.

A view of Ambergris that had remained essentially unchanged for centuries. Had survived early incursions by the Kalif, the cavalry charges of Morrow back when it had a king instead of the F&L. Had even survived the Silence.

But could not survive the Rising.

The gray caps have a kind of see-through paper. A slight greenish tint, barely noticeable. It feels light as a leaf, but is very strong. Finch has stolen two sheets of it, taped them together to form an overlay to his old map. On this overlay he charts the changes he has observed, using a dark pencil that he can erase at will.

In the evenings, when too restless to sleep but too tired to read, Finch will turn on the light in the study. Or use a lantern if the electricity is out. Review the overlay. Search for what he knows has been made different again. Then render a section bare with handkerchief and water. Build it up again, redraw it all. A change in the lip of the bay. Or in the HFZ. A row of houses that has burned down. A drug mushroom that erupted from the pavement. A new gray cap house or cathedral.

Lately, he has been charting the retreat of the water. Right after the Rising, the canals from the bay into Ambergris had been like the fat fingers of a grasping hand. Now they are withered, the "thumb" almost dry, the others shriveling. Like his father's blue-veined hands in the clinic near the end. A disease he'd picked up early in life, fighting the Kalif. It got into his lungs first, and spread. No cure except death.

Remapping takes the kind of concentration that empties out the mind. In the old house, before they became vagabonds together, his father had created something similar in his locked study. Much bigger, with even more detail, laid out across a huge table fit for a banquet. Color-coded to show Hoegbotton and Frankwrithe territories within the city. Green and red. Along with blue for those narrow reefs of neutrality. Over time, his father would chart weapons depots on that map. Troop concentrations. Hidden storehouses. Usually Hoegbotton but some Frankwrithe positions, too. His father's overlay was actually a black sheet that perfectly hid the map. And a tablecloth over top of that.

How many guests invited into that place had been served drinks on that table, never realizing what was hidden beneath?

At seventeen, mad at his father for no longer using him as a courier, Finch had stolen the key. Started sneaking into the study when his father was out. Found the map. He used to stand there, it naked before him, and memorize the progress of the war in his head. It looked like lively abstract art. Symbols in search of context.

Finch doesn't draw directly on the old map because he doesn't want to forget the past. Hopes that one day that lost world will return. The overlay is only temporary, he keeps telling himself. Even as the changes become more and more permanent.

His map is a crude facsimile of the original. He has only the dark pencil to record the changes. Nor can his map chart the changes in the people around him. Or tell him what to do next.

One day, his father surprised him in the study. He stood at the door with a guarded look on his face. Finch stared back, frozen. There seemed to be nothing he could say. His father walked up. Put the black sheet over the map. Replaced the tablecloth. Muttered, "This didn't happen." Took the key from him. Escorted him out.

They never talked about it again. But in that moment of shock, when Finch heard the door open, it burned his father's map into his head. Every detail. Every nuance. And even now, looking at his own map, the overlay, he sees it. Sees that room.

Knows every inch of Ambergris. Even the parts he hasn't yet visited. Even the parts still changing.

3

Tracking down Bliss took three tries. Wyte had an address for a townhouse Bliss sometimes used for meetings, in an old Hoegbotton stronghold southeast of Albumuth. Finch could still see the slashes of faded paint on the pavement, left by groups of Irregulars. Who knew how old the marks were? A code that told a secret history of the city. *Gray cap passed by here Tuesday . . . Food and ammo in the second house on the left . . . Stay clear of this intersection after dark.*

They found the house on a street that had once been part of a wealthy district. Trees lined the sidewalk, but not a leaf on them. Gravel where grass had been. Silence all around. The houses to either side derelict husks. A burned corpse with no arms right on the steps. Which should've told them Bliss wasn't there. Flies had settled on the torn-up face like a congregation. A slender whiteness had begun to push up through the black. Stalks of fruiting bodies. Rising. In another twenty hours, nothing would be left.

"Nothing inside," Finch said, coming back out.

"Let's visit Stanton," Wyte said.

Stanton, one of Wyte's druggie snitches, lived a few blocks down. Behind Stanton, Finch saw a tarp draped over a soot-gray alley mouth. A bundle of his possessions to one side. A crumbling brick he used to protect himself at night. Before the Rising, Stanton had been a banker. Or, at least, that's what he'd told Wyte. Probably an addict then, too.

Wyte always kept a few extra purple mushrooms in his overcoat pockets. Stanton, in a kind of makeshift robe, clung to Wyte like *he* was the drug. Wyte a plank of wood in the River Moth and Stanton trying to stop from drowning. Except all he ever did was drown.

"Where'd Bliss go?" Wyte asked Stanton.

The thirty-year-old Stanton lifted his gaunt, balding head. Red-eyed, wrinkled face. "Down by the abandoned train station. Four streets over. Corner of Sporn and Trillian. He was just there yesterday."

Wyte put three purple mushrooms in Stanton's hand. Stanton received them like they were worth more than one day's relief. The huge red mushrooms that dispensed the drugs stuck to a strict schedule. Monday and Friday. Stanton had already gone through what he'd gathered the day before. Finch didn't think he'd last another month.

When they left Stanton, he was trembling under his pathetic shelter. Eyes wide open and dilated. Gone someplace better. Someplace temporary.

The train station was empty. But way in the back, under the shadowed arches populated by pigeons and bats, they found a gambling pit. Almost a grotto, for all the fungus surrounding it. Fuzzy clumps of muted gold and green hid the entrance. Cockfighting. Card games. Betting black market goods.

Not much of a conversation. Wyte stuck his gun up against the lookout's cheek. Convinced her it would be better just to lead them in. The hardened men and women they surprised, lantern-lit and reaching for knives or guns, thought better of it, too. But they had a hard time restraining the roosters. One fire-red, the other a muted orange. Razor talons moving like pistons.

A heavily muscled man in his twenties who had done some piecework for Bliss gave him up, quick. Called Bliss a slang word for foreign. Even though the muscled man looked foreign himself. Seemed to dare any of the others to argue with him. They didn't.

Wyte and Finch receded into the gloom. Shoved the lookout inside. Barricaded the door from the outside with a couple of heavy rusted barrels. Hoped there wasn't a second entrance. But knew there always was. Got the hell out before anyone could start thinking about an ambush.

"Fuck, but I hate this job!" Wyte exclaimed, as their boots kicked up water pooling between rows of bolted-down chairs alongside the abandoned track.

Said he hated it, but looked a lot happier than at the station.

The address turned out to be a modest-looking two-story apartment building west of the Religious District. Shoved up against more of the same, with the billowing dome of the northernmost camp beyond.

Finch recognized it as a former Frankwrithe & Lewden neighborhood. It had retained some sense of order. Of discipline. A few men with red armbands stood on the sidewalk like guards. While people traded goods.

Finch was nervous. Always worried when they went to F&L places that someone would tag him as an ex-Hoegbotton Irregular. Maybe want to put a bullet through his brain. He would've liked to have told the detectives in this sector what they were doing, but the gray caps frowned on cooperation. They liked to keep the stations as separate as possible. Make themselves the conduit.

It began to drizzle. Had been damp and warm all day. A mist gathered around Finch. Moistened his hair, his face. Green sweat had darkened the armpits of Wyte's shirt and now leaked through his overcoat.

Would Wyte hold up? Truff, please let him hold up.

Inside. Down the hall. Gun drawn. Leaking.

Wyte always went first now. He'd accepted that role voluntarily. It only made sense.

At the green-gold-purple splotched door of Bliss's apartment on the first floor, Wyte signaled his intent. The door didn't look that strong. Wyte would batter it down. Finch would storm through behind him.

A strange mewling whine came from inside. Just strange enough to make Finch shiver.

Finch mimed, *Wait.*

Took out his handkerchief, turned the knob.

The door opened.

Wyte was through before Finch could stop him, yelling, "Detectives! Hands up! Weapons down!"

Finch followed. Heart like a hammer. Gun squirting out a little between his hands in his hard double grip.

The first four rooms: empty, trashed. Someone had destroyed or ransacked everything. Tables, couches overturned. Books shredded. Torn pages everywhere. A smell of shit or rot or both. And blood. Lots of blood. Sprayed. Pooling. But no bodies. From the looks of the furniture, the arrangement had always been meant to be temporary. Or at least, it was now.

In the back bedroom they found the source of the mewling.

"Oh fuck," said Finch.

"Is that him?" Wyte asked.

"Yes."

Ethan Bliss had been nailed alive against the far wall, above a bed. His face was crusted with blood. White shirt red. Blood welling from his punctured extremities. His hands and feet still twitching as he tried to pull free of the green nails that looked like hard mushrooms. Whimpering and looking down at them through eyes crusted by something purple and brittle.

The eyes through the crust registered Finch, Wyte. A bright red mushroom had been rammed into his mouth. But he'd managed to get most of it out.

In a muffled roar: "Don't just stand there like a couple of fucking idiots. Get me down!"

Bliss began to weep.

Finch held Bliss while Wyte worked at the hands and feet. *Too close.* Sweat. Funk. Some underlying sweetness that was worse. For a sixty-year-old man, Bliss was wiry and muscular. Odd. To be here with someone who had been so well-known. Nailed to a wall. Blood all over the place. Would've been a scandal before the Rising. Now it was just another day on the job.

It took ten minutes to get him down. They tried to wipe the crust from his eyes. Managed to smear his face with green residue from his wounds. Looked like pollen dusted over the blood.

Wyte muttered, "Should we take him back to the station?"

Finch shook his head. "No. Let's do it here."

They took him to the couch in the living room. Pulled the couch upright. Wyte pushed the glass off of it using his sleeve. Finch found towels in the kitchen, brought them back and offered them to Bliss.

Bliss angrily waved Finch off.

"No, not yet," he said.

"For Truff's sake, aren't you glad to be alive?" Wyte said.

Finch gave Wyte a hard look. "He's probably in shock."

"Shock's overrated," Bliss said. "Hand me that red mushroom. The one they stuffed in my mouth."

It had fallen onto the bed. Finch went back and got it. Wondering if Bliss would recognize him. Probably not. Finch had changed his appearance completely, and Bliss had last seen him about twenty years ago.

Bliss smeared the remains of the fungus, soft cheese consistency, all over his hands and feet. Glistening. Already he had stopped bleeding.

"Now the towels," he said, taking them from Finch. He glared at Wyte, then Finch. "Who are you anyway? How did you find me? What do you want?" Even in anger, he had a youthful face. One of those faces that got more rigid as it aged. But you could still see the boyish features under the wrinkles. Under the neatly trimmed moustache.

Finch stood in front of Bliss. Wyte to the side, tapping his foot. Restless. Disturbed by something.

"I'm Finch. This is Wyte." Finch showed Bliss his badge. "You don't look happy. Should we put you back up there?"

"I wasn't dying," Bliss snapped. "Someone would have come along." Emphasis on *someone* made Finch think Bliss knew exactly who.

Bliss at the old desert fortress, turning slowly at his approach. A sound of metal locking into place. A kind of mirror. An eye. Then a circle of stone, a door, covered with gray cap symbols.

"Who did this, Bliss?" Wyte asked, kicking a broken chair out of the way. "Whose blood is all over the floor? Who'd you piss off?"

Bliss appeared not to hear this question. He stared instead at Finch. Measuring him. Like a light had clicked on behind his eyes. That weathered face had hardened remarkably, even as it managed a good imitation of a smile. Said to Finch, "You look familiar to me, detective. Do I know you? You obviously know me."

Wyte barged in, to Finch's relief: "Shut up. We're asking the questions."

Bliss registered Wyte as if for the first time. Said in a smooth voice that drove in the barb. "Why don't you find who did *that* to you, instead of wasting your time with me?"

"I said, shut up!" Wyte slapped Bliss across the cheek. Hard.

Finch had never seen Wyte hit a suspect who hadn't tried to hit him first.

Bliss took it quietly. Cursed. Put a hand to the mark. Like it had happened before. Or like pain was just an inconvenience to him. "What do you *think* happened, *detective*? They surprised us, lit us up, and didn't leave much behind. Ten of my best men."

Finch, supporting Wyte: "Answer the question, Bliss. *Who* did this to you?"

An exasperated sigh that seemed to signal a decision.

"A new man, from the Spit. He asked a lot of questions about gray caps. About the towers."

"What's his name?"

"He kept telling it to me over and over so I wouldn't forget. Even while they butchered my men. *Stark*."

"Just Stark? What's his full name?"

Wyte broke in. "I know about Stark. He's only been here eight weeks. He's from Stockton. New blood. He's been liquidating the opposition the past few weeks." Wyte was the station's Stockton expert. Ran a few snitches in that organization.

"And we've been *letting* him?"

Wyte shrugged. "Makes our job easier, doesn't it?"

Finch gave him a look that said *we'll talk more about this later.* Found it odd that Wyte knew something he didn't.

He turned to Bliss. "Why the hell did he leave you alive?"

Bliss shrugged. "Maybe he wanted to send a message."

I don't believe you.

"What kind of message? To who?" Wyte asked.

Silence.

"Take a guess about what he wanted, Bliss," Finch said.

"Part of what he wanted to do was to hurt me. He enjoyed that a little too much. I think he would have done it even if he hadn't wanted information."

"Anyone with him?"

"Just his god-awful muscle. His second in command goes by the name of Bosun, like on a ship. He's built like a kind of wiry circus strongman with a bullet bald head. Once you see him, you recognize him forever. He's the one who lifted me to the wall with one hand and drove the nails in with the other while Stark watched. All this *before* they asked me any questions."

"What questions, Bliss?" Wyte asked.

No response.

Finch showed Bliss the photograph of the dead man. "Do you know him?"

Bliss stiffened, glanced up at Finch. "Again, it would be nice to know *why* you're here?"

"Look at the photo, Bliss." Bliss looked.

"This man is dead."

"Yes, but do you know him?" Finch asked again.

Bliss shook his head. "I've never seen him before."

Lying? Or truly confused?

"What about these words?" Finch took out a piece of paper on which he'd written *bellum omnium contra omnes.*

Saw the surprise on Bliss's face. Saw that surprise change to something vaguely cat-like and unreadable. Knew whatever Bliss told him would be truth diseased with lie.

"Stark asked about something similar," Bliss said, gaze distant. "But I wouldn't know anything about that."

Wyte made an exasperated sound. "Let's finish this at the station. Interrogate him there." To Bliss: "If you cooperate, maybe it won't come down to a bullet and a memory bulb."

Most men would've gone a little pale. Bliss just sat there staring daggers at them. A defiant little man who had once run half the city.

Finch pushed. "Maybe you're right, Wyte. I'd like to know what deal you made with Stark for your life. You don't mind a trip to the station, do you, Bliss? You've got nothing to hide, right?"

Bliss erupted up off of the couch like a man twice his size, flung the lamp at Wyte, knocking his gun away. Completed the motion by slamming Finch on the side of the head with surprising strength. Dazed, Finch fell over a low table, banging his knees. Bliss bolted for the kitchen while Wyte was still scrambling for his gun.

"Fuck! Finch, stop him!"

Finch got up off the floor, drew his gun, stumbled toward the kitchen. Wyte was two steps behind.

Beyond the kitchen: a flight of stairs leading down. Finch could hear running footsteps but couldn't see Bliss. Had no choice but to charge down the stairs, only to be greeted by another hallway. Then a quick, tight corner. Wyte had caught up, and they barreled around like a couple of slapstick comedians, sliding into each other.

Caught a glimpse of Bliss's white shirt through darkness.

"Bliss! I'll shoot! Don't think I won't!" Could Bliss even hear him?

He lost Bliss in the shadows again, but got off a round or two. Hit nothing but wall. Cursing himself for not having checked the rest of the apartment. Collided with Wyte taking a second corner. Wyte was already breathing hard.

They collected themselves. Opened the door that greeted them. Another long corridor, with a door at the end.

"Fuck! How big is this place?"

They sidled up to the door. Finch got down low on his haunches, put his hand on the knob. Now he was breathing hard, but not because he was winded.

"Cover me high," he said, glancing up at Wyte. Blood singing in his ears, fingers a little numb.

Wyte nodded, face impossibly long and thick from that angle, chin jutting, expression priest-solemn. Finch turned the knob and pushed the door open. Slowly rose, knees already aching.

"Goddamn it."

An empty room ten feet square, the walls made of cinder blocks painted white. A single bulb for light. No windows. No other door.

They kept circling it with guns drawn, like Bliss would appear out of nowhere.

Never lost.

Except now he was.

4

Where had Bliss gone? The question haunted Finch as they left the apartment. Didn't know if anyone had heard the shots. Or if Bliss still had people who might be watching. "Secret door?" Wyte had suggested, almost as if it didn't bother him. But they'd found nothing. They'd have had to tear the place apart. Brick by brick. Didn't have the tools or time for that.

They passed addicts with the familiar purple stains across their skin. Men in the ill-fitting uniforms of janitors for the camps. Somebody pissing in an alley. Faded posters on a long crumbling wall, showing pictures of members of the short-lived puppet government. Another blood-red mushroom looming over them big as a tree. Every week there seemed to be more of them. Next to it, a blossoming flower of a building atop the squashed remains of the local grocery store. Soft humming sounds came from an interior obscured by fleshy window flaps.

Where had Bliss gone—and how was he involved?

Finch replayed that moment over and over. Bliss running for the kitchen. Bliss in his memory bulb dream. Trying to reconcile those versions with the Bliss he remembered from before the Rising. The way Bliss's gaze couldn't settle on one thing. As if his mind worked faster now. A growing sense that this new Bliss hadn't been stripped of prestige and security but had *traded* it for something else.

Wyte seemed agitated, and Finch thought he knew why. So he said, "It's my fault. We should've taken him in from the beginning, like you suggested. I didn't need to question him first. And I forgot to check out the rest of the apartment."

Wyte's neck had an orange stain on it. Fingernails that had turned black. A smell like a distant sewer drain. But he'd been worse.

"I hit him, and I spooked him," Wyte said. "I'm as much to blame as you. Maybe more. But that's not the point, Finchy."

Here it comes.

Wyte stopped walking, faced him. Finch had his back to a crumbling wall veined through with fungus so blue it looked black. An overlay of scattered bullet holes. Across the street, a laughing pack of Partials shoved a couple of prisoners ahead of them. A middle-aged bearded man with a bandage across his forehead and angry rips in a shirt discolored pink. A woman who could have been the man's wife, her long black hair being used as a leash by one of the Partials. Just a jaunt around the block before getting down to business.

"Look, Finch," Wyte said. "I'm your partner. And you keep *keeping* things from me. I hadn't even seen the photo of the dead man until you showed it to Bliss. And where's the list Heretic gave you?"

Wyte will never adjust. It made Finch sick deep in his stomach.

Finch pulled Wyte back to the wall with him. The Partials had moved on ahead, oblivious to anything but their prisoners, but he didn't want to take any chances. In a whisper: "Listen to me. I'm just trying to protect you."

Wyte stared at him for so long that Finch had to look at the ancient dislodged stones of the sidewalk. A sudden hunger for a past when Wyte hadn't been this way. A feeling so strong he felt water in his eyes.

Each word meant to wound, Wyte said: "I don't need protecting, like I've told you. Back in the day, *I* protected *you*." Then self-importantly, when Finch said nothing: "I'm going to work for the rebels soon. I know someone who knows someone."

This shit again. Once every few weeks.

Something snapped in Finch. Felt it in his head like the sudden eruption of a migraine.

He shoved Wyte up against the wall. Didn't care who was watching. Felt the air go out of the older man's lungs. Those eyes scared by what they saw in Finch. Skin clammy. Some of Wyte's shirt wasn't really a shirt.

Finch said as calmly as he could: "You are not going to be a fucking spy for the rebels. You are not going to be a fucking spy for the rebels. Ever. *Do you understand?*"

"Get the fuck off of me!" Wyte hissed. Twisting in Finch's grip. Head angled toward the sky. Shoulders arched back like he was trying to take off his coat but had gotten his arm stuck.

"You're not. And do you know why not? Because you've been colonized. And it's gone too far. *And they'll never take you." Never take you back. Never want you now. Too late.* "And if they did, you'd probably be spying on them. For the gray caps. Without even knowing it. Which is why you can't." *And you'd be leaving me with a station full of detectives who hate me because I didn't abandon you.*

He released Wyte, pushing off of him. Creating space between them in case it turned into a fight.

But Wyte stayed up against the wall. What was the look on his face? Didn't matter. It was the way he stood. Finch had seen the same tired stoop in workers from the camps. Seen it at times in Rath.

Continued on now that it made no difference: "The closest you'll get to working for anyone is wringing intel out of that ragged bunch of Stockton contacts you call a network." Trailed off.

Wyte's self-disdain when he turned to Finch made him look angry or righteous. A darkness there that might have been spores coming up through his skin.

"Better than doing nothing, like you."

"I don't do nothing. I do what I *can*. There's a difference." Hands clenched into fists. Face contorted. Close to being out of control. *What if he's right?*

Stood there while Wyte opened his mouth to say something.

But Wyte didn't say anything, just let out his breath with a shudder. Finch watched warily as Wyte reached into his overcoat pocket with a hand that trembled slightly and took out a flask made of battered silver and tin, the once-proud H&S insignia marred by fire burns.

Finch had given it to Wyte on his birthday ten years ago. Emily hadn't liked it. Thought her husband drank too much anyway. Didn't need to "make it into a ritual" as she put it. But that didn't stop her from joining them when they'd stood on the step outside of the house to share a smoke and whatever Wyte had put in the flask. Remembered its quick glint as it picked up the sun or a streetlight.

"It's got good brandy in it, Finchy," Wyte said. "The last bit I've been hoarding."

"You're not going to hit me?"

"What for, Finchy? What'd be the point?"

Finch grimaced. Managed to transform it into a thin smile. "Some brandy might be a good idea." He patted Wyte's ruffled overcoat back into place. "I'm sorry, Wyte. I'm sorry."

And he meant it. Turned away. Disgusted with himself. Who had the bigger burden? The one who had to watch the other person endure or the one who endured?

Wearily, Wyte said: "How could you know? What it's like living with something else inside me. While on the outside I keep changing."

Worse than a dead man talking to me?

Finch didn't want to think about it. Took the flask. Downed half of it in a gulp. Felt the liquid rage through his capillaries. Like a forest fire that left ice behind it. He handed the flask back. "Good stuff." They started walking again.

Wyte laughed. "Still can't really hold it, can you? Any more than you could when you were working for me."

Slapped Finch on the back hard enough to make him stagger.

Fair enough.

* * *

Wyte. The story.

He'd gone to investigate a death about a year ago. By himself. No one else in the station. The call sounded simple. A man found dead beneath a tree, beginning to smell. Could someone take a look? Most days, not worth bothering with. But it was a slow morning, and Wyte took the job seriously. The woman seemed upset, like it was personal.

The body was down near the bay. Beside a cracked stone sign that used to welcome visitors to Ambergris. *Holy city, majestic, banish your fears.* No one was around. Not the woman who had called it in. No one.

The man lay on his back. Connected to the "tree," which was a huge mushroom. Connected by tendrils. The smell, vile. The man's eyes open and flickering.

Wyte should have left. Wyte should have known better. But maybe Wyte was bored. Or wanted a change. Or just didn't care. He hadn't seen his kids since they'd been sent out of the city. He'd been fighting with his wife a lot.

He leaned over the body. Maybe he thought he saw something floating in those eyes. Something moving. Maybe movement meant life to him.

"Who knows? Just know that it's a dumb move."

A dumb move. That's how the detectives would say it during the retell. At their little refuge, not far from the station. Blakely had discovered the place. In front of what used to be the old Bureaucratic Quarter. Looks like a guard post. Nondescript. Gray stone. Surrounded by a thicket of half-walls, rubble hills, and stunted trees. With a moat that's really just a pond that collects rainwater. From the inside, it's clear the structure is the top of a bell tower pulled down and submerged when the gray caps Rose.

Always half out of their minds with whisky or homemade wine, or whatever. When they told the story. *A dumb move.* Like they were experts.

"Point is," Albin would say, because Albin usually told the story, "he leaned over, and the man's head exploded into spores. And those spores got into Wyte's head."

White spores for Wyte. Through the nose. Through any exposed cuts. Through the ears. Through the eyes.

Although he fought it. Twisted furiously. Jumped up and down. Cursed like the end of the world. So at least he didn't just stand there and let it happen.

"But by that time, it was too late. A few minutes later and he's just somebody's puppet."

Wyte became someone else. The "dead" man. Someone who didn't understand what had happened to him. Wyte ran down the street. Taken over. Screaming.

"Screaming a name over and over. 'Otto! I'm Otto!' because that was the dead man's name. Wyte thought he was Otto."

Or most of him did. Wyte, deep inside, still knew who he was, and that was worse.

Sometimes, out of a casual cruelty, a kind of boredom, one of the other detectives, usually Blakely, will call Wyte "Otto." Until Finch makes him stop.

"Well, they found him a day later. Once they figured out who the dead body was. Cowering in a closet. Saying 'Otto' over and over again."

In the dead man's apartment.

"A caution to us all."

Then they would clink glasses and bottles, congratulating themselves on being alive.

Truth was, they told the story less to humiliate Wyte than to keep reminding themselves not to take any chances. *Ambergris Rules.* No dumb moves.

Wyte got Otto out of his head. Eventually. Most of Otto. But not the fungus. That became worse. The gray caps couldn't or wouldn't help. Maybe they saw it as some kind of perverse improvement.

No one had ever found out who had lured Wyte there. Or why.

Finch knew they never would.

They split up. Wyte headed back to the station. Finch decided to return to the apartment on Manzikert. He'd have more than his fill of the station later.

"Do I mention Bliss?"

"If it comes up, no. His file's already being pulled. That's enough for now."

"He made us look like fools."

"We made ourselves look like fools."

Black trees. Odd fruit. Pissed-off cat. Hallways that still squeaked from wax. The stairwell still collected darkness. But a silence had crept in, too. An emptiness that hadn't been there before. No sounds of a mother and child. No smells of cooking.

On a hunch, Finch stopped at the fourth floor again. Knocked on the door of the man who had dressed up for Finch's mild interrogation. Held his badge up to the peephole.

The door creaked open. A Partial stood there. Stockier than the one who had catalogued the crime scene. His face even paler. Red teeth. As if he'd been eating raw meat sloppily. Dressed in black dyed leather, but wore beige boots. Like he'd been caught trying on someone else's clothes. In the belt around his gut, two holstered guns and a hammer, of all things.

Finch held the badge in front of him.

"I'm the detective on the case in apartment 525," he said. "Where's the old man who lives here?"

The Partial considered him for a moment. The glittering black eye was flickering madly. But the rest of him was like a chilled tortoise. Arms at his sides. Almost paralyzed.

"Gone," he said slowly. Making the syllable linger.

"Gone where?" Finch asked.

"Gone somewhere else," the Partial said with an effort.

Like you, my friend. Wondered if the flickering eye meant his attention was elsewhere. *Reviewing not recording.*

A new thought, horrifying him. "Are they *all* gone?"

The eye stopped flickering. Blinked twice. In a more normal voice the Partial said, "The building has been cleared."

Cleared how? Escorted out and rehoused? Sent to the camps? Liquidated?

But he didn't ask, just nodded. Smiled. Stepped back.

The Partial parroted the nod and receded from him into darkness. Shut the door.

Finch stood there a moment. This place was now a Partial stronghold. *No witnesses.*

He took the stairs to the fifth floor in leaps. As if running fast might prevent the crime that had brought him here. Bring back the old man in the too-tight suit.

The door. The gray cap symbol, glistening and obscene. The hallway. The bedroom, empty. The living room; no sign of the Partial.

The bodies.

Correction. Body.

The gray cap's body had disappeared.

Finch stood there a moment, brought up short. Trying to process that sudden . . . *lack.* Then realized: Heretic must have removed the body. If not, they'd send Finch to the camps. *Scapegoat.* Returning: the chill that had come over him talking to the red-toothed Partial. It hit him as it hadn't before. This case was a threat to his life. To the little security he had. His apartment. His relationship with Sintra.

But the man was still there, under a blanket someone had thrown over him. *The dead man sat in the chair next to him, smiling.* In the same position. The blue of the preservatives still stippling his features. *The man laughed again. Blindingly, unbelievably bright, a light like the sun shot through the window. The night sky torn apart by it.*

Finch went over and pulled the blanket back from the man's face. Sat on the couch, looking at the body. He would have to meet with Heretic soon. The thought unnerved him. Wished now he'd asked Wyte for the whole flask. Wished he could just go home. Find Sintra waiting for him.

"You know what those nonsense words mean," Finch said to the man. "You know why it's important."

Peaceful. The man looked peaceful, to be so dead. How perfectly preserved in the light from the open window. Ignoring how that light changed as it was interrogated by the space between the twinned towers in the distance.

Finch got down on his knees. Searched the body again. Not the careful search of yesterday. *Fuck the spore cameras. Fuck the Partial.*

Roughly, he rolled the body over and went through the pockets. As if he'd killed the man himself.

There must be something else.

But, no, there wasn't. Just lint in one pocket. A few bits of sand and gravel, maybe a grain of rice?, in the other.

He began to rip up the fabric. It tore easier than he would've thought. Hurting his hands. Red lines on his palms. Aching wrists. Still nothing. No hidden pockets. He forced himself to stop tearing.

The upturned corners of the man's lips seemed to say, "You'll never solve me."

I'm not a detective.

But he would be judged as a detective. Convicted as a detective.

A desert fortress. The HFZ. A phrase. *Never lost.* Falling from a great height. A gray cap even the gray caps couldn't identify. An operative from Stockton who was on the same trail. Another operative, probably from Morrow, attacked by Stockton spies and appearing in a dead man's memories. Now disappeared.

Stark. Bosun. Bliss.

It would drive him mad, he realized. If he let it.

I need a better gun.

Looked at his watch.

5:20.

Time to leave.

Let the horror show begin.

5

Back at the station.

5:50.

No sign of Wyte. The other detectives had left, too, except for Gustat, who was frantically packing up his things. Finch looked at the smaller man with a kind of scorn. Gustat ignored him in his haste. Strange horse-like footfalls across the carpet. The croaking bang of the door behind him.

Then it was just Finch.

Soon the curtains at the back of the room would part. Night would truly begin.

Wyte had placed a hasty typo-filled report on Finch's desk about the situation in Bliss's apartment. "John Finch" typed at the bottom. *Brave of you, Wyte.* A blotch of purple obscured a few words in the middle. A smudged green thumbprint on the left corner. Wyte had tried to wipe it away, which just made it worse.

Under it, another sheet, handwritten, with some crude facts about Stark.

"Stark is now the operational head of Stockton's spy network."

Stating the obvious. No one started liquidating the competition unless they were already secure in their position.

"He carries a sword."

Who didn't, these days? Thought about pulling his own sword out. As he did several times a week, when he thought the others weren't looking.

"He has a taster for his food . . . He's a psychopath . . . He's been seen . . ." well, practically everywhere and nowhere, if Wyte's information was correct.

Nothing solid. Nothing that linked Stark to the case except Bliss saying Stark had asked him about those words they'd found on the scrap of paper. *Bellum omnium contra omnes.* Wondered what Bliss would've said if he'd shown him the symbol too.

Finch kept a stack of cigars in his desk in a box converted to the purpose. He took one out. Trillian brand. Several years old. Common and popular in its day. A little dry now.

Nothing new in this city. Not whisky. Not cigars. Not people.

The kind of thing his father used to say.

He cut the tip. Used his oil lamp to light it.

The ash was even. The burn slow. He puffed on it, waiting. *The congregation will be here soon enough.*

His thoughts went back to Wyte's flask. In a flush of inspiration, Finch went over to Blakely's desk, opened the top drawer. Sure enough. Something plum-colored in a bottle. Homemade cork. He pulled it off. Took a whiff. Rotgut, but good enough. Took a couple of swigs right from the bottle. His throat burned. His tongue felt numb.

Saw double for a second. Another puff on the cigar fixed that. Went back to his desk.

Waiting this way, helpless, his vision became apocalyptic, false. In his mind, mortar fire rained down on the city. Artillery belched out a retort. Blasted into walls, sending up gouts of stone and flame. The war raged on, unnoticed by most. He was an agent of neither side. Just in it for himself.

Tried to think past the evening's torment. The walk back to his apartment afterward. In the dark. Thought of who might be waiting.

If he didn't screw up before that.

A little after six, the gray caps began to arrive. *The night shift.*

The first one pulled aside the curtain. Had emerged from the awful red-fringed hole at the back. Perfect parallel to the memory hole. Only much larger. Finch could see the gray cap's face under the hat. Pulsing. Wriggling. The eyes so yellow. What did they see that he could not?

The gray cap stepped forward, onto the carpet.

In the light of day, on certain streets, Finch could almost pretend that the Rising had never happened. But not here. Not now. Any fantasy was fatal. Any fear.

Finch walked out onto the carpet. Puffing. Feeling the brittle squeeze in his chest even as he released the smoke from his mouth. Let the cigar burn down toward his fingers to feel the distracting pain.

A strong scent of rotting licorice as the gray cap pushed past him. Ignoring him as it sat down at a desk. Gustat's desk.

One.

Nine more. One for each desk. Along with whatever familiars they had decided to bring with them.

Finch wished he had a club. A knife. Anything. The fungal guns didn't work against gray caps. Thought again about the sword. About bringing it across Heretic's rubbery neck.

He drove the image away as irrational. Heretic had asked him to be here. If Heretic ever wanted him dead, he'd send a present to his apartment. Or dissolve him into a puff of spores in front of the other detectives.

Five times he'd stayed after hours. Survived each encounter. But talking to a single gray cap during the day was different from being among many of them after dusk. It brought back memories of the war. It reminded him of night duty in the trenches, the crude defenses House Hoegbotton had created for its soldiers. Sighting through the scope at some pile of rubble opposite. Hoping not to see anything. Feeling the sweat and fear of the others to each side. The flinch and intake of breath at the slightest movement.

Two.

Three.

Four.

Moving past him. Soft rustle of robes. Hushed sigh of their breathing, as if they slept even while awake. Oddly heavy footfalls. A smell that ranged from sweet like syrup to rank and disgusting. Did they control it? Were there signals they gave off humans could never read? *Those eyes. That mouth. The ragged claws on the doughy hands.*

Sitting at the desks like distorted reflections of their daytime counterparts. He had never learned their names. Thought of them only by the names of the humans who'd been assigned the same desks. Or once had. So there sat Dorn, and there sat Wyte, and there were Skinner and Albin.

The fifth was Heretic. He'd brought something with him. On a leash. Finch didn't know what it was. Couldn't tell where it started or ended. It had no face, just a sense of wet, uncoiling darkness. Like an endless fall off a bridge at night, under a starless sky, into deep water. That one glimpse and Finch never looked at it directly again.

The light in the room had faded to the dark green preferred by the gray caps.

"Do you like my *skery*, Finch? Do you find my *skery* pleasing to the eye?" Heretic asked in a voice rough yet reedy, standing in front of Finch. Emphasis on *pleasing to the eye*. As usual when Heretic tried out a turn of phrase. "No? That's a shame. The *skery* is a new thing, and useful to us. Very soon, it will save us a lot of effort, allow the Partials to do other work."

Finch had no answer for that.

Together, Finch, the gray cap, and the *skery* went to his desk. At night, Heretic walked with a kind of effortless forward movement. More at ease and more deadly. As if daylight affected a gray cap's equilibrium.

Heretic sat down, dropping the leash. The *skery* went right to Finch's memory hole and began worrying the edges with its wet gobble of a mouth. Cleaning it of parasites.

Finch put out his cigar in the ashtray at the edge of the desk. Stood in front of Heretic. *Take the initiative.* In a calm, flat voice, he said: "I went back to the apartment. The body . . . one of the bodies was missing."

"I took it away." A clipped quality behind the moistness. Some continuing thread of amusement. The eyes looked as though embedded in a rubber festival mask. "We're testing the body for a variety of — —." The word sounded like *tilivirck*.

Finch nodded like he understood.

"We also harvested another memory bulb from the man."

Utter paralysis. Unbidden: an image of Sintra's face as he entered her. The way she sighed and relaxed into him. As the blood of his tears dropped onto her cheeks, her lips.

"What did you see?" Finch asked.

Heretic shook his head. A simple motion rendered alien, frightening. "Perhaps you should tell me first, Finch. What you saw."

"It's in the report," Finch said. Too quickly.

"The report. It's all in the report. How could we forget? Perhaps because the report was disappointing. Very disappointing, and not what we've come to expect from you." Still a secret amusement there, mingled with the threat.

His stomach lurched. The room felt hot. At the other desks, the last of the gray caps had sat down. At their feet, their familiars curled, mewled, foraged.

"It's only been a day," Finch said.

"Finch," Heretic said. "Are you telling me everything?"

Bliss had disappeared from a ten-foot-square room. With no windows.

"I left out nothing important," Finch said. "Up to that point."

Heretic said something in his own language that sounded like a child arguing with a click beetle. Then, a half-expected blade held to the throat: "What about the scrap of paper the Partial says you took from the body?"

The symbol. The strange words. What would Heretic tell him about the Silence if he asked? Nothing. He'd kill Finch. Or worse.

Out of sudden fear, a strange calm. Later, he realized it felt like losing control even as he gained it. An echoing faint laughter that became the sound of hammers working on the two towers in the bay. That became water slapping against the wall in Rathven's basement.

Words left his mouth. "There was a man in the memories I recognized. I didn't put it in the report because I wanted to investigate first. It related to the paper in the dead man's hand." Lying.

Falling through cold air and he couldn't feel his legs.

"Explain."

"A man called Ethan Bliss." And then the flood: "A Morrow agent active for Frankwrithe & Lewden, during the War of the Houses. I tracked him down today with Wyte, but he . . . slipped away. I'm following up. I put in a request for his file along with my report."

If we can't find him, we'll go after Stark.

Heretic seemed to consider that, then asked, "And the scrap of paper?"

"I'm still investigating what it means. I'll put it all into my report for tomorrow."

"And the list I gave you, of people who lived in that apartment?"

Finch relaxed a little. "I'm still working on it. By tomorrow afternoon I should know more." *If Rathven's finished by then.*

Heretic considered this statement for a long time, then said, "You have withheld information from me. You haven't even finished with the list. From now on, you will report every day. You are to tell me *everything*. Do not leave it to your judgment."

Finch opened his mouth to speak. Heretic said words that sounded like *kith vrisdresn zorn*. Snapped his fingers.

The *skery* wound itself around Finch's legs and tightened. Sudden tingling paralysis. He could not move away. Could not fall. Choking on his own breath. The paralysis brought with it an image of an endless field of dim stars, one by one extinguished. A gulf and a void. Finch was as afraid as he had ever been in his life. Because he didn't know what he was looking at, or why.

Try to breathe. Slowly. Breathe slowly.

The *skery* curled its way up to his chest. Around his neck. It pulled tight so he was gasping in his motionlessness. He felt something like sharp leaves or thorns up against his neck. An impression of lips. A sharp, smoky scent. Half the field of stars had gone out. There was more darkness than light.

From behind Finch's desk, from a thousand miles away, from behind a thick wall: Heretic. Saying, "A *skery* is not as bad for you as what I could bring with me."

The *skery* curled back down Finch's body. Released him. He stumbled forward, hands on the desk to stop from falling. The field of stars so bright he almost passed out. Then the desk came into focus. Prickles of sensation came back into his legs. Neck already sore and throbbing.

"Do you understand me, Finch?" Heretic said. "We can make it quite clear who you really are. To everyone. Or we can just put you in the camps. Or we can do much, much worse."

Finch had killed a gray cap once. As an Irregular. Before the Rising. Out in the confusion of civil war. With a knife and a gun. He thought about that now, looking at Heretic.

Heretic: "How did Bliss manage to escape you? I expect that in your report by tomorrow night. You will leave your report on your desk. I will read it. If I am not satisfied, I will visit you. Find ways to convince me that you are more valuable alive than as a memory bulb. Do you understand?"

"I understand," Finch managed after a moment. Throat sore. Burying his anger deep. Just wanting to be away from there. Just wanting to be somewhere he might fool himself into calling *safe*.

The gray cap rose. "You'll find Bliss's information in the 'memory hole' by your desk in a few minutes."

Heretic walked toward the back, holding his *skery*. Rivulets of golden spores swirled up from his footfalls. Sparkled in the murk like tiny blinking eyes.

Against all good judgment, against his shock at the *skery*'s touch, Finch spoke. "What happened when you took the dead man's memory bulb?"

Heretic half-turned, the look on his face murderous. "I did not eat the memory bulb. That was another *fanaarcensitii*. He saw nothing. He died within minutes, in horrible pain. Apparently, you are very, very lucky, Finch."

A long peal of that awful laughter before Heretic disappeared behind the curtain.

Afterward, Finch couldn't sleep. Stomach churning. Couldn't get rid of a crawling sensation. Half his mouth felt numb. The other half tingled like a faint electric shock. His legs moved slowly, a deep ache in both muscle and bone.

Had returned to his apartment to find a note from Sintra shoved under the door: *Can't make it tonight. Tomorrow night.* Found that a bad mood could get worse.

He went up to the roof of the hotel, a fifth of whisky retrieved from his kitchen, and let a nagging Feral come with him. Carried the cat's comforting weight, like a purring loaf of bread, in the crook of his left arm. In his other hand, the file on Bliss.

The stairs above his floor had been so colonized by moss and lichen that they didn't creak. Dark. Dangerous. But Finch didn't care. He'd lost his way anyhow, was in need of something sturdier than self-pity.

A hatch in the ceiling where the stairs ended led to the roof. He switched Bliss's file to under his arm, next to a protesting Feral. Set down the whisky long enough to push open the hatch without losing his balance. Picked it back up, and stepped through with Feral. Into a bracing wind. A wash of stars set against the black-and-green-tinged sky.

Except for the bit obscured by the dilapidated sign, Finch could see the whole city from here. One reason he'd chosen the hotel. The view from the roof helped him with his map overlay. Made him feel more in control, being able to see so much from one place. The soldier in him always wanted the best possible recon.

Muted lights from the buildings to either side. Like he saw them through a black curtain. Even the two towers seemed dulled, the emerald glow humble. A few sparkling clouds of spores, in blue and yellow, danced far out in the sky, to the south. Otherwise, just the inward-focused white of the camp domes, balanced to the north by the humming glitter of orange-green HFZ. The air didn't carry the smell of mushrooms. As if a fresh breeze had come from outside the city.

A tall figure stood near the edge of the roof, looking out. Finch stiffened, making Feral hiss. He groped for the gun he had left in the apartment, Feral jumping from his arm. Then Finch realized it was just the Photographer, Rath's brother. The man who liked to take pictures of water and ran a black market store out of his apartment.

Finch had seen the photographs. Stacked up next to the cameras. Plastered to the walls. Blown up, miniaturized, blurry, in focus. On anything that might serve, or re-serve, as contact paper. As if the Photographer looked for one particular thing in the water. As if not interested in water at all, searching for something he hadn't found yet.

A fifth of whisky was enough for two.

The Photographer turned as Finch approached. A slow, unconcerned motion. Finch had never seen him anything other than calm. Or maybe his mood was always resigned to whatever new thing came next. Didn't know what had happened to him in the camps. Didn't know much about him at all, except that he trusted the man. Which made little sense. He was so clearly damaged. So indifferent to Finch's help in getting him out of the camp.

The Photographer nodded.

Finch passed the bottle to the Photographer. The man took a sip and handed it back. He stared at Finch with an unreadable gaze. A white face and a watchful mouth, with an upturn to the lips that could make him look devilish. The eyes and cheekbones didn't match the mouth. The eyes were almost vacant, except for a deep-set glint. Finch thought of that glint as curiosity or obsession. The high cheekbones gave the Photographer an aura of deep or deeply denied suffering.

"Anything new out there?"

"A few things." His voice a thin reed.

"Anything I should know about?"

The Photographer shrugged, looked out at the night. "More activity at the towers, just a little while ago. An emergency? Quickly solved, if so. Nothing there now. A few spore discharges to the west. Can't tell if they're human or mechanical. But not much, no . . . What happened to you?"

An involuntary snort. He must look as ragged as he felt. The Photographer had never asked after his health before.

"I came across something that didn't like me," Finch said. No desire to share the details. Thinking about how he had to hold out for another day before seeing Sintra again.

The Photographer nodded as if this made sense. Returned to his contemplation of the view. Didn't care much for small talk.

Slowly, stiffly, Finch lowered himself into a chair. A few feet away, Feral was munching on something he'd caught.

A couple of light bulbs hung near the rotting sign. The outer arc of their light just barely caught the edge of the chairs. Enough to read by.

Eyes adjusted to the dim light, Finch began to go through Bliss's file. Two laughably old photographs. One so dark it was just a silhouette with a hint of jaw leering out of a smudge. The report itself was brief, pithy, in the spidery script of gray cap transcriptions. Translated from their original files. *Which took what form?* Probably were worse things than memory holes down below.

Finch already knew most of what was in the report. Bliss's rise within F&L ranks. The compromise with Hoegbotton. The alliance with the Lady in Blue. But he was somehow surprised that the gray caps knew it. Made him wonder about the extent of their intel before the Rising.

Buried in the middle of the report, Finch found a list of aliases under which Bliss had operated: *Charles Dinley, George Graansvoort, John Letcher, Grant Shearwater, Dar Sardice.* And, most improbably, *Jasper Marlowe Anthony Blasio.* A typo? An error in the transcription?

Dar Sardice proved the most interesting. The other names had been ways of disguising movements across checkpoints within the city. Dar Sardice had been used much earlier, during Ambergrisian-Hoegbotton campaigns against the Kalif. "Dar Sardice" had been Frankwrithe's man keeping an eye on the progress of the war. From behind the Kalif's supply lines. The cover? Independent merchant and businessman. With an established trade route that cut through over eight hundred miles of desert dotted with fortified towns. The whole Western Front. Against which the Ambergrisian Army had thrown itself with unparalleled ferocity. From which it had eventually retreated. *"It was just too large," his father had said once. "It was overwhelming. The wide, hot, empty spaces. The strangeness of the towns. The fact we didn't speak the language."* Left a trail of broken, bombed equipment behind. Trucks. Tanks. Mortars.

A desert fortress. A fall from a great height. Ethan Bliss as Dar Sardice, turning up in every major theater of a desert war. Then appearing again not long after as F&L's man in Ambergris. Popping up in the dead man's memories. Had disappeared when cornered, after having been nailed to a wall just a few minutes before.

Was he looking at a secret that should be obvious? If so, it eluded him the more he tried to pin it down.

Beside him, the Photographer stirred. "I am going to go back inside. Do you need anything from me?"

"Just information," Finch said, and downed some whisky. He enjoyed the way it spread out from his throat, his stomach. Settling him as it mixed with the afterburn of the cigar.

"What kind of information?"

On a hunch, feeling like his back was exposed: "Seen anyone strange around the hotel recently?"

The Photographer replied with a kind of odd regret, as if speaking out of turn: "Yes, I have."

Suddenly more alert: "Describe them?"

"Two of them, today. They came separately. The first I saw around noon. A tall Partial. He was on the stairs when I saw him. Coming down." A look of disgust on the Photographer's face.

The same Partial?

"Coming down from where?"

"I don't know. I was on the fifth floor. He was coming down."

Could've been anyone. Could've been here for any reason. And nothing he could do about it.

"The second?"

"He stayed outside the building. It was late afternoon. A bald man. Dangerous-looking. He talked to the madman by the statue. Didn't like what the madman told him. Then looked up at the windows for awhile. He stayed off to the side smoking a cigarette. Got impatient and walked into the lobby for a moment, came back out, and left almost right away."

A description that matched what Bliss had told them about Bosun, Stark's muscle. Which meant they'd had watchers on Bliss's place. Watchers who had identified Finch incredibly fast. Now they were checking out where he lived. He didn't like that. Didn't like it at all.

Definitely time to have a talk with Stark.

"Tell me if you see them again? Or anyone else who doesn't live here?"

The Photographer nodded. Then he was taking long strides to the hatch, as if he suddenly needed to be somewhere. The hatch creaked open, and he was gone.

Off to Finch's left, Feral was stalking something new around a couple of wooden boxes. Finch went back to his whisky. Wondered if Bliss/Dar Sardice leading them to Stark meant Stark would lead them back to Bliss. And who was Stark, then? Just another Stockton man, or something else?

All the while trying not to think of the *skery.* Curling up his leg. Wound around his neck.

Failing.

WEDNESDAY

I: When did you first decide to contact Stark? Before or after Bliss?

F: I was just investigating two deaths. Following orders.

I: And to you that meant scheming with *all* of the city's enemies?

F: No, that's not it at all. That you—

[screams, garbled recording]

F: *Why did you do that?* Why? I'm *talking*. I'm *talking*.

I: But you're not saying anything.

1

On their way the next morning to track down Stark . . .

Wind and spray of rain against Finch's face as they sped across the bay toward the Spit. Glad of the cool water soaking his hair. But he had a hard time keeping the filter-mask over eyes, nose, and mouth from clouding up. It itched, made him sweat. Made Wyte, as he turned toward Finch, look like something meant to frighten children. But better safe than dead. Even the gray caps didn't know what lived in the air above the bay, the water corrupted by runoff from the HFZ. *Tiny assassins. Cell disruptors and breath-stealers . . .*

Finch stood at the prow of the gray cap boat, the only kind allowed out on the bay. Wyte beside him, skin on his arms green. Not from being seasick. The boat was big enough for eight or ten. Empty with just the two of them. Slight upward lurching push as it expelled water below the surface to propel them forward. Looked like any other boat from afar. *Except it acts like it's alive.* Route preplanned by the gruff Partial who had met them on the shore. Who had shoved a mushroom into an orifice on the hull that looked uncannily like a memory hole. Somehow the boat knew where to go. How to return.

Finch's shoes were sinking into the loamy sponge of the "planks." Tried to remember to bend his knees to keep his balance. But balance was a precarious thing. Tongue dry, stomach aching. The *skery* had done something to his muscles. Made him feel like he'd wrestled a giant all night. Didn't like that. Didn't like being robbed of his natural river-legs. Finch had liked the water, once. With childhood friends, names now lost—*Charlie? Sam?*—he'd gone down to the docks to fish. Pushed a canoe out into the current. Later, working for Wyte, he'd gotten up close to the big ships docking to unload and take on board H&S goods.

Ghosts of early-morning conversations with Wyte ran through Finch's head.

"Most of my informants have gone dark. Stark's influence. Taking care of leaks and stirring up hornets."

"You've got to know more about Stark than what you left on my desk, Wyte."

"No. Not a thing. We don't even know if that's his real name."

"Nobody's real name is just Stark, Wyte."

Wyte had arranged for a Stockton operative named Stephen Davies to act as a go-between with Stark. They'd approach the floating pontoons at the northeast edge of the Spit. Much safer than from the land side. A maze of ruins there. Ideal for ambush. No cover. No way to retreat.

Spies came into Ambergris simple and alone, first stop the Spit. Over the water. In the darkness, as if newly born. With nothing on them that the gray caps might want. Nothing that their masters wouldn't want taken. They built up their resources over time. Using whatever money or influence they'd brought from Stockton, Morrow, or even more distant lands. Sometimes the Spit was the last stop, too.

"Truff love foreigners, trying to take advantage of our fucked-up city."

"Stark'll be no different. Where was Stockton during the Rising?"

"Waiting to pick the bones clean."

Trying to pump themselves up. Convince themselves they were still loyal to Ambergris. Hated how the masks made their voices tinny.

"Davies seems in awe of Stark."

"Sure it's not fear? Though most of them are probably past fear or awe by now . . ."

Wyte just shrugged. Finch knew he didn't want to think about that. Didn't want to know what shit might be waiting on the Spit.

Hints of bobbing islands in the waves now. Some of them too close to ignore. Yet Finch ignored them. Corpse islands made from workers who had died in the camps. Reborn as floating compost for fruiting bodies. And far, far below them, the decaying docks, the drowned part of Albumuth Boulevard. All of the dead, still in the buildings where they had worked or lived, the onslaught of water so sudden. Slamming into them. For a time lit up by the strobing of the giant squid that had patrolled the bay. Long since gone, driven out by the pollution. Finch couldn't take it. Not this morning.

"Water can behave like a person," his father used to say. Treacherous. Tides and swirls and eddies. Sucking boats down with them.

The past didn't seem like another world. The past seemed like it had never happened. Couldn't have happened. The leap to *this* too hideous, too nightmarish. Better to have no past at all. Suddenly, he needed Sintra. Needed her badly. Could almost smell her perfume. Wanted to be back in his apartment, next to her.

"Where do you live?"

"A place with four walls, and a ceiling."

"What are the neighbors like?"

"Noisy. Sad. Temporary . . ."

Resented Wyte irrationally for a moment. As if Sintra could've replaced him on the boat. Backed him up. Except she couldn't.

"What can you hear from your window, Sintra?"

"The sound of detectives asking questions."

"Finch." Wyte made it sound like a warning, jolting him from his thoughts. "Over there." Pointing, like he wanted a distraction, too.

Just behind them: another boat. Much larger, coming in from the southeast. Flat-bottomed. Lagging in the water.

Finch had brought his gun against his own better instincts. Drew it now. Then looked closer and holstered it.

"Just prisoners," he said. *Could as well be us.*

Wyte took a second look, nodded.

Soon the boat slid past their prow, heading for the towers. It held about thirty people from the camps. Guarded by two gray caps and a Partial. The men and women dressed in the dull sack robes of their status. Some wearing old-fashioned masks that might or might not work. Heads bowed not from prayer but from hopelessness. Thin, with light-green skin. Shoulders slumped.

"During the *day*?" Wyte said, almost pleading to be told he was wrong.

"During the day," Finch said, annoyed. Best just to be thankful not to be in the camps.

The Truffidian priest in the back of the boat caught Finch's attention. In full regalia, down to the golden chains. The same priests had walked side by side with Ambergrisian infantry invading Kalif lands. The gray caps had broken them. Treated them almost like pets now. Their eyes locked, the older man bowing his head to avoid Finch's stare. Noted the hooded look. The slight shake. He was on the gray caps' drugs. Did this in return for his fix. *Turncoat.*

Wyte: "In the old days, he'd have died for that. And not quickly."

And so would we.

"What?" Wyte said.

"Nothing."

Against his will, pulled to it by the immensity, Finch's gaze slid beyond the work camp boat. To the towers in mottled green, with darker blues writhing through. Protected by scaffolding, they seemed to flutter and be alive. Portions like lungs. Breathing. The tops, two hundred feet high or more, lost in clouds and rain and odd magenta shards of lightning. A wide pontoon bridge led out to the towers. A semi-permanent island at the base housed the workers. Several boats had docked there. Dozens of gray caps stood guard.

Past the towers, back the way they'd come, Finch could just make out the hunched group of buildings that included the apartment with the dead man and gray cap. Was the Partial there, staring out at him? Talking to Heretic? *Hiding something from Heretic?*

"When will they know the towers are finished?" Finch wondered aloud.

"Roofs, Finchy. When you see roofs on top. That means it's done."

Joking? Serious? Didn't know anymore when Wyte was lucid and when not. Didn't know what to encourage.

The *wrongness* of the railing at the prow suddenly got through to Finch. Should be grainy, splinters needling his hands. Instead: soft, fleshy. He took his hand away like the railing was boiling hot.

Through the rain, the Spit was revealing itself. Gone with surprising quickness from a brown line in the distance to something with substance and texture. Rows of boats moored side by side by side, twenty or thirty deep. Still floating, bobbing, even as they were falling apart and half-sinking. A leaky sovereignty. A chained-together legion of convicts treading water. All of it shoved up against the shore, against the remains of the Religious Quarter. If the gray caps ever decided they wanted to truly cut off citizen from citizen, they'd burn the Spit, place a wall between it and the Religious Quarter. They'd root out the dogghe and nimblytod from the Quarter like so many weeds. Shove them all into the HFZ and be done with it.

Limits to what they can do? Or to what they want to do?

The boat began to slow. Soon they bumped up against the docks, gently. Prow kissing wood. Finch jumped off the boat as it lay wallowing there, followed by Wyte. Took off their masks. Breathed in the metallic air. Tossed their masks back in the boat. The boat sighed, shutting down until their return. Didn't know what would happen to anyone who tried to board it while they were gone. Knew it would be bad.

No sign of Davies. An avalanche of other boats before them, a scattering of tall buildings, natural and not, dull-glistening far beyond, through the rain. Buckets tied to the dock gurgled and filled, emptied. A blue dinghy. Oily water. Rotting planks.

"Got a plan if Davies doesn't show up, Wyte?"

Wyte didn't answer.

A bald man appeared at the edge of the empty docks, weapon holstered. Just appeared. Finch couldn't tell where he'd come from. Wyte drew his gun for both of them.

Face like a boxer's, the nose wide from repeated blows. Scar over the left eye, under the right eye. *Same knife stroke?* Barrelchest. Thick arms. Wearing a blood-red vest over a dark-green shirt. Black pants, blacker boots.

The man came forward with hands held in front of him. Like he wanted to be handcuffed. Something was in his hands, though. *An offering?*

He dropped what he'd been holding onto the ground. A wooden carving of a lizard caught in some kind of trap.

The man said, in some misbegotten blend of accents, "I'm Bosun. Davies couldn't make it."

Close enough now that his face was like a carved oval bone.

Scrubbed clean of anything except directness. Some sort of spice on his breath. A smirk Finch didn't like any more than the name.

Wyte gave Finch a glance. Knew Wyte was thinking the same thing. Bliss had named Bosun as Stark's right-hand man. Someone who didn't flinch from torture. Who seemed to enjoy it. Who'd helped wipe out Bliss's whole team.

"What happened to Davies?" Wyte asked, stepping back to create a little space. Finch faded to the right, so he'd be out of Wyte's line of fire. Kept his hand on his belt. Near his holster.

"Davies couldn't make it," Bosun repeated. "Stark's waiting. Come. Now."

Bosun started walking back toward the maze of gathered boats. Didn't seem to care about Wyte's gun. Finch wondered who might be watching from the row of dark glass windows that formed the first wall of boats.

"What guarantees do we have?" Finch called after Bosun. Wanted to ask, "What's with the lizard, you fucking lunatic?"

Bosun, without looking back: "None, beyond this: We won't hurt you unless you try to hurt us. And we won't try to fuck you, either. Unless you try to fuck us." A deep rasp similar to laughter. Him receding further toward the maze while the two detectives stood there.

Finch stared at Wyte. Wyte stared at Finch.

"Are we really going to go in there?" Wyte asked.

Finch looked back across the bay, saw how far they'd come. *Who on the Spit would risk angering the gray caps?* Thought about the *skery*. About how easy it would've been for them both to go down in a hail of bullets if someone waited behind the windows of the first line of boats.

Shrugged. "Just think of him as Davies if it makes you feel better." Hiding his own unease.

They stepped around the lizard carving like it might do harm. On impulse, Finch went back and stooped with a muttered curse. Picked it up. As Bosun had no doubt intended him to do from the beginning.

Followed Bosun into the darkness.

* * *

Once, Finch's father had shown him an old tobacco pipe. "This pipe contains the world," he said. Finch might've been fourteen, still running errands like a loyal son. His father was ten years removed from the campaigns against the Kalif, and rising fast within House Hoegbotton. They sat at his ornate desk in the study of the old house. Dad on his soft red silk chair. Finch on a stool to his left. Souvenirs his father had brought back from the desert served as grace notes. A rifle used by the Kalif's men. The steering wheel from a tank. A scimitar that he had promised would one day be his son's.

A sunny spring morning, mottled shadow coming into the room from the long bank of windows against the far wall. Faint honey smell from the tiny white flowers that came with the manicured bushes that lined the avenue in front of the house.

"A pipe?" Finch said. Incredulous. Expecting a trick. Maybe a magic trick.

His father pointed to a hole in the side of the pipe. "Look inside."

Warily, Finch put the pipe to his eye. Gasped in delight. Because the glass magnified the image revealed through the hole. And the world did indeed exist there. A whole map of the known world. There was a dot for Ambergris. The line of the River Moth. The city of Morrow marked to the north, Stockton some fifty miles south, on the other side of the river. The Southern Isles down below the Moth Delta. The Kalif's empire covering the whole west beyond the Moth. Exotic city after city marked in that vast desert, the plains and hills beyond. To the east, jungle and mountains that remained uncharted.

"There's a hole on the other side, too," his father said.

Finch turned the pipe around. Stared into another tiny piece of magnifying glass. Black-and-white photos of twelve men and women confronted him.

"Who are they?"

"Spies," his father said. "The owner of this pipe ran a network of spies. The map on the other side is really a code. It tells the owner something about the spies whose pictures you're looking at. Each one lives in a different city marked on the map. But you have to know the code to know which goes with which city. And what other information is being given to you."

Finch took his eye away from the pipe to look at his dad. "How fun!" he said, because he didn't know what to say.

"No," his father said, frowning. "No, it's not fun. Not really. It's deadly serious." A look like he was trying to tell Finch something Finch just couldn't understand at the time.

Finch remembers that pipe when he's working on his overlay. That tiny view of a huge world, which makes him realize the limitations of his map. That beyond it, beyond Ambergris, there's something more. Though it's easy to forget.

It's the pipe he's thinking about as he enters the Spit with Wyte. About those spies, who had led exciting, dangerous lives all across the world. But who were still, at the end of the day, captured inside a pipe.

Bound by rules.

Moved around a board against their will.

Or thought they were.

What's the difference?

2

Through the doors of boats. Through many doors. Always with sudden water between them. Gray, blue, black, depending on the shifting clouds above. The distance wide enough to make them jump. Then narrow as a line of blue. As the boats rocked, lashed together by rope that groaned. A marsh smell. A fish smell. Mixed with the odd old-new smell of paint curled back in a snarl or crisply flat.

Into spaces seeping water from old wounds, the texture of warped planks beneath their feet weathered in a hundred ingenious ways. Across decks that announced them through the creak caused by their weight, wood singing a dull protest. Up or down steps always too deep or too shallow.

Following the wide back of their silent guide, Wyte the worse off for being taller, having to contort his frame into whatever shape awaited him. The doors got smaller then larger, then smaller again. Oval. Rectangular. Square. Inlaid with glass. Gone, leaving only gaping doorway and a couple of rusted hinges. Once, a flapping triangle of canvas with an eye painted on it in green and red that seemed to follow Finch's stumbling progress.

And what in Truff's name is this supposed to represent? The thought came to Finch more than once, looking down at the whittled wood from Bosun. The trap. The lizard caught in it. The carving brought his thoughts to Sidle, made him feel, absurdly, like Bosun had been inside his apartment. Who created such things? Who had the *time*?

Bosun stopped suddenly, turned back to look at them from just inside a doorway.

Wyte ran into Finch before he could stop himself. Lulled by the stilted rhythm of their progress. Finch just able to stop falling.

"What? Are we there already?" Wyte asked, peering over Finch's shoulder. Could feel his breath, hot and thick.

Bosun smiled. A thin smile. Nothing humorous about it.

They stood precariously outside the doorway, on a tiny deck, backs to a cabin wall. A trough of water lapping between boats. A heron croaking through the slate-gray sky.

"Toss your guns," Bosun said.

"Why should we?" Wyte asked.

"No guns allowed with Stark."

"Too bad," Wyte said.

Bosun said, "Drop them in the water. Or I'll leave you here."

Framed by the doorway, gray water shadows leaking all over him, Bosun didn't look human. Didn't look real. Seemed to be receding from them while all around the sounds of the Spit became stronger. Like a drumbeat that faded in one place, picked up with a different tempo in another.

Wyte said, "Again, why the *fuck* should we do that?"

"Because," Finch said, "we don't know where we are." *And if he'd wanted to kill us, he'd have done it already.*

Bosun's smile widened while Wyte cursed, said, "Do you know who we work for?"

We work for monsters. We work for ourselves.

As if in a dream, Finch watched himself toss his gun into the water. It entered like a diver, head first. The water parted for it. Disappeared without a splash. A kind of relief came over him. A kind of acceptance. *The gun had been nothing but trouble. The gun had always caused problems.*

Wyte gave Finch a look of betrayal. Hesitated. Bosun receded further. Wyte could shoot Bosun. Then they'd be lost, in hostile territory. Or Wyte could miss and Bosun would be gone anyway. Or Wyte could get rid of his gun and Bosun would leave them. But Finch didn't think that would happen.

He tugged the gun from Wyte's reluctant hands. Threw it in the water as Wyte muttered, "A mistake, Finch. A mistake."

Finch demanded it of Bosun: "*Stark.*"

"Stark," Bosun said, nodding.

Then Bosun was just a wide back again, a kind of door himself. Leading them somewhere dangerous.

But a few minutes later, Bosun stopped again. This time inside an old tugboat. Finch right there beside him, back sore from stooping. Wyte behind them, still in the last, much larger boat. Exuding a muddled aura of defeat.

Then he was gone. Finch could sense it. Wyte there, behind him. Then not. A kind of wind or impact punching the air. A muffled shout. Cut off. Finch turned and saw just the outline of doorways receding in a ragged infinite number back the way they'd come. Nothing but shadow otherwise. Whirled around to Bosun, deck rising and falling beneath his feet.

Bosun stood there. Arms folded, watching.

Finch fought the urge to close the distance. To hurt Bosun. Fought it. Knew that self-control would save his life. Maybe save Wyte's life. Knew now, too, that Stark didn't give a shit about gray cap retaliation. Didn't care that Heretic would be after him if he snuffed out two detectives.

"Where's my partner? Where are you taking him?" Tried to keep his voice level.

If you hurt him . . .

Bosun shrugged, said, "Doesn't want to see him. Just you. Wyte's not safe. We don't know where he's been. You'll see him later. Take off your shoes."

"Take off my *shoes*?" It was unexpected enough to make Finch forget Wyte for a moment.

"Shoes and socks. Need to see your feet. That going to be a problem?"

"Why the fuck would I care about my shoes after giving up my gun?"

Over the side went Finch's shoes and socks. Stood there, hopping, as he showed Bosun the bottom of first one foot, then the other. Wondering where this would end. Furious, worried, scared.

Another part of him looked down from a great height, puzzled.

When did being a detective mean this? He was investigating a double murder. He was working for an occupying force that could make Stark disappear in a burst of dandelion-like spores. And he didn't have his shoes. He didn't have his socks. He didn't have his gun.

"Are we done?" Finch asked. "Is this almost over?"

Impassive bullet of a head swiveling toward Finch. Dark eyes glinting. "Turn out your pockets."

"Why?"

Bosun pulled out his gun. "No good reason."

Finch raised his left arm, palm up. "I'll do it. I'll do it."

There was a lot more than he'd thought. A copy of the photo of the murder victim. A folded up note from Sintra, the first and almost only thing she'd ever written to him. *Dear Finch—I made you coffee. Thanks for a great night. Love, S.* His current identity papers. A few semi-worthless paper bills from before the Rising. A strange coin, notched along the edges, that he'd kept for luck. A scrap of paper with nonsense words written on it, an odd symbol on the back.

In the end, Bosun returned all of it to him.

"Worthless."

But he'd lingered on the scrap of paper. Far longer than necessary to read it.

3

Thirty minutes? Longer? Finch lost count of the doors. Lost count or didn't care. His back throbbed from hunching over. From crawling, then climbing, Bosun's form always ahead of him. They were in the heart of the Spit now. Bigger boats—almost ships—lay near the center, places where you could forget you were on the water. Masts rose up like barren trees. Warrens of rooms, through which Bosun walked sure-footed, never losing his bearings.

Passed through a bar of sorts, with homemade booze in reused bottles. Women flirted with dull, rumpled men with beards and strange black hats. A few loners with a calculated threadbare appearance. Beyond the bar, the sound of spirited bartering in back rooms for black market goods. Selling guns, food, maybe even information.

Where was Wyte now? How far behind or ahead? Still alive, or thrown over the side to follow their guns? Began to wonder if Wyte would wind up like Bliss or like Bliss's men. Nailed to a wall? Bleeding fungal blood?

Even stranger ideas began to enter his head. That Rath in her basement, doling out information, was someone he'd made up out of convenience. That Sintra had no mysterious life beyond his own. That he'd written the words on the scrap of paper pried from the dead man's hands. That the soreness around his neck came not from the *skery* but from sleeping in the wrong position. That he would wake up to find Sintra was his wife. The gray caps had never Risen. He still worked for Hoegbotton & Sons as a courier, but Wyte was an obedient wire-haired terrier he'd bought for Sintra. There was no Spit. No bay. No towers.

Instead, they reached Stark's headquarters: through one last doorway, hinges splinters of wood, the door missing. *Ripped apart? How long ago?*

Bosun straightened up, Finch beside him. Stepped into a room aboard some kind of ferry. Passenger seats stripped out leaving the metal skeletons of chairs. The high, curving ceiling showed in faded paint a scene from an opera, people in balcony seats applauding. Below that hung a chandelier from which almost all the glass was gone.

A long wide space stretched out before them. Like a dance floor. Timbers stained with dark red swirls and smudges. The soft smell of soap couldn't dull the sharp assault of the blood.

At the far end: a couple of chairs, a desk, and a large figure hanging a painting on the wall. As they approached, Finch recognized the painting as a reproduction. It showed the Kalif of another age demanding fealty from a defiant Stockton king. Back when Stockton had kings. Hunting dogs stood in the foreground, but fiendish, with forked tongues and jowls curling back to reveal metal daggers. The composition more surreal than photographic. All of it the echo of a time lost to the present.

The large man nodded to them even as he kept moving the painting. Trying to catch it on the nails in a wall covered with bullet holes and dark bloodstains. Splatter had swept across the divide between wall and floor.

Finch noticed now the dark sheets in the farthest corner. Roughly man-sized.

"You found Bosun, I see," the man said. A deep voice. "Or he found you. Either way, you're here. Finally." The painting caught on the nails. Held. "There."

The man turned toward them. "You can call me Stark."

Stark made a tall space look small. A height that warranted a girth that could have been muscle or fat. Or both. The truth of it hidden by a trench coat. Frankwrithe & Lewden army issue. With old medals from the Kalif's empire pinned there: black glint with a hint of gold against the steep gray of the trench coat. A hawk face, with dark pupils swimming in too much white. A strong nose and a chin that jutted: two halves of the same beak. A knife in his left boot sheathed in a silver scabbard that shone as if polished every hour. Finch mistrusted that knife immediately. Reminded him of the squeaky floors at 239 Manzikert Avenue. *Look at the knife while the blow comes from somewhere else.* What else did the trench coat hide? A sword?

Stark didn't come forward. Didn't offer his hand. Just stood there. The painting behind him. Now Finch saw that Stark hadn't been trying to hide the bullet holes, the blood. Instead, the painting had been placed between them.

"Sit," Bosun growled, shoving Finch forward into a chair. Stark sat down behind the desk. Bosun stood to the side, reaching for a piece of dark wood on the desk. One of many. Started carving. Quick, accurate cuts. So fast his hands were a blur.

"Where's Wyte?" Finch asked.

Stark pursed his lips, ignored him, and said, "What did you think would happen? I'm curious. You thought you two would just walk in here, into *my place,* and you'd take me away to your shitty little station for questioning? Come back with an army if you want that, and come in shooting."

Finch, pressing: "What have you done with Wyte?"

Stark stared to the side, exhaled loudly. He seemed to breathe through his mouth. "John Finch. Why do you think people are so stupid?"

"Are they? Stupid?" Finch said, too aware of his bare feet. The floor was cold.

"Take my predecessors," Stark said. "They knew I was coming. They knew their superiors weren't pleased with them. Yet they took no precautions. They were *still here* when I arrived. I think they deserved what they got, don't you?"

Anger rising. "If you've hurt my partner . . ."

Stark dismissed his concern with a wave of his hand. "Don't start making threats you can't back up. Wyte is fine. You'll see him soon enough. But he's a tad too . . . fungal . . . for my liking. Or yours, from what I've heard."

"What about my gun?"

Stark smiled, revealing teeth stained red. Finch recognized the signs of addiction to a stimulant found in the bark from a tree that grew in both Ambergris and Stockton.

"You can join your gun," Stark said, "or you can shut up about it. I'm not here to talk to you about *guns*." The stained teeth made Stark resemble one of the shambly dogs latching onto its prey in the painting behind him. But the way he stared at Finch wasn't doglike. It reminded him of the older men in the Hoegbotton Irregulars. They too had looked crazy. Like a black flame burned within them.

"Taking my weapon might lead to strong actions by my superiors." Hated Stark for forcing him to use the gray caps as a shield.

Bosun dropped a carving of a cat onto the desk, stepped back. It looked like Feral to Finch. Made him obscurely worried again. Behind him, the sounds of knife on wood again.

Ignoring Bosun, Stark said, "We all know what *superiors* you mean, Finch. You mean those fey, gray-hatted, walking talking shit-stalks. But the fact is I don't care. I haven't cared since I came here, and I will continue not to care until I leave. With as much of Ambergris smoldering behind me as I can manage. So here's a question for you: Why do you work for them? I mean, really? *Why?* Besides fear, of course. Besides a leaky roof over your head and a plate of mashed-up mushrooms on your kitchen table. Do you *like* working for them?"

Finch had never answered that question. Asked: "Why did you leave Ethan Bliss alive?"

Stark nodded in appreciation. "My question is better than yours, but, still—good for you, changing the subject. I took out his team because I don't like surprises, and Bliss seems full of them. Why'd I leave him *alive*? Well, maybe I thought Bliss made enticing bait. Maybe I wanted to see who would come creeping around if I left him alive . . . and here you are."

The smile was a little too painted on, the comment too blunt.

"What did Bliss promise you? And where can I find him?"

Stark sighed. "You're not getting it, Finch. Bliss reminds me of a toy I once had. A mechanical toy. By the time I got it, who could tell what the hell it was or what it was supposed to do. Its uniform or fur or whatever it had wasn't there anymore. It had no eyes, just eyeholes. Mostly it mumbled and marched in place when you wound it up. Who knows what Bliss started out as. I doubt he even remembers. So, where is he? It doesn't matter to me. And if you take my advice you won't let it matter to you, either."

Sudden anger burned in Finch's chest, kindling for pride. "I'm not here to ask your advice."

"Oh, but you are, *detective*. You want to question me about that nasty double murder you're investigating. You want to know things only I can tell you. What is that but asking advice?" The black flame lit up his eyes. Lent his speech a subdued yet incandescent fury.

Finch leaned forward, into the teeth of Stark's strength. "What do you know about the murders?"

Stark chuckled. "Finchy—that's what Wyte calls you, I think. *Finchy*, I've been here two months. Why would you think I'd know anything about the murders, except that they occurred? Why, I'm just an immigrant, still getting my land legs. Imagine how many questions I have for *you*."

Finch reached a decision. Slowly pulled the photo of the dead man from his jacket pocket. Slid it across the desk.

"Do you know this man?" The more questions Finch asked the fewer he'd have to answer. Or so he hoped.

Stark made a show of examining the photo, waved it at Bosun, who said, "Already saw it," and went back to his whittling. Stark returned the photo to Finch.

"No. I don't know him. But he looks peculiar. Like he's having a very bad day, and it might get worse. Like he's also sick of this freak show you call a city. Like he might just have decided to hang it all up and go on vacation."

"Is that so?" Finch said, staring at the painting on the wall. "Maybe you should leave with him." The blood. The bullet holes. Did Stark actually *know* anything? Tried to set aside his irritation. Knew he was just sick of Stark insulting his city.

"Don't try to be clever—it doesn't suit you. Here comes another one," Stark said, glaring over Finch's shoulder.

Bosun had finished his next carving in record time. Set it on the desk with something akin to sincerity. A man with a mushroom head. *Wyte?*

"What about the words *bellum omnium contra omnes*?" Finch asked. "Why did you ask Bliss about them?" Bosun had already seen that, too.

"Bosun," Stark said, "did you ask Bliss about that mouthful? Bella . . . bella . . . Finchy, a little help?"

"Bellum omnium contra omnes."

"No," Bosun said. "Don't know what that means. Just nailed him to a wall. Didn't ask him anything."

"You're lying."

"I don't lie," Bosun said, smacking Finch across the back of the head.

Stark spread his hands in a cryptic gesture. "See, detective? You really don't understand who you're dealing with at all. But now *I've* got a question: Why didn't you arrest Bliss? Bosun says you and Wyte came out of his apartment empty-handed. When Bosun went back inside, Bliss wasn't there. Where'd he go? Did you reach some kind of agreement with him? Except if you had, you wouldn't be asking me where he'd hidden himself."

Confirmation that Bosun had been following them.

"What would I arrest him for? He was the victim. He'd been tortured and his men liquidated."

"Torture's a strong word, Finch," Stark said. "And you're not telling me everything, I'd be willing to bet. You Ambergrisians are naturally clever. Like a fox is clever. Like a rat is clever."

Ignored Stark. Changed tactics. Asked, "Why did you come here?"

"Vacation."

"How long do you plan to stay?"

"As long as my vacation lasts."

"Why did you target Bliss?"

"For fun."

"Do you have any information about the double murder we're investigating?"

"In the apartment on Manzikert Avenue? No."

"Do you like the camps enough to live in them for the rest of your life?"

Stark rose suddenly, seeming to increase threefold in height. "Threats, detective? Come on! You can do better than that. You have no other clues. You're getting pressure to solve the case. Or maybe not. Maybe you just want to know what's going on because it's eating you alive, not understanding what you're looking at. Such a big mystery, so many ways to disappoint your bosses, only one way to please them. But, then, I'm not here to guess at your motivations."

"Again, then, *why are you here*?"

"Isn't it obvious?" Stark said, gesturing at the blood, the bullet holes. "I'm here to fucking clean house. Clean house and, along the way, maybe make my mark. Nothing wrong with a man turning a profit and helping his country at the same time." Stark pulled a file out of a desk drawer, tossed it across to Finch. Then leaned forward, hands on the chair. "Here's a little something to help us both."

Finch picked up the file. "What's this?"

"A transcript of a . . . conversation . . . two Stockton operatives had a couple of weeks ago. With a gray cap."

That got through. Incredulous: "You interrogated a *gray cap*? Are you insane?"

Stark: "Sane as a lamppost, Finch. Sane as a lamppost. And come to think of it, the whole experience was a little like interrogating a lamppost. A lamppost with teeth."

Some private joke passed between Stark and Bosun that made them both chuckle.

Bosun said, "Grays don't like us much."

Stark, smirking: "No, they don't. Not that you'd ever find me in a room with one of those things. You don't have to teach me, not old Stark. Bosun might be able to take one on, but there's nothing subtle about his approach. It's like a wolf ripping into a pheasant.

"Now, I'm giving you a copy of this transcript because whether you believe it or not, I *like* you . . . even if your name probably isn't Finch any more than mine is Stark. And I especially like you because according to rumor you've killed a gray cap or two before. I imagine you haven't forgotten how? So take a look. See what you think. Does it help with your murders? I can't tell you what to think. But understand this: I'm doing you a favor. I'm bringing you closer to the truth. You might even have a chance of getting out of this alive if you do your job right. That should be valuable to both of us."

Finch, through clenched teeth: "Why shouldn't I give you up to the gray caps?"

Another carving. A woman. Reclining. Crudely made to emphasize her breasts. Didn't want to know who it was meant to be.

"You could. But will I be here when they come? Maybe I won't. Maybe I'll be at your apartment. With a gun. Or maybe I'll be over at *Sintra's* place. *You* don't know where she lives, do you? But maybe *I* do. Maybe I'll be there. She'd be worth the trouble I think. She might even like it."

Finch started to rise. *To do what?* Bosun just as quickly pushed him back down, shoving a gun hard into his ribs. Grinding pain. He stifled a grunt.

"Not smart," Bosun said.

Stark hadn't moved. "Just something to think about, Finch, that's all."

"Where's Wyte?" Finch asked. Because if he didn't ask that question he'd be screaming at Stark.

Stark's smile faded. He ran both hands beneath his eyes, as if to clear cobwebs. "That's such a dull question. Here's a better one. Ever wonder why they let anyone *stay*? On this godforsaken 'Spit'? Why they don't just raid it and wipe us all out? No clue? Seriously? Well, I'll tell you anyway. It's because they want to send spies back with us, Finch. Little grimy bastards. Most of them too small to see with the naked eye. But luckily not small enough to escape a microscope. And they're spying on everything. Even you. While you're just trying to do your job. How about that, Finch? How does that make you feel?"

"Fuck off," Finch managed, trying to stanch the torrent of words.

But Stark wasn't finished: "For that reason, as much of a shit hole as this city is, I don't look forward to going back to Stockton when this is all over. They put you through hell for decontamination. Weeks. Some spend months. So, to answer your question: you'll get Wyte back soon enough. He won't know where he was or what he saw. But he'll be intact. Except for some skin scrapings. Just in case."

Bosun placed a carving of a boat on the desk. "We get your boat, too," he said.

"No, no, Bosun," Stark said, irritably. He shoved the boat off the side of the desk. "That would be mean of us. Almost cruel. How will they get back to the station otherwise? Can you imagine how cut up their feet would be? How sick they'd be of squishing down on something soft and not knowing if it was a banana peel or something alive and deadly. Why, they might not make it back *at all* by land, going through that gauntlet with no guns, no shoes. No nothing."

"Thanks," Finch said. Making it sound as much like an echo of "fuck off" as possible. The sudden thought that he might have to kill Stark to be free of him.

"Time to leave now," Stark said with a big neighborly smile. "Just know we'll be watching you. Watching and checking in from time to time. I've given you information. You owe me information back."

Almost against his will, biting on the inside of his cheek: "How do I contact you?"

"Oh, you don't, detective. I'm only here on the Spit to finish cleaning up. I'm not staying on the Spit. That would be suicide. I'll be in touch. Or Bosun will." Pointed with his head to the pile of bodies under blankets. "Poor Davies there, I'm sorry to say, did not clean up well. You might not want to tell Wyte about that, although I'm sure he can guess."

As Bosun led him out, Stark said, in an uncharacteristic tone, like a wistful afterthought, "The towers will be done soon, Finch. Ever wondered about what *that* might mean for this miserable city?"

4

Silence as they took the boat back across the bay. Finch lay on the deck of the boat. Not giving a shit about how it breathed into him. Staring at the sky. Gray cloud ribbons, the rain now just mist. A hint of cold, something unexpected for the season. Wyte stood above Finch. Fuming. Livid. Jut-jawed about how easily they'd abducted him. Bruises on his face and hands long and narrow from that foreshortened angle.

Finch felt the smooth glide of the boat through thickish water. The way the deck gave a little under his weight. Like he was lying on top of another body.

No gun. No shoes. Just what was left in his pockets, because Bosun didn't want it.

Stark: "I'm here to fucking clean house."

Heretic: "A skery *is not as bad for you as what I could bring with me."*

Bliss: "You look familiar to me, detective. Do I know you?"

And the dead man laughing at all of them.

Beside Finch's head, Wyte's feet. In black boots dirty with algae-like fungus. A tiny community. A miniature of the city. Finch imagined he could see creatures there. Creatures who lived out their unaware lives in a state of naive happiness. A sharp smell, like petrol mixed with pepper. The friction of their discourse on that slick black hillside.

He turned his attention back to the sky. Ignored the three crimson tendrils coming out from under Wyte's overcoat. The weariness wasn't from confronting Stark. The weariness was from continually being threatened.

"Wyte. Just so we're clear—you're not thinking about making a deal with Stark. To replace Davies and your other Stockton contacts?"

"No." Didn't sound convincing.

“You’re so full of shit, Wyte.” Exasperated because back in the day Wyte was the one lecturing him about being naive. Telling him not to trust the ship captains at the docks when what was in their hold didn’t match the invoice. Always warning him about getting fooled.

“I’m not going to make any deals!”

Pressing: “What did Stark’s people talk to you about then, Wyte? Scratch that—*who* are Stark’s people?”

“Nobody! No one,” Wyte protested. “They didn’t talk to me. I had a hood over my head. I never even saw them. And how do I know you didn’t decide to trade information with Stark?”

“Because I didn’t, Wyte. You know why? Because he’s not like your Stockton contacts from before. You can’t really deal with someone like Stark. He’ll cheerfully sell you a knife and then slit your throat with it before you’ve even given him the money.”

“I *know* that. Tend to your own house.”

“Fair enough.”

A silence that spread and spread until it reached the sky. Not really mad at Wyte. Mad at Stark for making him powerless. For humiliating him.

Thick stalks of green appeared at the left edge of his vision. He turned his head. It was the underside of the two towers. The cross-section of scaffolding and support. It seemed alive. Made of vines wrapped around sinews that convulsively wove and rewove themselves together. Thought he saw a dead fox in there. Thought he saw a face.

Then they were past, and it was just the gray again.

* * *

Everyone has a theory about the two towers. Finch has heard them all, mostly at the detectives’ nameless refuge. When they first decided on the location, they’d had to take the bell out of the bell tower to make more space. A grunting, straining ordeal. To get it down. To shove it out of the one window without destroying the place. It had sunk slowly. Much to their mutual amusement. “It should’ve sunk like the stone it is,” Blakely had said. “Something about the clapper," Wyte had said. "The air trapped inside?" Finch: "Bullshit. It's just being difficult." Could still see it in the water below. Dark and rippling. A shape like the bullet head of some monstrous fish.

Talk of one tower had led to talk of the others.

Skinner: "I hear the towers are being built over the ruins of the old gray cap library. For some ritual."

Wyte: "I heard it's a power source for more electricity. When it's done, the whole city will be lit up again. They're nothing if not practical."

Gustat, snorting his disdain, "Lit up for sure, because it's a weapon. Why else out in the bay? From there, it looks over the whole city. It'll shoot out some kind of energy. Another way to control all of us. First thing they'll do is destroy the Spit."

Blakely: "You're full of shit. It's a huge statue to their god. Or a memorial. Whatever, those are just its legs."

The "island" around their refuge is just floating debris that has matted round. Encouraged by them. Camouflage. Stability. Some day, the whole thing is going to rot. They'll have to go elsewhere. Or maybe by then the city will be theirs again and they'll have their pick of pubs. Won't have to be part of the same chain gang, the same galley crew.

One day they might even get around to building a bridge. But for now, the detectives have built a place to moor a boat, and used the boat to bring across an amazing amount of booze. Salvage from every murder scene. Every call of domestic abuse. A history of Ambergris in alcohol, from Smashing Todd's to Randy Robert's. A smell like sweat and beer. Better than the smell of the station. No electricity, but they've hidden an icebox in the waters below the rotting floorboards at the far end of the main room. Keeps cold enough. They bring food as they have it. Stock the place with gray cap rations too. Tastes like crap, but the food—if that's what it is—never goes bad.

Gustat: "What god? They don't worship a god. They're too practical, like Wyte says."

Albin: "Too practical? By what measure? This is just them working up to another Silence. Better hope the rebels get to it first."

Dapple, uncertainly: "Not true. They can kill us all now if they want to. They don't need more help."

Albin: "Not enough of them for that."

Blakely again: "Some people think it's some kind of gate. They swear late at night you can see things moving through it. That you can see strange stars."

The detectives never talk about work. But, rumor? Rumor is like news from some far distant, more exciting place. Especially about the two towers.

Once, Finch offered his opinion. "They've got limits, first of all. You can see that already. They couldn't control the effects of the HFZ. They need help from the camps to build the towers. When the towers go faster, they put up fewer other buildings. The electricity goes out. Or their radio station goes silent. They have *limits*."

Blank looks. Not getting it. Much easier to think of the gray caps as some implacable force. Like the weather. Something that can't be fought. Because the fact is: if the gray caps want, they can disappear your friends, your family. It doesn't take unlimited resources to do that.

Wyte and Finch aren't allowed at the hideout anymore. Once it became clear Wyte would never really get rid of his affliction. Ever since Finch decided to back him anyway.

5

Finch and Wyte returned to the station in time to witness the end of a rare fight. Blakely and Dapple had gone at it. Under the glow of spectral lamps, the gaze of the tiny windows. Not caring if the gray caps were watching.

Blakely faced them. Standing on the mottled green carpet right where it reached the desks. Nose bloodied. Dapple with his back to them. Hair rising in tufts like he'd been startled. Fists up, too. Albin watching from his desk. A peculiar look of interest and boredom on his face.

Back when it had mattered, Dapple had been a Hoegbotton man. Blakely had been with Frankwrithe & Lewden. Both stared at each other now across a battlefield of other people's betrayal.

The other detectives gathered around.

"I won't do it," Dapple was saying.

"You've done it plenty of times before. Looked behind the curtain," Blakely said with a kind of cruel confidence. "What's different now?"

"I was forced to those other times. None of you did anything to help."

Finch doubted the fight had started there. Or that either remembered what it had really been about. Blakely was famous for baiting others. Daring them to look behind that damned curtain. *Enter the haunted house. Walk through the graveyard at night.*

After Stark and Bosun, Finch felt like he was watching Blakely and Dapple from on high. Children or midgets. Heard Wyte mutter from behind him, "Dumb fucks."

Blakely saw them first. Lowered his hands. Tension losing out to puzzlement.

"What happened to your shoes, Finch?" Said with contempt.

Dapple turned, looked too. His eyes were red.

"Nothing as exciting as what was happening here," Finch said, pushing through them, Wyte tightlipped behind him. Over his shoulder, "Whatever play you're practicing for, I'm not paying to go see it."

That got a laugh, though not from Blakely or Dapple. Spared Finch from having to talk about his shoes.

As he and Wyte sat down, Finch tossing Stark's file onto his desk, they got plenty of stares. Looks that said *you'll get questions later*. For now, though, the Blakely–Dapple spat was still more interesting. Skinner was already trying to get them going again, asking Dapple, "Are you just going to take that from him?"

On top of the clutter on Finch's desk: a note to call Rathven. Felt a spark of excitement. Picked up the receiver. Dialed the number. Waited while it rang. Stomach growling. Didn't think he could take more gray cap rations, though. Might wait to eat until he got home. Hunger focused his thoughts. Made him sharper. For a while.

Still ringing.

Wyte, searching through drawers: "I've got an extra pair of shoes somewhere. Too big, but . . ."

Still ringing. He'd try later.

"If you find them, I'll take them," Finch said. No hesitation. Didn't want to take another step without something on his feet. Too easy to pick up something nasty. Sudden memory of his father kneeling to tie his shoelaces. Eight? Nine? Saying, *"Mud between your toes in the river, no one cares. Set one foot outside this house onto the street, I'll never hear the end of it."* Sounds of his grandparents in the background, arguing about something long forgotten. Father's bristly face inches from his, mouth transformed by a smile. *"Let's go for a walk, shall we?"* Never knew when that meant his father had to meet someone, or if it really was just a walk.

Finch called another number. A number Sintra had given him. None of the phones on their way back had worked. Felt a helpless need to tell her she might be in danger. That "a man named Stark" might be following her.

Experienced an odd relief when no one picked up. Because, really, how could he tell her? Without telling her too much?

All you have to do is play along with Stark and he won't touch her.

How *had* Stark known about Sintra? Bosun casing the hotel? Then following her home? Along with the unworthy thought: *Maybe that's what you should do.*

A perverse pang of jealousy.

A sound of triumph from Wyte, who had produced a scuffed old pair of shoes. "Socks still in them!"

Wyte tossed them at his feet. Wyte had left his fingerprints all over the socks. Blotches of red and black. With a grimace, Finch put on the socks, then the shoes. Too big, but they'd serve.

"Thanks."

"Sure." In a whisper: "Now we just have to get new guns. There might be some in the supply cabinet, but Skinner has the key on his desk."

"Lost your guns, too?" Never live it down.

Finch shook his head. "No. I'm going to get a real gun. Something more reliable. I'm done with guns that leak."

Wyte raised an eyebrow at that. "You sure that's a good idea?"

"If I put a bullet in Stark, I want it to count."

"If you put a bullet in Stark, make sure you've got a good reason. And that you've taken care of his men," Wyte said.

Finch had no answer for that. He looked around. Blakely was by the coffee-maker. Laughing at something Gustat had said. Dapple was hiding behind his desk, pretending to work. Trembling. Let the gray caps figure that one out from their surveillance. Skinner and Albin had disappeared for the moment. Good. No one except Wyte was watching.

Picked up the file. Opened it. Saw the Stockton logo. "TOP SECRET" stamped in red across the top. Scrawled note from Stark, in a spidery script: "My gift to you, Finch. Let me know when you crack the case. If it doesn't crack you first." *Bastard.*

"What is it?" Wyte asked.

"I don't know." And he didn't. Not really.

He started to read, hesitated, then began handing pages to Wyte as he finished them. Wanted to say, "Don't share this with anyone." Instead said, "Remember, Wyte, you told me not to protect you . . ."

And, if you have made a deal with Stark, you'll just be feeding back to him what he already knows . . .

REPORT 2A-ATC-001
Originating Agents: Classified, pending investigation
Interrogation location: 22 East Lake Street
Transcription: Classified
Details:
*** 14.3 minutes of a damaged 60-minute tape.**
*** Breaks in the tape--of unknown length--are indicated in the transcript by "***."**
*** Brackets around a word or phrase indicate poor sound quality and therefore doubts as to the actual word or phrase.**
*** There are three voices on the tape, labeled Agent #1, Agent #2, and Subject.**

***

Agent #1: Is that thing turned on?

Agent #2: Of course it's fucking well turned on. It might say something we need to remember.

Agent #1: Then remember it. Don't put it on tape ...

Agent #2: No. I want it all on the tape. So we don't [forget]...

Agent #1: That Stark's orders?

Agent #2: What the hell is that?

(Sounds of a struggle, followed by labored breathing. Tape turned off, then turned on again.)

Agent #2: Get ... that thing away from me.

Agent #1: Goddamn it they're tough bastards. Even I forget sometimes. Okay, put it on the tape. Doesn't really matter, does it?

Agent #2: You want to ask it the questions?

Subject: I will [answer] no questions.

Agent #1 or #2: Shut up.

(Loud slap. Sound of a chair falling down?)

Agent #2: Be careful. Be careful. It hasn't even started talking yet.

Subject: Long and painful for you ... your insides will explode, your lips and cheeks split open. Your brains feed the birds.

Agent #1: Cheery fucker, isn't he? And they're all like that.

***

Subject: I do not know the answer to your questions. Your question sounds like a [question]. It does not sound like an answer. Do you have an answer?

Agent #1: What were you doing when we caught you? Simple question.

Agent #2: Oh, do it right. Do it right ... For the record: Subject was intercepted and brought to this location after stepping out of a strange door. Like a secret panel or something, which closed up after him.

Agent #1: You stupid fucking mushroom. Answer the question. Answer now and save yourself.

Agent #2: For the record, the Subject drew a symbol on the table. In some sort of golden dust. Kind of a half-circle then a circle then a line with another line across it. Then two more half-circles at the end. I'll draw it later.

Agent #1: More bullshit. Shove some more water into it. Only thing that works.

(A sound like water being poured from a jug. Splashes. Sounds of gasping. A cracking sound. A shriek. Silence for a long time, but no cut in the tape.)

Agent #1: Can you hear [me]? I know you can hear me.

Subject: I hear [you]. [You will] all die. I will myself see you afloat in the canal. Cultured. You are not--

***

Agent #1: Just more water then.

Agent #2: It'll die.

Agent #1: Don't care.

Agent #2: Don't you think Stark should--

Agent #1: The hell with Stark. He's been here, what? Three seconds?

Agent #2: Record shows [name redacted] authorized additional water torture on the Subject.

Agent #1: Shut the fuck up and help with this.

(A gurgling, thrashing sound. Spluttering. Silence.)

Agent #1: Now, once again, where'd that door come from?

****

Subject: ... been where you were not. But you'll never read them. Not before we finish the towers.

Agent #1: What is behind the door?

Subject: Nothing for you. Too late.

Agent #2: Now I'm getting impatient with this. Maybe this will help you. Remember.

(Long, prolonged scream. Not human.)

Subject: Don't do that again. Don't do that again. Don't do that again. Don't--

****

Agent #2: He doesn't [know] what he means. I should just kill him now.

Agent #1: Not yet. Not yet. Tell me, mushie, about this gold. Where'd it come from?

(From here on, Subject's words are more garbled, as if its mouth had been damaged. Accuracy of transcript compromised.)

Subject: Not a [filo] left. Not one. What [indecipherable] would take me like this?

Agent #2: What about the gold?

Subject: Yes, lots of gold there. Lots of gold other places, too. Gold is everywhere. Gold and green. The light, the water...

Agent #1: Do you mean the door? Or do you mean real gold?

Agent #2: Should we start on his legs? Fucking thing [smells] like shit. I think he's rotting.

Agent #1: Other places? What do you mean, other places?

Subject: Someday we will move other places but you will still only be here.

Agent #2: Give it up. He's hallucinating.

Agent #1: Just wait. Mushie--tell me just a little more, and maybe we'll let you go. Back underground where it's safe. Would you like that?

Subject: No place is safe. For you.

***

Subject: No more. No more. You, maybe if you [know] what it says there. Maybe you will not [indecipherable gray cap word].

Agent #2: We'll let you go if you just tell us--what is this weapon the rebels have?

Subject: [stream of gray cap swear words]

Agent #1: What about this address, then? The chapel at 1829 Northwest Scarp Lane. This rebel safe house. Ring a bell? Has it got something to do with the weapon? Our sources say it has something to do with the weapon.

Subject: Make me sleep. Burn me. Take me back to where I was.

Agent #2: He doesn't know anything about it. That much is clear.

Agent #1: Start on his legs.

(Prolonged screams.)

***

Agent #1 (panting): It's done. It's over.

Agent #2: Where do you think you're going?

Agent #1: He's not going to say anything else. If he is still alive--and I doubt that--kill him and throw him in a canal. No, wait, cut him up. Dump him somewhere they won't find him for a while.

Agent #2: And what the fuck will you be doing while I'm doing [that]? That's going to take me a long fucking time.

Agent #1: I've already got plans. And they don't include waiting around here. We've gotten all we're going to get.

Agent #2: You're staying. Stark's orders. I'm telling you--

(Sounds of something heavy falling over.)

Agent #2: ... Not dead! It's got a hand free.

Agent #1: Shit. Get that other light on. Get it on quick.

(Banging on the door. Calling out to some third agent.)

Agent #2: Open the fucking door! This isn't funny. I don't see it now. It was here just a second ago. Is it in the fireplace? Dammit, at least throw a gun back in here. And unlock the fucking door. I can't see a fucking thing.

Subject: But I can.

(Screaming for three minutes, then tape cuts off.)

6

Finch stared at his desk for a while after he'd read the last page. A kind of primal horror rose even as he tried to tamp it down. Mixed up with a question: *What does Stark want me to take from this? How does it help* him *for me to have this?*

Wyte finished. Handed the pages back like they had been dipped in poison. "How'd they think they'd get away with that?" he said. Voice haggard. "Killing a—"

"Don't say it." Finch stood. "Let's go for a walk." Took the file with him. Wyte trailed behind. Down that emerald carpet, past the crumbling marble tables at the front that once served as cover for receptionists. Through the massive, worm-riddled double doors, gold leaf long since peeled off and sold. Along with the inlaid iron bars.

Walked out into the light. Onto Albumuth Boulevard. Above them rose a sharp finger of red bricks, jutting. Only sign the building had ever had five stories instead of two. Ahead, the rough stone barricades that discouraged suicide bombers. Lichen sensors in purple-and-green dotted their surface. Beyond that, the dirty street. Just a few people in gas masks walking past. Huge black insect eyes. Trench coats. Gloves. Hunched over. Not looking in their direction.

Finch pulled Wyte to the side. Against the faded brick wall. Who knew if it was safer. But it felt safer. Reminded him of when Wyte used to bring him out here and patiently explain how he'd screwed up back when he worked as a courier.

"Why don't you tell me what you think."

Wyte looked at him for a second as if to say "You really want my opinion?" Then, slowly, "Two Stockton agents kidnapped a gray cap who came out of a secret door. Maybe a door leading to the underground? One of the agents worked for Stockton before Stark arrived. The other probably came with him. There was a third agent outside as a precaution while they interrogated the gray cap."

"Water torture," Finch interjected. "Take note of that. Not something I'd've thought to use." Thinking of his encounters during the war.

"So they interrogate the gray cap. Pretty brutally. And they ask him about the door, and the gray cap seems to make a connection between this door and the towers."

Agent #2: For the record: Subject was intercepted and brought to this location after stepping out of a strange door. Like a secret panel or something. Closed up after him.

"And there's another connection, Wyte. If you can appear out of a strange door that disappears, you can *disappear* out of a door that *appears*, perhaps."

Wyte: "Bliss?"

Bliss or Dar Sardice. Warming to this task now. Relishing the idea of figuring it out. "Remember that Bliss knew exactly which mushrooms to use for his wounds."

"True," Wyte said, but he frowned, like he didn't totally agree. "So then they talk about gold, but not real gold. The gray cap seemed to be taunting them a bit. And after that, they're following up on information that led them to believe the gray caps know about some weapon the rebels have."

Agent #1: Do you mean the door? Or do you mean real gold?

Agent #2: We'll let you go if you just tell us—what is this weapon the rebels have?

"And there's that mention of the two towers." Finch searched through the pages, found it. "Here—'been where you were not. But you'll never read them. Not before we finish the towers.' And then one agent asks about the door again. What does that mean?"

Wyte shook his head. "I don't know."

They stood there. Looking at each other. As if the answer might appear between them through sheer force of will.

What did Stark know? Maybe he didn't know anything. Maybe he was flushing out information like he'd flushed out two detectives by messing with Bliss.

"A rebel weapon. Strange doors. Gold that isn't gold. The two towers." Finch laughed. "Fuck if I know what it means." And he didn't, not really, even though answers kept niggling at the edges of his thoughts.

"But maybe we know how Bliss escaped," Wyte said.

Using magic. Using trapdoors. Maybe he turned into a door himself. Finch put that aside for later.

"Heretic is going to want another report. By tonight." He'd promised not to leave anything out. Didn't dare leave anything out. "At least we've got a couple of addresses." Finch wondered if Wyte was as relieved as he was at the prospect of having real leads.

"Want me to check them out?"

Finch: "Just the one."

Wyte: "Which one?"

"Where they tortured the gray cap."

Where they both died because they didn't finish the job properly. Searched for it in the transcript, pointed to it with his finger: "22 East Lake Street. But for Truff's sake, *use a proxy*. Get one of your snitches to do it for you. Watch from down the street just in case. If the gray caps have the place under surveillance, you don't want to just walk right up to it."

"What about the other address?"

Lowering his voice as a Partial passed by on the other side of the street: "If it's a real lead and not something Stark stuck into the transcript to fuck with us, it's too dangerous. A rebel safe house? Not even clear the gray cap knew what they were talking about? Wyte, that's a job for Partials. I'll put that in my report to Heretic. But I have to leave out the part about a tortured gray cap, and where we got the information. Which means, we need to check out the torture address ourselves."

"What am I looking for?"

"I don't know."

Wyte didn't seem to care. "Shouldn't take more than an hour or two there and back. Maybe a little more if I check in with some of my snitches along the way." His expression had become tighter, more defined. As if Finch was filling him with purpose, the thing encroaching on Wyte beaten back. For now.

Finch clapped him on the shoulder as they went inside. Wyte grabbed his coat. Lumbered over to Skinner's desk, swiped the key as Skinner watched. Went over to the supply cabinet. No longer caring what they thought. Got a gun, loaded it, and headed for the door with what almost looked like a skip in his step.

Blakely stared at the door Wyte had disappeared through: "What, you finally agreed to marry him?" With a leer.

Finch ignored him. Time to call Rath again.

Rath's voice crackled and hissed through the bad connection. Sounded like she was buried deep in a watery cave.

"Finch," she said. "I've got news. I think I've found out about—"

"What I wanted to know?" he said. Before she could say "the dead man."

"Yes."

A prickle of excitement. Along with a sobering wave of caution. He still didn't know for sure who had given up Sintra to Stark.

Kept his voice calm. "I'll come by after work." Fought the urge to say he'd be right there.

"You don't want to know now?" Disappointment in her voice.

"Busy. I'll catch up with you later." Hoping she'd understand. *They're listening.*

Click. Either Rath had hung up or the line had gone out.

A sudden elation wouldn't leave him. Made him give out a little laugh. Even though he knew it was premature. Usually you knew who the dead person was to begin with. The trail was three days cold by now.

How to frame it all for Heretic?

Finch thumbed through Stark's report again. Thought about his encounter with Stark on the boat. Bliss's disappearance. Bliss's appearance in the memory bulb dream.

What could he tell Heretic?

Blakely, Skinner, and Gustat were working at their desks. Once upon a time, he might've consulted with them. But the Wyte situation made that impossible now. Sometimes he thought they even liked Wyte better than him. Wyte couldn't help it. Finch could help it. Didn't have to side with Wyte.

The phone rang. He stared at the receiver for a second. *Sintra? Rathven?*

Finch picked it up.

"Hello."

"Finchy!" Stark's voice. Strong and smooth. A shock hearing it on his station phone. "I see you've read the transcript of our little drama, since Wyte's already hot-footing it over to where Number One and Number Two heroically sacrificed for the greater good."

Finch leaned forward. Shielded the receiver with his hand. In a low voice: "How did you get this phone number? Don't you know—"

"Don't I know what, Finch? That I'm one of your informants, calling in as scheduled? To ask: Did you like what you read?" A mischievous lilt to the words. Blood behind it.

Play Stark's game or just hang up? Blakely was giving him an odd look. Dapple too.

Finch turned his back on them, phone on his lap. "Yes, I did. I did like it. So long as it's true. I would have liked to hear the conversation myself."

"Oh, I don't think so," Stark said. "I don't think you would've liked that at all. It's quite melodramatic. Practically bathetic. The kind of thing that would've lent itself to opera, back in the day."

Except then I'd know if you'd left anything out. Or put anything in.

"How about the Subject?" Finch asked. "Did the Subject get away?" *Does Heretic know about any of this?*

"Alas, the Subject didn't get far. A tragic case of smoking in bed. Happens all the time. After the Subject finished with our poor agents, the Subject went to sleep. A sound, sound sleep."

"I don't know what that means."

"Oh, you know what it means, Finch."

"What do you want, then?"

"What do I want? Nice of you to ask." Stark's tone had gotten colder. "I want lots of things. So many things it's hard to know where to begin. Money's always good. Especially *gold*. I could also use a *weapon*. You know, to defend myself against the rebels. Think you can deliver that? After all, I've delivered for you."

"What you've delivered are rumors," Finch said. "What you've delivered is information we don't know will lead to anything important."

A pause. Then, "I'm not sure I like your attitude, detective. Maybe I should be working with someone else. Maybe I should be working with your girlfriend. Or your friend Rathven. Or your partner, Wyte. Or even that madman who lives right outside of your hotel. Would you prefer that?"

Managed a calm tone. "No. I think the arrangement we have will be fine." Realized he'd curled his free hand into a fist. Knuckles white. Nails biting into his palm.

Laughter on the other end. "I thought you might say that. I thought you might see it my way. It's all on you now. Just remember: we'll be watching."

Hung up before Finch could reply.

7

Back on the roof of the hotel. Where Finch could see it all from on high. See it clean and remote. Banish pointless images of ripping out Stark's throat. Shooting him dead in the street. If Heretic doubted Finch, killing Stark wouldn't help anything. He'd filed his report before he left. Stuffed it down the memory hole with misgivings. Would it be enough?

Wanted clarity before he saw Rathven, knew he wasn't going to get it.

The sun was going down. Watched the orange-yellow shimmer. Tried to ignore the towers, but that was impossible. The light made them a fuzzy green, as if dusted with pollen. The glare hurt his eyes.

The Photographer would be coming up soon. Finch had knocked on his door on the way up. Thin shadow through slit of door. Pale face rising from someplace submerged to meet his request. Told him that what he wanted would take thirty, forty minutes.

Too restless to sit. Hands in the pockets of his jacket. Left hand clenched around a piece of paper, a timeline:

Stark arrives—disappearing door—gray cap tortured—two murders—strange phrase on scrap of paper—Bliss—men murdered—Bliss disappears—two towers near completion—Stark gives us information—Heretic presses re the case . . .

How much of it was really connected?

Agent #2: For the record, the Subject drew a symbol on the table. In some sort of golden dust. Kind of a half-circle then a circle then a line with another line across it. Then two more half-circles at the end. I'll draw it later.

Now he had to reconsider the gray symbol on the torn piece of paper. Had preferred the case when it all seemed to be about Bliss.

Within the hour, he'd know the identity of the dead man. Part of him wanted to know. Part of him thought he wasn't going to like the answer.

He'd included almost everything in the report for Heretic except the tortured gray cap. *Put some heat on Stark.* And nothing about Rathven. After all, Finch hadn't even spoken to her yet. But he'd had to mention the words on the piece of paper. Called it a possible password.

Wyte had returned before Finch had filed the report, with nothing to add but a bad mood. Looking like shit again. His informant had found nothing at the address, because the building had burned to the ground. No witnesses. "Nothing except this." Wyte had tossed a carving onto Finch's desk. Crudely like a gray cap. Along with some information from his informant: Bosun was Stark's younger brother. Known in Stockton as a brawler and boozer. *Interesting, but what to do with it?* Stark was still a question mark.

The hatch behind him opened. Out unfolded the gawky frame of the Photographer. Once upright, he walked across to Finch. Holding something that seemed to absorb the light in his long fingers. Compact. Functional. Deadly.

"Here, take it," the Photographer said. As if Finch needed prompting.

Finch loved the weight as his right hand closed over it. Had a cold, comforting heft. A Lewden Special: a vicious snub-nosed semi-automatic. He'd used one during the wars. Taken it off a dead man. Liked it. Liked it almost too much. Could reload quickly. Accurate fire. Used bullets that ended things. Bullets that exploded inside the body. Would cause even a gray cap an acute case of indigestion. Finch hadn't expected something this good.

Gave the Photographer a sly look. "What, exactly, did you do before the Rising?"

On the Photographer a smile looked grim. "I took photos." No other information was forthcoming.

Finch looked at him for a moment, then dropped it. "Ammo?"

"Yes," the Photographer said. Handed over ten clips. Twenty bullets in each.

Finch's eyebrows rose. He'd only asked for five clips. Looked at the Photographer as if to say *What do you know that I don't?*

"How much?"

"Nothing now. Maybe a favor, later."

"Just make sure to ask while I can still grant favors." Wry laugh.

"Or while I still need them." The Photographer's expression revealed neither humor nor the lack of it.

Listening with only one ear. Thoughts wandering back to the transcript. The two towers. A strange door. *The rebels have a weapon.*

Which rebels? came a question from a voice in his head. *The ones in Ambergris or the ones in the HFZ?*

They turned to watch the city at dusk. The unexpected phosphorescence in places. As if the sun's death throes. The now-dull green glow rippling from the bay. The towers were still being worked on nonstop. Finch could almost imagine them complete now.

"What do you think the towers are for?" Finch asked the Photographer.

A gleam of interest entered the Photographer's dead black eyes. "Sometimes I dream. I dream it's a giant camera. And it's taking pictures of places we can't see."

Rathven let him in without a word. She locked the door behind them quickly.

"There have been strangers in the building the last couple days," she told him.

"I know," he said. *Some of them may even have been here to visit you.* Glad of the weight of the gun in his jacket pocket. Trust wasn't something Finch gave up lightly. But he was willing to give it up.

"Why do you think they're here?"

"No idea." Not entirely true.

The water had receded for the moment. Leaving odd marks on the floor and walls beyond the main room that gave evidence of tides and eddies. Remains of minerals. Remains of books that hadn't survived. A broom leaning against the wall, used to sweep away water. The stacks and stacks of books. That odd darkness of a tunnel leading . . . *where*? And where did she sleep?

Rathven took two books from an old sofa chair. Put them on the table. An old oil lamp flickered across the books, which were tattered and stained. Mold and worms had been at them. A thick mustiness made Finch sneeze. The gray caps' ridiculous list lay sprawled beneath the table.

She asked him to sit. He didn't like that the chair was so comfortable. Felt like he could fall asleep in it. Wanted to ask, in a conversational way, "So, did a man named Bosun visit you? Maybe a man named Stark?" But didn't. That conversation could wait. As for warning her, she had plenty of reasons to be careful already.

She pulled up an old wooden chair. Turned it around, leaning her arms against the back. Looking tense. Unsettled. The straight, unflinching stare she gave him undermined by quick glances toward the tunnel. Was she expecting someone to appear?

"Do you need tea or coffee?" she asked. He only liked tea now for some reason, but wanted neither at the moment.

"I'm tired, Rath. I'm not in the mood. What did you find out?"

Rathven winced. "Just the information, right?"

"What's wrong?" he asked, feeling he'd insulted her. "Something's wrong."

She stared at him with those large hazel eyes. "You're not going to like what I found out."

Finch laughed. Until the tears came. Doubled over in the grip of the chair. "I'm not going to like what you found out? I'm not going to *like* it?"

Glanced over, wiping at his face with his sleeve. Saw her confusion.

"Rath, I haven't learned anything I *liked* since Monday. There's nothing about this case that I've found *likable*. Nothing. This morning I went out to interrogate a suspect and came back without my socks, my shoes, or my gun."

That brought a curling half-smile, but her eyes were still wary. As if the idea was both funny and horrible to her. "Your socks? Walking around in your bare feet? *In Ambergris*?"

He nodded. Sobered. "So, what did you find out?"

A deep breath from Rathven. She looked like a creature used to being in motion stopped in midstride. Asked a fundamental question about its own existence.

"Yesterday, I read all of the names on your list. That took a long time. Then I made a much shorter list of any names I recognized."

"Like?"

"People with any historical significance. I didn't recognize anyone I knew personally. But there were a few names from the past. A minor novelist. A sculptor. A woman who was a noted engineer. I thought I'd look them up in various histories. See if they had connections to anyone in the present."

"A long shot." But he admired her for having a process.

"Yes. At the same time, I also started checking names from the past thirty years with what city records still exist. But I didn't get far."

"Why?"

Rathven leaned forward, balancing on two chair legs. "Because I came across information about one of the names on the list. Someone who lived in that apartment a long time ago."

"Who?"

Rathven said the name. It meant nothing to him, but rang in his head like a gunshot.

"Duncan Shriek," he repeated. "Who was he?"

"Good question. It took some research, but I thought I'd heard the name before. Not sure where. I had to borrow a couple of books to find out."

"And?"

She seemed reluctant to answer, which made Finch reluctant, too. As if he needed her to go slow to protect himself. From a feeling that had begun to creep up from his stomach. Tightening his chest.

She sucked in her breath, continued: "And I did—I found out a lot about him. Shriek was a fringe historian. He had some radical ideas about the Silence. About the gray caps. They wouldn't seem radical to us now. They'd seem mostly right. But by the time anyone would've been able to see that, he was gone. Disappeared. Over a hundred years ago."

Suddenly, Finch felt disappointed in her.

"What's the connection to the here and now? How does this help me?"

Rathven leaned back again. "Take a look at the two books on the table."

The feeling in his stomach got worse. Finch looked at her. Looked at the table. Back at her. Straightened in the sofa chair. Picked up the books gently. Felt the dust on his hands. Turned to the title page of the first. *Shriek: An Afterword,* written by Janice Shriek with Duncan Shriek.

"Janice? His wife?" A strange emotion was rising now, unconnected to the feeling of dread. A formless sadness. A watchfulness.

"No," Rathven said in a flat tone. "No. His sister."

"Is it fiction? Nonfiction?"

"A kind of memoir by Janice with comments by Duncan. She was an art gallery owner. A major sponsor of many artists back then. She went missing, and so did her brother. Both around the same time. But it's the other one you really need to look at."

Finch put down *Shriek: An Afterword,* picked up the other book. "*Cinsorium & Other Historical Fables,*" he read. "By Duncan Shriek." Felt a twinge of irritation or resentment. Couldn't she get to the point?

"Look at the inside back cover. Of the dust jacket," Rathven said.

Turned to the back. Found the author's photo staring out at him. A confusion overtook him that snuffed out rational thought.

The man could've been forty-five or fifty, with dark brown hair, dark eyebrows, and a beard that appeared to be made from tendrils of fungus.

"Fuck."

The man laughed again. Blindingly, unbelievably bright, a light like the sun shot through the window. The night sky torn apart by it.

The photo was ancient. Stained. Falling apart. But it didn't lie. The face in the back of the book matched the face of the dead man in the apartment.

Lightheaded. Cold. He sat back in the chair, the books in his lap. *Cinsorium* closed so he didn't have to look at the photo. *Never lost.*

"When did he live there? *Show me the entry.*"

Rathven reached down to get the list. "It's already folded right to it." Handed it to him.

> SHRIEK, DUNCAN, OCCUPANCY 17 MONTHS, 5 DAYS, 15 HOURS, 4 MINUTES, 56 SECONDS—WRITER AND HISTORIAN; LEFT SUDDENLY, DISAPPEARED AND PRESUMED DEAD.

"That's impossible," Finch said, letting the list slither out of his hands to the floor. "That's impossible."

Felt exposed. Vulnerable like never before. The semi-automatic at his side was no protection at all. *Stark, lips drawn back in a leer. Bosun and his psychotic carvings. Bliss as a young F&L agent staggering across the Kalif's desert. A dead man talking to him, flanked by a cat and a lizard.*

Rathven nodded. "It's impossible. But it's him."

The books felt too heavy in his lap. "Or his twin. Or his great-great-grandson."

"Do you really believe that, Finch?" Rathven asked.

"No."

No, he really didn't. Not in his gut.

Suddenly, the double murder had a sense of scale that expanded in his mind like Heretic's list. A timeline almost beyond comprehension.

How to escape this?

I am not a detective.

He understood Rathven's look now.

Haunted.

* * *

Being haunted had started for his father during the war against the Kalif's empire, in the engineering arm of the Hoegbotton army. Something had gotten into his lungs during that time. The doctors at the clinic, toward the end, still couldn't find a solution. Something about dust. Different kinds of dust. Dust from the road to empire, thousands of years old. Dust from the retreat. Dust from trying to hold Ambergris together. Dust from betraying it.

Earlier on during the campaign there had been a feeling of optimism, a heady confidence. House Frankwrithe had been beaten back to

Morrow. The gray caps seemed once again in decline, and because of the war effort Ambergris now had a powerful military.

As his father had said once, "They didn't want it to go to waste. And they feared that the young officers might be too ambitious left at home. And there was this kind of claustrophobic restlessness hard to understand now, perhaps. People wanted to be part of Ambergris, but to be *out* of it at the same time. They felt cramped, hemmed in—and the eastern flank of the Kalif's empire was so close, and the Kalif spread so thin, defending all of that territory. It was too tempting. Too easy."

One of his father's first tasks was to get the Hoegbotton army across the Moth in a way that allowed quick return. He accomplished this with boats, with floating bridges that could be taken apart and reused in other ways. From there, "the Fixer," as he came to be called, participated in more than a dozen battles. Helping take defensive positions. Solving how to get across supposedly impassable mountains. Whenever they needed an engineer, he was there. And he had the photographs to prove it, the ones Finch had since consigned to the flames: his lean, clean-shaven figure posing in front of a canyon, a cityscape, a smoldering tank. If the posture seemed more stooped, more resigned, the smile a little more faded as time passed, it could have been the natural process of aging. If not for Finch knowing that, eventually, what his father had found there would kill him.

He'd told Finch one day that he'd imagined he would be able to quit the military, take on the civilian projects that he preferred. Saw, he said, a grand new age of architectural expansion, as in the days of Pejoran. A city reimagined and rebuilt in a way that meant more than just restoration or renovation. Mineral deposits that fueled a war effort could fuel a peace effort.

But it didn't happen that way, as if the dust of empire that slowly changed his father had changed Ambergris, too. House Hoegbotton's race to acquire territory in the name of Ambergris meant not engaging insurgents at its exposed flanks: holding cities but not holding land. Until, finally, a slow collapse back to the River Moth, leaving behind as evidence of their passage more than a few half-breed children, abandoned equipment, and all of Finch's father's engineering projects. His father had had photos of these, too. In a separate album. He used to thumb through it at night with Finch on his lap, as if to deny what had happened next.

Images from some other life. A few of a woman with the distinctive features of the west. Faded. Worn. Lost.

His father had returned to an Ambergris exhausted in some ways, with House Frankwrithe eager to resurrect itself in people's hearts because House Hoegbotton neglected the home front to focus on the Kalif. Food shortages, electricity shortages.

In the decade that followed, Finch's father rose to become a strangely neutral figure. As the divide between Hoegbotton and Frankwrithe became narrower, as the city devolved into regions and factions and neighborhoods, he found himself working in government as a former war hero. For bridges. For reconstruction of roads. For anything that could bring back, even for just a month or a year, stability to a district or side.

"It was like fighting a guerilla war of engineering," he told Finch once. "I'd rebuild it. Someone else would smash it."

Finch believes that being found out was a kind of relief for his father. To give up the exhaustion of playing sides against each other. Of having to find work. Of having to be so secretive. Being a fugitive didn't weigh on him as heavily.

Thinks about this as he struggles with the mystery that is Duncan Shriek.

Is Duncan Shriek the dust, coming down across a century, that will kill him?

8

Could be a twin. Could be a great-great-grandson. But wasn't.

Finch walked up the stairs to his apartment, holding the two books. Rath had tried to get him to stay longer. As if she didn't want to be alone with what she'd found out. But *he* had to be alone with it.

Still at a loss. You could plod along for years thinking you were holding on, that you were doing okay. That you might even be doing a little good. Then something happened and you realized you didn't understand *anything*. A sudden shuddering impulse for Sintra that he understood was reflexive. Wasn't real. Was about forgetting. Even though he needed to remember.

The stairs seemed to go on forever. Like a throat swallowing him up.

Finch had shielded Rath from his confusion. Asked her to do more investigative work. Suggested there was a rational explanation. Even though he didn't believe it. Even intimated he knew something he couldn't share.

How long until Heretic knows? Maybe he already knows.

He came to the seventh floor. Saw that his apartment door was open a crack. Which drove Duncan Shriek from his mind and brought Stark back. Stark and Bosun. Unless it was Sintra?

Would she have left the door open?

Strange, how calm he felt. Had he played out the scenario of intruder in his mind too often to be surprised?

Finch placed the two books on the floor. Took out his Lewden Special and released the safety. Nudged the door wider. Saw the gray and black silhouettes of his living room furniture, the kitchen beyond, and the window directly ahead of him. A hazy green-white light came from outside.

No one there.

No sign of anyone having been there.

Maybe they'd already left.

Maybe he'd forgotten to close the door. *Not likely.*

Slowly, Finch entered, sighting along the gun's barrel. Still felt like ice water ran through his veins. Saw even the darkness in preternatural detail.

Stood to the left of the window. In the shadow of bookcases. Listening.

Heard someone breathing in the next room. Someone moving around. *What if it* is *Sintra?*

Decided to wait there. Let whoever it was come out into the living room. Now, finally, his heart pounded. Images of mistakes flashed through his head. Of Sintra with a bullet hole through her forehead. Or Wyte.

The bedroom door opened. Out came a shadow. Finch couldn't see the face. Couldn't see a weapon, either.

"I've got a gun. Stay where you are, or I'll shoot," Finch said.

The shadow stopped, quick glance toward him. Then ran for the window.

The window?

Already moving forward, Finch squeezed the trigger. The roar of the Lewden Special. A thick splintering sound from the bookcase opposite. He'd missed.

The figure leapt. Closing the distance, Finch leapt with him. A circle of green light had appeared. Rimmed with fiery gold. Shot through the middle with purest black. The figure went through the circle—and Finch went too, slamming into the shadow's back. Grabbing hold of the shoulders. Gun still in his hand.

The blackness extended. *Past the floor.*

Gasped, screamed. Overcome by the sense of falling. Held on to the figure, which was trying to throw him off. Finch's face felt like it was burning. The blackness was absolute.

Falling into the throat of a *skery*. Falling into nothing. Falling through the window. To their deaths. His stomach kept dropping and dropping. He kept screaming and screaming.

And still they fell.

Nothing lost.

All lost.

THURSDAY

I: Why do you hate Partials?

F: I don't hate them.

I: We all have a job to do.

F: I don't like cameras.

I: Where did you go during the party?

F: Nowhere. Home. I went home.

I: You were seen on the street after curfew. By a Partial.

F: It was someone else. No. No. Please. Don't! [sounds of weeping] I didn't go anywhere. I don't remember.

I: Who was it? Stark? The Lady in Blue? Bliss? Someone else?

F: All of them. None of them. Doesn't matter what answer I give. *Your* answer is always the fucking same.

I: I can make you remember.

1

Light. Blinding him. They both fell heavy and sprawling across some unforgiving surface. Gun skittered out of his hand. A shooting pain in his left leg, ribs. Cried out. Lost his grip on the man's shoulders. Every scrap of skin *crawled.* As if he'd passed through a cloud of hornets. Spasmed for a moment, his muscles not obeying his commands. Brain on fire. Worse than the *skery*. Came to rest gasping. Rough stones with something soft between them. An intense clapping sound rose up. Faded.

The other man rolled to the side. Started to get up. Finch reached out. Caught a booted foot. Pulled the man back down toward him. He opened his eyes just a slit against the terrible light. Saw the man's face.

"Bliss! Bliss!" Finch hissed. Still in the grip of darkness. He dragged Bliss closer as the man kicked, struggling to get free. Jumped on top of him. Punched him in the kidneys. Once. Twice. Three times. Knuckles aching. Bliss grunted. Finch delivered an elbow across the face, through Bliss's guard. Bliss went limp. Saw the man's eyelids flutter, his eyes almost roll back into his head.

Finch got up, staggering. *What did you do to me?* Keening. Kicked Bliss in the ribs. A bark of distress and Bliss curled onto his side.

Meant to launch another kick, but was brought up short. The ground around them had caught his attention. Dull red tiles. Yellow-green weeds thrusting up between them.

Looked up. In a sudden panic, he realized that the terrible light was the sun. He stood in the middle of an empty courtyard. A rusted, crumbling fountain. Blank azure-amber eyes of some long-dead hero astride a rusting horse. Mottled brown fish spouting air beside him.

Above the wall facing him: the looming white dome of one of the camps. Took a quick glance behind. The green shimmer of the two towers just visible through an archway leading out. A flock of pigeons circling. The clapping sound.

He was between the Spit and the Religious Quarter.

On the other side of the bay from his apartment.

The sun was out.

In the middle of the night.

Finch began to shake. Fought down nausea.

Said, gasping the words, "What the fuck did you *do*, Bliss?" Almost couldn't stop saying it. Taste of grit in his mouth. Skin still twitching.

Bliss raised his head, still on his side. Through blood-greased teeth: "Don't be frightened. We went through a *door*. Like any other door."

Finch kicked Bliss again for that. This time he didn't cry out, just lay there. Found his gun. Squatting beside Bliss, Finch shoved the muzzle against the man's left cheek. Forced Bliss's face against the stone.

"Answer my questions. Answer them without any bullshit," voice calmer than he felt.

This wasn't the first time he'd put a gun to someone's face. But he was threatening a man who, in his former life, had made speeches and led parades. A man now reduced to snooping in apartments after dark.

"I'll answer them! Stop hitting me." Startling bloodshot white of Bliss's eye trying to look up at Finch from that extreme angle. Face already darkening with bruises like a stormy sky.

"Get up," Finch said. He pulled the smaller man to his feet by one arm. Looked around. Two exits. The archway behind him. Another on the far side. Didn't trust the broken windows blinding him with the sun. Anyone could be watching.

Finch dragged Bliss into the darkness of the nearest archway. The contrast of shadows after the extreme light almost left him blind again. Black sunspots everywhere.

Pushed Bliss up against a whitewashed wall turned gray. Bricks exposed through the mortar like dark red teeth in a rotting mouth. Got close to Bliss so he could force the gun under the man's jaw. Pinned him to the wall with a fist wrapped around his shirt collar.

His hands were steady now. Shock hadn't set in yet. Maybe it never would.

Bliss was wheezing from the pressure of the Lewden Special against his windpipe. Trying to swallow.

"Now. Tell me what just happened." He eased up on Bliss's throat.

Bliss coughed. Managed, in a hollow voice, "Like I said, nothing to panic about. We just went through a door."

Something switched on in Finch. *Stark threatening him. Heretic and the* skery. *Falling through darkness with Bliss like moving through the doors on the Spit, like traveling through the gullet of a* skery *large as a behemoth.*

Smashed Bliss across the face with the Lewden. Felt a satisfying *give* as metal met flesh and laid open Bliss's right cheek. Bliss made a sound more like surprise than pain. Began to slump but Finch held him up. Blood flowed down the side of Bliss's face. Spattered onto his shoulder. Another puzzled sound. Like he couldn't believe Finch was doing this to him.

"You already said it was a door, Bliss. Tell me something new."

Bliss's head drooped toward his chest. Finch slapped him lightly.

"Stay with me, Bliss," Finch said. Released his grip on Bliss's collar. "Here." Handed him his handkerchief. "Keep it."

"Thanks," Bliss said, with more than a hint of something deadly behind the words. He held the handkerchief to his face, the gray-white soon soaked with red.

"If you tell me enough I'll let you go," Finch said. Tried to sound reasonable. As reasonable as he could while he kept the gun trained on Bliss. Truth was, he didn't know what he was going to do with Bliss. Or to him.

After a moment, Bliss said in a dull tone, "We went through a door to another part of the city. Across a kind of bridge."

"That's how you escaped the first time. There was no hidden exit."

"No, there wasn't," Bliss said.

"It was night just a few minutes ago." Couldn't keep the confusion from his voice.

"From the position of the sun, I'd say it's noon now. Maybe it's the next day."

"The next day?"

"Yes. If we're lucky. You surprised me. I didn't have time to be . . . specific."

Impossible. Like a story told about the gray caps to frighten children. Fought the urge to bring the gun smashing down on Bliss's face again.

Focus on what makes sense. Ignore the rest.

He was in a courtyard, the tiles warm and rough beneath the shitty shoes Wyte had lent him. There was a breeze. The sun was out. These things were real.

"What were you doing in my apartment?"

Bliss put more energy behind his words suddenly. "Finch, listen to me: you don't want to know. It isn't what you find out that's going to keep you alive. It's *where you're standing*. You're in the middle of things you can't control. It's too big for you. You shouldn't be worried about me, or what I was doing. You should be worried about yourself."

"Answer the question."

Bliss must have caught the returning menace in Finch's voice. He tried to smile sheepishly, as if embarrassed. Said in his polished but shopworn voice, "I was looking for information on you."

"What did you find?"

"Nothing. I didn't have time to find anything."

"Who do you work for?"

"I work for Morrow," Bliss said.

"I don't believe you." He didn't. Not really.

"My answer won't change no matter how you rough me up."

Finch doubted that. Bliss's face was covered in blood. But more damage could be done.

"Let's go back to what I asked you after we took you down off that wall. Why were you in the dead man's memories?" Bliss looked genuinely surprised. By the question? Or being asked it? "I ate the dead man's memory bulb. I saw you. I saw you near a desert fortress."

A kind of mirror. An eye. Pulling back to see a figure that seemed oddly familiar, and then a name: Ethan Bliss. *Then a circle of stone, a door, covered with gray cap symbols. And, finally, jumping out into the desert air, toward a door hovering in the middle of the sky, pursued by the gray cap, before the world went dark.*

"Memory bulbs are unreliable. You know that. You can see almost anything in them."

Finch would never be able to tell when Bliss was lying.

"What do the two towers have to do with all of this?"

"Who says they do?"

"Stark."

Bliss made a dismissive spitting sound. "Stark's a thug. He's nothing. Knows nothing."

"Yet he killed all of your men and nailed you to a wall."

Bliss grimaced, like he'd swallowed a mouthful of dirt. "That was beginner's luck. His days are numbered. In this city you adapt or you die."

Finch still didn't believe him.

"Like you've adapted? Gone from Frankwrithe spymaster to politician to something else?" Then, on an impulse: "What were you doing during the war with the Kalif? Working for F&L and Morrow? For Hoegbotton?"

Bliss smiled, though his eyes were cold. "I was doing my duty for my city."

"Which city?"

"Like I said, you adapt or you die."

"What did you promise to Stark to save your life?"

"Nothing. Stark's a smooth-talking thug. Anything he got I gave him because I wanted him to have it. Because nothing I have would've stopped him from killing me if he got it into his head to kill me."

"Then what did you want him to have?"

Bliss just shook his head.

"How do you travel between doors?"

"Maybe there are some things I'm never going to tell you."

The sunlight, the fact it shouldn't be sunlight, kept getting into Finch's head. Disrupting his thoughts.

"Let's talk about the towers again, then."

Bliss's expression had gone neutral. No one, looking at the spy's face, could've known what he was thinking. "The towers are close to completion. And the gray caps are putting all of their resources into those towers. Ignoring everything else. Even their Partials. But, still, they have an intense interest in this case. Curious, isn't it?"

"Any theories?"

"You already know more than you should. Enough to get you killed."

A weariness came over Finch. His skin still felt *wrong*. What would happen if he faded away with Bliss still there? Where would he wake up? The nausea was getting worse.

"Here's a theory. It just came to me. I might as well try it out on you. I think my murder victim saw you, Bliss. I think he saw you because you were somehow involved with his murder. Maybe you took him through a door like the one you took me through. Maybe the door closed on the gray cap. But you led the victim to his death. The only thing is: I don't know *why* you would do it."

But Bliss was done. He lowered the handkerchief from his cheek. "Are you going to try to take me to the station now? Or just start hitting me again?" Defiant. Almost smug.

For one terrible moment Finch had the sense he hadn't been hurting Bliss at all. That it was all an act. A light shone in Bliss's eyes that seemed shielded from the moment.

Finch let out a deep breath. Lowered the gun. Shoved Bliss away from him. "Go. Get the fuck out of here."

Bliss looked surprised. "Just like that?"

Finch gave a tired smile. "Just like that. I've run out of questions. And you'd just jump through a door before I got you back across the bay." He was going to be sick in a second. Didn't know how much control he'd have then.

"Letting me go doesn't make me forget what you've done to my face, Finch."

"I could've done worse. Don't come near my apartment again, Bliss, or I'll kill you." *Don't come near Sintra. Don't come near Rathven. No one.*

The spy's voice went cold, condemning. "When you see me again, it will be because I *want* you to see me. And not before."

Finch turned around. He really didn't want to see Bliss leave.

Bliss said, "You could escape, you know. You could just disappear."

"I tried that once," Finch said. "It didn't work. I'm still here."

A pause. Then a sound like darkness imploding on itself, a brief flash of green-gold light.

Bliss was gone. The scent of limes hung in the air.

Cursed and shuddered as he realized something: Bliss's hands hadn't been bandaged. They'd looked good as new. *Who healed that fast, even with fungal help?*

Bent over. Threw up his guts onto the courtyard tiles.

When he'd recovered, he sat down heavily on the edge of the fountain. Bone-tired.

Wondering what day it was.

* * *

Ten doors knocked on. Three doors that actually opened for him. Only the last one had a working telephone inside. An apartment a few blocks from the courtyard. He flashed his badge. An emaciated woman in a flower pattern dress let him in, checking first to make sure none of her neighbors on the ground floor saw her do it. Eyes large and bloodshot. Anywhere from forty to sixty. A purple growth on her left shoulder like a huge birthmark.

Inside, a bald man in socks but no shoes sat in a wicker chair facing the wall in a spare living room. Staring at a crappy painting of a beach in the Southern Isles. Wore a stained white undershirt and brown shorts.

The woman went to stand beside the man, protective hand on his shoulder, while Finch leaned on the kitchen counter.

Dialed the station. Wyte's number. Listened to it ring once, twice, ten times. His mouth was still dry, vision a little blurry. Jacket dirty. His hair full of grit. Wyte's extra pair of shoes scuffed from kicking Bliss. A sound in his ears he couldn't identify. Tired because he hadn't slept? Or because of stress?

A click, and someone said through the crackling, "Wyte's desk."

"Who's this?" Finch asked.

"Blakely. Who's this?"

"Blakely? It's Finch. Where's Wyte?"

"Finch. Where the hell have you been?"

Now he'd find out. "Have I been gone that long?"

"Just the whole damn morning." Blakely sounded rattled, and a little drunk.

Perverse relief. He'd only lost a half-day, maybe less.

"I had to follow up on a lead. Can you pass me over to Wyte?"

"Wyte's not here. Heretic came in. Smoldering mad about your case. He ordered Wyte to go investigate an address. It related to something in your report, I think. Wyte was told to take Dapple with him. Poor bastard."

"Crap." Consequences of being honest with Heretic. "How long ago did they leave?"

"An hour. Maybe a little more." That meant he could still catch up with them. He was already on the right side of the bay.

"By boat?"

"Yes. Western canal."

What experience did Wyte and Dapple have investigating rebel safe houses? Partials and their snitches usually followed up on those kinds of leads. A spark of anger and guilt. Anger at Stark for giving them the information. Guilt at himself for putting it in the report.

"Remind me of the address?"

"1829 Northwest Scarp Lane. Wyte made sure I wrote it down."

"Right," Finch said.

The edge of the Religious Quarter. Dogghe-controlled territory. A low-grade war still going on between the native insurgency and the gray caps. The war they'd all forgotten. Either the gray caps no longer saw that insurgency as a threat, or the towers took up all of their time now. Or Finch just wasn't in the loop.

"Putting Dapple and Wyte together. That's like a suicide mission."

"No shit, Finch. But Heretic wanted it done, said Wyte knew the area."

"Only because he was a shipping manager for Hoegbotton, Blakely." Twelve years ago. More.

"*I* wasn't the one who sent them out there," Blakely said, irritated.

The crackling became a roar, flooding the phone, then subsided after a minute.

"Blakely? You still there?"

"Barely. Listen, there were two messages for you. One from someone called Rathven. Another from a woman who just left her name as 'S.'"

"What'd they say?"

"Just to call them. You should get back here. Soon. People are saying strange things, like the towers will be finished this week. We're all on edge."

Didn't know you cared.

"I've got to find Wyte first."

"You're an idiot," Blakely said, hanging up.

The woman stirred. An accusing stare. Hand still on the man's shoulder. "Are you going to go now?" she asked. It didn't take much effort to realize the gray caps or the Partials had done something to her husband. No stretch at all to blame the stranger with the badge.

"One more call and I'll leave," he said.

She held his gaze for a second. Then turned to the painting as if it were a window.

Finch dialed the number Sintra had given him. Rathven could wait.

A voice answered after a moment. Finch wasn't sure it was her.

"Sintra?"

"Finch?"

"Yes."

"Finch." Relief in that single word, but also something that he couldn't identify. "I was worried. I went by your apartment. Your door was open. You weren't there. Are you okay?"

More than they'd said to each other in person sometimes.

"I'm fine." An ache rose in his throat. His hand on the receiver shook. No, he wasn't fine. Exhausted. Starving. Still trying to process losing twelve hours in a blink of an eye. Holding it together because he had no one to hold it together for him.

"Are you back home? I came by, and when I saw the door open I locked it."

"Thanks for that."

"Where are you, Finch?"

Where was he? Clinging to a lifeline. He'd meant to warn her to be careful. But, somehow, talking now, it felt like he was talking to a stranger. A voice in his head told him he should be careful. How had Stark found out about Sintra? What if *Sintra* had told Stark? About him? Was that possible?

"I'm working on a case."

"But why was your door open? Things were knocked over, as if there'd been a struggle."

"I'll tell you later."

"Can I come by tonight?"

Lump in the throat. "Sure," he said. "I just called to hear your voice. Tough day."

"Finch," she said. "Is everything really all right?"

"No," he said. Made a decision, leapt out into the abyss. "Not really. I'm about to go into a dangerous situation near the Religious Quarter. There's an address we're supposed to check out."

"Then don't go. Just don't go."

"I have to. I don't have a choice." *Not with Wyte out there with only Dapple for backup.*

"You're scaring me, Finch," Sintra said.

"I'm going to hang up now," Finch said. "See you soon. Be safe." A click as the phone cut out. Didn't know if she'd heard him or not.

The woman watched him without saying anything. Even as he told her thanks. Even as he left a gray cap food voucher on the counter. Even as he backed out into the corridor.

Relax your guard in this city and you were dead.

2

An hour later, Finch stood on the ridge and stared down. Far below, the dull blue snake of a canal. Two detectives in a boat. Slowly making their way northeast. Finch was about three hundred feet above them. Wyte was a large shadow with a white face, the boat a floating coffin. Dapple had been reduced to a kind of question mark. Not a good place to be. Anyone could've been on the ridge, looking down. Lucky for them it was just him.

A steep hillside below Finch. Made of garbage. Stone. Metal. Bricks. The petrified snout of a tank or two. Ripped apart treads. Collapsed train cars pitted with scars and holes. Ragged, dry scraps of clothing that might've been people once.

A dry smell hung over it all. Cut through at times by the stench of something dead but lingering. He'd been here before, when it had just been a grassy slope. *A nice place. A place couples might go to have a picnic.* Couldn't imagine it ever returning to that state.

The weather had gotten surly. Grayish. A strange hot wind dashed itself against the street rubble. Blew up into his face. Off to the northeast: the Religious Quarter. A still-distant series of broken towers, steeples, and domes. Wrapped in a haze of contrasting, layered shades of green. Looking light as mist. Like something out of a dream from afar. Up close, Finch knew, it reflected only hints of the Ambergris from before, the place once ruled by an opera composer, shaped by the colors red and green.

The canal led into the Religious Quarter, but Wyte and Dapple would have to disembark much earlier. Their objective lay just outside the quarter.

Finch's gaze traveled back down the canal, toward civilization. Zeroed in on a series of swift-moving dots some two hundred feet behind the boat. Dark. Lanky. Angular. Using the bramble on the far side of the canal as cover. Partials. Trailing Wyte.

Stared down at the story unfolding below him with a kind of absurd disbelief. Swore under his breath. Took the measure of the Partials down the barrel of his Lewden Special. But it was a long shot. Literally. He lowered the gun.

Maybe Wyte knew about the Partials? What if they were providing support? No. Blakely would've mentioned that. Blakely would've told him about Partials. Probably sent to make sure Wyte did as he'd been told. Was *the* Partial with them, or was he back at the apartment guarding a dead man?

For a moment, Finch just stood on the ridge, under the gray sky. Watched with envy the wheeling arc of a vulture like a dark blade through the air.

Easy to turn away. Heretic didn't expect him to be there. Wyte didn't know where he'd gone. Finch could say he'd been investigating some other lead. Could go back to the station. Forget he'd seen any of this. Wait for them to get back. If they came back.

Bliss: "It isn't what you find out that's going to keep you alive. It's where you're standing . . . You shouldn't be worried about me, or what I was doing. You should be worried about yourself."

Bone-weary. Hungry. Bliss's words still in his thoughts. The long fall through the door still devouring him. Finch looked back the way he'd come. Looked down at Wyte and Dapple. Remembered Dapple calm once, at his desk, stealing a moment to write a few lines of poetry. Remembered Wyte training him as a courier for Hoegbotton. His patience and his good humor. Long nights in their home, laughing and joking not just with Wyte but with Emily. Back before the end of history.

Now he was standing on top of a mountain of garbage, trying to figure out how he'd gotten there.

"Fuck," he said to the vulture. To the false light of the Religious Quarter. "Fuck you all."

Then he was descending the ridge at an angle. Trying to put enough shadow, enough debris, in front of him and the canal that the Partials couldn't see him.

This was going to get worse before it got better.

* * *

Finch caught up to them as they were mooring the boat to a rickety dock under a stand of willow trees. Shadowed by a lichen-choked, half-drowned stone archway that led nowhere now. The canal had a metallic blue sheen to it. Nothing rippled across its surface. The gray boat had that mottled, doughy look Finch hated. Like it was made of flesh.

He said nothing. Just came out of the shadow of the trees and leaned against the arch. Waiting for Wyte to see him.

Looping one last length of rope round a pole, Wyte did a double take.

"Finch?" he said. "Finch." A slow, hesitant smile broke across his troubling face. A sincere relief that softened the sternness of his features. "It's good to see you."

Dapple jumped off the boat. "How'd you know where to find us?" he demanded. The anger of a desperate man.

"Relax. Blakely told me," Finch said. "I was already on this side of the bay."

But Dapple's face darkened at the mention of Blakely. He looked more nervous than usual. The body language of a mouse or rat. Twitching. Had two guns. Both gray cap issue. One drawn. One stuck through his belt. He wore a mottled green shirt too big for him and black trousers shoved into brown boots. Like a doll dressed for war.

As ever, Wyte hid himself in a bulky, tightly buttoned overcoat. An angry red splotch had drifted down his forehead. Had colonized half of one eye. Cheek. Chin. The splotch had elongated and widened his face. Made his head more like a porous marble bust. He wore black gloves over his hands. Red and white threads had emerged from his sleeves. Wandered of their own accord.

As Wyte trod heavily closer, he extended his hand. Gave Finch a thankful look as they shook. Wyte's grip was strong but *gave*. Like the glove was full of moist bread. Finch suppressed a shudder from the sense of *things* moving inside each finger.

"Where were you this morning?" Wyte asked. Dapple stood behind him, eclipsed.

"I'll tell you later."

"Why not tell me now." Finch heard the fear in Wyte's voice.

"No," Finch said, laying the word down hard.

Wyte considered that for a moment. Like it was a wall between them. Looked back toward the boat as if thinking about getting back on it. "Did Blakely tell you our mission?"

"I told Wyte we should just. Should just run," Dapple said, breaking in. "That this is going to. Going to get us killed." Sometimes Dapple stopped in mid-sentence. Like an actor trying to perfect a line.

"Listen, Wyte," Finch said, ignoring Dapple. "I came down off the ridge. There are Partials following you. A few hundred feet behind. They're probably watching us now."

Or they've got a spy on you, Wyte, and they don't need to watch us.

Wyte grimaced. Dapple stared at the water like he expected something to erupt out of it.

"What do we do?" Dapple asked. Didn't seem to expect an answer.

"Shut up, Dapple," Wyte whispered.

"Carry out our mission. Come home alive. Like always." Finch putting emphasis on *our*. An ache in his throat. Knew Wyte would understand that Finch wouldn't have come down the ridge for anyone else.

No matter that you're not always the Wyte I remember.

A sudden spark in Wyte's eyes. Something that glittered. Began to fade almost as soon as it had passed through.

"Like old times," Wyte said. A wry grin. "Like when I taught you how to deal with ship captains down at the docks." His voice was crumbling like a ruined wall. The edges of words worn away.

Finch was too tired to take the brunt of that. "We should get moving."

He wanted action so he wouldn't have to think.

About any of it.

3

The haze of the Religious Quarter came closer and closer. A fake fairytale city-within-a-city above them. Of those following, no sight. Just the sound of gravel once, dislodged. A distant muttered curse.

After a climb, the ground leveled out. They came to a long, tall wall parallel to a rough road. Ahead, the wall ran on into the distance, buckled and cracked in places. Like it was having trouble restraining what it had been made to hold back. Coming over the wall: the lime scent, the rich greens of the Religious Quarter. Fungus and trees wedded in a vast alliance. Looked like nothing more or less than a fiery explosion, frozen in time. Bullet holes in the wall, in dozens of places. The blackish spray of old blood where someone had gotten unlucky. Under it all, a latticework of fungus. Faintly visible. Faintly green-glowing.

"This is Scarp Lane," Wyte said. "I was here before the Rising. Tree-lined. Nice homes. Bars and restaurants and dance halls. Little alcoves for people to put up offerings to their gods. You could indulge in your favorite vice and then walk right over and pray it away. Between the wars, it used to be a nice row of wrought-iron streetlamps and sidewalk vendors."

Finch frowned. *Used to be.* Wyte didn't usually indulge in *used to be.*

Nothing for it but to follow the wall.

People began to appear in doorways. Leaning against rusting lampposts. On balconies. Dark in complexion. Wore strange hats. Stared you in the eye. Challenged silently why you were here. Sometimes as many as six or seven. Loitering on a street corner. Any time Finch saw more than four people gathered in one place, he figured the gray caps had used their resources elsewhere.

"Put your badges away," Finch said, suddenly.

Dapple had been holding his badge so anyone could see it. Protested, even after Wyte made his own disappear.

"Seen any Partials here?" Finch asked.

"No."

"Seen anyone who would give a shit about your badge?"

Dapple didn't respond.

"And you won't, either," Finch continued. "Not this close to the wall. Except for the ones following us."

They'd be heavily armed. Probably with fungal weapons. Moving in a tight formation. If they were doing more than shadowing Wyte and Dapple, gray caps might be following, too.

From below.

The chapel at 1829 Northwest Scarp Lane pushed out from the wall. It had once been a modest two-story church topped by a silver metal dome. Now that dome was speckled and overgrown with rich burnished copper-bronze-amber mold that met a sea of mixed sea greens and blues creeping up. Little rounded windows in the dome. Perfect firing lines.

Beneath, the green-and-white paint of the rounded walls had peeled away to reveal dry dark wood beneath. In the center, a large ornate double door. To either side, hollowed-out alcoves that Finch didn't think led anywhere. In front of all three, a facade of archways.

A horseshoe-shaped barricade of six or seven tanks with a sandbag wall curved from just beyond the side of the chapel to around the front of it. The tanks nestled together as if sleeping. Been there seven years at least. Burnt out. Crumbling. Faithful old Hoegbotton insignia still visible on the sides. Delicate snow-white mushrooms had overtaken them. Fernlike green tendrils grew from their rusted tops: all that was left of the men that had been flushed out.

Less than one hundred feet between the chapel entrance and the sandbag wall. Anyone could have manned it. At any time. Rival armies and militias had marched and retreated across that damaged ground for more than forty years.

No one in sight now, in either direction. Yet another kind of sign.

"Great fucking place for an ambush," Finch said, as they stood outside the chapel. At their backs, beyond the tanks and sandbags, a warren of streets. Burnt-out schools, apartments, abandoned businesses.

"I don't like it, either," Wyte said.

"What if it's a test? A test to prove our loyalty?" Dapple said. "And it's not a rebel safe house at all."

"Shut up," Wyte said. Shifting his weight from foot to foot as if something pained him. To Finch: "If anyone is in there, we ask a few questions. Try to get some information to satisfy Heretic. Get out."

Finch nodded. If anyone was in there, Finch didn't know if they'd get many words in before the shooting started. Rebel safe house. Three detectives working for the gray caps, with Partials backing them up. Be better off turning in their guns, asking for mercy. Maybe.

Dapple looked close to tears. "We should get. The hell out now."

"Changed your mind? Then why don't you stay out here," Finch said. "Guard the door. Duck inside and tell us if you see anything suspicious." Dapple would be less dangerous as a guard than backing them up.

"With Partials out here?" Dapple protested.

Finch checked the magazine in the semi-automatic. Released the safety. "You'll do it, Dapple, and you'll be happy about it. And Dapple? Don't run away. We'll find you."

"Enough!" Wyte said. "Let's get this over with."

The language of men scared shitless.

Wyte put his hand in the huge left-side pocket of his coat. The one with the growing verdigris stain. The one with his gun in it.

He walked through the middle doorway, Finch behind him.

Dark and cool inside. A second door just a few feet after the first. Wyte pushed it open. Finch covered him.

As his eyes adjusted to the gloom, Finch let the room come to him. The smell of moist, rotting wood. A high ceiling that made every step echo up in the rafters. Two sets of pews, in twelve rows. Leading up to a raised wooden platform with an ornate, carved railing. Beyond that, red curtains. The supports for a chandelier hung down from the ceiling. But there was no chandelier. On the right side of the dais, an iron staircase curled up toward the dome.

"What the hell is that?" Wyte said, pointing.

As his eyes adjusted, Finch could see that a long, low glass-lined counter ran along the right side of the dais. Couldn't tell what was inside it.

"I don't know."

Finch drifted ahead of Wyte. Walked up the carpet with Wyte behind. Climbed onto the platform from the steps built into the right side.

The counter. Under the smudged glass, a series of arms and heads. The arms looked like prosthetics. Didn't understand the heads with their hollow eye sockets any better.

"Why in a church?" Wyte asked.

Finch shushed him.

Beyond the counter: a doorway covered with a tapestry of Manzikert subduing the gray caps.

Finch motioned toward the tapestry with his Lewden Special.

Wyte shook his head. Too dangerous. Too unknown.

Finch nodded.

Wyte retreated into the shadows to the left of the counter. Pulled the gun from his pocket. It looped spirals of dark fluid onto his overcoat. Finch bent at the knees, put the counter between his body and the doorway. Aimed at the tapestry.

"Is anyone there?" Finch said. Loud enough to be heard in any backroom.

Something fell. Like a jar or tin.

"Is anyone there?" Finch repeated. His heart felt like a fragile animal inside his chest. Trying to get free. Being battered in the attempt. Kept switching the gun from hand to hand. So he could wipe his sweaty palms on his shirt.

A kind of hesitation from beyond the doorway. A kind of poised silence. Then a careful movement swept aside the tapestry. A short, thin woman walked out.

She stood behind the counter as Finch rose, gun at his side. Wyte reappeared from the shadows.

The woman's gray hair had been pulled back into a tight ponytail. She wore a formless blue dress with a black belt. Her face was heavily lined. Her mouth drooped on the left side as if from a stroke. Or an old wound. Finch thought he could see the whispering line of a scar across the cheek.

"Point your gun somewhere else, detective," she said, staring at Wyte. Her voice had gravel in it. Finch had no doubt she'd commanded men before.

The seepage had become a constant spatter against the wooden floor. But Finch couldn't tell if it came from the gun or from Wyte.

Wyte lowered his gun.

"Who says we're detectives?" Finch said.

Her eyes were the color of a knife blade. "That's a gray cap weapon."

"We're investigating a murder," Finch said. "That's all we're here for."

"All?" she echoed.

Finch wondered what they looked like to her. Wyte transforming. Him tired and dirty. In Wyte's crappy shoes.

Wyte asked, "What's your name?"

No answer.

"We could bring you in for questioning," Wyte said.

"But you won't, because I'm an old woman," she said in a whisper. "Because you're decent men."

Wyte snorted, losing patience. "A night in the station holding cell might make you more talkative."

The full, hawklike intensity of her stare focused on Wyte. "You want a name? It's Jane Smith."

Wyte opened his mouth. Closed it again.

Finch gave Wyte a wary look. Said to her, "What are all these parts doing here?"

"This is a business. People who've been released from the camps come here if they've lost a leg. Or an arm."

"Or a head?" Finch asked.

"You seem to be keeping yours, detective," she snapped.

Wyte said, "Are you the Lady in Blue?"

Finch knew he'd meant it as a kind of joke. But Wyte's voice couldn't convey a joke anymore.

A look of disbelief spread across the woman's thin features. The wrinkles at the sides of her eyes bunched up. She began to guffaw. The roughest, crudest laughter Finch had ever heard from a woman.

When she had recovered, she said, "You should leave. Now."

"*Bellum omnium contra omnes,*" Finch said. Put as much weight as he could behind the words. As if he meant to physically move her with them. Couldn't have said where the impulse came from, to say it. Wyte gasped.

Her eyes opened wide. The color in her cheeks deepened.

"*There is a way,*" she said. Hesitated. As if she'd made a mistake.

Finch repeated the words: *bellum omnium contra omnes.*

Her features hardened. "I don't think I know what you're talking about after all."

"I think you do," Finch said. He hadn't given the right response, but he'd been close.

Wyte pulled out his gun, brushed past Finch, and shoved it in the woman's face.

"Wyte . . ." Finch said in a warning tone.

"No, Finch," Wyte said. "I'm sick of this. Sick of it. She's lying. You want this to go down like Bliss all over again? Well, I don't." Wyte pushed the muzzle into the woman's forehead until the discharge dribbled down her face. She closed her eyes, winced, said again, "I don't know what it means. I don't."

"Wyte, *this won't get you what you want,*" Finch said.

Turned his pale, monstrous head for a second. "Hell it won't."

"For Truff's sake, Wyte! Put down the fucking gun!"

"If I do, she's going to kill us," Wyte said. The gun slipping in his grasp. Finger still tight on the trigger. "Can't you feel it? We're going to *die here* because of her." Voice small and low. His shape beneath the overcoat in the grip of some terrible insurrection.

The woman's eyes fluttered, closed again. Waiting for the bullet while Wyte waited for his answer.

No way to get to Wyte before he shot her.

Saved by Dapple calling out in alarm from beyond the door. "Partials!"

Wyte looked toward the door. Lowered the gun. But something

was swimming in his eyes. Something that wasn't part of him. Not really.

The woman leaned down, fast.

The front of the counter exploded in a cloud of dust and debris.

The force threw Finch up against the rail, drove Wyte down to one knee. Wyte's gun skittered across the floor. A piece of wood had grazed Finch's left arm. His ears rang from the blast. Through the wreckage of the counter, Finch could see the cannon of a gun that had done the damage. Mounted on a metal stand.

The woman had leapt to the spiral staircase. She was shouting to someone above her. Coughing, Finch got off a shot that bit into the steps at her heels. Then the darkness took her.

Wyte recovered his weapon, started to move toward the stairs. Finch followed, then stopped. Pulled at Wyte's coat sleeve.

"Fuck. Wait."

"Wait, Finch? *Wait?*" Straining against his grip. "Goddammit, *she's getting away*!"

The sound of gunfire. Coming from the top of the chapel. And a torrent of boots on steps from beyond the tapestry door.

"No! Didn't you hear Dapple? And there's a whole fucking army coming."

"Shit," Wyte said. No longer pulling away.

They ran back down the carpet. Past the pews.

Bullets sprayed in a torrent against the outside of the chapel walls. A muted cry from Dapple.

Brought them up short at the double doors.

Finch looked at Wyte. Wyte looked back at him. Knew they were thinking the same thing. *Better outside with Partials than trapped inside with the rebels.*

Finch heard the sound of the tapestry parting just as they burst through the double doors. Out into the light. Stumbled over Dapple lying on his back in the dirt between the doors and the archways. Face slack. Clipped by a fungal bullet. Left shoulder turning black. Neck covered in looping veins of dark red that made him look like an obscene map. Convulsions already. Eyes distant. Muttering through a mouth flecked with spit. His guns beside him.

Finch looked up to see Partials behind the sandbags, amongst the tanks. Dozens of them. Pale faces. Dark clothing. Aiming up at the top of the chapel and the sharpshooters pouring fire down on them.

Frozen for an instant. Caught between two bad choices. Didn't know how Dapple had gotten hit.

Then a roar from next to him. *Wyte* was roaring. Standing straight up. Not caring if he got hit. Finch could just see the Partials moving back and forth behind their shelter. The liquid muzzle flashes.

"No, Wyte!" But it was too late. Wyte was shooting at them, and shooting and shooting. Bullets stitched through the dirt. Smacked into the stone of the archways.

No chance for finding common cause now. They had to get away from the front door.

"Wyte! Come on!" Shoved Wyte toward the alcove to their right. Finch dragging Dapple, who had gone silent with shock. Wyte still blazing away with his gun, gone mad with the pressure. Goading them. Laughing at them. Their confused pale faces in Finch's confused vision like smears of fat.

Between the alcove and the archway in front of it: enough cover to get Dapple out of sight and Finch mostly out of the line of fire.

But Wyte, oblivious, was beginning to scare Finch. A fungal bullet ripped right into Wyte's arm as he shot back at them. The bullet just stuck there. Absorbed by Wyte's body.

Finch got off a couple of shots at the Partials. Semi-automatic bucking in his hand. Smelled the acid smoke of the aftermath. None of the Partials went down. Had about ten bullets in the gun. More clips in his pockets.

But they'd still get shot to pieces. Now the double doors had opened. Rebels were firing back at the Partials. From the doors. From the dome.

Wyte jammed another bunch of sticky nodules into his gun from his right front pocket. Kept right on firing. The noise was hellacious. Wyte's bullets made an echoing thwack sound. Finch's a deeper crack. The Partial's return fire was like wood popping in a fire. The smell of the fungal bullets musty and metallic.

A scream from one of the Partials. Another scream. Finch, back up against the wall, shielding Dapple, had only a partial view.

A fungal bullet hit the dirt well to their right. Veins of red spread out across the ground. Seeking. Searching. Stopped next to a lizard sunning itself, oblivious to the threat.

"What's happening, Wyte," Finch shouted above the roar.

"I'm fucking killing them. Killing them all," he roared.

A conventional bullet clipped the side of Wyte's head. Left a bloody track. A runnel of flesh coming off. He roared again—this time with pain. Directed his fire to the left, toward the rebels or more Partials. The response was a fresh hail of bullets that sent even Wyte back into their shelter for a moment. Finch kept squeezing off rounds blind. Trying to aim high but not too high.

Wyte's face shone bright. His eyes were large and dilated and he was smiling.

"The bullets don't hurt," he kept saying. "They don't hurt at all."

"They'll hurt you eventually, dammit!" Finch got off another round.

Dapple convulsed. Blood rushed out of his mouth. His eyes stared toward the sky. Lifeless.

"Fuck."

Finch grabbed Wyte's shirtsleeve. Pulled him in close. Green pallor. Tongue purple. Eyes like black marbles shot through with gold worms. A bullet lodged in his left cheek. Coin-shaped. Like a curious birthmark.

"Wyte! We've got to get out of here. *Do you understand*?"

Wyte seemed to wake up. Spittle came out of his mouth as he said, "We'll go right through the Partials." Firing with his straight right arm as he talked. Bullets slamming into his side. Finch could hear them making impact. Being absorbed. "There's an alley behind them. Up or down the street you're dead. But if we're fast, right through the Partials works."

"How the fuck does that *work*?" Finch shouted at Wyte.

"I go out first, shielding you," Wyte said impatiently. Almost with a snarl.

"With your body?" Finch said, incredulous. "That's crazy."

Grinned at him. One eye on the street. "It's all fucked up. What's one more thing? Trust me, Finch."

"You'll die if you do this, Wyte," Finch said.

"No. I won't." Never heard Wyte so confident.

A bullet spiraled into Wyte's left thigh. He didn't even flinch.

Grim smile. "I love you, Wyte." And he did, he realized.

A smile back from Wyte like it was the old days before the Rising.

* * *

Later, in memory, it would be a fractured mix of shouts and screams and bullets flying and Finch running into the back of Wyte to keep as close as possible. Tripping over the things crawling off of Wyte's legs. Wyte exploding out from their shelter, overcoat thrown aside to reveal a body become *other*. A garden of fungus. Arms ballooning out into sudden wings of brilliant purple-red-orange. Legs lost in shelves and plateaus and spikes of green and blue. Back broader and insanely strong and gray. Head suddenly elongated and widened. As he ran a high-pitched scream came from his mouth that frightened Finch and bloodied the ears of the Partials.

The bullets. Wyte kept taking them like gifts. They tore through his limbs, lodged in his torso. Leaving holes. Leaving daylight. That closed up. And running in the shadow of that magnificence, as Wyte's scream became a roar again and they were assailing the ramparts of the Partials, he felt as if he were following some sort of god, his own gun like a toy as, from the shelter that was Wyte, he shot back at the chapel to keep the rebels pinned down.

Wyte's voice came out incomprehensible and strange now. Guttural and animal-like. No part of him in those moments that was human. Once he looked back at Finch to make sure he was still there. The whites of his eyes colonized. His pupils looking like something trapped. Trapped forever inside its own flesh.

For a while it was as if Wyte had lent Finch that kind of vision, because he could see the bullets coming. As if Finch were floating overhead, watching. And it was ecstasy or some kind of odd heaven. The surprise that eclipsed the Partials' pale faces as Wyte overran their positions. Wyte trying to outrun something he couldn't outrun.

Tendrils from his chest racing out to impale them. The weeping muzzle of his gun taking them in the legs, the heads. Faces trampled under his charge. Fungal eyes still clicking and clicking as the bodies lay dead. While even the rebels' fire had become scattershot from the shock of the new. From seeing the glory that Wyte had become. The monster.

Then it all came crashing down and Finch was in his skin again. In that one last look back he saw it all as a crazed tableau of men fallen, falling, firing, or running at an impossible speed. Almost distant enough as they made it to the warren of streets beyond to think of them as the silhouettes of broken, spasming dolls.

Realized he was roaring, too, like Wyte. As the tears ran down his face. As he kept firing behind him long after the enemy had faded into time and distance.

4

Breathless. Aching. Side hurting. Wyte trailing bits of things into the rubble behind them. Waiting for a bullet in the back of the head that never came. The acrid smell of spent ammo. A shambling halt under the shadow of the arch. The boat still tethered in the canal. The sky dark gray.

Wyte was still coming down from whatever had possessed him. Voice slick with some hidden discharge. Muttering: "Like wheat. Like paper. Just shredding them. Just running through them."

Finch babbling back. Exhilarated. Heart still beating so hard in his chest.

Wyte's face had regained a semblance of the normal, skin sealed over the bullets. Already now looking drawn, diminished. Finch kept seeing Wyte killing the Partials.

Wyte had rebuttoned his trench coat. The lining torn. Hung down below the hem. Mud-spattered. Blood-spattered. About a dozen bullet holes in it. Small orange mushroom caps peeked out from the holes. Others had burst through the fabric. Around the buttons, purple fungus rasped out, probing.

"Wyte, Dapple's dead," Finch said.

"I know, Finch. I saw. Get in the boat."

Finch climbed in and sat down. Held himself rigid as Wyte made the difficult negotiation of casting off and jumping in without capsizing them. Wyte sat down opposite. The boat glided across the water, back the way it had come. Like magic.

"You saved my life, Wyte," Finch said. And it was true. Monstrously true. Kept staring at Wyte with a kind of awe. Wyte's strength had manifested in a way Finch still couldn't quite believe.

"But not Dapple," Wyte said. "Dapple's dead. And I feel beaten and bruised all over."

Had Wyte passed a point of no return? More things that had colonized him peered out from the collar of the coat. Spilled out from his pants legs. Erupted in red-and-green patterns from his boots. A stench of overwhelming sweetness. Of corruption.

"Don't go back to the station," Finch said. "Not today."

"We were sent there to die, weren't we?" Matter-of-fact.

For my sins.

"Maybe we weren't," Finch said, thinking about the Partial standing over Shriek's body. Lecturing him about how Partials saw more than gray caps. "Maybe it's all falling apart. In front of our eyes. Everything."

Wyte made a wet clucking sound. He was trying to laugh. "Didn't it fall apart a long time ago?"

Knew Wyte was thinking about his wife, his kids, the little house they'd shared together so long ago.

Finch didn't want that in his head, shot a glance up toward the ridge. Anyone could pick them off. Anyone. "Stay at home. I'll figure it out. Call you."

Wyte nodded again, almost slumped over in his seat. A kind of glow had begun to suffuse his features. Green-golden.

Or you'll call me. Suppressed a shudder.

Finch's vision blurred. Too many things to keep inside. Every time he thought he'd tamped down one thing, another came rushing up.

A long silence. A complex smile played across Wyte's blurring lips. Finally said, "You know, Finch, I think we're a lot closer to solving this case."

A double take from Finch. A stifled smile. "Yeah, Wyte. Sure you do. Rest now. Sleep. I'll keep watch."

Wyte nodded. Closed his eyes.

A flake of something floated onto Finch's shoulder. Then another and another. He looked up to see that it was snowing. It was snowing in Ambergris.

As the white flakes drifted down, Finch on a hunch looked back. The white dome of the farthest camp had disappeared, replaced by an impression of billowing whiteness. An outline of what had once been. Realized that bits of fungus were raining down on them.

Raindrops followed, thick but sparse. Finch blinking them away. He laughed then. A wide laugh. Showing his teeth.

The "snow" still coming down. Falling onto Wyte's slack face. Melting away. Into him.

5

By the time Finch made it back to the hotel, he was almost asleep on his feet. Keeping him awake: left shoulder on fire. A bullet hole through the right arm of his jacket. Would've nicked him if he'd been a fatter man. A sharp pain in his ankle when he climbed the steps to the lobby. Stomach empty and complaining. Even after he bought some sad-looking plums. On credit. With a threat. From a woman who'd set them out on her stoop like a row of Bosun's carvings. Ate them on the way back to the hotel. Slowly.

Passed the Photographer inside. Grunted a hello. The Photographer just stared at him.

Lots of love to you, too.

He turned left in the courtyard, descended. Stopped at Rathven's door. Knocked.

A slow, reluctant opening. Long wedge of light. When Rathven looked up at Finch he thought he saw the secret knowledge they shared shining through her eyes.

A frown hardened her face. "What do you want?" She had one arm behind her back, hiding something. Wore severe pants and a shirt that almost made her look like an Irregular.

"You called me. Remember?"

She seemed to consider that. Almost as if she couldn't tell if he was lying. That she couldn't remember making the call.

"Can I come in?" Finch said, pressing.

"No. I mean, *not now*. You look like a wreck. What happened to you?"

Felt exposed there, in the hallway.

"Just let me in," he said, pushing at the door. Seeing if it would give. Seeing if she would give. "Of course I look rough. It's been a rough day."

"Stay where you are," Rathven said. She was stronger than she looked. The door hadn't even trembled. Or she'd wedged something behind it. "Are you drunk?" she asked.

Brought up short by the question, he shook his head. "No, of course not. At least tell me why you called." Felt like he had stone blocks attached to his legs. His vision was swimming. The words he said came both fast and slow. Didn't wait for her hesitation, said, "Don't tell me it was nothing. Something's obviously wrong. You're not yourself."

A fire in her hazel eyes. A kind of scorn in the set of her mouth. Her rigid stance. "Do you blame me?" she spat out. "And you—you're not 'yourself' either. I don't know who you are. You work for the gray caps but you help me get someone out of the camps. You help people in this building but then you go off and do Truff knows what during the day. For them. For *them*. You're in a good humor. You're in a bad mood. Sullen. Distant. Suddenly friendly. You like coffee, then suddenly you like *tea*. Why *wouldn't* I be wary?"

The words hit him like a blow to the head. Felt the corridor swirling.

"I have to sit down," he said. "If I have to, I'll sit down right here." The nausea had come back. Kept seeing Bliss and the tunnel they'd fallen through. Holding onto Bliss's shoulders had made it real, hard to shake off.

Rathven, continuing: "You bring me these lists. These lists of dead people. And you say research them, and it turns out you're investigating the murder of someone who *couldn't possibly have been alive*. It's a burden knowing that. Thinking that maybe you're not even working on a murder case. That maybe you're just crazy."

Each word like a length of rope Finch tried to hold on to as he fell. Slipping away under his grasp. Burning his palms.

He saw the floor coming up on him, then the ceiling above as he managed to land on his back. Shoulder feeling crunchy, like ground-up glass. Hand scraping against the floor. Crumpled into darkness. But, thankfully, not Bliss's darkness. Weightless. No nausea here. No thoughts.

Except the original one: *What was Duncan Shriek doing in that apartment?*

Ghosts of light pearling across the uneven surface of ceiling beams. Came to his senses in his own apartment, on the couch. A lamp on the stand by his head. Rathven leaning forward to stare at him. Her gun on the table between them. A battered old revolver. Heavy. The kind of thing that at close range would take your heart out, throw you across the room. Not what Finch would've expected from her. Curled up next to it, Heretic's list, returned, along with *Shriek: An Afterword* and *Cinsorium & Other Historical Fables.*

With an effort, he pulled himself into a sitting position.

"How long was I out?"

"Just a few minutes." Rathven wasn't smiling.

A sudden, suspicious thought. "How'd you get me in here?" Reached for his own gun. Found it still there. Tried to make a graceful motion away from it. Too late. Looked up to see Rathven frowning again.

"What are you afraid of?" she asked. "That I'm really strong or that I had an accomplice? Or that I'm going to shoot you?"

"No, I meant—"

"My brother helped bring you in here."

Finch nodded, ran a hand across his face. His hand felt like lizard skin. In his head a sound like waves.

Slowly realized the apartment didn't look the same. Thought it was him at first, vision blurry. But no: books tossed on the floor. Paintings smashed or askew on the walls. His other furniture knocked over. The kitchen trashed, too. Winced from pain in his shoulder.

"Shit, Rathven. What happened?"

"I don't know. It was this way when we came up. There've been too many strangers in the hotel lately. Why do you think I'm carrying a gun now?"

"You didn't before?" Ignored the look she gave him. "I've got to get cleaned up," he said.

"I'll wait."

He checked the table in his bedroom, with the maps on it. On the floor. The overlay was torn and had a boot print on it. Of the Partial? The one he hated? Much as he'd hoped during Wyte's mad charge, he hadn't seen the man.

The map his father had given him was intact. Still on the table. The bed was tossed. Pillows on the floor, sheets pulled back. Mattress had knife marks in it.

Finch considered that for a second. Then went into the bathroom. Shower didn't work. A thin trickle of water from the sink. He took off his clothes slowly, knees creaky. Like an old man. Washed himself clean with a washcloth. Waiting patiently for the water. Cold. Bracing. A lot of sandy dirt. Especially on his feet. He put on clean clothes. Same jacket. Bullet hole and all. Found some socks and an old pair of boots. Felt a little bit more human. Still, the face in the mirror looked defeated, pinched. Eyes he didn't know stared back at him.

He walked into the living room to find Rathven with a broom, sweeping up broken glass in the kitchen. She'd already wrestled many of his books back onto their shelves.

"Rath, you don't need to do that," Finch said.

"No, I don't," she said. Kept sweeping.

Whoever had trashed the apartment had left Finch's whisky alone. He found a glass. A generous pour. Let the taste burn in his mouth. *Sterilize me.* Grimaced as his shoulder tightened. Could've been worse. Could've been the right shoulder. Interfered with drawing his gun. Or his sword.

He picked up a chair with his good arm, righted it. Sat, watching Rathven in the kitchen. Admired how she could focus so single-mindedly on the ordinary.

"Seen Feral?" he asked her.

"No. I'm sure whatever happened scared him."

"Was the door open when you brought me up here?"

"No, it was closed. And locked. I had to get your key out of your pocket."

Locked? How?

"Do you know a man named Ethan Bliss?" Had to ask the question.

A break in the rhythm of her sweeping. "Bliss? No."

Finch wasn't convinced. "Ethan Bliss. Smaller than me. Dark eyes. You might have known him as a Frankwrithe & Lewden supporter before the Rising . . . He was the one in my apartment last night." *Although he didn't have time to trash the place then.*

No reaction. Which was a kind of reaction.

"We fought," Finch continued. "It's part of why I look this way."

Rathven leaned on the broom. Eyes narrowed. "How does *he* look?"

"I don't follow y—"

"Because I wouldn't know. I've never met him."

"Never even seen him? He used to be a powerful man for Frankwrithe before the Rising."

"No."

Hard to read her. Had, for that reason, sometimes been tempted to request her file from the gray caps. Resisted the urge. Didn't want to have Heretic asking him why.

In a low voice, "Are you investigating me?" Her tone said, *After all the help I've given you.*

"No, of course not." Scrambled for cover: "Could you do me a favor? He has a couple of aliases I need checked out."

Finch searched for a piece of paper. Wrote down *Graansvoort, Dar Sardice.*

The truth: he couldn't really imagine Rathven hurting him. Not on purpose. Suspected her of hiding something. But that might have nothing to do with him. Everyone in the city kept secrets.

She looked at the names on the piece of paper.

"It's all getting more and more complicated, Rathven. Hard to keep it all clear in my head."

"More complicated than Duncan Shriek?"

"Much more complicated." *Doors that were more than doors. Wyte become something greater and lesser than human.* Suddenly, the city was several cities. Time was several times. As if he'd been looking at his map and the overlay, and suddenly realized *more* overlays were needed to really see Ambergris.

The confusion must have shown because she gave him a half-smile.

A kind of peace offering. "I'll be finished soon. Then you should get some sleep."

In the apartment Bliss can visit anytime he wants to?

He tried to smile back. "But why did you call? Really?" Teetering now. *Two towers. Heretic's* skery. *Wyte's improbable charge. Dapple sprawled in the dirt. Dead.*

She held his gaze for a moment longer than was comfortable. As if trying to convey something to him that could not be said aloud.

"Sintra came by the hotel this morning."

"I know. She told me."

"Did she tell you she came down to see me?"

Finch, suddenly alert: "No . . ."

"Did she tell you she asked about your case?"

"It was a short phone call." Already marshaling stones, sandbags, the wreckage of tanks as a barricade.

"Well, she did, Finch," Rathven said. "She asked me about the case. We talked about it."

"And you told her about Shriek?" Incredulous.

Flat, dead tone. Not a glimmer of humor in her eyes.

"No. She already knew."

Feral came to the door scratching about ten minutes after Rathven had left. Frantic as Finch undid the locks on his apartment door. Complaining about the tragedy of not having been fed. That there should be such injustice in the world. Despite himself, Finch smiled.

Finch locked the door behind Feral. Once again shoved a chair up against the doorknob. Put down twice the normal amount of food for the cat. Then lay down on his couch, forcing himself to eat a packet of gray cap rations. The packet was porous. The contents a swelling purple. In his mouth, it tasted like onions and salt and chicken. Knew it was not.

Welcomed the utter fatigue. It emptied his head. Made it hard to think about unthinkable things. He'd go back to the station in the morning. Sort it out. Somehow. The apartment still looked like shit, but not as much like someone had trashed it. Actually found himself hoping it had been Bliss, come back to finish the job. Otherwise, Stark was already upping the pressure. Or, there was an unknown element out there.

Too tired to sleep. Poured himself another whisky. Sat down with *Shriek: An Afterword* and *Cinsorium & Other Historical Fables*. He was facing the apartment door, with his Lewden Special wedged in beside his left leg. So he could reach across his body to draw it. Sitting upright eased the pain in his shoulder.

Cinsorium looked like a kind of abridgment of Duncan Shriek's theories. He started to read it, then put it down. Needed something first that gave him more of a sense of Duncan's character.

He picked up *Shriek*, began to skim it. Saw at once the conceit: Duncan's voice in parentheses, commenting on Janice's history of a broken family and the first war between the Houses. Skipped to the end, read the editor's afterword. Duncan's disappearance. His sister's disappearance and possible death. The manuscript found in a pub Finch figured must've gone under or been destroyed years ago. With notes scrawled on the pages by Duncan. Which meant he'd still been alive when Janice went missing.

Finch turned back to the beginning. Charted Duncan's rise and fall as an historian, a believer in fringe theories about the gray caps. Almost all of them now proven true. Obsessed with a student at the academy where he'd taught history. A long, unhappy love affair. Duncan turned into a stalker. Discredited. Become unbelievable. Skipped Janice's own rise in the art world. Beside the point to Finch. He found Janice an exasperating narrator. She hid things, lied, delayed the truth. To undermine and slant. Like a particularly crafty interrogation subject.

Gradually, he got a sense of the tragedy of Duncan's life. How close Shriek had been to success. To being a kind of prophet. An injustice, his fate working at Finch's sense of fairness. A staggering sense of an opportunity lost. A path not taken. An Ambergris where Duncan Shriek was lauded and the Rising had never happened. Or been defeated. A horror at the idea of nothing really changing in a century. The Houses had gone from war to war. The city was more fractured than ever. Would still be fractured even if the gray caps disappeared tomorrow.

All depressingly similar, and yet he remembered the brief years of peace more vividly than the war. No matter how hard he tried to forget. *A better life. A better way.*

Kept searching Duncan's asides for anything that might point to *why* the man would wind up dead a hundred years later in an apartment he'd once lived in. Found a reference to switching apartments to evade the gray caps. Another reference to working as a tour guide while living in an apartment in Trillian Square. The place had been destroyed long before the Rising. Finch wondered if the few children growing up now even knew who Trillian was anymore.

Then there was Shriek's obsession with Manzikert. With the Silence. And with Samuel Tonsure, the monk who accompanied Manzikert underground and who never returned, although his journal—half evidence of an ill-fated expedition, half the ravings of a madman—reappeared sixty years later.

> I became convinced that the journal formed a puzzle, written in a kind of code, the code weakened, diluted, only hinted at, by the uniform color of the ink in the copies, the dull sterility of set type.

A quote from a book Duncan had found helpful called *A Refraction of Light in a Prison* had an uneasy resonance with the desert fortifications from Shriek's memory bulb:

> Where the eastern approaches of the Kalif's empire fade into the mountains no man can conquer, the ruined fortress of Zamilon keeps watch over time and the stars. Within the fortress . . . Truffidian monks guard the last true page of Tonsure's famous journal.

Could Zamilon be the place he had seen in the memory bulb vision?

He read, too, about Duncan's own explorations underground, following in Tonsure's footsteps:

> I could disguise myself from the gray caps, but not from their servants—the spores, the parasites, the tiny mushroom caps, fungi, and lichen. They found me and infiltrated me—I could feel their tendrils, their fleshy-dry-cold-warm pseudopods and cilia and strands slowly sliding up my skin, like a hundred tiny hands. They tried to remake me in their image.

Like Wyte. A few pages later, a section Janice had taken from Duncan's journal. About doors. About a door. A kind of recognition from deep within that stirred him to read carefully.

> A machine. A glass. A mirror . . . But it hasn't worked right since they built it. A part, a mechanism, a balance—something they don't quite understand . . . Ghosts of images cloud the surface of the machine and are wiped clean as if by a careless, a meticulous, an impatient painter. A great windswept desert, sluggish with the weight of its own dunes. An ocean, waveless, the tension of its surface broken only by the shadow of clouds above, the water such a perfect blue-green that it hurts your eyes . . . Places that if they exist in this world you have never seen, or heard mention of their existence. Ever . . . After several days, your vision strays and unfocuses and you blink slowly, attention drawn to a door . . . The distance between you and the door is infinite. The distance between you and the door is so minute you could reach out and touch it.

Skipped a few pages. Found a section where Janice related a conversation with her brother.

> Duncan: The door in the machine never fully opens.
> Janice: What would happen if it did?
> Duncan: They would be free.
> Janice: Who?
> Duncan: The gray caps.
> Janice: Free of what?
> Duncan: They are trying to get somewhere else—but they

> can't. It doesn't work. With all they can do, with all they are, they still cannot make their mirror, their glass, work properly.

And, then, on the Silence:

> You learned it wrong. That's not what happened. It didn't happen like that . . . They disappeared without a drop of blood left behind. Not a fragment of bone. No. They weren't killed. At least not directly. Try to imagine a different answer: a sudden miscalculation, a botched experiment. A flaw in the machine. All of those people. All twenty-five thousand of them. The men, the women, the children—they didn't die. They were *moved*. The door opened in a way the gray caps didn't expect, couldn't expect, and all those people—they were moved *by mistake*. The machine took them to someplace else. And, yes, maybe they died, and maybe they died horribly—but my point is, it was all an accident. A mistake. A terrible, pointless blunder.

Also, mentions of the symbol from the back of the scrap of paper: "Manzikert had triggered the Silence, I felt certain, with his actions in founding Ambergris. Samuel Tonsure had somehow catalogued and explained the gray caps during his captivity underground."

Throughout, Finch caught a refrain by Janice. Didn't know if it was Duncan's refrain echoed by Janice: *No one makes it out.* And near the end, with Duncan apparently lost underground again, this sentence: "There may be a way." What the woman had said to him when he'd blurted out *bellum omnium contra omnes.*

No one makes it out. Yet *There may be a way*. Janice had thought Duncan meant metaphorically. Spiritually. Maybe it was literal.

Couldn't help thinking of the words on the scrap of paper in Shriek's hand: *Never lost.* Like a call and response. *There is a way. Never lost.* Was that what he should have said to the woman?

Absently, he petted Feral, who'd leapt onto his lap, nudging his head up against Finch's chest. Tossed back another shot of whisky. The alcohol had begun to numb his shoulder. It also helped push worry for Wyte into the back of his mind.

Returned relentlessly to the facts.

A man last seen alive a hundred years before turns up dead in an apartment he once lived in. There's a dead gray cap with him. The gray cap has been cut in half as neatly as if he'd been killed in a slaughterhouse.

The dead man is Duncan Shriek, former discredited historian and explorer of the underground. The Stockton spymaster Stark believes the apartment holds a rebel weapon, but the only thing left in the apartment is the body of Shriek.

Stark kills all of Bliss's men, but leaves Bliss alive. Bliss travels through the city using doors that aren't doors—doors that when you come out the other side, it is the future.

And Shriek, the center of it all, believed the gray caps had built a door to another place, and the Silence was a result of that door malfunctioning.

Finch took out the photo of Shriek the Partial had given him. Stared at the photo on the dust jacket of *Cinsorium & Other Historical Fables*. Hadn't looked at either that closely before. Not like he was looking now. Shadows of light and dark in both. Framing a man with eyes shut, eyes open.

Who is he? Who was he?

Eyes Shut had a beard made of fungus. A hard face. A well-preserved quality to it. Weathered in the way of someone who has lowered his head into the wind too many times. Eyes Open had a close-cropped normal beard. A kind of naive quality to the face. The smile perhaps too self-satisfied. The look of a martyr-in-waiting.

Eyes Shut's smile was that of someone with a secret.

6

Woken by a sudden shifting of shadows. A vague awareness of a figure. A sound like a thousand soft gunshots. Dreamed he'd gone down the hole behind the station's curtain. Into the underground. Found the gray caps there. Sleeping on their sides. Heads down like resting silverfish. Heretic and the *skery* lying peacefully on a mattress made of curling ferns. Finch went to join them and immediately exploded into spores. Was everywhere and nowhere all at once.

Finch had a headache. Mouth felt thick. The sound: a thunderous rain. A woman knelt in the gloom beside his bed.

"Sintra."

The sharp smell of grass and water on her skin. Wanted to fall into her. Hold her like he was holding onto Bliss as they fell into darkness. Not caring in that moment what Rathven had told him.

But couldn't decipher the look on her face. Somewhere between watchful and sad. Made him hold back.

"I could've been anyone," she said. "You're too trusting."

Teasing: "But you're not anyone."

Sintra rose and dropped something onto the bed. He picked it up. The extra key to his apartment.

"Keep it." Offered it back to her.

"No," she said.

Frowned, kept holding it out to her. "It's yours. Not mine." Disturbed by her now. Calm disrupted. *There are doors and there are doors.*

"Someone broke into your apartment," she said. "I don't want you to think it was me. Keep the key. Maybe I'll take it back later."

Finch turned on the lamp next to the bed. Could see her clearly. A white blouse that revealed the curve of her breasts. Black pants that ended in stylish boots she must have bought long ago. Over that, a deep green trench coat ending at the knee. And still that expression on her face. Almost grim. Almost frowning.

Lowered his arm. The key felt cold and small in his palm. Made him weak to think of her without it.

"Are you sure?" Couldn't risk more than that.

"Yes," she said. Folded her arms.

He got up. Reached out to touch her hair. She pulled back.

"What's wrong?"

"I don't want to stay here," she said. "I want to go out." Not looking at him.

So this was how it would go down. What could he do but let her.

"Okay, so we'll go out, then."

"You don't have to," she said. As if suddenly undecided. Thought he understood. But he felt reckless. They'd only gone out twice before.

"I want to." And he did. Wanted to be out in the world. Even if that world was completely fucked up.

"I can go out by myself."

Touched her face with one finger, to brush aside a strand of hair. To feel the softness of her cheek. Brought her close. Kissed her on the forehead.

"Let me get some clothes on. We'll go. Wherever you want to go." No matter how far.

Wouldn't burden her with the details of his day. *Wyte erupting from ruins of his own dissolution to save them both. The mad charge to safety. The "snow" falling on them both.* A whole world of torment he wanted to leave behind.

"We'll go wherever you want to go," he said again, from the bedroom as he dressed. Savagely. Like he didn't care. Putting it on her. Apartment wasn't safe anyway. A solid wall could become a portal. A man could die and keep dying for a hundred years.

Came back out and made a show of sticking his Lewden in its holster. Put his arm around her, despite the pain in his shoulder. Opened the door. Feral shot out through the gap and was gone.

Made a show, too, of locking the door behind them with Sintra's key.

"You look rested," she said as they went down the stairs. "That's good."

Didn't feel rested. Not anymore.

* * *

Sintra: "There's a black market party tonight. We'll go to that. I know the way. There will be signs."

An urgency to the night. A dangerous pace to it. In the sky at some distance: the green towers, lit up like a glistening festival display. They rose impossibly high. In another city, at another time, that stained, blurry light might have seemed romantic.

The rain made it difficult to look for signs that didn't look like signs. A line of white paint in the gutter. A sudden fracture of light from a door. A muttered phrase from a drunk collapsed on a corner. At night, only about half the streetlamps worked. But all across the skyline phosphorescence draped and bled and hazed in and hazed out again. Ragged groups of camp refugees were gray smudges. A smoke smell, and a strong whiff of acidic perfume that came from a blossoming fungus like a light blue wineglass. No umbrellas. They looked too much like mushroom caps.

They huddled in awnings. Ran across open courtyards. Hugged the sides of buildings. Splashed through puddles. Loosened up enough to laugh about it. Like kids. Like the Rising had never happened. Like she'd never returned the key.

They crossed a bridge over a canal. Lights from both sides careened and cascaded through the water rippling below. Stood there for a few minutes. The rain had let up. Came in waves now, with calm between. The night had turned cooler.

He took her hand. Took in her bedraggled hair, the way the rain had moistened her cheeks. Wanted her. Badly. While another part of him wanted to ask, *"How did you know about Duncan Shriek?"*

"It's almost a normal night," he said.

"What's a normal night?" she asked. But she was smiling. A little.

"A night when my apartment isn't trashed twice," he said.

"What do you think they wanted?"

"Money, probably," he said. Unable to look at her while he was lying.

"What about you?" he asked.

"I had a day like any other." She smiled at him. Revealed near perfect teeth. Wondered again if the dogghe skill with herbs helped.

Couldn't take it anymore. "Sintra, *what do you do*?" Such a naked question. It split the air like a thunderclap.

She studied him. The light from the canal reflected in her eyes. Anything from rotted leaves to dead bodies could lie at the bottom.

"I could be anyone, John," she said. "I could be someone you wouldn't like very much."

"I might have a better idea than you think."

"No. You don't. What if I have three children? What if I'm a trained assassin? What if I'm a prostitute?" In one swift motion: she had his gun and was pointing it at him. "What if I'm somebody who wants you dead?"

Took a step back, had his hands out in front of him. Too surprised to do more.

But a flick of her wrist and she was offering the Lewden back to him, grip-first. While his heart dealt with it.

"Point made," he said. Taking it. Swallowing. Hard.

"Maybe I should tell you I'm a spy for the rebels. I think that's what you'd like me to say, isn't it? But why does it matter. Why now?"

"I don't know," Finch said. Except he did. She'd given back the key. While everything was falling down around him.

They stood facing each other. Like friends, or enemies.

"What do you want to know?" she asked. "And *why*?"

"Whatever you can tell me," Finch said. *Something that makes you more real.*

She looked out over the shimmering water. "You don't really want to know. There's nothing I can tell you that will help you more than what's already in your head."

"What's wrong?" he asked. "What's really wrong?"

She didn't blink or turn away. But she didn't answer, either. Just took his hand.

"Do you still want to follow me?"

She led him past an abandoned factory lit up like a burning ship. As if displaced from the Spit. Windows slick with the spray of rain. Came closer, saw that a neon-red fungus had colonized it. Heard Partials hooting and mocking someone a couple streets over. Even saw a couple of quickly disappearing shadows that might've been gray caps. Part of the risky thrill of finding a bootleg party. Like they were doing something dangerous. Kept his hand on his gun the whole time.

Finally found the guts of a building whose roof had been blown off. Every inch of its exterior glittered with graffiti. Finch had completely lost his bearings. Was trusting Sintra.

The weight and sound of the rain lifted off of them. They were sopping, but didn't care. So was everyone else.

"It was a theater," she whispered, moving up against him. "I saw a play here once about Voss Bender's life. I saw it with my father when I was fourteen. Afterward, we got ice cream from a sidewalk vendor. Then we took a long walk down to the park. There were so many people around. The night was beautiful. It was one of the first times I'd dressed up for anything. My mother was sick, so she didn't come along. But I spent all night telling her about it."

"Stop," Finch said.

"A year later, the war broke out again and the park was gone. The people couldn't come out onto the streets. It was too dangerous. My mother had gotten better, but my father had lost his arm to a fungal bullet. He couldn't work for a long time he was so depressed. He'd been a journalist. I knew about my native heritage, but it wasn't until then that I learned more, because my father returned to his roots. It was a way of making himself whole again, I think."

"Stop," he said again. Each detail making her more distant.

"What about you, John?" she asked. "What do you want to tell me? Is there anything you want to tell me?" Tone between bitterness and sympathy. Maybe even affection.

"No."

"Does it make it better or worse if I tell you these things?"

Daring him to look at her. But he wouldn't.

"Worse," he admitted. Defeated.

"Because you can't tell me anything back," she said. "Because you don't trust me. Shouldn't trust anyone."

Because then you're not who I need you to be.

Hugged him then. Whispered in his ear, "Do you understand now? We're alone, John, even when we're together." Kissed his cheek.

Didn't want it, but took it.

"Let's just find the party." Needed a drink. Bad.

Down a stairwell. Through a hallway picked clean of detail. The deeper they went, the more light. From gas lamps. From naked bulbs. From flurries of candles unwinding along their path.

People began to appear out of the half-light. Couples kissing. Sidewalk barbers, driven inside. A man leaning against the wall, offering cigars. More vendors. Wine. Drugs. Food. Candy. Pots and pans. Watches. Fabric. The smell of something spicy.

Finch bought a bottle of wine with three packets of gray cap food. The man popped the cork for them. Finch handed the bottle to Sintra. She took a manly swig, laughed, pulled him close as if in apology. Kissed him, her tongue in his mouth. Connected to every nerve in his body. She pulled away to hand him the bottle, whispered, "Isn't that better than *words*, John?" He drank long and deep. Sweet, full-bodied. Exploding against his taste buds. Coursing into his body. Followed by a bitter aftertaste. But he didn't care. He really didn't care.

Down more stairs. The sounds of the party now muted, now blaring. As if they were getting closer, then further away. They came to a doorway with a black sheet draped across it. A small man with a slurred, gritty voice and dirty black hair took their payment: three food pods and the pocketknife Sintra had brought. Let them through, into light.

A raised platform, looking down at a huge room that must have been used for storage once. Hundreds of people occupied that space now, the sound of their voices muffled yet deafening. Gray archways surrounded the room. No way to defend the space. From anything. Oil lamps hung from each archway, made a buttery light that created shadow even as it swept away the darkness. A strong smell of sweat.

A band played in the far left corner. Cello. A drum made from trash can lids. An old accordion. People were exchanging pieces of paper nearby. Probably stories, poetry, artwork. The gray caps didn't care, but the Partials did. Noticed a few silent, large men at the fringes. Probably bouncers hired by the vendors.

Finch took another swig of wine. The last time he'd seen so many people in such a small space he'd been fourteen and his father had taken him to a reception thrown by the Frankwrithe viceroy three months after an armistice with House Hoegbotton. Stiff and cramped in a suit. His father had introduced him to each dignitary, and afterward, while they were distracted, Finch had snuck into the viceroy's rooms and taken the papers his father needed.

Recklessly, he crushed Sintra to him, put his arm around her neck, let his hand touch her breast. She turned into him. Shouted in his ear, "Should we go down there?"

He nodded, and they descended into the chaos. Relaxed into it. Despite seeing the tawdry cheapness of it. Too good at playing a role not to know when another role was being played out in front of his eyes.

The frantic, almost hysterical dancing of the women. The faces rising toward them mask-like in that half-light. The hesitant rhythm of the band. As if the Partials would break in at any second. How much alcohol everyone was drinking. Quickly, just in case.

More wine. Another kiss from Sintra. Thought he saw on her face a look close to desperation. Or was it resignation?

They made their way to the far end. Next to the band. Joined the dancers. A man and woman, both shirtless, careened into them. Disappeared again in a whirl of arms. Another couple up close to each other, slow as the music was fast. The pungent tang of some drug. A smell like incense. The bodies around them became like one body. Only to fall apart, like the limbs in the rebel safe house. Heads. Legs. Arms. *Wyte charging out to meet the Partials.*

Finch needed more wine, then. For both of them. Smiles from people around them. A shared secret. *Life could be good. If you could only get far enough out of yourself.* Abandoning. Forgetting.

A song ended. As it had ended before, and before that, too. But this time Sintra said, "Follow me." Led him by the hand into the darkness of a doorway where a lamp had failed. The sudden touch of cold stone. On the other side, a catacomb of rooms. The light from the party already receding. Snuffed out. Men and women had paired off here. Moans, murmurs, a sudden heat.

They found a section of wall around a corner. Drank the last of the wine. Let the bottle fall, and, broken, roll to the side. She was unbuttoning her white blouse, a wild light in her eyes. He was helping her, suddenly frantic in his need. His mouth was on her breasts. Tongue on her delicate brown nipple. Coming back up to her mouth with his. She gasped. Unbuttoned his pants. His cock throbbing as she took it in her hand. He let out a long sigh. His fingers curled through her hair.

He pushed her up against the wall. Pulled her pants down. Got his arms under her, ignoring the pain in his shoulder. Slid into her tight wetness. Groaned. Her hand against the back of his head. Her arm around his back. Nails digging into him ecstatically. Thrust hard up into her like an animal, muttering obscenities into her ear. While she encouraged him. His tongue into her mouth. Finding her tongue. Pulling back to look at her sweat-tinged face in the dark. A shadow. A wraith. Those eyes. She leaned into him, both arms around him, and sucked on his ear in a way that drove him mad. Everything receded to just that point at which he was entering her. Then expanded until he was everywhere at once. Suddenly she came, biting his shoulder and he, snarling, telling her to bite harder. The feel of her teeth on his skin made him cry out, come deep into her. Held there by her long after he was spent. She was spent.

With reluctance, Finch let her slide back to her feet. Pulled up his pants as she pulled up hers. Buttoned her blouse. Kissed again. Salty and deep. Shocked him.

They walked until they stood in the archway, staring into the main room. With its loudness. Its light. Its movement.

"Stay here," she whispered. "I'll get more wine and be back."

"Now?"

"Now. I need another drink." She threw her arms around him. Clung to him like a child. Whispered in his ear, "Be careful, John."

When she pulled away she looked so vulnerable Finch almost told her everything he thought he knew. She looked like she was receding from him at a great speed. And he was suddenly frightened.

Then she was gone. Beyond his grasp. Out into the crowd. Lost. And he was standing there. Alone.

He started after her. Didn't know why. She was just going to get more wine. Not leaving for good. But a familiar face stopped him.

Bosun. Entering from the raised stage opposite. Five tough-looking men in trench coats stood behind him. Bosun was scanning the crowd. For him?

Looked again for Sintra but couldn't find her. Decided to step back into the archway. Out of sight.

A hint of movement behind him. A hand over his mouth. A sharp pain in his arm before he could react. Falling as the lamps shuffled through his vision, became the scrap of paper pulled from Shriek's hand, bursting into flame. Became the candles on a cake from his eleventh birthday. Began to blow out the candles. And with each, another clue snuffed out. Shriek going dark. Stark's transcript extinguished. His father's face, hovering just beyond the candles. Mysterious. Shadowed. Smiling.

7

Someone slapped his face.

"Wake up. Wake up."

Finch opened his eyes. Night. Lying on his back. In the grass. Staring up at a field of green stars. He shivered. It looked nothing like the sky over Ambergris.

A woman's face blocked out the stars. For a second, in the gloom, he thought it was the woman from the rebel safe house. She had a gun. Didn't recognize the make.

"You . . ." he said, still woozy.

"Don't make me hurt you," she said, then stepped out of view.

Hands roughly pulled him up. They shoved his arms behind him. Handcuffs slid into place. Cut into his wrists. Felt almost as bad as he had after following Bliss through the door.

"Where am I?" Finch asked.

"Shut up," the woman said.

Wyte, saying to him once, "You know what they say about the rebels? A rebel is just a Hoegbotton who made the mistake of marrying a Frankwrithe."

They stood on the side of a grassy hill. Below them, a crushed tangle of tanks and other military equipment. Glistening darkly. The wind through the hundred metal husks made a distant, warped, singing sound. Beyond, he could see the black silhouette, jagged and *wrong*, of a ruined city. In the middle: a dome of dull orange light.

"Is that Ambergris?" Incredulous.

"Shut up," she said.

Two men appeared to either side of him. They wore dark pants tucked into boots. Camouflage shirts. Ammo belts. Rifles slung over their shoulders. Military helmets.

"Or are we inside the HFZ somehow?" Finch asked. His gun was missing from its holster. His mouth was dry. His arms already ached.

"No one is in the HFZ, John Finch," the woman said.

"Why am I here?" Tried hard to bite down on a rising fear. *I'm here because I work for the gray caps . . .*

"Walk," said one of the men. Shoved him in the back.

"We're going to the top of the hill," the woman said, from in front of Finch. "Don't move too fast, or we'll shoot you. Understand?"

"Yes," he said. "I understand." Understood, too, that Sintra had betrayed him. Realized he'd been expecting that ache for a long time.

Some of the stars in the sky were moving. Slowly moving back and forth. The wind was very cold. The grass whispered around his boots.

They reached the top of the hill. In the shelter provided by the ruined wall of an ancient fortress, a tent served as a windbreak for two chairs. A table with a pitcher on it. Two glasses. A couple of dim lamps, placed so they couldn't be seen from downhill.

A figure beside the chairs. In a long, dark robe. Graying hair lifted slightly by the wind.

The Lady in Blue.

Unmistakable. Finch just stared at her. Disbelieving. Forgot his captors shoving him from behind. Forgot the danger he was in. He had never seen her before, and now he was seeing her by starlight. On a hill under a strange night sky. Surrounded by some kind of dead city.

In the Hoegbotton Irregulars, the promise of meeting her had been held out like a guarantee of better times. As they lay in the trenches. As they went from house to house, rooting out insurgents. As they ate hard, stale bread and molding fruit. Made soup from glue, water, and salt. That whole past life overtaking Finch as they marched him up in front of her.

She was shorter than Finch. Maybe five-six. Late fifties or early sixties. Thin and in good shape. Wrinkles at the corners of her eyes, across her forehead. Accentuated by the lamplight: a near perpetual wry smile, a sad amusement to the eyes. A look that seemed to say she was here, in the moment, but also a dozen other places as well.

The Lady in Blue said, "You are, supposedly, John Finch. And I am, reportedly, the Lady in Blue. You have questions, although I may not have as many answers as you'd like. Let's sit." She spoke with the quiet, weathered quality of experience. Mixed with a bluntness that was nothing like her radio broadcasts. It came as a jolt. Thought for a moment that she might not be the Lady after all.

His captors uncuffed him. Shoved him into a chair opposite the Lady in Blue. Withdrew out of the light.

Finch rubbed his wrists. Sitting in the chair a kind of weight dropped onto his chest. Didn't know if it was some after-effect of how he'd gotten there. Or the presence of the Lady in Blue.

"Where are we? Why am I here?" Aware he sounded weak. *Because I am weak.* Sintra's scent was still on him. Felt trapped.

"Where are we?" echoed the Lady in Blue. "Maybe it's a place you know. Maybe it's, to pick somewhere random, a place called Alfar. Or one version of Alfar. Does it matter? No. We could be anywhere. That's one thing you'll learn."

She leaned forward, poured a clear liquid from the pitcher into a glass. Offered it to him. He took it but didn't drink.

"Go on. If I wanted you dead, you never would have woken up."

"Maybe you're cruel," Finch said. But he drank. The water was cool on his throat. Drove away the lingering nausea.

"Do you know why you're here, 'Finch'?" she asked, leaning back. An appraising look.

"Only you know that." The way she said "Finch" made him feel naked, exposed. His awe was fading. Replaced by a kind of perverse resentment. This woman had helped ruin his father.

"*Bellum omnium contra omnes,*" she said, and the little hairs on Finch's neck rose. "Maybe I say those words to you three times and you wake up from this dream you've been living and remember your mission."

"I don't believe you," Finch said. Waking up to the fact that he'd been kidnapped. That he was in a dangerous situation. She'd hinted she knew his real name. She knew he worked for the gray caps. Knew he'd been at the rebel safe house.

The Lady in Blue laughed. "Of course you don't, because, unfortunately, you're correct. You're not a secret agent for the resistance."

"What do the words mean?" Asking questions meant he didn't have to answer any.

"Maybe it's in a language from another place, a place the gray caps don't know about. Maybe we're the only ones who can understand it. 'War of all against all,' that's what it means. Though we won't be using it again after today. You've made sure of that."

"*Never lost* is the countersign."

"*Part* of the countersign." She wasn't smiling.

"We were just doing our jobs," Finch said. "We were going to ask some questions and leave. We wanted to stay alive."

The wind coming from the city below had faded. Finch could hear strange mewls and moans. Then a sound like a million leaves rustling.

The Lady in Blue folded her arms. "Maybe we should talk about your murder investigation instead. Such as it is."

"You're not the first to be interested."

Her smile was as humorless as a knife blade. "Then one more won't hurt, will it? Tell me what you know."

Remembered the transcript Stark had given him: "There's a weapon in the apartment where we found the dead man. You, the rebels, lost a weapon there."

"We lost an agent there, Finch," the Lady in Blue said flatly.

Duncan Shriek.

"What's his name? The man?" Finch asked.

A look of profound displeasure from the Lady in Blue.

"Now that is disappointing, Finch. Disappointing in three ways. First because I don't have much time and you're wasting it. Second because I suppose this means you're going to try to survive by giving me scraps. And third because I'm not your unimaginative little gray cap boss." Unable to keep disgust out of her voice.

"You left," Finch said. "You left all of us behind. We've had to live in that city *for six years*. Survive any way we could."

You abandoned us. Curled up inside that outburst all the bottled-up frustration from nearly eight years of playing a role. A role inside of a role.

The Lady in Blue nodded as if she agreed, but said, "Do you think we've been having a party out here, Finch? Do you think we've been sitting out here waiting for the end times? No. We've been learning things. We've been gathering our forces. Waiting for the right moment. It's been as hard for us as for you. Harder maybe."

At least you've had a change of scenery.

When he remained silent, she said, "Tell me the name of the man in the apartment. Think of it as an exercise in trust."

They already knew. He had no leverage.

"It's a man named Duncan Shriek. Except he died a hundred years ago. That's what I don't understand."

The dead man sat in the chair next to him, smiling.

"Was there anyone with him?"

"Half of a dead gray cap."

Falling through cold air and couldn't feel his legs.

"Is the body still in the apartment?"

"Not the gray cap, but Shriek's is."

"Is there any visible sign of injury to Shriek?"

"Not really."

"How did he die?"

"I don't know. He looks like he might have fallen. Twisted his neck a bit."

"Don't you feel better, telling the truth?"

"Yes," he said. Meant it.

She paused for a moment, as if marshaling hidden forces. Then said, "While we're telling the truth, Finch, I should let you know something: I knew John Crossley. *John Marlowe Crossley.*"

A sharp intake of breath he couldn't control. Too long since he'd heard that name spoken. Hadn't uttered it in years, either. Had tried to unthink it.

The Lady in Blue continued: "John had a strange idea of honor. He had genuine disagreements with us. With everyone, really. That's why he fell so hard. Why no one could protect him. It would have been easier if he'd been a simple spy, one side against another, not working for the Kalif."

"I don't know what you're talking about," Finch said. Although he knew it was hopeless. He felt like a hermit crab being pulled from its shell.

The Lady in Blue nodded, but not to Finch.

A slamming blow came down on Finch's bad shoulder. He cried out, fell from his seat into the grass. Moaning in pain. Turning to protect his shoulder.

The Lady in Blue had risen. Stood next to him. Suddenly more threatening, more terrible, than anyone he had ever seen. "You *do* know what I'm talking about, James Scott Crossley. *You do know.*"

Like looking in a mirror and seeing a double that didn't really match up. He'd been Finch for so long that he didn't know James Scott Crossley anymore. Not really. Some stranger who hadn't survived the Rising. Some poor bastard who'd never made it back, like so many others.

She pulled the chair away from the table and sat down. "Do I have your attention?"

Through gritted teeth. "Yes." He didn't want to remember Crossley. Crossley was dead. Both of them.

"You've changed your look. Your hair is lighter, and you've shaved the beard. You're heavier. Older, of course. But it's still you. What would people *do* if they knew? With your father's reputation for treachery? Even now, maybe they'd be firmer with you. Maybe they'd stop what they're up to long enough to settle old scores. One thing to protect the key to a weapon. Another to find out the key has close ties to someone who betrayed the city to a foreign power. Maybe you'd wake up to a bullet in your brain. And know this, too, John: your father brought it on *himself*. Don't delude yourself about that."

"Fuck you," Finch said. "Fuck you, *Alessandra Lewden.*"

Got a kick in the ribs for that. Lay there, saying nothing. Pinned to the ground by her words. Shoulder knifed through with broken glass.

She relented then. Said in something close to a kindly tone, "But that's not why you're here, 'Finch,' if that's what you'd prefer I call you. A year ago? Maybe. But now? No."

Through gritted teeth, "What do you want, then?"

"We've time enough to talk about that," she said. "Soon we'll be leaving here. It's never safe to stay in one place for long. Get up."

Finch stood. Holding his shoulder.

"Look," the Lady in Blue said, pointing out past the ruined hulks of tanks. Toward the dull orange dome.

"What am I looking for?"

"Just wait."

As she spoke, the dome exploded. A thousand streamers rising in intense shades of red and orange. Like some kind of land-bound sun. The tendrils arched into the sky. Hung there. Then disintegrated into a vast cloud. A roiling mass of particles. Discharging light until a steady humming glow suffused the city in a kind of dawn. There came in reply from the city a hundredfold bestial roar. Strange fractal creatures began to grow at a frenetic pace across every surface. Straining up toward the light. While the orange dome, much reduced, seemed to breathe in and out. Beyond the particle cloud the darkness continued unabated.

"Dawn, Finch," the Lady in Blue said. "That's the kind of dawn they have here."

"Yes, but what is this place?" Finch asked, almost pleading. "Where am I?"

"It's a place where the echo of the HFZ—*just the echo of it*—destroyed a city. Subjected it to this perpetual artificial dawn. There's no one living down there now. No one. Just flesh that serves as fertile soil . . . for something else. The HFZ is like a wound where the knife cut through more than one layer. And that's really all you needed to see. No, it hasn't been *fun* out here for six years, Finch. Not really."

She nodded to someone behind him. A man came up and got Finch in a choke hold. He struggled against it. Kicked his legs. Frantic. The woman came around front. Stuck a needle in his arm.

The stars swirled into a circle, then a haze.

The world disappeared all over again.

* * *

James Crossley had been callow, self-absorbed, impatient, a ladies' man. Finch was none of those things. Finch was direct, brusque, had a dark sense of humor. Crossley had been, for a while, finicky about food. Finch had cured him of the last of that during the worst times, with stew made from leather belts, made from dogs and rats.

Crossley never swore. Finch had trained himself to swear to fit in. To break up the rhythm of his normal speech patterns. Crossley liked the river. Finch kept waiting for something to leap out of it. Both liked cigars and whiskey. Both were as dependable as they could be, indifferent to music, and hated small talk. Although Crossley had had more chances to hate it than Finch.

Crossley had been part of his father's network as a youth, something he'd only known later. Even if he'd had an inkling.

His father passed information on Frankwrithe to Hoegbotton, and information on Hoegbotton to Frankwrithe. Built things for Hoegbotton only to give Frankwrithe the intel to blow them up. Used the contacts to feed Hoegbotton sensitive information on troop movements from supposed "sources." Neither side having any sense of the level of betrayal until they came together to fight the gray caps. After which it became clear John Crossley had been given his orders by someone working for the Kalif. Creating chaos while providing the Kalif's secret service with an inside look at both factions.

And why? *Why?* Neither James Crossley nor John Finch had any idea. Their father had never told them. Just said once that being a powerful man meant you made enemies. "Too many people get the wrong idea," he'd said. While he hid out in an abandoned mansion in northern Ambergris. Coughing up blood from the sickness he'd first contracted while on campaign in the Kalif's territory.

"Look," he'd said to Finch, showing him, "I never knew my face would be printed on playing cards." One of fifty most-wanted men and women. On the rebels' list.

Remembered again the pipe his father had shown him.

Crossley was the past. Finch was the present, waiting for the future. For the air to clear. For all of this to go away.

But two things they agreed on.

Both still trusted in their father, couldn't bring themselves to shun him. Even knowing what he had done.

Both had loved him.

8

Finch woke with an uneven, sharp surface cutting into his back. Above, a wavery light showed a shelf of rippling black rock. Glittering stalactites pointed down at him.

"We're in an underground cave system," a voice said from nearby.

He sat up. The walls of the cavern glowed a deep, dark gold. Traveling across them, in the waves of illumination, Finch saw what looked like strobing starfish. A smell like and unlike brine came to him. Colder, more muted. He still didn't have his gun. Felt vulnerable, small. *She knows I'm Crossley. And she doesn't care.* Which meant she was going to ask him for something big.

The Lady in Blue stood beside him. Wearing the plain uniform of a private or Irregular, all in muted green. Short-sleeved shirt. Tapered pants. Holding a lantern, staring across an underground sea. It stretched out into a horizon of swirling black shadows and glints like newborn stars. A rowboat was tethered to the shore.

"Stop drugging me," Finch said. He felt sluggish.

"The less you know, the better."

"How long was I out for?"

"It doesn't matter."

"It does to me."

"We drug you because there are things we can't let you know."

"You mean if I'm interrogated. By someone else."

She ignored him, indicated the cave with a sweep of her hand. "This is where the gray caps left Samuel Tonsure," she said. "You know who Tonsure is? Not everyone does."

He nodded. "The monk Shriek was obsessed with. The one who disappeared."

"They took his journal from him right here. Left him to make his own way in their world."

Duncan, in his book: "I became convinced that the journal formed a puzzle, written in a kind of code, the code weakened, diluted, only hinted at, by the uniform color of the ink in the copies, the dull sterility of set type."

"And where exactly is that?" Finch managed with a thick tongue. His head felt heavy. Whatever they'd drugged him with had quieted the pain in his shoulder.

"You might be better off asking *when*, but it's your question. Answer: we're *everywhere*. But at this moment, we're deep beneath the city. Or, at least, *a* city."

The Lady in Blue stepped into the boat, hung the lantern on a hook in the prow. "Come on," she said. "We're going on a journey."

Finch hesitated. Suffered from too many journeys. From a shoot-out on an Ambergris street to falling through a door in time and space. Stepping onto the boat felt like a kind of slow drowning. Into yet another dream.

"You don't have a choice," the Lady in Blue growled. "I don't want to have to force you. But I will."

She was alone. Finch couldn't see a weapon, though she'd picked up a long pole from the boat. But he didn't doubt she could hurt him.

Awkwardly, he got to his feet. Stepped into the boat behind the Lady in Blue. It wobbled beneath his weight.

"Sit down," she said. He sat.

She began to pole them across the little sea, with a strength he hadn't noticed before. He could see the outline of her triceps as she pushed off with the pole.

Over the side, by the lantern light, needle-thin fish with green fins shot through the water. More starfish. A couple of delicate red shrimp. It wasn't very deep; he could see the silver-gold flash of the bottom. The unreal translucent light confounded him. A glimpse of a kind of peace. Fought against relaxing. Was still in danger.

"Where are we going?" he asked. "What does this have to do with Duncan Shriek?"

"Eat something," she said. "Drink something."

Sandwiches and a flask by his feet. He unwrapped a sandwich.

Chicken and egg. Ordinary. Normal. Tasted good. The flask had a refreshing liquor in it. It warmed him as it spread through his body.

"And while you eat, listen to me. Don't talk. Just *listen* . . ."

[*She said:*] For a moment, imagine everything from the gray caps' point of view, John Finch. James Scott Crossley.

In the beginning. Once upon a time. A small group of you became separated from your world while on an expedition. In a word, lost. A problem or mistake in the doors between places. Suddenly there are hundreds or thousands of doors between you and home. Suddenly you're adrift. You find yourselves washed up on an alien shore, along the banks of a strange and magnificent river. You can't find your way back to where you came from, even though at first all you do is try. And try and try.

After a while of trying and failing, you decide to settle down where you are, establish a colony that we will later call "Cinsorium." It's a better place for you than other choices for exile. You live a long time but procreate slowly so the isolation is good. No competition. No real threats. You create buildings that remind you of home. No corners. All circles. You bend the local fungus to your will, because you're spore-based and everything you do is based on this fact. Plenty of raw material to use in and around Cinsorium.

But, still, you're always looking for a way back, a way out. You might even have been close at one point—right before Cappan Manzikert sails upriver with his brigands. Because as soon as Manzikert appears, it's back to square one for you. Even less than square one. He destroys your colony, drives you underground. He burns your records, all of the information in your library. Not just the clues you've gathered of how to get home, but your whole knowledge base. Essential things.

Ironic, really, Finch. Because Manzikert's a barbarian. Yet as far as I can tell, he saved us all with that one brutal act. Something even Duncan Shriek didn't understand.

So you stay underground to rebuild. You're cautious, you're far from home, and there aren't very many of you. Will never be very many of you, no matter what you do. You let the people above become comfortable. You lie low, so to speak.

Then you try again. At last. And because you're cautious you build it underground. A door. A machine.

But the door doesn't work. Something goes wrong. Who knows what? It could've been anything. Maybe it's the wrong location. Maybe it was always a long shot. Many of your own people are killed. And everyone in Ambergris disappears, except the ones in the fishing fleet. Either dead or taken *elsewhere*. Scattered across worlds and time. Unable to get back. (Think about that, Finch—somewhere out there, there must be a colony or two of Ambergrisians who survived. Can you imagine what they might be like now, after so long? Stranded. Vague tales of another place, one crueler, kinder, more hospitable, less so.)

Maybe it's then that you believe, *this is the end. We're doomed to die out here, in this backwater. We'll never be found.* But, still, you're patient. You're clever. You're hard-working. You spend a long time learning from your mistakes. Sometimes you venture out during festival nights. You do experiments related to your goal. You even kidnap humans, use them as test subjects. Always trying to convey a sense of dread in those who live aboveground, always trying to make yourself larger in their minds—like a wild cat that puffs itself up in front of an enemy.

When the opportunity comes, it's because Hoegbotton and Frankwrithe have exhausted themselves against each other—sometimes even using weapons you provided to them—and the city lies in ruins. You take a huge gamble. Why a gamble? Because there still aren't enough of you, not compared to the human population.

You pour all of your resources into the Rising. You're hard to kill, but you can't possibly hold a whole city for long against an armed resistance, not if it means a true occupation. But you don't *need* it to last for long. You just need to create the *impression* of overwhelming force.

And it works. You Rise. You use your re-engineering skills and knowledge of the underground to flood the city. You use your spores like a kind of diversion, a magic show. Yes, you can kill people, but not all of them, and not as fast as the enemy thinks. Besides, fear is even more useful to you—it's how your agents have worked throughout Ambergrisian history. Preying on the imaginations of a people raised to fear you. (Often for good reason.)

You force the combined Hoegbotton and Frankwrithe army arrayed against you to fight on your terms, on your turf. You even leave an escape route so that no one needs to fight to survive. They can just flee.

Again, it works. The resistance retreats—and when they're far enough away, in one more spasm of energy and expertise, you cast the HFZ over your enemy, like a net, and you disperse them across the doors. Thus ending effective armed resistance, and creating more fear.

For the actual occupation, you are clever and resourceful. You enlist the remaining population to police itself, to govern itself—as much as it is able. When the situation is stable except for isolated pockets of unrest, you start to build your final attempt at a door. A way home. Two towers, which aren't really towers but a kind of complex *gateway*. Situated precisely where you need them to be for success.

Meanwhile, you stall. You go through the motions. You provide electricity, food, drugs on the one hand. Camps, the Partials, and repression on the other. You don't need to control territory in the normal way. You don't see the city from the sky looking down, like humans. You see it from the underground looking up. And you control the underground. That's your homeland away from home. You can choose what you hold onto aboveground and what you don't. So long as you rule everything below. So long as you can *block* access to whatever you like.

You leave the burnt-out tanks on the streets, don't clean up the HFZ *not* as a warning to the human population, but because you don't have the *personnel* to do that and keep working on the towers, too. And because, on some level, you don't really care about any of it. Not *any* of it. Especially not governing. All you care about are the two towers.

And do you know why? Because we might have called it a door all this time. "A window. A machine." But it's more complex than that. It's not just a door. It's a *beacon*. Because, you see, Finch, they don't *need* a huge door if they've found a way home. Not according to our intelligence. No, they only need a door this big if they're planning to use it to bring *more* over here. To Ambergris. To the world.

The Silence? All of what Duncan Shriek said in those old books—it's true. Except he was wrong about this one thing. *They've found they like it here.* They want to stay. Permanently. In numbers.

Now, is that *exactly* what happened, and how it happened? No, probably not, because we can't actually imagine how they think, or what they think about. And it might not even be a door yet. It might just be a beacon. If they haven't found their home yet.

But what I've told you is close. Close enough, according to our sources.

. . . You may not believe me, Finch-Crossley, but I don't take any of it personally. Not really. They behave as their nature and their situation warrants. I can respect that. There's a sick kind of honor in that, really. But that still doesn't mean I don't plan on finishing what Manzikert started. Because, as you've guessed, we now have a new weapon. A new weapon that is very old.

They'd reached the far shore, the sea giving way to land. The boat nudged up against a lip of flat rock. Which led to an overhang carved out of the black stone. The ancient fossilized remains of a fireplace out front. Beyond the fireplace, evidence of habitation.

Almost as unreal as the story the Lady in Blue had told him. The air moist and cold. Finch shivered.

Didn't know whether to believe her or not. Didn't know if it mattered. Nothing she'd said sounded any more or less plausible than what Duncan Shriek had written in his books. Understood, too, the weight of everything she had shown him. Knew it in his gut.

Wanted to tell her he lived in a different world. The world where Stark wanted to hurt people he loved, where Heretic could have him killed on a whim. Where Wyte's condition went from bad to worse. All of it gritty and immediate, with immediate consequences. He wasn't Crossley's son anymore. He was Finch, and there was a reason for that. *Survival.*

"You're too quiet," she said.

"I've heard worse theories," Finch said. Because he felt he had to say something. Because he felt overwhelmed.

The Lady in Blue gave him a curious look, head tilted to the side. "Not convinced? That's a shame, because you can disbelieve it all you want. It'll get you nowhere. Now get out of the boat and help me," she said.

The shocking cold of the shallow water woke him up. They pushed the rowboat up onto the shore. The Lady in Blue unhooked the lantern, walked forward.

"What is this place?" Finch asked as his boots found dry land.

"Wait and see," she said. Ushered him toward the overhang.

A cozy little space, sheltered by the rock. A thick layer of dust covered the uneven floor. Looked fuzzy in the lantern light. A welter of numbers and words had been carved into the far wall, all the way up to the ceiling. So many marks that they struck Finch like a cacophony of noise. Made him claustrophobic.

In the far corner, a skeleton on top of a blanket had disintegrated into a thicket of fibers and fragments. Intact. Yellowing. Human. Delicate, almost birdlike. Curled up in a position of sleep. On its side.

Looking at those small bones, Finch felt a sudden, inexplicable sadness. "Is that the monk?"

Words from the man's mouth in the clicks and whistles of the gray caps' language. And then, a sudden and monstrous clarity that can never be put into words.

"Yes, according to Shriek, that's Samuel Tonsure," the Lady in Blue said. "This is where he died. A hermit. In exile. Truff knows why the gray caps left him to this fate. Blind. Alone. He must have gone mad in his last years."

She pointed to the other corner. To a large pockmark in the floor. Light green. With rings within rings. Like a cross section of tree trunk. "And that's where Duncan was found. We didn't even know that he was human, or alive. He looked to us like a gray cap whose legs had been fused into the ground. When he was brought to me, I don't think he even knew who he was. He'd learned to walk among gray caps undetected. He'd traveled through the doors for many,

many years. And then he'd come home here, alone, lonely. To give up being human. Half out of his mind. Attuned to the rhythms of mushroom and spore. Here, by Tonsure's side. Like a dog guarding the grave of its master. I think he thought he'd wake up in a thousand years and everything would be *different*. Or that he'd never wake up at all."

Remembering Duncan's words: *"They found me and infiltrated me—I could feel their tendrils, their fleshy-dry-cold-warm pseudopods and cilia and strands slowly sliding up my skin, like a hundred tiny hands. They tried to remake me in their image."*

"And you found a way to use him." An echo of his voice against the stone. A place more like a memorial than a home.

"Yes. After a while. After we managed to remind him that he was human. Amazing how long that part took."

Finch said, "What happened next?"

Pain in her smile. "Do you want to know a secret?"

He leaned in toward the Lady in Blue, humoring her. This close she looked somehow *off-balance*. Something in her eyes. The faint smell of cigars. Masked by the freshness of some subtle herb.

"Duncan Shriek isn't dead," she whispered.

Then she jabbed something into his neck.

No time for surprise. No time for anything but falling through the gullet of the *skery*. Again.

9

Came to: On the battlements of a fortress at night. Gun emplacements dark and menacing.

Duncan Shriek isn't dead. For a moment he was losing his balance. Then someone propped him up from behind. *I don't believe it.* Not Crossley, not Finch.

Cold, with a wind blowing. Above, the heavens, laced with stars that seemed to be falling in together. A wash of silver and gold across the sky. Beyond the walls, a vast empty space. A desert? In that space, a thousand green fires blossoming. He knew this place—he knew it. It had been in his memory bulb dream. Shriek's memories. *Bliss was here.*

The Lady in Blue stood beside him again. Surrounded by dozens of soldiers. Intent on moving supplies, guard duty, or cleaning weapons.

"This is the monastery fortress of Zamilon, or at least a *version* of it," the Lady in Blue said, as if reading his thoughts. "Abandoned for many decades, until we came along."

Duncan: "Where the eastern approaches of the Kalif's empire fade into the mountains no man can conquer, the ruined fortress of Zamilon keeps watch over time and the stars. Within the fortress . . . Truffidian monks guard the last true page of Tonsure's famous journal."

Below the battlements, the great hulking shadows of some kind of machinery. Engines of war flanking a wide road that led to a huge door. Looked like it was made half of volcanic rock and half of charred book cover. Set in the door, a smaller door, and a small door set into that one.

Painted and carved into every surface, radiating outward, the symbol from the scrap of paper:

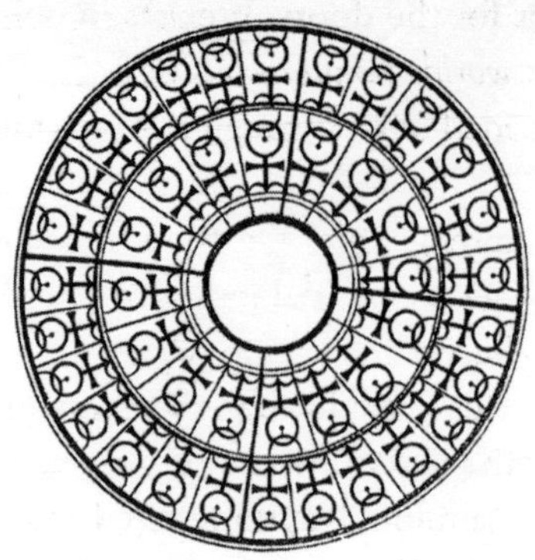

Finch pointed to it. "What's that?"

"It's part of how we travel through the doors. Part of the . . . mechanism. But it means something different to the gray caps. It doesn't work the same way for us as for them. Thankfully."

Turned to the scene beyond the battlements. Furtive movement out there. Occluding the fires at times. A suggestion of long, wide limbs. Of misshapen heads.

"And all of *that*?"

"Those are the fires of enemy camps. Not gray caps. Not human. Something else. They don't know what to make of us. And we don't know what to make of them. But we have to hold this position. Do you want to know why?"

Felt again like he was falling. "I'm not sure."

The Lady in Blue pulled him around. Held him by the shoulders. A vice-like grip. An almost inhuman strength. He understood now, on a physical level, how she had held on, and kept holding on, all this time.

"You don't have that luxury, James Scott Crossley. *That* out there is nothing. It's just the latest thing to make us falter, to make us doubt ourselves." She released him. "When we started out, we didn't really understand. We had to learn fast."

"You read Samuel Tonsure's journal?"

"That and other things. Shriek's books after we found him."

"And you learned about Zamilon?"

"Sometimes by hard-earned experience. But now we know:

Zamilon is a nexus for the doors. It exists in our world, *but it also exists in many other worlds simultaneously.*"

"And Duncan needed to go through it for his mission? He was on a mission for you?"

"Yes. But he's unpredictable. We think he went somewhere he shouldn't have. Triggered a trap. I'm not sure we'll ever know what went wrong unless Shriek chooses to tell us."

"So it's dangerous to travel through the doors?"

She stared up at the wash of stars. "It can be. We only use doors leading from or to Zamilon. Anything else has resulted in disaster. We don't know why. But Duncan has no such constraint . . ."

Remembering the Spit: *Through many doors . . . The doors smaller then larger, then smaller again. Oval. Rectangular. Square. Inlaid with glass. Gone, leaving only gaping doorway and a couple of rusted hinges.*

"Who knows about the portals, the doors?"

The Lady in Blue laughed. "Duncan Shriek knew. Maybe some people have always known. Ambergris's early kings may have had the knowledge and lost it. Every schoolchild used to know. Because every scary story about the gray caps implies that they can move quickly from place to place . . . So far we've kept it from the rebel cells operating in the city. There's too much risk of them being captured by the gray caps and made to talk. And on the other side, the gray caps seem to have kept the doors hidden from the Partials."

"How much do the gray caps know about you?" *How much does Stark know? Or Bliss?*

"They know we're out here. But we're blessed by their concentration on the towers. It makes it easier for us to operate."

"Tell me why I'm here," Finch asked. The question he didn't want answered.

The Lady in Blue's features tightened. She looked away. "What I'm going to ask from you is dangerous. I wanted you to understand fully. So you'd know it in your *gut.* What's at stake. Because the war we're fighting right now isn't in Ambergris. It's out here. It's about opening and closing doors. Holding positions around places like Zamilon. With the few soldiers we have.

"We don't have a functional army here." She gestured around her.

"Maybe a thousand well-trained men, if that. The rest are scattered. Twenty thousand soldiers, Finch. Marked by the HFZ and scattered across the doors. Imagine. Each one flung somewhere else, like a pearl necklace shattering on a marble staircase. Only, the moment after that necklace shatters there are thousands of marble staircases and one bead on each."

"They're not dead?" Finch, incredulous.

The Lady in Blue shook her head. "No. Most of them are just lost, and we need to bring them back . . . When Duncan didn't complete his mission, when we figured out where the bodies had turned up, where Duncan was, some wanted to cut our losses. Abandon the mission. Try to sabotage the towers. I said no. I said, I knew your father. I knew him well enough to know that, in this case, we could trust you. That you'd understand. That I'd make you understand."

"Understand what?" Finch said. "What is there left to understand?" A fury rising in him. "Understand that when I go back I have the secret services of not one but two countries working against me? That the gray caps will kill me if I don't solve this case? That my partner is probably dying? *What is it that you want me to understand?*"

The Lady in Blue looked at him in surprise. As if no one had spoken to her like that for a long time.

"I understand, Finch," she said slowly, biting off each syllable, "that you are the only one who can get back to the body while they're watching. It's a trap for anyone else. A fatal trap. And you and I both understand now that Duncan Shriek is alive. And I'm telling you that if you can get to him, you can bring him all the way back and help him complete his mission."

"What kind of weapon is Shriek? Is he a bomb?" Only thing Finch could think of. Like the suicide bombers the rebels had used in the past.

"No. He's the kind of weapon that's also a beacon. Also a door." She smiled. A wide and beautiful smile that cut right through Finch. There on the ramparts. Overlooking the desert. In a place that might or might not be part of the world. *"There may be a way."*

"Just *say* it."

"We mean to force the door, Finch. To hijack it. To come through in numbers. Duncan Shriek is going to find our lost men and bring them through the gate formed by the towers. Before the gray caps can bring their own people through."

"That's insane. The risk . . ."

"If we had a better plan, we would use it."

"Even if Shriek *is* alive, how do you know he can do it? Bring the soldiers back?"

"He's shown us some of what he can do already."

"How will he find them?" Each question cut him off from one more avenue of retreat.

"They are all marked, or tagged, by the HFZ event. Each man. Each woman. He will find them through the doors, and we will return to Ambergris triumphant."

A strange light had entered her eyes. Like someone who had been dreaming of something that they'd never thought could happen. And now it was happening.

"What if they kill me? Eat my memories?" Finch asked. "What then?"

The Lady in Blue turned the full force of her gaze on him. "What's really bothering you, Finch? Is it fear? Or is it something else?" She turned to look out at the desert again. "Those things out there," she murmured. "They're gray caps, and they're people. Combined. How? I don't know. Maybe they came here during the Silence. Possible. But even though I don't know, I understand. Because *we're changing, too,* Finch. There's no one under my command who hasn't been altered in some way. The question is how much you change. Change too much and you're no different from Shriek, no different from a gray cap. And then even if we win, we lose. But adapt just enough? That's what I need from you. To adapt just enough."

An answer for everything. Yet Finch knew he'd always be searching for the next question. He felt a hundred years old. Like the weight of everything had piled on his back at once.

"What if I say no? What if I want you to just leave me the fuck alone?" *Stop fighting,* some part of him advised. *Just fall into it and keep falling.* But he couldn't. Not yet.

The Lady in Blue sighed. "You know, it's no good for the Kalif, either, if the gray caps come through. I don't care who you are or aren't working for. I don't care about your father's spying. I just know you hate Partials and your father had no love for the gray caps."

"How are you going to protect me?"

"We can't protect you. But we can make sure you don't get caught."

"You mean you can kill me." Feeling ill. Realized that in some ways the Lady in Blue was no different than Stark. *Apply pressure. Squeeze. Get what you want.*

The Lady in Blue looked somehow both stern and compassionate. In a quiet voice, she said, "I mean you know too much, John Finch. Sometimes we have to take the cards we're dealt and make the most of them. You can't throw away the cards now—you've already looked at them."

There it was. Stated directly. Somehow Finch admired her more for it. A bitter laugh of appreciation as he stood there, facing her down.

"So I have no choice."

"If it's any consolation, maybe you never had a choice. Maybe there was never a point at which you could have turned back." She had the good grace to look away as she said, "Our man will be in touch when the time comes."

Finch anticipated the needle a second before it entered his neck.

* * *

When they released Finch back into the crowd at the black market party, everything was different. The sound soared over him at first. Then it was as if he couldn't hear it anymore. Looked for Sintra but didn't see her. Looked for Bosun but didn't see him, either. Didn't know how much time had passed. But the band was taking a break.

An urgency to the night, but he'd brought it with him. Couldn't get the image of the Lady in Blue out of his head. On a hill. In a boat. At the wall of the fortress. The images stabbed at him, threatened madness. *What didn't she tell me?*

Finch crossed the room on unsteady legs. Wary of Bosun. But still no Bosun. Felt for his Lewden Special. Relief. It had been returned to him.

Made his way through corridors. Gaze unfocused. Seeing nothing.

Out into the rain. The towers a steamy green above the tops of buildings. The street nearly empty.

Two steps onto the street and he met an immovable force. Bosun, appearing out of darkness. Pulling his right arm behind him. Inexorable, the man all muscle. Felt Bosun's other hand looking for his gun. Felt it taken. Again.

Bosun's hot breath at his ear as Finch was marched toward a side alley. Helpless as a child.

"Find my carving?" Bosun muttered.

Against the discomfort, twisting, "For Truff's sake, you don't have to break my arm."

"So you didn't find it." Bosun seemed disappointed.

"What carving?" Grunting. Contorting to try to get relief.

"Stop moving. In your apartment. Left it there while we took the place apart. Would've done in your cat if he hadn't hidden."

Another mystery solved. One that didn't even matter anymore.

"Fuck you. Your breath smells like shit."

Bosun just laughed. "Be lucky if yours doesn't begin to smell like blood."

In the alley: Stark. With five other men. Bosun shoved Finch forward, releasing him.

"Finch, what a surprise!" Stark said. "I know you're just coming from a party, but we're having our own little party out here. Glad you could make it."

Bosun punched him in the gut before he could react. Fists like stone. Sent him slumped over onto the ground. Begging for air.

Got to his feet slowly, not sure if he should. Could've used Wyte coming out of the darkness in that moment.

Stark's face was a vicious half-moon in the dimness. Hard to believe Bosun was his brother.

"Where'd you go, Finch? Where'd you go for an hour and a half? Bosun says you were there and then you *weren't*."

The question so much smaller than the answer. Contempt for the interrogator. What kind of spymaster came in person for this kind of ambush? Only someone who'd never gotten past the simple art of the shakedown. Came in hard and fast and thought that was enough.

Not here it isn't.

Secret knowledge gave him strength. "Just enjoying the party."

Stark circled him. "I'll bet you were. Saw your exotic girl leave. She looked well satisfied. Did you give her a good time in there? You should be glad I'm a man of such refinement, Finch, or we might've given her a better one."

"Is that all you came here to say?" Finch asked.

Bosun nodded and two of his men wrenched Finch's arms back. Painfully.

"No, not really. We've some more serious matters to discuss. Like, did you know there's a bounty on the head of the Lady in Blue?" Stark came close, looked him in the eye. "I think you do know that. It applies to anyone who associates with her—on my side or yours."

"I don't know what you're talking about."

Stark nodded. Bosun punched him in the stomach again. Grunted. Fought through the pain. The thugs held him up.

"I think you do, Finch. I think you do. At least, those two thought so. Show him, boys."

They dragged him closer to the wall. Saw four pale feet, the rest of the bodies hidden by shadows.

"The two morons that Bosun saw spirit you away. They didn't say much before they died. But they said enough."

Finch didn't think they'd said anything at all. "I don't even know who they are."

"Of course you don't, Finch," Stark said with disgust. "You never saw their faces. Let alone their feet. So, again, where did you disappear off to?"

"Nowhere."

Stark looked at him a second. "Nowhere? Nowhere. Next you'll be saying you've made no progress on the case."

"There is no progress, Stark."

"Even after I gave you that juicy transcript? I think you're lying."

Finch, reckless: "I think you fed us that address in the transcript. It almost got us killed. For nothing. And I wasted a day. So I've got nothing for you, either."

Stark pulled back a second, as if to get a better look at Finch.

"Are you serious, Finch? Because that's not what I heard. I heard Wyte blew it for you. Your man transforms into some huge fucking monster and charges the stage. That's what I'm told. Not exactly proper procedure. Not exactly what you'd expect from a detective. Or maybe it is. Maybe it's the old quick-change comic theater routine. Maybe that goes over big in this shit hole. What is Wyte, anyway? Some kind of secret weapon?"

"He's sick," Finch said.

"Any sicker than Duncan Shriek?" Stark asked, with a knowing leer. "Because I hear Mr. Shriek is dead. And holed up in a certain apartment on Manzikert Avenue. Writing his ghost memoirs." Stark's refinement was slipping. A rougher voice, with a gutter accent.

"Why not go look for yourself," Finch said. "Maybe you'll turn up some clues."

Stark kneed Finch in the groin. Finch groaned. Couldn't fall down, held by the two men. "Think you're funny? I know that's a kill zone. You don't get me, Finch. Do you think I give a fuck about this sewer of a city?" Stark whispered in his ear. "I don't give a fuck about this dump. I don't care if it all goes up in pillars of flame. It's not my fucking town. But I don't like being lied to. And I don't like people getting in the way of what I want."

Apparently no one did. Not Stark. Not the Lady in Blue. Not Heretic. Finch was tired of it.

Stark wrenched Finch's head back by his hair. "They're working all night on the towers, Finchy. All night. Like there's a deadline suddenly. Driving people past their limits. Until they're dying. Until they're falling from the scaffolding. Why are they doing that, Finch? Why are the towers so important? And what's it got to do with that apartment, Finchy? And what's that got to do with the rebel safe house, Finchy? And how is all of this going to benefit me?"

With every question, Stark seemed smaller. More brutish.

A wash of stars. An underground sea. A thousand green lights out in the desert.

"You're the professional spy, Stark. Why don't you figure it out?" Made professional sound small.

Somehow that made Stark laugh. "I'm trying, Finch. Believe me, I'm trying. But people like you make it so difficult." Stark nodded.

They let him fall to the ground. Bosun tossed his gun back to him.

Stark leaned down. "There are no professionals here, Finchy. We're all amateurs. That's what makes us dangerous. Now, you'd better start getting results. You'd better start thinking about your future. What's left of it. Or all the lovely people around you are going to suffer. Starting sooner than you think. And if that doesn't work, we'll just come for you. There's not much time left. This is your last warning."

Had the feel of a well-worn speech.

Stark stalked off, the rest behind him. Leaving Finch beside the two corpses.

Above them all: the towers. Finch saw that the blackness between them was different than to either side. Showed no stars. Blurred, with the vague impression of shadowy nighttime scenes sliding across. Fast.

Now he knew why.

Back in the hotel. Near midnight. Didn't know for sure. Approached the landing below the seventh floor. Heard Feral hissing at something. Saw a flickering, golden light that projected a circle of fire. Elongated and slanted down the hallway. Distorted further by the fungus on the walls. A rank smell, like too-strong perfume.

Bliss? The Partial?

Already had his Lewden out. Slowly walked up the steps. Saw Feral, fur puffed out, standing a few feet from his door. Staring up the source of the light. The thing had attached itself to the door. It looked like a golden brooch with filigree detail extending out in wavy branches or tendrils. From that angle, he could see the transparent cilia underneath. Almost looked like a larger cousin of the starfish he'd seen in the underground cavern.

Came closer, gun aimed at it. Arms shaking a little.

Feral saw him and scurried over to stand next to him. Now a low growl came from the cat's throat.

From ten feet away, the front of the organism had the look of pure gold. A rough flower pattern. In the middle, a closed aperture divided into four parts.

A beam of light flashed out from the thing. Blinded him for a moment. Withdrew.

"Finch!" Heretic's voice. A ghostly quaver.

Finch lowered his gun. Didn't know whether to be relieved or angry. "Not worth your time, Feral." A message from Heretic. A little more dramatic than usual.

The aperture dilated. Out leapt the *skery*. Finch screamed. Stumbled back. The *skery* reached its full length an inch from his face. Receded. Bobbed there, long and black. Curling downward. Until he could see it wasn't the *skery* at all. Just a sick joke. In another second, it broke off and fell to the floor.

Feral came forward. Hissed at it, smacked at it with his claws. Jumping back even as he did so.

No one stirred in the apartments to either side. Finch didn't blame them.

The oval in the middle widened. An approximation of Heretic's face appeared. He looked almost jolly. As if he'd known how horrified Finch would be of the *skery*.

"Finch," Heretic rasped, "you've been gone a long time. Almost long enough for me to suspect you had left us. I thought you'd run. Until you appeared again shadowing Wyte—"

But most of the rest was lost. Whatever it was supposed to be. Reverting to a series of clicks and whistles and moist suppurations. The garglings of a monster. As if Heretic didn't care anymore whether Finch had orders or not. Or something had gone wrong when recording the message. Or everything was falling apart.

Finch listened to the obscene chatter for a minute. Then he put a couple of bullets in Heretic's face. With a sigh the golden organism slid slowly to the hallway floor. Began to curl in on itself.

Picked up Feral, opened the door, locked it behind him, and went to bed.

FRIDAY

I: When did you first realize how deeply you were involved?

F: I didn't. I mean, it wasn't clear. I mean, I never did.

I: That is a lie. You're hiding things again.

F: Then kill me and use a memory bulb to find out the truth. Bastard.

I: We can only kill you once. And once you are dead, all we would have is your bulb. They're unreliable.

F: Then trust me.

I: People lie. They lie and they keep lying. Eventually, they can't remember the truth. Is that your problem, Finch?

F: I'm not really a detective. That's why I can't answer your questions.

I: Once they made you a detective, you *were* a detective. Why did you never understand that?

1

The bed shuddered beneath Finch, almost seemed to gasp. He reached for his gun as a deep thudding vibration shook the hotel. An after-sound like shredding or tearing. Timbers settling and creaking like an old ship. Thought for one sleep-muddled moment it was his damaged shoulder.

Took a moment to realize the impact came from outside the building. He pulled on pants. Ran to the kitchen window as another shuddering thud struck. Looked down through the smudged pane. Nothing on the street below, just a few people running. Checked from the bathroom. No one in the courtyard.

A commotion outside. People on the stairs. All he could think was: fire? Or, worse, Partials rounding up people. Wished Wyte were there with him.

Threw on and buttoned a shirt, put on shoes without socks. Feral meowing round his feet. Agitated. A burning smell in the air now. Or was he imagining it? Shoved his gun into his waistband. Went out the door fast.

Stumbled over the remains of Heretic's message, curled up like a husk. Residents were shoving their way up the stairs to the roof. While his neighbor, the old man, stood watching them from the hall. Framed by a rough stain of blue-gray fungus on the wall.

"What's happening?" Finch asked.

"The towers!" The man spat out the words. "The towers are starting a war. Everybody wants to go watch. Idiots! I'm staying right here."

On the roof the burnt smell was stronger. A cloudless sky. Searing blue. More hotel residents in one place than he'd ever seen before. Black market vendors. Clinic workers. Camp guards. Scavengers.

Druggies. All holding on to their gas masks. Just in case. All looking out toward the bay.

No longer muffled, the thud had a growling rasp to it. An immediacy. Like a cannon was going off near his head. With each new thud a murmur rose. Of concern? Of awe? Shoved his way through the crowd until he was near the edge of the roof.

Out in the bay, an emerald light shot out from the tops of the towers, combined into one oddly thick ball of sparks. Hurtled toward the Spit. Smashed into the boats. Sent up steam and fire. Seemed to *cling* there. The Spit. Burning. Some would say "long overdue," but what would come after? A fireworks display to the few children, who were clapping.

A slightly unreal aspect to it. Watching it from afar. The Spit so tiny. Each boat a sliver. A toothpick. Rocking on a vast sea. The tyranny of distance. A few boats had become unmoored and were drifting across the bay. Aimless. Half on fire. Were Stark and Bosun still on the Spit? Desperately moving from boat to boat. Making for shore. Finch didn't think so.

Wondered if Wyte was watching somewhere or still dealing with his condition.

The sky between the towers had become darker, shot through with shades of amber. In the backdrop: a flock of strange birds and the silhouette of an island that shouldn't exist.

The people around him were talking about the green light.

"Getting rid of that nest of spies. Should've done it a long time ago."

"No friends of Ambergris. No friends at all."

"But what's next, then? Where does it stop?"

Finch looked over at the HFZ. Violent strands of strobing orange-red fungal mist rose into the sky. Like an infection running rampant. Remembered the hill he had stood atop with the Lady in Blue. The image came back with a vividness that took over his vision for a moment. *A roiling mass of particles. Discharging light until a steady humming glow suffused the city in a kind of dawn. There came in reply from the city a hundredfold bestial roar.*

"Why do they ever do anything?"

"They're all dead by now. Or dying."

Could the Lady in Blue be both right and wrong? Could Duncan Shriek be alive but the towers have some other purpose altogether? Under that sharp blue sky, he didn't know the answer. What if he was bait? A distraction? Once again, the disconnect hurt him. Between what she'd shown him and Ambergris as he knew it. *An ethereal beauty that no longer lives here.* A dream to believe or deny. A vision as different for him as it was for Wyte or Rathven.

"The city fighting itself. Pointless now . . ."

The Photographer came up next to him. Binoculars hung from his neck. He carried a small pouch by the drawstring. "Breathtaking, isn't it?"

"No," Finch said. "No, it's not. It's fucking awful."

The Photographer said, "Just look at the way the water reacts. Look at the patterns." Almost giddy.

An orange eruption of flames over the Spit. Accompanied by spirals of black smoke. Another blast. Another. The building didn't shake as much now. As if used to it. Or as if Finch were.

"When did it start?"

"Twenty minutes ago? Suddenly most of the workers climbed down from the top of the towers. They're at the base now, still constructing something."

A sudden spark of hope hit him hard. Hadn't realized he still had the capacity for it. "So they aren't finished yet."

"Almost. And so is the Spit."

Finch stared sharply at the Photographer. But there was no hint of triumph in him.

"It's a strong warning," the Photographer said. "They're clearing the way for something."

"I wonder what they'll do when they've finished off the Spit," Finch said, almost to himself.

The Photographer pointed to the east. "What's missing?"

The other camp dome was gone. Had left behind only a kind of ghostly white outline, broken by mottled gray. With that lack, the greens of the Religious Quarter burned even stronger in the sunlight. And through that entanglement lay the distant echo, the distant shadows, of cupolas and minarets. *Like a dream. Like a trap.* Was Sintra watching from there even now?

"Fuck."

A new phase of the Rising.

The crowd had begun to realize the roof might be dangerous. Thinned out. Just a few left. A woman in her fifties dressed in a bathrobe, arms wrapped tightly round herself. A couple in their twenties who had never, Finch realized, known anything but war or the Rising. Three old men in their best clothes, watching solemnly.

Better for most to hunker down in their apartments and not see the end coming. Or go out onto the streets in one last gasp of defiance. *Against what?*

The towers continued to pound the Spit. A white smoke had overtaken the black smoke. It looked now like the thick green spheres slamming into the Spit were dissolving into a cloud bank or a thick mist.

"I have something for you," the Photographer said. Put the pouch in Finch's hand. "It looks just like a memory bulb, but it isn't. Keep it with you at all times."

Finch stared at the pouch. Stared at the Photographer. Taken completely by surprise.

The Photographer said, "If you aren't caught, you'll need it for your mission. If you *are* caught, take a bite. Just one bite."

"And then what?"

The Photographer's face was as blank as the side of a wall. "There will be nothing left of you. Nothing they could trace. Nothing they could *read*."

Nothing left. No pain. No concealment. Nothing.

"We're changing, too, Finch. There's no one under my command who hasn't been altered in some way. The question is how much you change. Change too much and you're no different from Shriek, no different from a gray cap. And then even if we win, we lose."

Instinctively tried to give it back to the Photographer. The man stepped away, hands shoved in his jacket pockets.

"Don't talk about this in your apartment," the Photographer said, as if nothing had happened. "Don't write down anything while in your apartment."

"Why not?"

"The message last night left intruders. We can't run interference on them without leaving a trail."

Didn't even bother to examine that, turn it over in his mind. Just one more intrusion in a life littered with them. No anger left to shed.

The Photographer continued: "Later today someone else will approach you with the rest of what you need."

Assuming I'll do it. But standing there, pouch in hand, it seemed impossible he wouldn't do it. The only way out. To take control of the case before it imploded. *Let it not be a case anymore. Let it be something else.*

"I always thought it would be the madman out front," Finch said.

A thin smile from the Photographer. "He's just a madman."

"Do I need to stay here?"

"Follow your usual routine. You'll be followed. We'll know where you are no matter where you go."

After a pause: "Does Rathven know?"

"No," the Photographer said.

"She's not even your sister, is she?"

"Goodbye, Finch," the Photographer said, and stuck out his hand. A stronger grip than he'd imagined, and more final.

He wasn't coming back.

"What about your photographs?"

"You can have them if you want them. I don't need them anymore."

Then he was gone, walking down the stairs.

In the bay, the towers had fallen silent. There was just the heavy wall of black smoke from the southeast shore. Already he could hear the sound of angry voices from below. Could see, at intersections far below, crowds gathering.

Finch stood there awhile. Looking out over the city. Not sure whether to believe he held its future in his hands.

2

At the station, Blakely had barricaded the door with a couple of filing cabinets and an empty desk. Finch slid through a narrow gap that Gustat quickly closed behind him. Blakely had the smell of whisky on his breath, masked by coffee. The flushed face of someone trying desperately to get drunk for a long time. Behind him, Gustat was fiddling with his radio, with no luck. No sign of Wyte. Or Albin or Skinner.

"What the fuck is going on?"

Blakely: "You've seen what's happening. We'll be targets. We're thinking we might fortify the bell tower. If things don't get better."

Finch just stared at him. "Fortify the tower?" *Make one last stand.* Wait out the siege in a pathetic excuse for a tree fort, a few dozen bottles of whisky and beer for comfort. Had a flash of Blakely as a bullying, pimply faced child, strong-arming his way into the local clubhouse.

"You have a better idea?" Blakely asked.

Saw the fear in his face now.

"There are no better ideas," Finch muttered.

But Blakely had a point. The mood on the streets had been fearful, murderous. He'd kept his detective's badge in his hand the whole time. Other hand on his gun. Hating the way the sky made everything so clear, so clean-looking. Hating the weight in his pocket of the thing the Photographer had given him. Partials had been rounding up anyone still in a camp uniform. Bashing in heads. But no statement had been made by the gray caps. By a stroke of bad luck, it was also another drug mushroom day. Everyone wanted them now, to stock up against disaster.

Finch walked toward his desk. Bodies had been stacked in the holding cell. On top: a man of about thirty-five in a lacerated brown suit and a woman in her twenties, wearing a fancy red dress. A plate-like lavender lichen had begun to cover up their faces. A dozen others under them. All dead. Thought he recognized one or two from the chapel.

"What's this about?" he demanded.

No response for the longest time. Then Blakely spoke up. "Heretic said they were traitors. With the rebels. Brought them here last night. They had to be liquidated, Heretic said."

Gustat wouldn't look at Blakely. Wouldn't look anywhere.

"So Heretic was here?" Finch asked.

"Yes, he was. Last night."

"And you just plan on leaving the bodies here?" Failing to hide his disgust. *At them? At the situation?*

"He told us to."

Gustat spoke up. "There's talk of the gray caps getting ready to cleanse whole neighborhoods with spore clouds. They've closed off the streets nearest the bay and the towers. The towers will be done in *the next day or two*." The words said with a mixture of awe and dread.

"They're pretty well done already," Finch said. "They took out the whole fucking Spit this morning if you hadn't noticed. Where are the others?"

"Told to go work on the towers, so I guess they aren't done," Blakely said.

Finch sat down at his desk. Anger building in him. For having to go through the motions. At the casual cruelty of his position.

New case notes on his desk. In Blakely's hand. A domestic dispute. A mugging. Someone had stolen someone else's food. Someone's dog had gone missing and the owner had filed a missing person's report. Amazing how the mundane shit never ended. While the world went to hell. Again tried to chart the sequence of events that had led him to this moment. Couldn't.

"Heard anything from Wyte?" he asked, to distract himself.

"He's alive?" Gustat seemed shocked.

"Yes, he's fucking well alive." Then realized he hadn't called in to the station after the shoot-out. *Need to call Wyte.* "Dapple's dead, though. We had a shoot-out with rebels and Partials." The words came out so matter-of-factly. So easily.

"Dapple's dead," Gustat said, hand still on the radio tuner. A blank stare into the distance. Began to cry. As if Dapple had been his best friend, instead of just tolerated.

Harsh laugh from Blakely. "Sorry we didn't have a chance to catch up on your exploits before now. But last night we were too busy sticking it out here in the station next to a pile of corpses."

"It happens, Gustat," Finch said. With a toughness he didn't feel. Ignoring Blakely. Hadn't expected Gustat's tears. Hadn't expected a lot of things. Wondered how much longer he could endure it. When would whatever kept him going run out?

"Look in your memory hole, Finch," Blakely said.

A message? He leaned down. Pulled the pod out uneasily, with the other two watching. Went through the ritual of opening it. Just a note. From Heretic.

PLANS HAVE CHANGED. FILE A FINAL REPORT ON YOUR CASE. THEN REPORT WITH WYTE TO THE TOWERS FOR WORK DETAIL.

A vast improvement over the last message.

Blakely's face held fear and smugness all at once. "You're off the case. He told us before he left. The case is over."

Incredulous: "Who is taking it over, then?"

"No one. Working on the towers is punishment for what happened at the safe house. If you ask me, you got off light. He was in a good mood. Calm. Almost happy. Even when he put them to sleep." A tilt of the head toward the holding cage.

"You've got to work on the towers," Gustat said, still messing with his radio. An odd look on his face, halfway between a frown and a smile.

"Thanks for the reminder," Finch said. "Now fuck off."

"Cheer up," Blakely said. "I don't think Heretic's coming back. I don't think anyone's coming back."

The clock ticked. The phone on Finch's desk rang a few times. Mostly people scared because of the destruction of the Spit. Even though the towers had done nothing since. Some of the people who called even had some small hope he could help them. But they were living in the grip of memories of the old days. A past that had never really existed.

Finch worked on his final report. Going through the motions. Sticking to routine. Waiting for someone to tap him on the shoulder and tell him the rest of the plan. He would call Wyte soon, too. Just working up the nerve.

Started out with pen and paper. Wrote drivel. *Fuck you . . . Am I just the bait? . . . There's nothing here you can use . . . You're monstrous . . .*

Paralyzed for a moment by the thought of the look on Sintra's face as she walked away from him for the last time. Clinging now to what she'd told him even as he'd told her to stop before. *"My mother had gotten better, but my father had lost his arm to a fungal bullet. He couldn't work for a long time he was so depressed. He'd been a journalist."*

Threw away his pointless notes. Went to the typewriter. Soon had a real report that while bland made a kind of sense. Was it good enough to satisfy Heretic while he completed his mission? Had no idea. Read it over one last time.

There are no definitive conclusions to be drawn in this murder case. I have found no information on the identity of the dead gray cap. The man may be related to a fringe historian, Duncan Shriek, who lived in the apartment more than a hundred years ago, but this appears to be a coincidence. Two names came up repeatedly in investigating the case: Ethan Bliss, an operative for Morrow, and "Stark," the alias of a spy working for Stockton. Their relationship to the case is oblique at best, but both appear convinced that the man carried a weapon created by the rebels for use against Fanaarcensitii. I remain convinced that the man fell from a great height and was moved to the apartment—that he died elsewhere. Both Bliss and Stark may know more, but they remain fugitives, and we have not been given the resources to track them down. If the dead man was

part of a rebel conspiracy, then it appears to have failed. I would suggest that the Fanaarcensitii put all of their resources into tracking down Bliss and Stark. Interrogations of both parties might provide more information. All other intelligence can be found in the attached notes and prior reports.

--Detective John Finch

Short. Protective of those it needed to protect. Giving up those who were asking for it.

Cowardly. Masking death, despair, destruction.

Put it aside.

Typed, pushing the keys down hard:

EVENTS ARE MOVING BEYOND YOU. THERE'S NOTHING YOU CAN DO. YOU'RE NOT EVEN THE CRAFTIEST BASTARDS IN THE ROOM. YOU'LL ALL GO DOWN WONDERING HOW IT HAPPENED. I'LL NEVER UNDERSTAND YOU, BUT YOU'LL NEVER UNDERSTAND US, EITHER.

Felt like a child. Took that message, too, and walked back to his desk. Pondered both of them, lying there like some kind of judgment on his integrity.

A few minutes later, still thinking, the phone rang.

"Finch." Wyte. The voice barely recognizable. As human. "You've got to help me."

"When the time comes, right, Finch?" "Sure, Wyte. When the time comes."

"Finch. Are you there?"

"Yes."

"It's time."

Every memory of Wyte invincible the day before cracked into pieces. Finch's throat tightened. The world around him spun, lost focus. Blakely hunched over his desk. To the left was a splotch of ruddy white. The windows seemed to contract.

"Are you sure?"

"I'm sure."

"Okay, Wyte. Okay."

"And, Finch, I don't think I'm going quietly. Not like Richard Dorn."

The voice, once so deep and gravelly, had changed since they'd first met. Become soft and liquid, lighter yet thicker.

"Where are you?"

"At my apartment."

"You'll know what to do." "I'll know what to do."

"I'm coming," Finch said.

Wyte hung up.

Sat there a moment. Leaned forward a little over his desk. Elbows digging into the wood. Marshaling his strength.

You can do this. You have to do this. You promised *him.*

Finch raised his arm. Smashed his fist into the desk. Just to feel the pain shoot up through his shoulder. Stood. Swept everything off of his desk. Made a sound almost like a roar. Almost like a moan. While Blakely and Gustat, standing now, just stared at him.

Tonsure's bones in the little house by the underground sea. Strange stars. Falling with Bliss into darkness. Emerging into light. Heretic's skery *crawling up his leg. Sintra disappearing into darkness.*

"What the fuck are you looking at?" Finch snarled. He began to break everything on the floor into pieces small enough to feed into the memory hole. Bits of pencil. Torn paper. The gaping jaw of a stapler. Shoved them into it. The hole rasped and protested.

Then tore up his report and his pathetic message. Put them both down the hole as well.

"Do you like that, Heretic? *Do you*?" Might have been screaming it. Didn't care.

Blakely pulled him away, hand on his shoulder. Finch shrugged it off. Whirled on him. Looked at Blakely like he didn't know him. Saw Blakely had his gun out. Controlled himself, arms outstretched, palms down.

"It's okay, Blakely." But it wasn't okay. How much else could fall apart? What was left? "I just need some things from my desk and then I'm gone."

The Photographer had said they'd be watching him. Now they'd have to watch him deal with Wyte.

Blakely backed away. Didn't put down his gun. "You're crazy, Finch," he said. "You're crazy." Gustat stood there, mouth open.

Finch reached under the desk. Pulled the ceremonial scimitar in its scabbard from its hiding place.

Blakely backed even farther away. "What the hell is that?"

"It's my sword," Finch said. Brought the belt with the scabbard around his waist. "Never seen a sword before, Blakely?" Already had his gun. Didn't really need anything else. Never would again.

At the door, he planned to turn and say something. What, he didn't know. But there was nothing to say. Instead, he just pushed the filing cabinet aside.

Left Blakely and Gustat standing there, looking like two lost boys in a room suddenly grown huge.

3

Wyte's door had a sagging "17" on it. Half shadowed, half in sunlight from the decorative stone wall running parallel to all the apartments. The blue paint had a rust-like stain running through it. An old bullet hole decorated the upper left-hand corner. A faded, torn welcome mat. Sweat and mold and the fading stench of piss. It depressed Finch. He'd only visited Wyte there a few times. Late-night drinking sessions. Bold statements about escape or joining the rebels that nobody remembered in the mornings. Commiserating with Wyte over his estranged wife. His far distant children.

Finch had taken the long route, trying to shake any watchers.

Knocked once. Twice. Gun in one hand. Sword in the other.

Nothing.

Knocked again.

Heard a sound this time. Like a voice. A voice drowning as it spoke. Awash in strange tides. Might've said, "Come in, Finch."

Inside: cracked yellow wallpaper. A photo of Wyte's wife on a rickety table. A short hallway leading to the galley-style kitchen. A couple of crooked paintings showed faded watercolor scenes of Hoegbotton ships hunting the king squid. Fables of a bygone era.

Then the living room. Almost no furniture. As if Wyte were already gone.

But he wasn't. He lay in the corner of the living room, the weak light of an old lamp dribbling across his body. The lamp had come all the way from the Southern Isles, brought by Wyte's grandmother. Shells were still glued into the base.

Wyte dwarfed the lamp. Slumped there. Monstrous. Huge. Spilling out in peculiar ways. As if a mossy hill had been dropped into the room. Wandering tendrils as outliers. Above, looking down at Finch, the face within the face. The tiny eyes. White against the encroaching dark. Staring out.

Who'd laid the trap for Wyte? In the beginning? He'd laid it for himself, in a sense. By falling into it.

Wyte spoke. Guttural. Wet. Dissolving. "Thanks for coming, James." Like everything were normal. *Four days ago we were tracking down Bliss.*

"It's going to be okay, Wyte."

"You don't have to lie to me. It's not going to be okay. It's not. I know that. Even if Otto doesn't." A gruff, coughing laugh.

"You're among friends, Wyte."

A kind of seismic shift from the thing in the corner. Laughter?

"It's nice to call you James again. That might've been the hardest thing. Remembering to call you Finch. Or John."

"You didn't give me up, Wyte. I'll never forget that."

A shambling shrug from the mound in the corner. *From the thing with Wyte's eyes.*

"Tell Emily. Tell her . . ."

"She knows. *I* know, Wyte. No one needs to be told anything." Finch didn't even know where Emily lived anymore.

Creature. Monster. Other.

Finch's hands were shaking. Could he do this? Searching himself. Both Crossley and Finch. *Can either of us do this?* Kept thinking of Wyte behind the desk at Hoegbotton's so long ago. Showing Finch the ropes. Patiently explaining the job.

A world extinguished as thoroughly as a spent match in the gutter.

"James?"

"Yes?"

"Like I said on the phone, I can't control myself anymore. There's not much of me left. The rest might fight back. But you have to know that's not me."

Telling Finch in a candid moment months ago, "I don't want to hurt anybody. I don't want to lose control but still be there, knowing what I am doing."

"I know, Wyte," Finch said. Grinding his teeth. Biting his cheek until the blood came. A soundless scream building inside of him. "It's going to be okay."

But it wasn't.

Finch closed the door behind him.

Drew his sword, tears streaming down his face.

* * *

What it took to kill a man transformed that way was almost what it took to kill a gray cap. Finch had killed a gray cap once. Before the Rising. When he was James Crossley. When it was just House Hoegbotton against House Frankwrithe & Lewden. Just poorly trained Irregulars patrolling neighborhoods. Making sure the enemy didn't take hold in the cracks. Weeding them out from derelict, firebombed houses. Abandoned theaters. Courtyards that still held memories of massacres. Official Hoegbotton policy called gray caps "noncombatants" unless a unit felt under threat. Unofficial policy encouraged patrols to engage and drive off, "damage," or kill. Back then, the gray caps supplied arms and ammo to Frankwrithe & Lewden.

Crossley was in charge of the patrol that night. They'd emerged from a warren of streets into a junkyard, surrounded by burnt-out buildings, that had once been a playground. Right after detaining and then releasing three youths without papers. The three had done enough to convince Crossley they belonged. Or enough for him to not want to arrest them and have them wind up in a holding cell where they might not last until morning.

They had only the light of a half-moon and the reluctant streetlamps burning a hundred feet away. But Crossley caught sight of something moving herky-jerky through the junkyard.

Seven in the patrol. Exposed. He wasn't sure what he was seeing at first, because gray caps rarely came out into the open. It was like seeing a dolphin in a public pond. So he'd given the signal to spread out without knowing what they faced. Circle round. Converge.

He crept up, over broken girders and garbage, to find: a gray cap. Wandering in a circle. Talking to itself. No obvious injury. But something wrong. Like it was drunk.

When the gray cap saw them, it broke off its wandering dance. Tried to escape. But they had it hemmed in by then. Its teeth, needle sharp.

Claws on its fingers. It expelled a fungal mist, but they were already wearing gas masks.

Crossley was the first to shoot it. It lurched. Righted itself. Ran toward another point of the compass. Two bullets. Another lurch. But absorbed. A cry. A leap like a dancer, then. As if finally realizing the danger. Crossley-Finch would never forget. It whirled past one man and then another. But instead of escaping, it turned to close the distance. As if enraged. Or sick. The light in its eyes green and everlasting. Tore into one man with its claws, slapping away his rifle. Took another bullet for its efforts, but scooped out the Irregular's throat. The man crumpled to the ground. Crossley, scrambling to aim and fire, thought he saw a glint of a smile from the creature.

Darted. Flitted. Was gone. Then back again. Far then close. Each of them struggling to keep up with that speed. Grunting and cursing and sweating, as if it were something normal. Like digging a ditch or a grave. Too invested now. Knowing they couldn't retreat, and that the gray cap had decided to fight.

Wherever the thing stepped, a golden dust rose up from its tread. Clouds of red-and-green spores radiated out from it like steam. Their gas masks protected them.

Low on ammo. They kept shooting it, and it kept taking the bullets.

Knives out. Finch shouted the order to fix bayonets. Down to four. Against one. Reminded them not to let the bayonets get stuck in gray cap flesh. It would reel them in, finish each of them off. But, still—one man's rifle got stuck. Forgot to let it go. The gray cap jerked him forward, disemboweled him, then turned, stung by fresh cuts from all sides. Down to three men. Flesh sloughed off its body, but no blood. It did not wince. Kept shouting in its language. Sometimes mixing in human words. In a hissing, sibilant voice.

They kept at their task. Too busy to be afraid. Too busy to scream. Inside, its flesh was black, accordioned. Crossley saw as he came in close at its back. As it bit and kept biting another man. Finch brought his hunter's knife down across the back of the gray cap's leg. Felt the blade cut through something hard and thick. He pulled it out, taking a wedge of black flesh with it. The gray cap limped away. No longer as agile. A snarl. Finch and the others shot it in the face, the chest, the arms, the legs.

Still, it kept coming. Dancing in and out, its face a discolored mess. Eyes peeking out from the ruined flesh. Crossley lunging, driving his blade deeper into the leg as it turned to face one of his men. Dashed out as the creature tried to turn.

There was a *give,* and a wash of purple blood.

He stood back. Saw the gray cap standing on one leg.

"Murderers," the gray cap crooned. "Murderers. In our city."

Crossley wanted it dead in that moment. To shut it up. Caught in a blood lust so primal that the enemy looked fey and beautiful in the moonlight. Distant and removed from what they were doing to it.

Now they converged, the three of them. It couldn't evade them. Did it weep as they tore it to pieces? Did it make any human sound to make them stop? No. All it did was stare up at the hard stars as if they were but an extension of its eyes. Arms hacked and pulled off. Cut at. Peeled away. Tossed to the side. The red of its leg. While still it stared. While a cloud of spores erupted from the top of its head, puffing away, disappearing. Hacked, too, at the torso until there was just a head attached to a wreckage of neck. Still the thing smiled. Still it seemed to live. The reflexive life of a gecko's tail.

Now they cursed and sobbed. Unable, as the bloodlust left them, to understand how they had been brought to this. How they could have done this. Even as they still wanted to kill it. Screaming. Shouting. Not caring if an enemy could hear them. Just wanting to keep on killing it until it was dead.

Finally, they burnt it, until it was just dead eyes laughing, asking if it had been worth it.

Soon even that burst into spores.

4

Nothing remained of Finch when he was done with Wyte. Not really. Blood or something like blood drenched him. His left hand gripped the sword tightly, the guard thick with gore. Wyte wouldn't get a funeral. Wouldn't get much of anything. He'd already begun the short, sharp process of becoming one of the forgotten. Nothing anybody could've done to save him from that.

Finch's left shoulder sang with pain from the blow Wyte had given it. Left knee unsteady from having his legs taken out from under him. Toward the end. One last reflexive lunge from a creature that didn't want to die. The whole time it had felt like it was happening to him. His steps were heavy from the weight.

The sounds had been horrific. Something had lived inside of Wyte. When it came out, Finch shot it. Then sliced it apart as it squealed. Was it part of Wyte? Was it the remnants of Otto? Finch didn't care. He had just wanted it dead. Wanted to make sure Wyte wasn't coming back.

No relation to the family man and husband Wyte had once been, before the Rising. No correlation between his life then and his death now. Something crazy. Something beyond prediction. Never sat on the stoop of Wyte's former house, drinking out of his silver flask, and said, casually, "You're going to turn into a monster, Wyte, and I'm going to kill you with a ceremonial sword forged by the Kalif's empire."

Would the resurrection of Duncan Shriek be the opposite of this? Better or worse?

The phone rang inside Wyte's apartment as Finch was leaving. He hesitated. Went back inside. Closed the door. Locked it.

The phone was in the kitchen. He avoided looking in the corner. The stillness was oppressive. The smell thick, physical. Had to pull his shirt collar to his nose.

Picked up the phone with his bloody hand. Waited.

"Hello. Finch?" Stark. Almost cheery.

"What do you want?"

"You sound a little shaky. What's wrong?"

"What do you want?"

Realized then that Stark's people had followed him there. Told Stark where he was. *And that Stark knew Wyte's phone number.*

"It's not what I want," Stark said. "It's what you want. And, apparently, you want me to *keep hurting you*. Apparently if I keep hurting you more and more, I'll get what I want."

A barking laugh from Finch. "The city's fucked. The Spit's destroyed. The towers are almost done. Whatever you want won't matter in a day or two."

"My dear Finch, that's exactly my point. You need to tell me *everything you know*—by the end of today. Otherwise, don't waste your breath lecturing me about the state of this shitty city," Stark said in a silky voice. "Because what you should be worried about is: we could've gotten to Sintra easily enough. If you don't reveal all by nightfall, she's dead."

The same Sintra who betrayed me to the rebels. The one who is still in my head, fucking up my thoughts. Giving me this pain in my chest.

"But you didn't get to Sintra yet," Finch said. "Which means you don't know where Sintra is." *Any more than I do.* Finch's voice had risen to a shout. The back of his throat hurt. Every part of him hurt. *How had Stark known Wyte's number?*

A long, low laugh. "Finchy, I want whatever's in that apartment with Shriek. Today. So make it happen. Or Sintra's next. Or Rathven. I don't care which. Look what we did to Wyte. True, he was almost there already. We just gave him that final push. Want to know how? Look around before you leave. Maybe on the counter, maybe in the sink. Just take a look. Get a sense for just how desperate your friend really was. And who you're up against."

"There's nothing in that apartment but Shriek," Finch said.

"Then bring me Shriek," Stark said.

Finch hung up.

Hated himself for looking, for taking Stark's suggestion. Found nothing on the counter. Nothing in the sink. In the garbage under the sink, though, he found a small white envelope and a note.

In an embellished script, the note read, "Take these, Wyte. They'll help. As promised. Love, Stark." Inside the envelope, the crumbly remains of something fungal. Something that hadn't helped Wyte at all.

Forced himself to imagine it. Wyte. Terrified by the quickening change. Making a deal to trade information, even though Finch had warned him against it. Wyte maybe thinking that giving Stark some of what he wanted would take the pressure off of Finch.

Then Stark had given Wyte some kind of mushroom he knew would drive Wyte over the edge. The note was dated two days earlier, so that meant Wyte had come back to his apartment two straight nights. Looked at Stark's note, the possible solution. Trusting it. Not trusting it. Desperate for something that might save him for a time. Driven to it by the gun battle. Driven to it by every careless, cruel comment by his supposed friends, Finch included. Wyte, too embarrassed, too ashamed, to tell Finch what he'd done. How stupid he'd been. Even at the end. Especially at the end.

For a moment, Finch's self-disdain was boundless. Threatened to bring the ground crashing in on him.

The phone was ringing again. Finch ignored it.

Blood dripped down from his hairline into his eyes. His blood. A claw must've caught him in the scalp as Wyte was shifting from shape to shape near the end. Wiped it away. Went back to what remained of Wyte. Wasn't much. Already beginning to rot. But he rummaged in his jacket pocket. One last thing he had to do now. It wouldn't change anything. Not really. But it might, in the end, satisfy his sense of justice.

Now it was time to take care of Stark.

Ambergris Rules. Take out the immediate threat.

Two hours later, Finch was done. He pulled the curtain back a sliver. Looked out with one eye shut against the glare. Dazzling sunlight. The grainy gray of the wall and a curving narrow strip of archway. Showing the street beyond. Weeds between sidewalk tiles. A row of dank, rotting warehouses on the other side. A lone tree. Crooked and bare of leaves.

If he had watchers, they'd be impatient by now. They'd have to come in closer. Especially if they had another reason.

Took out his gun. Fired a single shot into the room behind him. Lodged in the wall next to the kitchen. The sound was loud, like the others had been. Now they'd heard him with Wyte. Seen him come out, then go back in. Heard the shot. Followed by silence.

That might be enough to bring them.

Thirty seconds passed. Then two men came into view on the sidewalk. Dark clothes. The bulge of weapons under their jackets. Tallish. If Stark had a team on him, say four, they'd split up. Two would keep watch outside. Another one would walk up to the door, with the fourth covering him from the wall. Or they'd have one on the back window. Except Finch had checked the back, and there was no cover. Just a long, narrow alley filled with parts from motored vehicles. No one watching from what he could see poking his head out. Too dangerous. They probably didn't know the area, either. Might not even realize there was a back window. Beyond the narrow alley lay a taller building, more apartments.

They'd be coming right about now. Imagined he could hear footsteps. He went into the bathroom. Stood on the toilet. Hoisted himself up and through the window, ignoring the ache in his shoulder. Dropped into a crouch in the alley. Surrounded by worn tires and metal viscera. Everything but the motored vehicles themselves. Smell of rubber. Distant smell of oil. The long, tall wall of the building next door close enough to reach out and touch. No one watching. Unless they waited out of sight.

Gun drawn, heart beating fast, he made for the far end. The slice of blue sky above. The dull gray-brown of the buildings beyond. Made it, peeked around the corner. No one. Ran parallel to Wyte's apartment complex, into the streets beyond. Doubled back until he was looking around a corner at the wall of archways that hid Wyte's apartment.

Just in time to see, in glimpses, broken up by the wall, a man come out the front, walk down the corridor. Short. Muscular. Looked oddly burnt. Then another man came out from around back, where Finch had just been. Taller, thinner, bald. Weapon out. Finch drew back into the shadow of a stoop until the man was safely past a line of sight where he could see Finch.

The shorter man was now clutching at the front of the taller man's jacket. But the taller man gave way, and suddenly the shorter man was down on his knees, being sick into the ruins of the garden. Wyte had made an impact.

A hand signal from the taller man brought the two lookouts to their side. A quick conference. A few nervous gestures. A head bowed in exasperation or pain or some emotion Finch couldn't interpret. Either way, they'd lost their man and now had to report their failure back to Stark.

After a few moments, they headed off down the street, away from Finch. With as much stealth as possible, he followed. Erring on the side of too much distance between them rather than too little. Until the streets around them began to get more crowded. Mostly former camp prisoners. Still wearing their uniforms. Some had crutches. A few bandaged around the head or arms. Most with that pinched, withdrawn look around the eyes from hunger, stress, or worse. Birthmarks they'd picked up in the camps shone mossy and bright.

They made it much easier. Buried. Following.

As he walked, Finch saw hints of Wyte in the faces of passersby. It sustained his anger, and his grief. *Living against the odds.*

5

Stark was using a mushroom house as his headquarters. Off of Aquelus Street. About a half-mile from Albumuth Boulevard. About a mile from Wyte's apartment. Maybe a little more back to the station. Positioned so Stark would also have a straight shot, as straight as he'd get, back down to the Spit. A route that meant nothing now.

Using a mushroom house hinted at a rough genius in Stark, and a kind of insanity. It was three stories high. Light green with striations of metallic blue that gave it an ethereal sheen. Except for the tendency of the walls to curl and curve, the windows to flutter without a breeze, it shared a close resemblance to the normal houses on either side.

Finch stood on the opposite side of the street. Four houses down. Hidden by the stoop behind him and in front by a few high bushes with leaves shaped like shovels. An F&L neighborhood before the war. Protected from the worst predations of the wars. A quiet street. Little foot traffic. The mushroom house had probably scared people off. Or Stark's people had done it.

The men he'd followed had gone in. A few minutes later, Stark and Bosun had come from the opposite direction. They stood for a moment on the steps in front of the house. He couldn't hear what they were saying, but it sounded violent, like flames or swords. Then they went inside. He'd been waiting ever since. Going through the options. No way he could storm the house by himself. There were no guards at the front door, but that would've drawn too much attention. They'd even left garbage and debris out front. Let the fungus overgrow everything in sight.

He could just see the shadow of two men sitting back from the windows on the third floor. More men inside, of course. Possibly in the house opposite, on Finch's side of the street. Watching. Finch didn't particularly care. You could defend whatever position you wanted, but if the enemy hit you somewhere else, you were still fucked. He cared more that most of Stark's men would be muscle bought after he'd arrived. Take care of Stark somehow and many of them wouldn't be too keen to hunt Finch down. Too busy looking after their own interests.

An hour later, Stark and Bosun emerged from the house. With the short man who'd gone into Wyte's apartment. The tall man who'd come out the back. Headed his way, on the other side of the street.

"You never gave me up, Wyte. I'll never forget that."

"I can't control myself anymore. There's not much of me left. The rest might fight back. But I don't mean it if I do."

Quick and neat is how he wanted it. But that's not quite how it went down.

They passed by his position. He ran out firing, the sound so loud it shocked him. Put the bodyguards down. One shot in the chest, crumpling into oblivion. The other from a leg wound, blood spurting out. Screaming. Spasming.

Bosun turned at the same time as Stark, in time to get clipped in the shoulder. Registered extreme surprise, but recovered. Took off running, hunched over, cursing.

Bad luck. Finch didn't have time for another shot. Stark had about gotten his gun out. Finch smashed into Stark, twisted the gun out of his hand. Then hit Stark across the face. Saw the pain and anger as Stark bent to one knee.

"Bosun!" Stark shouting it like an order.

Slammed Stark against the side of the head. Started to drag him away as the other two lay on the ground. Grunted with the strain of Stark's bulk. Stark muttering, trying to get his senses back. Couldn't see where Bosun had gotten to. Had to get off the street quick.

A bullet kicked up dirt near his feet. Turned with Stark partially shielding him, the weight more awkward than he anticipated.

Bosun was across the street. Using a lamppost and a pile of junk for cover.

"Let him go and I won't kill you!" Bosun shouted. Had a gun in each hand. And not shitty knockoffs. Looked like custom-made revolvers.

Stark, muttering: "Go ahead, Bosun. Take the chance now."

Finch pulled Stark up. Shoved his Lewden Special against Stark's head. Other arm around Stark's waist. The man was still dazed.

"I'll kill him," Finch shouted back. "I'll kill him right here."

"You'll kill him anyway!" Bosun, anguished.

Backtracking toward the alley. Hoping nothing nasty waited there. Stark's weight awkward, hard to control. Didn't want to fall during this crude shuffle. Bosun would be on him in an instant.

Bosun fired off a couple of shots over his head. "You're a dead man if you hurt him."

Could already hear a commotion coming from the mushroom house. It had all happened in a couple of seconds. But Stark's men were good.

"Come after me, and I've got bullets enough for both of you, you bastard!" Finch shouted back.

Made it to the alley. Got off a couple of rounds to keep Bosun back.

The alley split into three directions just a hundred feet back. Hustled Stark around a corner. Pulled Stark's left arm behind his back. To the point of breaking as Stark groaned. Shoved the muzzle of his gun under the taller man's chin.

"Just keep going. Keep walking." Didn't want to talk. Didn't want to hear.

Guided Stark through a welter of back streets as confusing as any number of doorways on the Spit. Until they were far enough away that Finch felt comfortable stopping. Bosun didn't know Ambergris as well as Finch. And he'd know he had to be careful looking for his brother.

Finch released Stark face-first against a plain brick wall on a tiny side street. Windowless walls of fire-scarred buildings, rectangular and unimaginative. Crowding out the light from above. Stairwells running up their sides like rusting spines. Water on the pavement. A leering shelf of pink fungus jutting from the wall a couple inches from the ground. Stark's boots had cut into that ridge, the fungus staining the leather.

Stark started to talk. Finch came at him from the side. Punched him in the kidneys. Stark crumpled forward, air driven from his lungs. Wobbled, regained his balance. Breathing heavy.

"If you've killed Bosun, I swear . . ." The verbosity had left him for the moment. As if he'd been playing a role.

"Your brother was coming after me the last I saw. With just a nick in his shoulder. But you've got worse problems."

"So do you, Finch, unless you let me go."

But Finch was past that point. "If you just hadn't kept pushing, Stark. If you hadn't *kept at it,* maybe you wouldn't be here now. Take off your shoes."

"What?" A kind of pulsing rage threatened to make Stark's face unrecognizable.

Finch put the gun up against Stark's temple. "Now!"

With a show of repugnance and disdain, Stark removed first one shoe, then the other.

"Empty your pockets."

"Why?"

"Just do it." Realized he was shouting. Realized his hair was still clotted with Wyte's blood.

Stark spat as he pulled out his pockets. He didn't have much. Some money. A photograph of an old woman. A few keys.

"I don't like to be weighed down," Stark said.

Nothing there to tell Finch anything more about Stark.

Finch took a memory bulb out of his packet pocket. "Do you know who this is?"

A kind of savage, jaded amusement at seeing the bulb. Which faded. Quickly. Replaced by something Finch hadn't seen in Stark before. Uncertainty.

"It's from Wyte. Wyte's memory bulb. Now why do you think I made it?"

"Fuck you," Stark snarled. "Fuck you. Why don't you eat it, Finch. Eat it and be damned."

"You wanted information. You wanted me to help you. So I'm

going to help you. You're going to live inside of Wyte's head for awhile."

"I won't eat it," Stark said. He'd gone pale. The eyes flickered from side to side. Looking for a way out.

"Why didn't you kill Bliss, Stark? What did the two of you talk about?" Still curious.

"We talked about petunias, Finch," Stark said. "We talked about art and literature and what the weather was going to be like. What the fuck do you think we talked about? We talked about why I shouldn't kill him."

"And how'd he convince you?"

"Said he'd get me information, money, influence. Gave me the address of that rebel outpost for starters. He was going to help me clean out the whole area. But I haven't seen him since, the bastard."

Regarded Stark for a moment. Looked him in the eye. Believed what he found there. Or believed if it wasn't the truth he'd never get it out of Stark anyway.

"On your knees."

"No."

Finch pressed the gun up against Stark's cheek. "Guests get to choose. You're new here, so you're a guest. Bulb or bullet? Bullet or bulb?"

Slowly, Stark sank to his knees. Tried again. "I can make you a rich man, Finch. I can even get you out of Ambergris. There are still a lot of choices here."

"Do you think so? I don't."

"Do you know who I am, back in Stockton? Do you know what happens to you if you hurt me?" Stark's lower lip was quivering.

"No, I don't know. Because you won't tell me who you are. Open your mouth."

Stark's stare in that moment contained a kind of limitless, unhinged hatred. A kind of poison that willed itself to close the distance. To enter Finch. He grabbed the bulb from Finch. Crunched down on it with a kind of arrogant defiance. Finch realized Stark thought he could survive it. That he was bigger than whatever might happen to him.

A minute for the bulb to take effect. Finch placed the gun's muzzle against Stark's face. "Any last words before you don't remember who you are?"

Stark gave out a little crumpled laugh. A kind of regal contempt. "Not a one for you, Finchy. Except you'll pay for this, one way or the other. I'm the crown prince incognito. I'm an enchanted frog. Somebody will come after you."

The man's hostility began to fade as the memory bulb took effect. Finch looked into his eyes. Found nothing there. Nothing worth saving. Just an outsider who'd decided he wanted to profit off of the city's misery. A thug who thought he was tougher. Playing a game where his only strategy was to keep turning the screws. Finch didn't care who he was anymore. Just wanted him gone. Wondered without interest what Bosun would do now.

Stark's pupils had begun to dilate. Eyelids flickering like hummingbird wings. Said, as if from a faraway place, "No, I won't. I don't want to." Fell back on his heels. Arms slack.

Finch came close. Held Stark's head back. Took out another pouch. Poured preservation powder all over Stark's tongue. Like sand. Held his mouth shut even as Stark struggled, lethargically. Made him swallow. Once. Twice.

Released him. Stood back. Both times Finch had seen Heretic force a bulb and the powder on a prisoner, they'd died within an hour.

Stark convulsed, smashed his head back against the wall. So hard he left blood and hair on the brick. His eyes rolled back. Fell over on his side. Began to thrash. Blood poured out of his nostrils. Began to talk in a low voice. Very fast. No distance between sentences.

Then Stark began to laugh. Quietly at first. Almost like a gasping whisper. But rising in volume, until he was shrieking. Rolling around on the ground guffawing his brains out. With blood still looping out from his nostrils. Arms tight around himself. Mouth in a half-moon of involuntary mirth. It didn't really sound like laughter anymore. It sounded like screaming. Someone screaming as they were cut apart by knives.

A voice drowning as it spoke. Awash in strange tides.

What did Stark see? Was it Wyte? Wyte's memories? Distorted further by the powder? Or something else entirely?

Finch stepped back, in a firing stance. But he could not fire. All the rage in him had left. The madness.

Finally, lowered the gun. Left Stark there. Writhing in the mud and water. Boots kicking. Fighting with himself. The laughter raw and rasping. Like something had gone wrong in his throat.

Stark would not come back from this. And before the end he'd be in a kind of hell, like the hell Wyte had experienced. Like the hell Finch was in now. Would Bosun come after him? Didn't know. Didn't care at the moment.

Ambergris Rules.

* * *

You could close your eyes forever and still never be anywhere but where you had always been. Finch saw his father's capacity for violence only once. When he was twelve. *A hot night.* Made so by the rumbling excesses of heavy artillery off to the south. Brown smoke highlighting gouts of orange flame erupting around the silhouettes of buildings. The distant whumping sound of shells and tank retort. House Hoegbotton and House Frankwrithe engaged in a struggle none yet knew was pointless. The cease-fire hadn't held.

They'd had to move from their house, gotten caught in a war zone. Finch was hunched down by the window of the third-story apartment they'd taken refuge in. Waiting for his father to return from hours of scavenging for food and other supplies.

The window, with its grimy gray frame, had become a kind of moving painting for Finch. As intense as any zoetrope. Below, Albumuth Boulevard, once one of the richest arteries of trade in the world, had become little more than a mass of rubble and ripped-apart bodies. A day before men and tanks had fought across that landscape, the light red-green at their backs. The moans and screams matched to the cruel intensity of colors. He would watch, unblinking. Sometimes catch glimpses of gray caps running along the periphery.

Behind him, the door burst open.

A sniper with the insignia of House Hoegbotton. Framed by the doorway. Only five years older than Finch. Face already ancient.

"Down on the floor," the sniper ordered, walking into the living room. He had long, delicate fingers. Golden stubble on his cheeks. Smelled of sweat and gunpowder. "Get under that chair."

Finch scuttled out of the sniper's way across the floor. Under the chair as ordered. Watched as the sniper pulled the curtains across the window, opened the pane a crack, and shoved the long, steel muzzle of his automatic rifle through the crack. From Finch's perspective on the floor, the sniper looked huge. The recoil of the rifle made a dull, satisfying sound. Discarded shells rolled across the floor toward Finch. Touched one. Brought his finger away burned.

The man cursed when he missed. Said nothing when he hit his target.

"Shouldn't you be in the militia?" the sniper asked him while reloading, back against the wall. No one had shot back yet. Later, Finch would wonder if the sniper had been shooting at shadows. "You're old enough."

He had no answer. No one had ever told him he was old enough before.

Then his father appeared in the doorway, pistol in his hand. The bright green eyes. The neatly trimmed beard and moustache. The broad shoulders. The calloused palms.

The sniper turned, began to raise his rifle.

His father shook his head. A grim, single-minded look. Finch had never seen that look on his father's face before. It wasn't the expression of an engineer. It came from somewhere more primal.

The young sniper saw it, too. Lowered the rifle. Stood up. Walked stiff-legged past Finch's father and out into the hall. Like a dog trying to make itself bigger.

Finch saw his father turn and aim at the back of the sniper's head. Saw him struggle with the decision. Then lower the gun and lock the door.

For a moment, Finch didn't want to come out from under the table. Didn't know this person who looked like his father.

6

Finch headed back to the station. Wyte's death lodged like a heavy stone in his throat. Constricting his breath. Making him reckless.

A mob came at him out of nowhere, around a corner. Broke around him like a summer storm. A torrent of shouting. Of sweat and dirt and fear. The armbands of a long-dead neighborhood militia reborn. Some dared to show the rebels' blue band on their arms. Sensing that their time had come. Had it? Finch didn't know. So many camp uniforms he began to wonder if the gray caps had released them just to create chaos. To somehow *obscure* what was going to happen. Focused on some objective other than him. Or they didn't like the look of him. Numb. Staring straight ahead. Gun in its holster, sword in his right hand.

Ambergris come alive again, but into tribes, not a city. Finch wondered what old scores would be settled first.

Less than a quarter mile from the station, a shuddering thud and crack rumbled through the world. A series of them, from everywhere. Some near, some distant. Followed by silence. The sounds jolted Finch out of a walking trance. The shock reverberated in his bones.

Had the towers unleashed their weapon again? Couldn't confirm that. Couldn't see the towers from there. Hidden by the dirty green marble of old luxury hotels taken over by lichen and flanked by tall trees with yellowing leaves. People leaned out of windows on the fourth, the fifth floors, holding flags and shouting. Pointing to the northeast, the northwest.

In the street, a tiny old woman in a faded flower dress. A grubby boy gnawing on a shriveled apple stood beside her. Three Partials staring at the sky. All waiting for the next blow.

But there was no green light. No second series of explosions.

Instead, a curling trail of black smoke began to rise into that perfect blue sky. Finch recognized it. Had seen it before when a rebel bomb left a signal to the rest of the city. Heard shouts and screams rising like the smoke. Muffled. Distant. Disguised.

Had an odd premonition. An awful tightness in his stomach.

Finch began to run toward the smoke. Past wounded storefronts. Past the abandoned wooden box and scissors of a sidewalk barber. Past a huge red drug mushroom whose shade snuffed out the sky, the gentle sighing of its gills both ominous and calming.

He crossed onto Albumuth Boulevard, and approached the station.

The remains of it.

Transformed into a couple of side walls. Smoldering blocks of stone. The kindle of shattered, crackling wood. A blackened hole near the back, expelling blacker smoke. A smell like kerosene. A smell like meat cooking.

A roiling mass of particles. Discharging light until a steady humming glow suffused the city in a kind of dawn. There came in reply from the city a hundredfold bestial roar.

Finch rushed to the edge of that broken space. Stopped short. Saw the scattered remains of bodies. A pant leg. A foot. A torso tattooed with dirt and blood. A pile of something he could not identify. Realized some of it came from the people Heretic had killed and left in the holding cell.

The tubes of the memory holes, torn and bleeding, glistened as they thrashed, whipping the ground back and forth. Others lay still and dusty in the rubble.

A couple of men Finch didn't know staggered through the mess. Looking for survivors even though they were both bleeding. Both marked by fire. Searching like they might find something alive.

Finch took a step forward. Then another. Walked through the rubble, still holding his sword. Became aware of a dull, booming roar from deep inside the smoldering black hole in the back. Through the swirling whoosh of the rising smoke.

Became aware, too, of someone laughing from the wreckage of the wall to his left. The bricks still went up maybe twelve feet high, ending in a broken snarl. Sheltering the table with the typewriter, which stood as if indestructible. Beside it, slumped against the wall: Blakely, hurt in ways beyond a doctor's care. But still alive.

Worse than war. Worse than stab wounds.

There would be no putting Blakely back together.

"The typewriter," what was left of Blakely gasped, between laughs. "The typewriter. It's still there. It's still there."

Finch kneeled down beside him. The closer he got, the less he was forced to see what had happened to Blakely. Not a scratch on the man's face. But Blakely's eyes knew. Finch could see death in them.

"What happened, Blakely?"

"Albin," Blakely said. "Albin happened." Laughed again. "Blew it all to hell. Came by to talk, he said. Had explosives strapped to him. Stood by the curtain, said something I didn't catch. Stepped inside. Blew himself apart. Threw me all the way across the room. Albin. Can you believe it? Can you believe it? Can you believe it? Can you believe it? Can you believe it? Can you believe it? Can you—?"

Finch returned his gun to its holster. Blakely's face matched his body now. No kinder mercy. The world getting smaller and smaller, even as it expanded.

Stood up shakily, feeling the shock in his legs. Waved to the men searching the rubble. "Get the hell out of here."

They saw his gun and his sword, woke as if from a trance. Picked their way through the rubble, the interrupted flesh. Disappeared as if never there.

More curls of black smoke now. Rising all around. Other stations hit. Felt a conflicting sense of loss and freedom. People were dying who'd just tried to feed themselves. Just wanted to stay alive.

The Lady in Blue: "We don't use suicide bombers anymore." But they did.

Partials would be on their way to the station. Gray caps. Struggling to dig out of the rubble of their underground headquarters. Maybe the sound Finch heard was just a subterranean fire or maybe it was some *fanaarcensitii* beast clawing its way to the surface. Finch knew his imagination couldn't compete.

Was it coincidence he hadn't been there when it happened?

Left the station to whatever demon was fighting its way out from under the bricks and stone.

* * *

The madman danced on the steps near his favorite statue like nothing had ever gone wrong in his life. Even while the black smoke continued to rise over the city. In the hotel lobby, people had gathered as if seeking shelter from a thunderstorm. They stood there, strangers to him, and parted before him and his sword. He barely saw them.

Unfinished business. Loose ends. Needed to know his back was secure.

Stood in front of Rathven's door in the basement shadows. A sudden need for his father to be alive, to be counseling him, canceled out an impulse to smash in that door. To pound on it until his fist was raw.

Tried to wipe the crusted blood from his face. Held the gun behind his back. The sword safely at his side. He knocked, gently.

No answer.

Knocked again. Smiled into the peephole. Knew it might come off as a crazed leer.

Finally, muffled: "What do you want?"

"Just to talk." Just a quiet talk. *With my sword and my gun, if it comes down to that.* Then, "Wyte's dead." Investing his voice with a grief that he didn't feel. It had already shot through him and left him numb. *Wyte charging the Partials like some immortal hero. Wyte huddled in the corner of his apartment, scared shitless. The truth somewhere between.*

The door opened. Finch resisted the urge to shove it open. The urge to hit her. To hit someone.

Rathven looked paler than he'd ever seen her. She was aiming that heavy revolver at him. Fought to steady it as the gun dipped and wavered slightly in her two-handed grip. Sudden flash of insight based on nothing real: Rath as a girl, an awkward tomboy with a sense of humor, who couldn't laugh at herself. Uncomfortable in a skirt. Smart. Hopeful. Easily disappointed.

"Your 'brother' sell you that relic?" Contemptuously brushed past her, the image of her as a girl dulling his anger a bit. Brought his gun forward, into the shelter of his body. Holstered it. Found a seat by the table. Facing the door. Didn't like the tunnel behind him, but liked the sound of the water. Figured he'd hear someone long before they came creeping up out of it.

Still holding the gun, she turned to him. In the flickering light. The cavern lit up in faint cascades of green. Made him think of the Lady in Blue. *In a boat. Crossing an underground sea.* Ethereal. A faraway kingdom, too delicate to exist in the real world.

"Wyte's dead," Finch said. Each time he said it, it seemed more remote. Then came back to him fast and unbearable. Like something rising suddenly out of the dark that was both friend and foe.

"You said that." Rathven knew Wyte as someone Finch had talked about. Maybe half a dozen times. Had kept Wyte from her. Why? "What happened to you. You're covered in blood."

"Sit down, Rathven," Finch said. "Try to relax." Talking to himself.

"What happened?"

"Stark gave Wyte a mushroom that put him over the edge. I had to take care of Wyte." Said as calmly as he could manage. *Give her something to think about.*

It surprised Finch when she lowered the gun. Some part of him had thought she would shoot him.

Rathven sat down opposite him. Rested the gun on her knee.

"I'm sorry," she said.

"Why?" Finch asked. "You had nothing to do with it, right?"

A fire in her eyes. "No, of course not."

A feeling of *hurt* came over Finch. A sense of betrayal. It fascinated him. Worried at it like a piece of gristle between his teeth.

"You should've been a detective," Finch said. "Down here with all of your books. With that tunnel as an escape route."

"I should have been," she said, dutifully. But there was nothing playful in her expression. "What do you want from me, Finch? The city is falling apart. They've even disbanded the camps." Said it with a mix of regret and wonder. "I might have to—"

"What? Leave? Like your 'brother'?"

She had the grace to look away. "I'm in a different place than you. You never went to the camps. You don't really know what they were like. It was a white lie. You wouldn't have helped him otherwise. He was still a friend."

"You mean, if I knew he worked for the rebels."

"Everyone works for the rebels," she snapped.

"Even Sintra?" *Even me?*

"Sintra I know nothing about," Rathven said. "Nothing. Except what I told you."

"Who else do you work for?" Finch asked.

"No one. Everyone. You. Myself." Wriggling in the trap. She softened her tone. A kind of misdirection: "I did check out those aliases for you. The Bliss aliases."

"Find anything?"

"Just that 'Dar Sardice' might not be an alias."

"What do you mean?"

"I mean, if you go through some of the books about the wars, and the books I have about it from the Morrow/Frankwrithe side, you don't find Ethan Bliss's name anywhere until after the first mention of 'Dar Sardice.'"

"Do you mean that Dar Sardice is his real name?"

"Either that," Rathven said, "or he killed Dar Sardice and took his name. And then his real name isn't Bliss or Sardice. Or, my sources aren't complete enough."

Bliss pointing him toward Stark. Bliss bringing him into the next day while Bosun trashed his apartment. Bliss throwing him off the scent.

"How about Stark?"

Thought he sensed a hesitation before she said, "No."

"That's funny, because when I mentioned Stark before you didn't even stop to ask me who he was. Like you knew."

"I thought you'd tell me soon enough," she said. "For Truff's sake, *you were telling me your friend was dead*!"

"A lot of people come to you down here in the basement, don't they?" Finch said.

"You knew that already. Don't do this, Finch," Rathven said. Almost convincing him. But the ache was too great.

"A lot of people the gray caps wouldn't approve of," he said, pressing on.

"You're tired, you're grieving," she said.

"People who want things from you," he continued.

She changed tactics, said, "Am I under arrest?" Was it disdain or an echo of hurt he saw on her face? Were they insulting each other or wounding each other?

"No," he said. "Where would I take you? The station was bombed today. It's gone. Matchsticks and stones. Everybody's gone."

She had no answer to that, must've known "I'm sorry" would just set him off.

"Wyte's dead," Finch said, "because Stark took him over the edge. Stark got hold of certain information to try to make me help him. How did he get it?"

For a moment, Wyte sat beside him, saying, "How far are you going to take this?"

"Finch." Pleading. For what, though? For him to trust her? To stop questioning her? To keep things the way they'd always been?

Finch leaned forward, reached out, and pulled her chin up when she tried to look away. She let him do it. "Listen carefully. Stark knew about Sintra. *You* told him. He found out about you from his predecessors, the Stockton agents he liquidated once he got here. He came, or he sent Bosun. They either threatened you or paid you, or both. And you told them about Sintra. About me. Maybe you tried to protect me, and that's all you gave them. You might even think you helped me. But you gave them *something*. I know you did. You're the only one who could. If I'm wrong, tell me. Tell me I'm wrong. Right now. *But don't lie to me*."

Her lower lip quivered. She pushed his hand away. "You have to choose a side, Finch. Eventually you have to choose a side, even if you pretend to be neutral. Even if you think giving out information is like selling smokes or food packets."

"And you chose Stark's side?" Incredulous.

"No! But Stark would've killed me if I didn't give him something. And he hates the gray caps as much as I do. And I didn't think it would hurt to tell him what he could've found out about you in a couple of days anyway." She looked small, miserable, utterly alone. But right then he didn't care.

"Stark's a psychopath," Finch said. "Only out for himself." Repeating what Bliss had told him.

"Maybe. Maybe not. Maybe I just told myself it was okay because I didn't want to die."

"Couldn't your 'brother' and his friends help you?"

Rathven shook her head. "Everyone comes to me for information. Everyone sees me as neutral because I give everyone *something*."

"And you don't know Bliss?"

"I know of him. He visited the Photographer a few times, but he never wanted anything from me."

Bliss. The Photographer. How did that work? And why?

"Finch?" she said, and he realized he'd been lost in his thoughts. "What are you going to do?"

It took an effort of will. But knew he had to do it. For himself as well as for her. There was no one else. Told himself: She delivered Duncan Shriek to you. She helped you when the memory bulbs brought you low. She never lied to you before. *There is no one else.* Not a soul.

"Stark's as good as dead," Finch said. "And, Rath, I'll forget the rest if you'll do me a favor. I need a favor."

"What kind of favor?" Abject relief in her voice.

He placed his extra apartment key on her table. "Take care of Feral for me. Take care of the things in my apartment. If I don't come back." Wasn't looking forward to saying goodbye to Feral. Wasn't sure that wouldn't be the final stupid little thing that broke him.

"Where are you going?"

Finch smiled. "Nowhere. Everywhere."

7

But he didn't get very far. Bliss waited for him in the courtyard. Came out into the late afternoon light. One arm shoved into the outer pocket of his short brown jacket. Wore matching pants. A wide-brimmed black hat. A dark green scarf. Face flushed. Almost disguising a thin line of dull red that ran up across his right cheek. Another wound around his hairline, disappearing under the brim. Another remarkable recovery.

Frost clung to his boots. Fast melting. A damp, wet smell to him. Where'd he been? Not here.

"Put the gun away, Finch. And don't even think about drawing the Kalif's sacred steel."

Finch had no illusions about the hand shoved into the pocket. Could see something bulky there. He holstered his weapon. Stood in the gloom with Bliss.

With Dar Sardice.

"Now what?" Tried to push away the thought that Rathven had set him up somehow.

"Now we go up to the Photographer's apartment."

"Not mine? I think you know where it is."

"I don't trust yours." Bliss motioned with the gun in his pocket. "After you." His face closed, angular, serious.

Finch walked past him, tensing for a blow. But it never came. Bliss followed a step behind. Thought about turning on him, but had no illusions about what Bliss would do.

The spy's voice went cold, condemning. "When you see me again, it will be because I want *you to see me. And not before."*

On the fifth floor, they walked to the end of the hall. Apartment 521. Half-hidden by the long stalks of slender lime-green mushrooms. Bliss tossed a key on the floor.

"Open the door."

Carefully, Finch bent down to pick up the key, unlocked the door. Went inside, Bliss following.

The room was empty, except for a stout table in the center. A bottle of whisky and two glasses.

Photographs covered the walls. Nailed there. A half-dozen in frames were stacked against the far window. Which was blacked out with paint. Some of the photographs were larger than Finch, made up of many smaller pieces of contact paper. All showed water. In puddles. In waves. Close up. From far away. Noticed now how many of them had the towers as a backdrop. How many seemed to have been taken from areas of the shore the gray caps had blocked off.

"Now lock the door."

Finch did as he was told.

Turned to find that Bliss had taken off his hat. Taken out a cigar. Lit it with a quick scrape of a match against the table. Poured two glasses of whisky. Moved to a position behind the table. Put his own glass down. Returned his left hand to his pocket.

Bliss took a puff of the cigar, said, "Whisky?"

Finch moved uncertainly forward. "A last drink for the condemned man?" Took a glass.

It was good stuff. Smashing Todd's, twenty-one years. Put into barrels near the end of one of the worst periods of fighting between F&L and H&S. Better than what he had in the apartment. So smooth it only burned a little on the back end. Tasted of Morrow peat. The River Moth.

"No, Finch," Bliss said. "A celebration. A kind of christening, even."

"What do you want?" Snapped it out. No patience left.

"*Bellum omnium contra omnes,*" Bliss said in a thin, reedy voice.

"*You're* my contact?" *Rathven saying "Everyone works for the rebels."*

"You're supposed to say, 'Never lost.' Then I'm supposed to give you what you need."

"I thought you worked for Morrow."

A quizzical look from Bliss. "I do? Did I ever say I did? There are no Morrow interests in this city anymore. Only Ambergrisian interests."

“What’s your real name, Bliss? Is it Graansvoort? Or maybe it’s Dar Sardice?”

“You must believe everything you’re told.” Said almost without scorn.

“Why were you really in my apartment?”

Bliss’s head tilted to the left. Considering Finch. “Checking you out. Seeing how you checked out. I found a lot of familiar books on those shelves. Familiar to me, at least. A curious lack of photographs. That’s what really gave you away.”

“Me catching you wasn’t part of the plan.”

“No. I’ll never tell you.”

“So what do you think you found out?”

A bit of the old facile cleverness shone in his eyes. “Familiar books. No photos. I told her, ‘He’s changed his look. Shaved the beard. The hair is lighter. He’s older, but still *him*. James. The son John helped hide.’”

“How did you know my father?”

Bliss sidestepped the question. “Your father knew how to keep a secret. I always admired that about him. He had his head on straight. He knew what was important. And what wasn’t. I think you do, too. Your father would have agreed to this mission without a second thought.”

“My father is dead,” Finch said through gritted teeth. Put down his whisky. Bliss knowing didn’t shock him. It was the rest. “You still haven’t answered my question.”

“I trusted your father,” Bliss said. “And he trusted me. If that wasn’t the case, I’d have suggested one of the others. Blakely. Maybe even Wyte. But your boss did make you the lead on the case. Much easier for you to get in there.”

“Dar Sardice,” Finch said. Didn’t know if he pursued it because he really believed it was important.

Bliss nodded. Didn’t seem surprised. “I met your father while using that name. Out in the desert. It was a complicated time. Many conflicting allegiances.” Seemed ready to say more. Stopped himself. Head tilted down. Eyes still on Finch. “But I’m telling tales when we don’t have much time. You need to focus on the present.”

He carefully laid the cigar on the edge of the table. Kept his other hand on the gun. Pulled something out of a pocket on the inside of his jacket. Put it down on the table. On Finch's side.

A piece of metal, about ten inches long. Segmented, it looked like it folded out into something larger. Like one of the surveyor rulers his father had always carried with him. Except it was made of a strange alloy, the color deep blue, almost gray. With the rainbow hues when the light caught it that meant it was very old. Odd symbols had been etched into every inch of it. None of them familiar. They didn't even look like what he'd seen of gray cap writing. The metal seemed heavy, substantial. But Bliss had lifted it from his pocket like it weighed nothing at all.

Finch said, "What is that? It doesn't look like something made by us. Or by the gray caps."

"It's not."

"Oh." Again, the world opened up. Became larger, wider, deeper, than before.

Let it flow over and through you or you'll be lost.

"Now give me the memory bulb the Photographer gave you," Bliss said.

"Why?" Sarcastically: "How am I supposed to kill myself without it?"

"Just do it. Trust me." In a pinched, irritable tone. Like Finch should know what was good for him.

Finch placed the pouch on the table.

From his pocket, Bliss took out a small glass vial with a blue crystal stopper. "Watch and learn," he said, finishing his whisky. Puffing furiously on his cigar.

He retrieved the memory bulb from the pouch. Broke it into pieces in his whisky glass. Filling it to the top with a hill of colored dirt. Puffed on the cigar again. Blew away the ash column until there was just the blazing tapered tip.

"They call that a dog's dick," Bliss said, laughing.

"Here we call it the Kalif's cock," Finch said.

Bliss stopped laughing. Applied the tip to the memory bulb dust. "Yes, well, they call *this* . . . well, they don't call this *anything* because your normal sort of person on the street never does this . . ."

The dust began to smoke, then liquefy. In a minute or so, the whisky glass was filled with a pale blue liquid. Bliss carefully shepherded it into the vial. Stoppered it. Put it on Finch's side of the table. Hard to think of backing out faced with something so specific. A procedure so matter-of-fact.

"In this form, it has a completely different effect," Bliss said. "You'll prop Shriek up when you get into the apartment and pour it down his throat, making sure he doesn't choke. He won't have a gag reflex, of course. It will complete the process of regeneration, taking maybe a minute."

Complete the process of regeneration. Shriek awake. An image of everything happening in reverse. Of corpses getting up, walking backward to wherever they'd come from. Unliving their lives. Becoming children. Forgetting how to walk. Returning and returning and returning until they were gone. *Never seeing Shriek or the dead gray cap. Never having to kill anyone, for any reason.*

"What then?" Finch asked.

"You will give him the piece of metal. He'll know what to do. Afterward, he'll leave it behind and you will take the piece of metal with you. And I will come to get it from you.

"Just know that in all of this *you must be fast*. You won't have much time. You'll get in because you work for *them*. And that still means something. For a day or two, at least. They've had distractions thrown at them all day. Dividing their attention. But you can't count on that. We don't have eyes or ears inside of that apartment complex. Too risky. They'd find their way back to the Lady."

"And what do I do then? Confess all? Throw myself on the mercy of the gray caps?"

Bliss shrugged. "If you have to, give yourself up, yes. If all goes well, you won't have long to wait. We'll be watching. But there's always that risk."

Up close, what appeared immaculate about Bliss was actually shopworn, threadbare. His pants. His shoes. A button missing on the jacket. Was it noble or sad that he was still out in the field, running games, networks, schemes?

"Who *are* you, really?" Finch asked.

The old eyes stared out from the well-preserved face. "Any spy worthy of the name would figure that out. *Any spy*. For *anyone*."

Bliss came around the table, too fast for Finch to warn him off. Then stood there looking at Finch.

"Sometimes you have to take a leap into the unknown, John. Sometimes you just have to trust that, plan or no plan, you have limited control over the situation. Now, it's almost dusk. Leave when it's dark. Take the route you think gives you the most cover. That means people, Finch. Lots of confused, frightened people. Not back alleys. *They* can see a lone man. A crowd's more difficult, even for them. But stay away from Partial checkpoints. They're on edge, and that means they're more dangerous and less predictable. Even with your badge."

Finch felt for a moment out of his league, Bliss growing in stature with each word. Had nothing to say in return.

Bliss took something out of his pockets. Put it on the table. "Last thing. Sandwiches. Eat before you leave. And *don't* go back up to your apartment. It isn't safe."

"But I have to change. I'm covered in blood."

Bliss's expression was grim. "You'll fit in better that way."

He walked to the door. Turned there, surrounded by photographs of water. Gave Finch a salute. "Good luck, Finch. And some advice: be prepared to kill."

Said it casually. Almost as if he'd said it many times before.

8

Back in front of apartment 525. Where it had started. Only five days ago. Everything was different. Everything was the same.

Had fought his way through chaotic streets. *Grim-looking men and women careening past in forbidden motored vehicles. Armed with everything from pitchforks and kitchen knives to rifles and semi-automatics.* Then passed through the double doors. *Bodies slumped on the steps outside the building. Strewn. Spasming in something between agony and ecstasy. An acrid smell lingered from whatever had poisoned them.*

Inside, no one in the corridors. The floor no longer slick. No one on the landings.

No sign of any Partials. Distant sounds of conflict from outside only made it inside as a thud or rumbling echo. Could hear his own heartbeat. Couldn't hear any sounds from inside the apartments around him. Held the gun up, two-handed grip, but it was the weight of the sword at his side that comforted him.

Same gray cap symbol glowing on the door.

Same hesitation, but more pain behind it. The light in the hall flickered crazily.

Finally mastered his fear. Held the gun in one hand while he turned the doorknob and pushed with the other. The door was unlocked. A prickle of unease up his spine.

He walked into the darkened hall with the empty bedroom ahead. A yellow, artificial light leaked into the hall from the doorway on the left.

No sound but his tread on the wooden floor. Just an expectant pause. Realized he was holding his breath. Let it out. An absurd whistling through his nose that was worse.

He came out into the living room. A lantern on a chair by the balcony window provided the light. Cast everything in buttery shadows.

The sofa. The chairs. The empty kitchen behind. A shape on the rug. As his eyes adjusted, he saw it was the familiar shape of Shriek, under the blanket. The rebels' great hope. *A weapon. A beacon. A human being.*

He walked into the living room.

A movement from behind. Before he could turn, the muzzle of a gun had been shoved into his back. Flinched. Felt like something alive was crawling onto him from the gun.

"Drop your weapon, Finch. The bag, too." A familiar voice. The Partial.

"I'm here on official business," Finch snapped.

"We both know that's a lie. Drop it now."

Heard the click of the safety.

Finch dropped the gun.

"Now the sword. Undo the belt. Let it drop."

Finch obeyed, trying to breathe slowly, not let panic take him. What moment should he choose? *This one? The next?*

The sword made a dull clank against the floor. The slap of the belt leather.

The gun muzzle withdrew from his back. "Now turn and face me."

He turned. Fast. Meant to rush the Partial. Get under his guard. Too late. Saw the Partial's gun coming down for far too long. The thin white wrist behind it. A thudding pain in his forehead. The buttery light became death-white, intense. Then faded out.

* * *

He woke facing the window and the lantern, the end of the couch to his right. Tied to a chair. Wrists and ankles burned from the tightness of the rope. Shoulders ached from having his arms wrenched behind his back. Head throbbed. Could taste blood. The jacket with the piece of metal and the vial had been tossed to the side.

The balcony was empty. So was the kitchen. What he could see of it. A series of knives had been set out on the counter. A pot of water boiled on the burner. A hammer had been tossed onto the couch.

Tested the rope, but it just bit in deeper. Tried rocking, but could tell he'd never get to his feet. He'd just fall over.

Heard footsteps. Winced. Expecting Heretic and the *skery*. But only the Partial walked into view. Started rehearsing lines in his head.

"Hello, Finch," the Partial said. He'd brought a second lantern, placed it to the side.

The same sneer. Same recording eye. Same ugliness. As thin and pale as something dead.

"I've disabled the cameras in here, Finch," the Partial said. "I've told the other Partials to give us some privacy, too."

"Why? We're on the same case," Finch said. "Untie me and we can go our separate ways, no harm done."

The eye clicked and clicked. The Partial moved to his left. Finch could see the gun now. Held in the Partial's right hand. A nasty hybrid. An older Hoegbotton revolver altered to fire fungal bullets. The faint red-green tips of the bullets naked in the barrel. Seemed to breathe as they expanded, contracted.

"You should have checked the bedroom first, Finch. You would have found me," the Partial said. "But I'm not surprised. You've been very sloppy. Take the shoot-out at the chapel. A lot of my people died there."

"That was Heretic's decision, to send us there. And this is still an open investigation. I'm the lead detective on it. Untie me and I won't mention this to Heretic."

"But it's not open, Finch," the Partial said. "You closed it yourself. I have your final report. Or bits of it. It doesn't mention a lot of things. Killing Wyte, for example."

Making Stark eat a memory bulb.

"Wyte was dying," Finch said. "It was a mercy."

"Convenient you weren't at the station when the bomb went off."

"I wouldn't call it that." Struggling with the ropes. Getting nowhere again. Had to get free. Reach the pouch. Help Shriek.

"When does Heretic get here?"

"Interesting question, Finch. When will Heretic get here? He's already been here. With his fucking *skery*. I killed them both."

"What?" At sea. In a new country. One where he didn't know the rules.

"You may be stupid, Finch, but you're not deaf."

"I don't believe you." And he didn't.

The Partial put the gun down. Picked up the hammer. Leaned forward. Brought it down on Finch's left knee. Fracturing pain. Finch screamed. Cursed. Jerked up and down in the chair.

"Fuck! All right! I believe you. I believe you." Rode through the aftershocks.

The Partial said, "It's easy enough to kill a gray cap. If you can just find a way to push them off a five-story balcony. It's all about breaking down what's inside them. Just pretend they're a sack full of meat and wineglasses. Then imagine that crashing down five stories. Banging into fire stairs. Smacking hard against the pavement. There's a good chance they won't get up again. It's the damn *skery* that was the hard part."

Pointed to the corner nearest the kitchen. Finch saw something long and black. Half-hidden by the drawn-back window curtain. Still twitching. Relief that the *skery* was dead. Followed again by panic. No time. There wasn't time.

"Imagine this, Finch," the Partial said. "Those things were going to *replace* us."

"Untie me. Untie me and I'll leave. Like I was never here."

The Partial slapped Finch across the face. It stung, but nothing like the pain in his knee.

"Bad idea, Finch," the Partial said. Went over to the kitchen. Took the pot of water off the burner. "I think that's hot enough."

"Why are you doing this? Why kill Heretic?"

"You know, Finch, we're almost on the same side," the Partial said, cheerily. Pulled up the side table. Set the pot on it. A hissing sound.

"I don't understand," Finch said. Still in shock.

"Heretic's a disappointment. All of his kind are. Traitors to our cause. Not committed to it, Finch." He went back for the knives. "They can travel by uncanny means. But won't tell us how. They can make spores do whatever they want. But won't tell us how. We only get to be walking, talking cameras. That wasn't the deal. Now they plan to abandon us. Having first made us. Heretic said as much. And I am not interested in letting it happen."

"I still don't get it."

The Partial looked for a second like he would slap Finch again. Instead, he placed the knives on the table. Next to the pot of water. "They're bringing more of their kind here. They've already begun to abandon us. We have no orders. We're having to create our own purpose, our own orders. Because they don't care anymore. They have no need of us. Any more than they need Unrisens like you."

"Is that what you call us?" Trying not to look at the boiling water. The knives. The hammer.

The Partial sat back. "You should thank me. Heretic would have killed you outright. But I want you alive. I want you alive to tell me what you really know. To tell me what Heretic would never tell me. What you've found out. All those times you went missing this week. Where I couldn't see you."

"I don't know anything that can help you."

The Partial frowned. "That's not true. I think you're just stalling. Maybe you still don't really believe me about Heretic. Maybe you think he's going to come walking through that door."

"No, I believe you!" Anticipating the hammer.

But the Partial stood up anyway. Got behind Finch. Pulled his chair around until he was facing Shriek's body under the blanket.

Stooped. Pulled the blanket away.

Revealing Heretic, and a couple of pillows. The hat missing. A head stippled with tiny mauve mushroom caps. His neck twisted. His face crumpled and torn. Eyes closed. One of his feet was on the wrong way. As if he'd fallen from a great height.

From a suffocating distance, Finch heard the Partial say, "See? Just like I told you."

Heard someone say, "Where's the body? Of the dead man."

Heard the response through the singing of the blood in his ears:

"Oh, we destroyed that yesterday. Too big a risk to their plans. Heretic's orders. When he was still giving orders. We spread the ashes over the base of the towers."

Then, thankfully, the Partial was hitting him with the hammer again.

And he was losing the thread again.

Going under.

Going deep under.

SATURDAY

I: Try to see it from my point of view. Because I'm trying to see it from theirs. They've got a vision that's extraordinarily deep and wide. A long view.

F: How you must admire that.

I: Does an ant mourn the passing of another ant?

F: Maybe. I don't know.

I: They see everything, everywhere, over thousands of years. And they work with spores and things smaller than spores—on a microscopic level. What's it to them if they reduce a life from a macroscopic to microscopic level. To its different parts. It's just life in a different form. Nothing's been killed. Nothing's ended because something else has begun. I find it liberating. If only they'd kept their word.

F: Does that excuse them?

I: After all you've done over the past week, Finch. Do you really think *they* need an excuse? Believe me, it's nothing personal. Now, I'm going to have to hurt you again.

1

Woke to a sack over his head. Woke to the Partial whittling a tattoo into his leg. Woke to his own shrieks. Wondered if the Lady in Blue had spirited him away. Waking and drugging him. Waking and drugging him. *Never lost.*

And always, the Partial asking him questions. *Who was Ethan Bliss? How did the doors work? Had he met the Lady in Blue?* Kept answering sideways, but after a while didn't remember what he'd said. Or not said.

After midnight. Maybe. Pitch black except for the lanterns. Except for the pale face of the Partial.

Part of his mouth didn't work right. Jutted out. Swollen. His vowels came out slurry. Couldn't feel his feet or hands. A kind of mercy. Because early on the Partial had cut off one of Finch's toes. Had busted up his knee again. Cut a slit in his right cheek that bled into his mouth.

"Confess," the Partial kept saying. "Confess."

Was he ready to confess? And to what? Duncan Shriek was dead. The mission dead with it. Changing his name, leaving Crossley behind, now seemed as pathetic as the plan to revive Shriek. What had he been doing but playing sides off against each other? Buying time working for one, working for the other. For what? More of the same? Maybe even less of it. And if he confessed that, would the Partial do more than blink in confusion? Half the time the Partial wanted information. Half the time he just wanted to inflict pain.

The Partial said, "My name is Thomas. You should call me Thomas. That's my name."

Laughter gushed up from deep inside Finch at the absurdity of that. Laughter he couldn't stop.

"I confess," he said. Screamed it. As the Partial went back to work.

The chair slowly rocking, rocking back and forth.

* * *

Rocking. Rocking. Back and forth.

Finch sat on the upper deck of a houseboat in the Spit. From the towers across the bay, green fire gathered. It leapt out at them. Became huge and sparkling over their heads. Burned into boats all around them. Splintered timbers. Sent up waves of flame. A fire that never seemed to reach them. And yet was inside him.

Wyte and Finch's father sat on a whitewashed bench opposite him. His father was the hunched-over specter he'd been at the clinic, in the last days. Coughing up blood. Wyte was, mercifully, as he'd been before the vainglorious charge from the chapel.

"Getting close," his father said.

"Getting close," said Wyte.

"Hang on," his father said.

"Soon it will be your turn," Wyte said. "Will you be ready?"

"Ready for what?" Finch said.

"Never lost." Now it wasn't Wyte sitting beside his father, but Finch as James Crossley. Youthful. Neatly trimmed beard. Eyes bright with confidence. The James Crossley who'd worked as a courier for Wyte.

Finch smiled. "It's been a long time since I've seen you. Could've used you earlier, James."

His father had disappeared. Duncan Shriek was sitting next to James now. Flickering in and out like a faulty bulb.

Finch stared at them both. While the Spit burned down around them.

Shriek said, "You can't survive much more of this. You've got to find a way out."

Finch grinned painfully. With each new bolt of green light another part of him was disintegrating. Falling away.

"Easy for a dead man to say. I'm still in the world," he said.

Something was calling. Some noise was exploding in his head.

"You'll be back," Shriek promised, fading into darkness.

Woke, finally, to the sounds of combat. Rockets. Gunfire. The recoil of a tank blast?

Through the window, through the blood in his eyes, Finch saw intense flashes of light. Nothing like the gray caps' spore clouds. Or their fungal displays. That light was more like a mist. This was harsh and sudden. Unforgiving.

Blood tickled his throat. The Partial had taken teeth. Each a raging agony in his mouth.

The Partial sat on the couch, tapping his foot. He'd turned the chair so it faced him.

Finch laughed. An unhinged laugh that ended on too high a note. Thought, "Could the interrogation be getting to the fucker?" But had said it aloud. The Partial crept behind him. Felt a soft sawing around his numb hand. A sudden flowing release.

Still the rockets went off. So they must be real. Not hallucinations.

No one's coming for me. No one.

The Partial placed Finch's bloody pinkie finger on the table. It looked like a white worm.

"Don't disrespect me again," the Partial said. Breathing hard. Something almost sexual in the way he swallowed. Let the tip of his tongue show through his teeth. "Or there's more where that came from."

A chuckle or the low sound of a moan? "Only eight, or nine. But I won't. I won't. I won't. Just untie me. I can't feel my hands. I can't feel my legs."

The Partial ignored him. Which meant slapping him a few times.

Nothing he'd told the Partial had stopped him. Nothing. Not once. Not any more than Stark had stopped Finch. Saw Bliss at the table in the Photographer's apartment, carefully creating the vial of liquid. Saw Sintra's face against the wall as they made love. Rathven's hesitant smile at their detective joke. None of it mattered anymore.

Began to cry. To weep. Slumped over. Head leaning toward his lap.

"Oh, there's nothing to cry about, Finch. Nothing at all," the Partial said. "We're just having a conversation. A kind of meeting of the minds. If it makes you feel any better, those sounds you hear—they're your rebels, Finch. They've abandoned you. They're attacking the tower. It won't work, but I almost wish it would. Except there's no place for me in their new world, either."

"I'm sorry the gray caps. Betrayed you." Mangled the words. Parched. As if he could drink forever and not be satisfied. But the Partial had only given him boiling water.

"Are you?" the Partial asked. "Really? Because all I ever got from you before was contempt. An aura of deep contempt."

"Not contempt. Ignorance."

"Ignorance?" Incredulous.

"Of what. You had to go through. To become a Partial."

At some point during the interrogation, if that's what it still was, Finch remembered consoling the Partial. Couldn't keep it straight in his head. His brain felt like it was outside of his body. Exposed and raw.

"It's nice of you to pretend," the Partial said.

If I ever get free, I am going to put out your eye with my hands.

Another flash. A recoil. But the attack seemed blunted. The explosions of light less frequent. Saw the Partial's serious, pale face in the half-light.

"I've told you all I know," Finch said. "Anything you needed to know." But not Sintra. Not Rathven. Not the Lady in Blue. Hadn't given them up. Still, couldn't be sure anymore.

She said she'd have watchers on me. She lied.

The Partial ignored him. "Don't worry, Finch. We're almost to the end. Almost to dawn. Just another couple of hours. You might even make it."

Couldn't help himself. "Fuck you. Fuck you. You psychotic little prick. You cock-sucking psychotic bastard. *You fucking coward!*"

Thrashing in his chair until it fell over onto its side.

Silence then. Waiting.

The Partial lowered himself against the floor next to Finch. Looked him in the eyes. Said, "We'll keep going until I see all of you. *All of you.*"

Finch tried to spit in his face. All that came out was a trickle of blood.

Am I dying? Is this what death is like?

The rest dissolved into a kind of distant burning.

A kind of despairing, raging ache.

* * *

Back on the Spit. On the roof of the houseboat. Dusk now, the sun almost gone, but lingering.

The Spit smoldered. Thick with flame and smoke. The towers were silent. From that angle, he couldn't see what lay between them. But strange birds flew out between them. Like parrots, but different. Flashes of green-blue-orange. Beyond that, the city, in an agony of bronzing light.

Opposite him on the bench sat Duncan Shriek. This time he had a long gray beard, white hair down to his shoulders. His beard writhed, alive. His overcoat wasn't made of cloth at all. Concealed a mountain of a body, reminding Finch of Wyte. No shoes. Shriek's feet seemed to blend into the wood of the floorboards as if rooted there. His image flickered in and out. Could not seem to settle into flesh and blood.

"Hello again, Finch," Shriek said.

Finch, bitter: "They burned your body. Spread your ashes over the towers. You're *dead*," Finch said. "You failed us. Thousands and thousands of people are going to *die* because of you." Angry at himself.

Shriek said, "Your body is shutting down, Finch. You cannot take more torture. You have to do something. All I can do for now is numb the pain."

Finch's legs were on fire. He couldn't put out the flames.

"There's nothing I can do."

Shriek pulled him close. Until his face was inches from Finch's. Drawn into the power of those eyes that were both more and less than eyes. Into the magisterial force of the experience and pain there. "Find a way. And when you've done it, *drink the vial you brought with you*. Even if you do kill the Partial you'll die there on the floor, otherwise."

"The Photographer said the vial is poison."

"It is. But it's life as well. You'll die, and then I'll bring you back."

"You can't do anything," Finch said. "You're just in my head."

"So are you," Shriek said.

He picked Finch up by the shoulders. Raised him high. Pushed and released him in the same motion. So violently that he was sent flying over the city. Where Shriek's hands had touched him, a healing numbness. Spreading.

Below, the fires crackling on the Spit were snuffed out. The black smoke turned white and then broke apart. Still he soared, over the twinkling green of the Religious Quarter, over the dull white remains of the camps, over everything.

So this is how it ends. How it really ends. But at least it ends.

Woke to darkness. Woke to blood caked around his eyes. To a broken nose. To the knowledge that his bowels had loosened. That he'd pissed himself. Dribbling hot down his thighs, itching through the numbness. Was able to move his legs a little. A veil now between him and the pain. It registered as an even, serrated glow around his body. No part of him hurt more than any other part. Allowed him to concentrate. Gave him energy.

"Not done with you. Not the right answers." Mumbled like a prayer from somewhere in front of him.

Right eye was swollen shut. Opened his left enough to squint.

The Partial's face was up close through that slit of vision. The abyss of the fungal eye. The orange lichen of the other. The stark white landscape of that face. Staring at him. A hand shaking him. Trying to see if he was still alive.

Too close.

The gun was on the table. The knives were on the table.

Erupted hard up and out. Caught the Partial on the chin with the top of his head. A grunt of surprise. Of pain. Finch fell on top of the Partial. Legs still too rubbery. Brought his forehead hard onto the fungal eye. Could feel it give. The Partial screamed. Tried to push Finch off of him. Battered his sides with his fists. But Finch felt none of it. Bit into the Partial's left cheek. Pulled back. Spit out the flesh. The Partial shrieking. Finch kept smashing his head into the right side of the Partial's face. Until the eye socket sagged and the Partial was moaning. The beating of hands at Finch's sides now more like the wings of a bird.

Finally, the Partial stopped moving. Maybe he'd been saying

something. Screaming something. Finch didn't know. Didn't care. The warm glow that surrounded him muffled sound. Muffled everything but itself.

Was the Partial dead? He would be. Finch picked up a knife off the table with his mouth. Positioned it between his teeth. Knelt. Bent his head to the side. Came down hard. Jammed it hilt-deep in the Partial's throat. Got out of the way as the blood came quick and heavy. The Partial convulsed once, twice, back bucking. Then nothing.

The pain was coming back. Everywhere. The veil fading. He backed up to the table. Got his hands around a knife. Tilted it downward. Cut himself free after a minute. Didn't care what he had to cut through to do it.

Stumbled past the Partial. Past Heretic. To his jacket. Found the vial. Opened it. Stood there, trembling.

The Photographer had said it was poison. Bliss had said in liquid form it would rejuvenate Shriek. Shriek was gone. But the figment in his mind had been right about one thing: one way or the other, he was going to die without help.

Downed it in one gulp. Tasted like dirt and chocolate. Sprinkled with some sharp yet familiar herb.

Fell heavily to the floor. Sat there as the energy left him. As his wounds laid him out flat on his back. As he gasped. Every inch of his body crying out in an endless agony.

2

Finch and Shriek stood in the cavern by the underground sea. In front of Samuel Tonsure's one-room shelter.

"You're a hallucination," Finch said. Wouldn't look at Shriek. "I'm dying. I'm having a conversation with myself."

Shriek said, "Remember how Wyte had Otto inside of him? In a different way, you have me inside of you. I entered your mind when you ate my memory bulb."

Something had lived inside of Wyte. When it came out, Finch had shot it. Then sliced it apart as it squealed.

"That's impossible."

"Do you *really know* what's impossible anymore?" Shriek asked. "Are you in a position to have an opinion that means anything anymore? You will still die there, on the floor, Finch, if you don't believe in me." Felt an immense pressure in his skull. A kind of pulse. "That's me," Shriek said. "Me, trying to get out." His eyes burned with a deep and abiding fire. "I was still regenerating. Healing. But I altered the memory bulb. I encoded it with a copy of me. When you ate it, I entered your brain. If my body had lived, if the real me had lived, I would have eventually become less than an echo. A stray thought. An impulse for tea instead of coffee. Unexpected sadness or joy. You would have carried me, decaying, for the rest of your life. But that didn't happen. They've killed me and I'm all that's left. Now it's my mission."

Tea not coffee. The strange surge of energy during the shoot-out. Sadness or joy. Emotions not his own. Not Crossley's, either.

"There is no mission now."

"You're wrong, Finch. Very wrong."

Finch, disgusted: "Like Wyte and Otto. I'll die and you'll come out of me. Like a fucking parasite."

Shriek frowned. "No. Not like Wyte and Otto. Not like that at all. Otto ate Wyte from the inside out. I'm just a passenger, gone soon enough. If you help me."

"Help you do what?"

"Manifest in the real world. Become flesh and blood. Complete the mission while there's still time."

"But you're just a . . . an *imitation*."

"It's not the best way. It's just the only way now."

"My mind's playing tricks on me."

"Listen to me, Finch. It was Bliss who found me in this cavern. Who brought me to the rebels. I wasn't even human anymore. I wasn't, in any sane sense, alive. I had learned so much about the world that I had decided to withdraw from it. If I could come back from a hibernation of so many years, then maybe you'll understand why a copy of me might be able to re-enter the world."

Bliss again. On the walls of Zamilon. Finding Duncan Shriek. Bending the ear of the Lady in Blue.

"When I wake up, you'll just be a memory of a dream."

"You're not hearing me. *You won't wake up*. Your body is shutting down."

"Then take over. It's a weak enough machine," Finch said with self-contempt. "How can I stop you?"

Shriek waved his hand. They stood on the battlements of Zamilon. No one there but them. Cold and windy. Out in the desert: shadows gathering.

"I can't force you. It would take too much time. We don't have that kind of time. You'd die first. And right now the Lady in Blue is holding off the invaders at Zamilon. She's waiting for a miracle. I'm that miracle."

"And if I said no? If I said no, you'd just fade away and this would all be over?"

"Yes."

Thinking again about Wyte. About Stark under the influence of Wyte's memory bulb. *At what price?* And: *You knew you might die. Why aren't you willing to do this?*

Because it's not real.

Looked out at the green lights beginning to appear. Above, the blurred gleam of stars obscured by dust.

"It's up to you, Finch," Shriek said.

"How do we do it?" Finch asked. "I cut open my own head and you pop out?" *And what happens to me then?*

"It's nothing like that," Shriek said. "Nothing like that. You open yourself to me, and then I open myself to you. Then you sleep for a while. When you wake up, I am out of you. I can feed off of moisture. Off of the air. What I take from you will be no larger than the weight of a baby. And I will do the rest. Then we go our separate ways. You'll never see me again." *Except when I look in the mirror.* "I know you're afraid. But what happened to Wyte was invasive. Hostile. He had a parasite inside of him. Something made possible by the gray caps."

This isn't invasive?

The green lights were closer. He could almost make out the forms of the creatures gathered out there in the desert. Waiting to take Zamilon for themselves. Who could say their cause was any less just? The Lady in Blue didn't even know what they were.

"How do I know you're not hostile? I 'open up' and you take over."

"I won't. I promise. I can't. It wouldn't last for long."

"What's the risk if I say yes?"

Shriek hesitated. Then said, "I won't lie to you. It's a sacrifice. I will be doing things to your body to make my own. Stealing from your tissue. Robbing you while you're already weak. You won't be the same afterward. Even after you recover from the torture. You'll have dizzy spells. Headaches. You may not sleep for a while. When you do sleep, there will be nightmares as your mind flushes out my memories. But you'll be setting me free. And I won't take it from you unless you let me."

"You're saying it'll almost kill me."

"And heal you, too," Shriek said. "In the short term, I can make your flesh knit faster. I can shield you from the aftershock of what the Partial did to you. And a part of you will always be with me. Even after you die, you will live on because I will still be alive." Shriek grinned, showing his teeth. "I'm hard to kill."

Lost time. Lost worlds. A man who had lived for more than a hundred years, only to die in a crappy apartment as part of a larger game by a species that had come from a place so distant they'd spent centuries trying to find it again.

A giving up. A giving in. That's what Shriek was offering him. It tempted him. He had nothing left. Nothing of worth. No master plan. No better life waiting. Just his own death. Too much for him, and too little, standing there on the battlements of a place re-created by a passenger in his brain.

Finch searched the face of the dead man for honesty or deceit. Saw himself reflected back.

"How do we start?" he asked.

"For you, it's easy," Shriek said. "A mental trick. Just think back to the time when you went from being Crossley to being Finch. Imagine that instant as exactly as you can. Every detail you can remember. While you concentrate on that, I will enter through the 'gap' created. That's as simply as I can put it . . . The rest you won't feel."

A hopeful expression on Shriek's face.

The thought that maybe this was happening in the seconds before his death. That the last week had taken place in a single moment in his head. That none of it was real. Even the parts that seemed real. Those least of all.

Finch shuddered. Closed his eyes.

"Let's get this over with."

* * *

The creation of John Finch happened at night. Cold for once. The flares and tracers of battle over the darkened skyline. The roar of the tanks. The gunfire of attacking infantry. A percussive music playing all over southeast Ambergris. Near the Religious Quarter. Heavy losses for the Hoegbotton side. A series of tactical mistakes.

They stood on the street behind the clinic, him and his father. Next to a burning trash can. His father was a hunched figure who kept coughing up blood. By then his father had been very sick.

John Crossley had a folder full of documents for his son. James had a suitcase stuffed with identity cards, certificates, incriminating photographs. Had checked John Crossley into the clinic under the name "Stephen Mormeck." Someone they'd picked out of the phone book.

A clinic in Frankwrithe territory. Because of the rash of refugees. Because F&L had less reason to hate John Crossley.

"Is there anyone you want me to contact?" he'd asked his father.

A shake of the head, the great mane of gray hair. "No, no one. Make a clean break. For both of us." A gruff laugh. By then, he was self-medicating with whisky early in the day. That night next to the trash can, John Crossley had been drunk for two days.

But his eyes were clear. His arm steady as he handed the folder to his son. "Everything you'll need. For John Finch. Including a way to rejoin the Hoegbotton Irregulars."

Two years before the Rising. Six months after Hoegbotton and Frankwrithe had joined forces against the gray caps. Five months since his father had been denounced as a Kalif spy and they'd had to go on the run. The posters were everywhere. One of a row of traitors.

"I didn't do what they say I did. Not the way they say I did it. I never got anyone killed. I never . . ."

His father had never told James how they'd come to be betrayed. Which of the many people who had come to the house in the valley over the years. And James didn't have a clue, because his father kept pushing him further and further away from that part of his life.

James reached down, opened the suitcase. Felt the click of the clasps against his fingers. "It's all here. Every last document. Every last photograph." From the old house in the valley. James had gone there earlier that night, snuck in. Returned to the clinic in an army truck, along with a few other civilians with ties to Hoegbotton's trading arm. Wyte had stood watch for him, then gone out the back way and melted into the night. Wyte knew every street in the city. He'd have been back home with his wife before midnight.

Two in the morning now.

"What are you waiting for? Start shoveling this stuff into the fire," his father said.

Still, he hesitated. Watched the smoky flames rising into the darkness, the sparks mimicking the flares in the distance.

"If we burn all of the photographs, I'll forget what you look like."

His father didn't miss a beat. "But not who I am. And if you don't do it, there's no clean break, son."

His father reached down, picked up a handful of documents and IDs. Shoved them into the fire. Which flared up for a moment.

"This is the best way." John Crossley had said it a dozen times that day.

Anything else of value that couldn't tie the son to the father had been put in a storeroom on the edge of the merchant district. A neutral area. James could retrieve it at any time. The whisky. The cigars. The books. The map. The ceremonial scimitar his father had gotten while fighting against the Kalif. *"Keep it hidden, son, but use it when you have to."*

After a moment, James joined him. Started tossing handfuls into the flames. Photographs from the offensive into Kalif territory. John Crossley on a tank. In a window. Walking through the desert. Old journal entries. Even the little tobacco pipe he'd shown James as a youth.

"They'll never forget, never forgive, no matter who the enemy is, son. Better just to start a new life. Be someone else."

They'd never talked about his betrayal. The son had felt that asking would have meant admitting that the father had done something horribly wrong. He didn't want to let that into their world.

"Is there anyone you want me to contact," he'd asked his father. "No, no one," the old man had insisted.

When the suitcase was empty, James stood back. Beside his father. Watched the flames die down. Then hugged his father close. Sour breath. Shaking arms. The rasp at the back of his throat. Knew he was going to lose him soon.

"Welcome to Ambergris, John Finch," his father whispered in his ear.

3

Still dark when he woke, except for the lanterns. Except for a hint of gray from the window. He lay on the floor. Felt hungry. Thirsty. As much as he'd ever felt in his life. Hollow, too. As if he were made of spores. Would blow away. Over all of that, the constant complaint of his nerves. Reporting pain. Everywhere.

The Partial lay facedown beside the gray cap. Arms out to the sides. On the table, the bloody knives, the pot of water. The empty vial.

He sat up and saw himself, naked, propped up on two elbows opposite. Feet almost touching. Shock. Sudden horror. Even in the dim light, the same dark hair. The rakish yet thickening features. The solid build on the edge of fat. But Shriek's features rose out of his own. The cheekbones a little higher. The eyes different. This other Finch had green eyes. This other Finch had a strange smoothness to him, a blankness. None of Finch's scars had manifested on him. Few of the wrinkles. Finch shuddered. Shriek-Finch looked like a man who had reached middle age without the physical signs of experience.

"The resemblance will fade," Shriek said. "I'll be able to take any form I like, soon." A scratchy voice. As if getting used to his vocal cords.

Shriek rose, and Finch rose with him. An imperfect reflection. Shriek held himself differently than Finch. Shoulders hunched from some invisible weight. A stare less guarded. More expressive hands. Light gathered around Shriek in unnatural ways. A gentle iridescent strobing rippled across his body. It reminded Finch of the starfish in the cavern by the underground sea.

"How do you feel?" Shriek asked.

"I feel light . . . and yet heavy," Finch said. Could sense Shriek's overlay lifted from his mind. Its presence only confirmed by absence.

While all of those things he'd thought himself numb to came rushing back in with a near-fatal intensity. Sintra. Wyte.

Teetered on the edge of an abyss.

Shriek's voice brought him back: "Let it wash over you. Let it wash out of you. It's not real. It's like a dam breaking."

Finch nodded. Vague resentment: How could Shriek know how it felt?

Shriek wrapped his nakedness in the blanket. Muted the strobing. A shimmer across the face. The arms.

"What now?" Finch couldn't stop staring at himself.

"Just what Bliss gave you. Just that."

The piece of metal was still in his jacket pocket. He handed it to Shriek.

Shriek nodded. "Perfect."

Perfect for what? An unease in Finch. That he hadn't thought it all through. An urge to pick up his gun and shoot Shriek.

A spark in Shriek's eyes that originated there. Not a reflection from the light.

"What *are* you?" Finch asked.

A low, wheezy laugh from Shriek. As if his lungs were filled with spores.

"Just someone who knows too much."

Finch watched Shriek assemble the metal strip. Must've been some button or other mechanism hidden in the symbols. Because in Shriek's hands the strip of metal clicked, and like some kind of magician he began to pull more metal out of it. Until he had a length of metal as tall as a man. As tall as Shriek.

"Whoever created this also created the doors," Shriek said as he worked. "But I've never found them. Granted, I was more interested in the gray caps."

"Where did you find it?"

"Bliss found it. Somewhere far, far away."

Bliss, again. Finch beyond surprise.

"What does it do?"

Shriek pulled it sideways, with a motion almost like pulling apart something soft, crumbly. A piece of bread or a biscuit. A frame began to appear.

"It focuses my abilities. Like a lens."

When he had persuaded it into a rectangular shape, roughly door-like, Shriek knelt. Pressed the frame into the air like he was hanging a painting.

Let go of it.

It didn't fall. Made a snapping sound and it stayed there. About two feet off the ground. No flicker or waver. Static. Solid. Still. An intense but narrow gold-green light invested the edges of the metal. Made the symbols glow. The space inside the frame continued to show the window beyond it.

"It will be a minute or two before I can leave," Shriek said. *Finch said.* As Finch had watched, it had almost been like watching himself do it. A ghost watching its body move about the apartment.

"What happens next?" Finch asked.

"I complete the mission. Time doesn't work the way we think it works. Not really. I'll go into the HFZ to pick up the trail. From there, I will journey years and worlds away and return. An army gathered with me. I will be the beacon, the light, that guides them."

Words came tumbling out Finch hadn't known were there. "Why? Why do it? What does it matter to someone"—*something*—"so old. Who is so . . . removed"—*alien*—"from all of this."

The intensity of his need to know shocked him.

A sad, lonely smile. "The truth? None of my books ever changed anything. Nothing I did changed *anything.* I always tried, and I always failed. But Bliss helped me to see that failing a hundred times didn't mean you had to fail every time."

"And you trust Bliss?"

"About this? Yes. Even if I am just an echo, this is the last chance."

"It's too late to put things right," Finch said. "Too much has gone wrong." Ruined neighborhoods. The vacant stares of the people from the camps. The fighting in the streets. The effects of decades of near-constant war.

"As much as they can be put right, Finch," Shriek said.

"And after? What then?"

Shriek's dark gaze, from a dark place. The rectangle hanging in the air like a magic trick. A terrible power. Something in between.

"After? After, I'll be gone. Somewhere. Everywhere. Nowhere. A pile of ashes at the base of the towers . . ."

"And I'll still be here," Finch said. It came out like an ache.

Shriek, forceful: "You are a man who did the best he could in impossible circumstances. That's all."

After Shriek left, he would be alone. Terrribly injured. In an apartment with two dead bodies. In a war zone.

The door lit up. Became a reflecting mirror.

"I'm leaving now, Finch," Shriek said.

"Wait!" A last burst of curiosity. "Tell me what happened. How did you end up in this apartment?"

Shriek's features softened. "I tried something dangerous. Something impossible. I tried to use the nexus at Zamilon to go back in time. I tried to change the past so I wouldn't have to change the future. But you can't do that. And the past caught up with me. The attempt almost killed me."

The door had begun to hum. An intense white light shot from it, silhouetting Shriek. The hum became a kind of unearthly music.

"And the gray cap?"

"He got caught in the door I'd made."

"What does that mean? I don't know what that means," Finch said.

"You might ask yourself who Samuel Tonsure really was," Shriek said. Then nodded at Finch, and stepped through the door. Disappeared into the light.

The light went out.

The rectangle clattered to the floor.

The metal fell in on itself.

Just a bar of metal again, as before.

Finch knew he would never be able to make it do what Shriek had done. Knew that he would never see Shriek again.

4

Sunlight. Warm against his battered face. Curled up on the couch. His ankles and wrists seemed made of broken glass. Could feel the fragile bones shifting. Sending the glass up into his arms, his legs. His whole body hurt. Ached. His jaw was sore. Couldn't feel his nose anymore.

A vast and formless rush of city sounds from beyond the window. Sporadic gunfire. The thud and shift of something heavier. Like a giant striding across Ambergris. But distant. So distant.

Someone had applied field dressings to the stumps of finger and toe using torn fabric.

Tried to get up. A hand held him down. A voice he knew said, "Don't get up yet." The accent more pronounced. As if she were no longer acting.

An arm propped up his head so he could drink from a cup of water. It tasted good. Even though he had trouble getting it down. Even though it mixed with the blood inside his mouth.

Sintra's face came into view. He looked up at her with what he knew was a stupid, childlike dependence. Everything stripped away from him. Couldn't raise his arm far enough to wipe his eyes.

"Just lie there," she said. An oddly clinical concern in her voice. She wore forest green. Camouflage pants and shirt. Brown boots made out of something soft. A long knife sheathed at her waist. A rifle in the crook of her left arm, muzzle pointed toward the floor.

"Sintra," he said. Turned his stiff neck to follow her as she got up for more water. Saw again the bodies on the floor. A moment of disorientation. A man and a gray cap. Looking like they'd fallen from a great height. Except the Partial, face down, was sporling the remains of his fungal eye out across the floor. An army of tiny, black, fernlike mushrooms with golden stems had traveled from the eye to colonize the back of his head.

A croaking raven's laugh at the unexpected sight. Even as he realized there'd still be a recording there, somewhere, in the mess.

Tried to say to Sintra, "How did you find me?" Wasn't sure it came out right.

Sintra gave him more water to drink. Perched beside him on the armrest. "The city is catching its breath this morning. There is no one in this building now. Not a single Partial. No eyes left in this apartment. Their attention is elsewhere."

"How did you know? To look here."

Her voice from above him, matter-of-fact: "I've followed you here before."

"When?"

He felt her shrug. "I've followed you everywhere. Especially the last few months. Before the towers started firing on the Spit. I have followed you so much I know more about you than you do." Not said like a joke. More like she was weary of it. Tired of being a shadow.

The words lay there, in the sunlight. Finch picked over them again and again. Didn't find what he was looking for.

"Did you kill them?" she asked. Motioning toward the bodies.

"One of them."

"But not before he got to you." Said it like he was a problem to be solved. Like a threat.

Finch thought for the first time about the sword on the floor. Looked toward it.

His own gun appeared in her hand. Again.

"Finch . . ."

"Are you here to finish me off?"

"No, just to stop you from doing anything stupid." She held out a pill to him. "You'll feel better if you take it. Maybe long enough to get back to your apartment."

Took the pill gladly. Willingly. A test both of him and of her. Swallowed. A vague warmth spread through his limbs.

The old absurd idea crept up on him with the warmth. *It still isn't too late. We can get out of Ambergris. Cross the river. Make it to Stockton or Morrow* . . . Readying himself to make the argument again. That if they left together they could leave their old selves behind, too. But he couldn't get the words out. Dust on his tongue. To say them would mean he was delusional. That he was pursuing a ghost.

"What happened to the man who was here before? Your case?"

A deep, shuddering breath. "First, tell me the truth," he said. Had no cleverness, no deception, left to him. "Whatever it is."

She considered the question for a moment.

"We work with the rebels sometimes, in exchange for other favors. Who was the man in this apartment? Was it Duncan Shriek?"

"Who is 'we'?"

"The dogghe. My people. Who was the man in this apartment?"

The dogghe. The Religious Quarter. She was part dogghe, part nimblytod. Had no known address. Came to him in the night. Seemed to move around the city with ease. Of course she worked for the dogghe.

"Yes, Duncan Shriek," he told her, because it didn't matter anymore. "Someone who is an expert with . . . doors. Why me? Why not Blakely or Dapple. Or even Wyte?"

The words still came out slowly. Mangled. It took her time to recognize them and respond.

"You had no record up until two years before the Rising, John. That made us curious . . . What was Duncan Shriek's mission?"

"To stop more gray caps coming through. What were your orders with regard to me?"

"Coming through what?"

"The towers. Was it always that way? Between us?" *From the beginning?* An ache now that wasn't from his wounds. A slow-motion treachery. A life concealed.

"Finch, what can you tell me about Ethan Bliss?"

"I *loved* you." Let go of the words now, while she couldn't really see his face. When it didn't matter anymore. He had nothing to say to her about Bliss.

Her slow response: "And I liked you, John. I really did. I wouldn't have slept with you, otherwise. No matter the mission."

A childish bitterness, but he was too weak to keep the poison out of his mind: "You left behind some of your notes once. I had suspicions, but I never went to the gray caps with them. I never told anyone."

A mistake. He could feel the retreat in her words: "You might never have had to find out. We could have continued having our fun. The mystery of it. You liked that very much, I know. But a normal life? Like regular people? We aren't regular people. We were playing roles."

"What roles?"

Her voice took on a harshness that he knew shielded her as much as him. "You were the protector. I was the exotic native girl you liked to fuck."

"That's not true." Wanted no part of what she was doing.

"Isn't it? None of you really *see* us, John. Only what you want to see."

"And what do the dogghe want? What do they want out of Ambergris?"

Anger in her voice. Desire and need, too. Just not for him. "This was *our* place, John. Before your people came. Before the gray caps. And maybe it will be again."

"The rebels will never let that happen, no matter how you help them," Finch said. "Neither will the gray caps."

"Maybe they won't have a choice. Maybe this time we will just *take* it."

Saw it now. In the chaos of conflict between gray caps and rebels and the Partials. The dogghe might hold on to the Religious Quarter. If they were lucky. If others weren't.

"I won't answer any more of your questions," he said. "You already know the answers, I think."

He sat up. Took her in while he still could. A beautiful but tired-looking woman in her early thirties. Hair messy, face long and pinched from stress.

"Did your father ever recover?" he asked.

"What?" The question, after all the others, seemed to take her by surprise.

"From his trauma. Did he recover?"

She looked down, away from him. "Yes, he did." Was that a tremor in her voice? "He's passed on now, but he had as good a life as anyone."

He reached out, touched her shoulder. Her skin warm. Like he remembered it.

She clasped his hand. Eyes bright as she met his gaze. "Clean yourself up. Find some place safe to be, Finch. The next time I see you, I might be forcing answers from you. And I really wouldn't like that."

He nodded.

A flash of those green eyes. She put his gun down on the table. "I'm leaving it for you, but I'm taking this." Held up the metal strip Shriek had used. Unmistakable that it, ultimately, was what she'd come for.

"You shouldn't." But beyond caring. "It'll do more harm than good." *To me.*

"John, I don't think you really know the difference." Then she was walking out the door, down the hallway. Gone for good.

Finch stared after her for a moment. Then hobbled to the window. Looked out.

The towers were complete. They shone with green fire in the light. Between them, impossible scenes flashed so fast he caught only glimpses. A vast blue dome like an observatory. Replaced by a mountain topped by a tower. A city of gleaming buildings taller than any he'd ever seen. A forest of vine-like trees. A roiling sea over which egg-shaped balloons floated, trailing lines of shimmering light. And on it went. Almost beyond comprehension.

At some point soon, the scenes would stop changing. They would settle in on one scene. They would settle in on the gray caps' home.

Would he know by then if he'd done the right thing?

5

The way home. So heavy, so light, he almost didn't feel the pavement. Wearing one shoe. Only a sock over his other foot because it hurt too much. Somehow easier to hold the sword. The gun shoved into his belt. Head felt like a balloon stuffed with rags. Ached all over, with eruptions of pain in the places most sorely used by the Partial.

Through a haze, saw:

Partials gathered in a black squadron, marching toward a barricade manned in part by a truck weighted down by a cannon that had to be a century old at least. Two anemic mules whose ribs stuck out stood placidly behind the barricade. Along with the pale, uncertain faces of the defenders.

Gray caps approaching, at their back a huge cloud of spores, gliding and shifting, a thousand shades of green. Of red. Of blue. Suffocating the street. A last few stragglers running out before them, anonymous in their gas masks.

The huge drug mushrooms transformed. Hoods drawn down to the ground, the red surface once so soft become hard as brick. Wavering lines of green energy sparked from their minaret-like tops. Shot out toward the green towers. Gray caps stood watch from tiny circles of windows. Across the sides of each stem, unending repetitions of the symbol Shriek had carried with him on the scrap of paper. Over and over again in a kind of madness. No flow of food or drugs now. No pretense of even caring. Just a sense of waiting. For what?

He took a side street, then an alley. Crept through a courtyard and walked into an apartment complex as a shortcut. Kept his face turned to the wall. If someone wanted to kill him, they could.

Finally reached the hotel steps. The madman lay sprawled there. Someone had slit his throat. His arms were thrown out to either side as if in welcome. Just another body. Already a sly fringe of tiny green-and-white mushrooms had sprouted up through his pant legs, his shirt, his face. In another day, he'd be a fucking flower bed.

Next to the madman's left hand Finch saw a little round carving. He picked it up. Crudely drawn, but unmistakably Stark's face, with its sharp features. The deep-set eyes.

Rathven telling him, "You have to choose a side, Finch. Eventually you have to choose a side, even if you pretend to be neutral. Even if you think giving out information is like selling smokes or food packets."

Through his fuzziness, a terrible thought.

Dropped the carving. Hobbled fast up the steps.

At Rathven's door. One more time. Only it was open now. Had forced the Lewden Special into his left hand, over the bandaged finger. Held the sword in his right.

Hobbled inside, trying to focus his fading attention. Through the hallway. Entered the room ringed by bookshelves. In one chair, facing him, Bosun. He'd abandoned his custom-made revolvers. Held a fungal gun on Rathven. Her back was to him, but he could see her raised arms. The glint of her own monstrous revolver. A standoff.

"You are fucking late," Bosun said. "We've been waiting for a while."

Didn't reply. Just walked around until he stood to the right side of them both. Bosun's bald head was bloodstained. Other people's blood? A yellowing bandage over his shoulder where Finch had clipped him. A nervous tic working its way across the corner of his left eye. Wore a dark shirt and darker pants, tucked into boots. Taken from a Partial? Some perverse form of camouflage?

Rathven was pale but composed. Gaze never wavering from Bosun. The battered old gun trembled only a little in her grip. A smell of sweat and fear came from both of them.

"Finch!" Relief in Rathven's voice. That someone was there. That she wasn't alone with the madman. "I didn't let him in. He took me by surprise." As if Finch might, even now, accuse her. Stress crackling into her voice as she glanced over. "But he didn't know I had the gun . . ." Her look turned to dismay at his condition.

"This is my fault, Rathven," Finch said. "I'm sorry."

Bosun: "Your fault? Because you didn't kill me when you had the chance?" An odd expression of sadness and contempt.

Not for lack of trying.

"No, because I ever went after you. I should've left you alone."

A snort from Bosun. "I don't believe you."

I don't believe myself.

The fungal gun complicated things. Even if Finch got a shot in first, Bosun's gun could go off in an unexpected way. Infect them both.

"Where's Stark?" he asked. Knew the answer. Had to start somewhere.

Flat, emotionless: "Gone, but you knew that. You didn't hide him well enough. I found him all crumpled up in the alley, thinking he was someone else. Then he died. There was nothing I could do . . . He's somewhere safe. For now."

A wave of dizziness washed over Finch. Let it come, bent at his knees to stop from falling. As if he were back on the boat with Wyte, heading out to the Spit to meet Stark and Bosun for the first time.

Said: "I wasn't trying to hide him. I didn't want to hurt him. But he, you, kept coming at me."

Bosun ignored that. "I came here to kill you, maybe kill her, too. I still could." In a speculative tone. Like weighing whether to skip stones across a river or keep their smooth weight in his pocket.

"You didn't bring your muscle." To remind him it was two-to-one odds.

A sharp, curt laugh from Bosun. "No muscle left. They wouldn't follow with Stark gone. Now it's just like old times. Or would have been."

Finch, in an even tone: "Why don't you just leave? No one gets hurt then. Because you'll get hurt even if you manage to take out one of us. You know that."

Could see Rathven was having a harder and harder time holding on to the revolver. Didn't want her to drop it. No idea what Bosun would do then. Even with Finch ready to put a bullet in his head.

Bosun looked up at Finch for a second. Nothing there but a low animal cunning. But unmoored somehow. The eyes older than before. "Here's a deal for you: give me the memory bulb powder and then I'll leave." Could sense the intent.

Something in Finch rebelled at that. Wyte resurrected, even as a shadow. Along with Stark and Otto. Each haunting the other inside of Bosun's mind. Dead but not put to rest.

"That might drive you insane, Bosun. All kinds of things might happen."

"He's my brother!" A shriek. A scream. Something horrible and lost rising out of Bosun. Finger twitching on the trigger. Finch saw now the incredible control Bosun was exerting over his own impulses. To kill. To strike out. Weighed against that the promise of seeing his brother again. No matter how perverse the homecoming.

Could hear Rathven's sudden intake of breath in the aftermath.

Finch nodded. "I'll give it to you." Took the last pouch of powder out of his jacket. Turned sideways, gun still trained on Bosun. Tossed it toward the open door. "All you have to do to get it is leave."

Mouth dry. Legs still shaky. Holding it together for Rathven.

Bosun: "Tell her to put her gun down. And put down your sword."

"Rathven, put the gun down," Finch said. Let the sword clatter out of his hand. Couldn't risk squatting to place it on the floor. Might just fall over.

"I don't want to put the gun down, Finch."

"Just do it. I've got him covered."

She hesitated, then, hand shaking, placed her gun on the table between them.

"Now I'll get up and move around you to the door," Bosun said.

"Be careful, Finch," Rathven said.

Bosun got up. Came around the table toward Finch. Stepping over the fallen sword.

Gun to gun. Bosun inches away from him in that enclosed space.

"Let's not see each other again," Finch said.

A map of anger and frustration on Bosun's face. "No promises," he hissed.

A hint of a movement as Bosun passed him, back to the door. A blossoming agony Finch couldn't at first identify because of all of the other pain. Then he realized it came from his side.

Knew he was reeling, losing his balance.

Bosun, at the door, stooping to pick up the pouch just as Finch realized he was bleeding. Rathven lunging for her revolver, turning to shoot at Bosun as he ran out the door. Missing. Tearing a chunk out of the ceiling. Rathven scrambling to lock the door behind Bosun.

Finch looked down to see bright red blood welling up from a cut in his side. Saw Bosun's long, thin knife there on the floor. It had been the lightest of touches. Not even a touch. A whisper.

Vaguely knew Rathven was next to him as he slumped to the ground. Felt the touch of his own sword against his exposed foot as he slid, her arms around him.

"Finch! *Finch!*" Her voice, keeping him awake when he didn't want to be awake.

She brought him close. Her body warm and solid and real. He thought she was shaking. Realized she was sobbing. Then she was pulling his shirt away from his side. Pushing something up against it. Felt something wet and sticky next to his left arm.

"What's wrong?" he thought he asked.

"You've been stabbed, Finch," he thought he heard her say. Her face way up near the ceiling, looking down. Her arms impossibly long.

A coughing laugh. "Have I?" A kind of lurching dislocation.

Rathven was wrapping something around his side. Gauze? Urging him onto his feet.

"You're going into shock. I need to get you somewhere I can help you," she said.

"I deserve better." A dry laugh. Everybody deserved better.

Lurched up, almost falling forward onto his face. Leaned into her.

Glints and glimmers in a dark pool. Past the battered, weathered book stacks. Past her little kitchen. Past her bedroom. A glimpse of green and purple. The brightness of a single bulb. Like a sentry.

A rough-hewn doorway. Water on the floor. Curved walls. Moisture. A cockleshell of a boat. Strange pale-blue eyes of mudskippers in the shallows. Glowing in the light from a lantern.

She said something to him he didn't understand. Took his arm. Guided him until he was lying with his back against the prow, legs out in front like useless matchsticks. She took off the oars, began to row.

Glimpses of roots, brick, and wood in the ceiling. His mangled hand trailing through the water. The wound in his side like a rip in a stuffed animal. All the sawdust coming out. Lulling him to sleep. Closed his eyes. She shook him awake. Nodded at her as if she'd said something he agreed with. But there was nothing left to say.

A thud as the boat knocked against something.

"We're here," she said.

Opened his eyes. Saw her tying a rope to a lock embedded in old stone steps. Beyond, a worn archway.

She forced him to his feet. Helped him up the steps.

A single large room at the top, dark except for Rathven's swinging lantern. Caught a glimpse of books, a table.

She led him to a cot at the far end. Fell heavily onto it. She asked him a question. Didn't hear her. Fuzziness around the words. Drifted. Curious about the dryness in his mouth. The way his vision kept blurring.

Said, "The towers are changing. Need to get to the roof."

Rathven saying "No," forcing him back down onto the cot.

Blinks of light and time.

Fading and coming back.

* * *

A few hours later. Awake on the cot. Looking out through his good eye. She'd cut his clothes off. Washed him. Bandaged his side. Could feel the edge of the wound like a mouth as he lay there with a towel around his waist.

He was at the back of a large room, looking toward the front and the doors. The archway. Rich, burgundy carpet and rugs worn but clean. The walls covered from top to bottom in bookcases. Every shelf was filled with books. Perfectly preserved. In neat rows. On the floor, more books. In careful piles. Beside boxes and boxes of black market supplies.

Next to him, medicine and food. Two more cots and another table. A one-burner portable kerosene stove and a pot on this second table. Along with a rifle and several boxes of ammo. His sword. His gun.

Between him and the doors: a globe of the known world on a rosewood table. Four ornate wooden chairs. Rathven sitting in one of the chairs. Watching him.

"I brought your maps down here," she said, indicating the table. "A cane to help you walk. A chamber pot. A bottle of your whisky. You need to stay here. Out of sight," she said. "You need to rest."

"Clean yourself up. Find someplace safe to be, Finch."

"What about Feral? Where is he?"

"I'll bring him later, if the boat doesn't spook him."

Outside, he could lose himself in the fight. Could join the rebels. Could join the militias. Could do something. But, overnight, he had become a broken-down old man. A pensioner well past the days of pensions. Waiting for better days.

I am not a detective.

"What about the towers? Has anything changed?"

"Nothing. Don't worry—I'll let you know."

"What is this place?"

"It's an old library," she said. "From above it's just rubble. You can't get to it. But this one room I found intact. Although it didn't have many books in it to start."

"Found the rest?" he managed.

"Yes. I brought them here from all across the city."

"Why?"

She had the look of the true believer, of someone who still had hope, as she said, "Finch, here you'll find every book I could salvage about the city. Every book by any Ambergrisian author. Every book of history, of politics. Biographies. Novels. Poetry. They're all here. Much of it knowledge that was lost in the wars, because of the Houses. Because of the gray caps. But someday, Finch, when all of this is over . . ."

Finch looked away. Ashamed by her passion when he had so little left.

"Ever afraid of being found out?"

"All the time."

"The cots?"

"Before they disbanded the camps, I'd shelter escapees here. Or people who had been released but were injured."

"And now?"

"Apparently, this is now a haven for cynical detectives."

That made him smile. A little.

She stood. "You lost a lot of blood. But I stopped the bleeding. It's your other injuries I need to work on now. I'm not strong enough to turn you over. I'll need your help."

She got gauze, bandages, and other supplies. Water from the underground channel. A kind of ritual and finality to the way she set the supplies on the table next to him. That made him shudder. Thinking of the Partial with his knives and scalding water.

She saw his look as she set a pot to boil on the little stove. "I have to clean the wounds, Finch," she said.

He nodded. "I know."

She began wiping away any blood that hadn't already come off. Ignored him when he winced. Stopped only if he cried out.

She looked different in that light. Older. Tougher. More experienced.

"I think two of my ribs are broken," he said.

"Or bruised," she said. "You might be lucky."

Tried not to scream when she washed the places where his toe and finger had once been. Replaced Sintra's field dressings with proper bandages. Cleaned his swollen eye. His broken nose.

He stared at the ceiling as she pulled the towel back and gently dabbed at his thighs. Past modesty.

"Oh, Finch," she said, betraying tenderness that had been disguised by action before. "Who did this to you?"

"A Partial."

"How did you get away?"

"I killed him . . . Will I live?"

Didn't answer. Just replaced the towel, said, "You have deep cuts on your arms and legs." She began to wash and dress the wounds. The warmth stung and comforted all at once. The smell of piss had faded. There was an antiseptic feel to the air.

"Turn over now," she said. "I need to check your back."

With a groan, he managed that delicate maneuver. Ancient, creaky, feather-weak.

"You have more cuts," she announced after a second. Her voice not quite as even. Not quite as under control. She'd stopped working. Knew she was staring at him.

"Is it that bad?"

"I've seen worse," she managed.

"Can't even feel it," Finch said. Shock? Infection? Some last blessing from Shriek?

She worked on him for long minutes. Finally, had him sit up. Wrapped bandages around his ribs. Her head next to his. Her arms stretched around him.

Slowly reached out to her. Wrapped his arms around her. Though it hurt him.

Rathven held him. Held him like a friend. Solid. Comforting.

"Why are you doing this for me, Rathven?"

"You saved my life."

"I put you in danger."

"We both did."

"I have to tell you something," he said.

"Whatever you need," she said.

Understood that she might give him more than he had any right to expect.

It was hard. Halting. But after he began, it was hard to stop. He told her everything. All of it. Leaving nothing out. Sparing no one, least of all himself. As if truly confessing. Needing it out of him.

He told her about the Lady in Blue. About how he'd left Stark.

Wyte's death. About Bliss. The Partial. How Shriek had come out of him. About Sintra. Heard his voice. Detached, normal. Wondered how it sounded to her. Rational? Insane?

She said nothing. Just held him. Listened. When he was done, she gave him water. Made him eat a little. Then gently pushed him back onto the cot. Whispered that she would bring him clean clothes soon.

He fell asleep as soon as his head hit the pillow.

SUNDAY

Fading in and out of consciousness. Restless and exhausted. A dryness to his skin. An attenuated feeling. The sense that he could blow away in the wind. Did it come from Shriek? From having given part of himself away? He didn't know.

Lying on a cot or sitting in a chair seemed like a kind of sloth. Also a kind of gnawing ache that was half for Sintra and half, perversely, for what the Lady in Blue had shown him. The sentimental thought that he had never had a chance to tell Wyte about any of it.

Strange, but when he closed his eyes he had an image of the hotel above them restored to its former grandeur. A concierge and porter in the lobby. Someone behind the desk waiting to take his key. Sintra in an evening gown. They'd be about to take a motored vehicle to the opera. The streets would be busy with merchants and people coming home from work. The buildings, the storefronts, would be bright and cheery with lights. Like it had been in those mayfly beautiful moments between wars, before the Rising.

Waiting for a bomb to fall through the ceiling. Waiting for Partials to come up the tunnel to kill or arrest him. Waiting for salvation or disaster to come tumbling out of the space between the towers.

When he couldn't stand what he was feeling, he shook the shadows from his head. Went over to the map of Ambergris and the overlay. Removed the globe and star chart to fit them on the main table. Didn't know if it was Finch or Crossley who liked working on the project. Or both.

Rathven had just left to get some more supplies. She'd told him it was Sunday morning. Ordered him to get back on the cot.

Whatever is coming through the towers, the world will change again.

Still, for now, the world had only changed a little. He used a soft cloth on the map to erase what had been lost. Slowly, with regret, removed the Spit. Knew that even if parts survived, no one lived there now. Erased the station. Removed the words "Wyte's apartment." Removed the words "bell tower." Didn't think any of the detectives would ever go back there. Each red mushroom on his map, he now changed to a symbol indicating a fortified position. Added Stark's mushroom house, whether occupied now or not. Added the towers in the bay, which he had resisted until he knew they were complete. Out of fear? He didn't know.

Question: *How could I know they would burn the body?*

Answer: *Because it would've been stupid for them not to.*

The memory bulbs he'd eaten. The feel of Sintra's body beside him in bed. The full and terrible force of Heretic's gaze. The Partial's scorn for his weakness. The look in the Lady in Blue's eyes as she tried to convince him. The ruined fortress.

Then: disrupting his thoughts, a flash of gold-green light. A fizzling, popping sound. The sounds of footsteps coming up the stairs.

Finch stood up beside his map, grabbed his gun.

Bliss appeared at the edge of the carpet. Dark smudges on his face. The ragged edges of his jacket had a burnt look to them. His dark pants had darker stains on them.

"I should be more surprised," Finch said. And he wasn't. Just scared. *Another test to pass.*

An odd dueling smugness and humility to Bliss's expression. "Rathven has fewer secrets than she thinks, and I have more. You look well."

No indication from those eyes of what to expect.

"I look like shit. I feel like shit."

"Better that than dead," Bliss said, walking into the room. "Since you're still alive, I assume the mission was successful."

"Wouldn't you know already?"

"The towers will be operational very soon. Then we'll know. Where's the piece of metal Shriek used, Finch?"

"You've healed well," Finch said, ignoring him. "Almost as if I never hit you."

Bliss pulled up a chair next to the map. "I took a vacation. Somewhere remote. Somewhere I expected would be a little less . . . exciting . . .

than it was. An enigmatic smile. "I see you are busy changing the map. A little premature, don't you think?" Bliss's features hardened. "The mission *is* complete?"

"Yes," Finch admitted. "There were complications. But it's done." Hesitant to tell him just how many complications.

Bliss nodded. "Nothing ever happens the way we think it will. Now, where's that piece of metal?"

"I have a few questions first."

"Questions?"

"I've been doing a lot of thinking," Finch said. "In between passing out. When I haven't been pissing blood. About things like whether or not you really work for the rebels. Maybe Ethan Bliss does, but not Dar Sardice."

A pause, then, as if deciding whether or not to play along with him. Then: "Very good, Finch. Keep going."

"You share information with the rebels, yes, but you don't work for them. Even if they think so."

"Excellent, Finch!" A kind of forced cheeriness. "So who *do* I work for?"

"You were Dar Sardice before you were Ethan Bliss. It's the oldest name you're known by. You knew my father. You said you worked with him. My father was deep in Kalif territory during much of the campaign. Working on engineering projects for the Ambergris army. Often shuttling back and forth behind the front lines. You met him then, I think, not after he returned to Ambergris."

Bliss gave him a look of mingled regret and triumph. "You're right, of course. I gave him that, actually." Nodded at the scimitar on the table behind Finch, beside its scabbard. "A reward for his good service. I was also your father's control in Ambergris. I ran him, along with other sources. But he was the best."

"Ran him for who?" Wanted to hear Bliss say it.

"For the Kalif, of course. Always for the Kalif. The Kalif has a long memory, Finch. And the Kalif never forgets anything. We turned your father in the desert, and he stayed turned. But you knew that."

The question he'd been homing in on, the one he'd never been able to ask his father: "Why did he do it?"

"He never told you? Why does anyone do anything? For money. For love. For our children. Because we think it's right. Your father, he met a woman. He had reservations about the war by then. He'd seen some of the excesses of the Ambergrisian army, had never felt comfortable with the power of the Hoegbottons before the war. And he'd lived in the desert for a couple of years. Observed the traditions of a culture thousands of years old. He was ready to fall in love—with all of it."

"And then what?"

An impassive gaze. "The woman died. Brutalized and killed by Ambergrisian soldiers, apparently. Her body burned in a fire." A kind of triumphant smile. "But you, Finch. You were saved from that fire. You were less than a year old at the time."

A shifting feeling in his stomach. A distant sense of confusion. Stared at Bliss across the maps. "That's a lie. My mother died in childbirth. She was from Stockton. She had no family."

Bliss shrugged. "Believe what you like. Hoegbotton, Frankwrithe—both right. Both wrong. Does it matter in the long run? Your father worked for the Kalif. As for *why*, look around you, Finch. This is a city founded on an attempted *genocide*, and everything that came out of that. The Silence. The Wars of the Houses. The Rising. This place is dangerous, Finch. Its people are dangerous. Ambergris will always need a counterweight. First through Morrow and Frankwrithe & Lewden. Now through the rebels, because the gray caps are in control. Either that, or Ambergris tries to take over the world. One way or the other. That's what the Kalif learned repulsing your offensive."

"Is that what my father believed?"

"That's what I believe. Your father believed that by playing both sides against each other he was serving a greater good. I've never been under that delusion."

Searching Bliss's guarded face for what was true. Trying to reject the idea of further treacheries.

"*You* abandoned him, then. You let him take the fall when Hoegbotton and Frankwrithe joined forces. I was there. He died alone. Except for me."

Bliss shrugged. "I couldn't stop him from being found out. Just from being *found*. Too many people on each side were talking, suddenly. But, Finch, he wouldn't *let* me help him. Wouldn't let me take him out of Ambergris. Because of *you.* And because he was dying."

"But you made sure nobody got to him so he wouldn't talk."

"I did what I could."

Something clicked. Even on the run, when his father was dying, he hadn't wanted Finch to contact anyone. *No help from anyone.* Because he didn't trust anyone.

"He didn't want you getting near me," Finch said.

"I could've found you at any time, James Crossley," Bliss said, leaning back.

"I wouldn't have worked for you. You couldn't have recruited me."

"Haven't I already?" Then shrugged. "But this is all beside the point. Where's the piece of metal, Finch?"

A gun had appeared in Bliss's hand. His regretful look said, *Just in case.*

"Maybe I left it in the apartment. Maybe you should look there."

"Maybe you should just give it to me," Bliss said. "It's not the kind of thing you want to leave lying around." Acid in his voice. A hard glitter to the eyes that chilled Finch. But it didn't stop him.

"Mostly, though, Bliss, I keep thinking about how good you are at *finding* things. You never told me that you were the one who found Shriek. Gave him to the rebels. Do you want to explain that?"

Bliss sat back, tapping his foot against the floor. "You want the truth? Shriek was dumb luck. A wild card. Something to hold in reserve. He was like a spigot once I found a way to pry him out of his protective shell. Like a man left on a desert island for a hundred years. He would've talked to anyone."

"And you found him next to Samuel Tonsure's bones, of all people. And then you 'found' that magical strip of metal. The one that wasn't made by us or by gray caps. You even found the doors before the rebels did. Did you also tell them the soldiers in the HFZ weren't all dead, just lost?"

A sly smile. "It's a skill, Finch. Finding things. Leveraging them. My goals and the goals of the rebels are the same. For the moment. Although it's a very long game we're playing here." The eyes not smiling at all.

"Where did you find the metal?"

A hiss of impatience from Bliss. "I understand, Finch. I really do. You won't be working for me. You don't care who your mother is. Your father is a hero, not a traitor. Now just give me that fucking piece of metal, or we'll do it the hard way. We'll do it the *hardest possible way*."

Finch turned away from a thought that truly terrified him. That Bliss didn't work for the Kalif at all. That Dar Sardice was just the first of the masks he knew about. That the "long game" was beyond comprehension.

The sounds of oars from beyond the open doors. Of a boat thudding up against the steps.

"That'll be Rathven," Bliss said. "Do you really want to involve her in this?"

No, he didn't.

"I don't have it. Sintra took it from me in the apartment," Finch said. Almost triumphant. Almost proud of Sintra. "There was nothing I could do. The dogghe have it now. I couldn't stop her."

Bliss erupted from his seat. Suddenly seemed twice as tall. Mouth open in an expression of rage beyond any caricature Finch had ever seen.

Flinched before it. Pushed back in his chair. Waited for the blow, but couldn't look away.

Bliss's eyes were dead. Something else shone through. Something hostile. Something alien. Like a mask had slipped. Peering out through the urbane little man's face was something *other*.

Then it was gone. Bliss was just Bliss. "No matter," he said, with a smile that cut. "A complication soon solved." But Finch didn't think it would be that easy. Hoped it wouldn't.

Footsteps walking up the stairs.

A reptilian smile from Bliss.

"You're just a spectator now, Finch. Just another pawn. But I'll leave you with this: Did you ever stop to think that maybe Wyte represents the future of this city? That maybe you're *the past.* Still living, but the past nonetheless. There will be a day you'll remember this conversation in a much different light."

Then he was walking into the bookshelves. Which turned into a door fringed with green and gold.

Which he stepped into.

And was gone.

Rathven came in, holding her gun and a disgruntled Feral.

"Was someone in here with you, Finch?" She let Feral down. The cat ran to him, rubbed up against his legs.

Finch shook his head. "Talking to myself." Leaned over to pet Feral. Felt like he'd escaped some great danger. Had come across the edge, the outline, of something that his map could not encompass. That neither Finch nor Crossley could ever understand.

Somewhere out there the Lady in Blue was readying for invasion.

Somewhere Sintra was bringing the strange piece of metal to her superiors.

Somewhere Shriek was trying to come home.

And he was in a secret room surrounded by books, petting a cat.

From far above, he heard the mutter of mighty engines coming to life. A groaning, rending roar. A rising hum behind it. A metallic scream like the cry of a raptor.

The ceiling vibrated. The floor rumbled. A plume of dust. Feral looked up, concerned.

"I was coming to tell you, John," Rathven said. "The towers are changing. The electricity is out. Everywhere."

Panic and a surge of energy. "I've got to get to the roof to see it."

She shook her head. "No, you don't. You're too weak. We can take the boat instead. The tunnel leads out to the bay."

Wincing, he settled into the boat opposite Rathven. It felt strange to be in a boat not made by the gray caps. The wood so stiff. The lack of give beneath his feet. She lurched onto the seat opposite him. Set the lantern by her feet. Two gas masks there. Binoculars, too. Feral paced on the steps, watching them leave. Rathven had left food just in case.

Ribs of light from the lantern sent across the ceiling made it seem as if they traveled down the gullet of a great beast. Cool, under the earth. Overhead, there might be violence. There might be mobs. Street sweeps by the Partials. Poisonous clouds of fungus. Almost anything. But down here, there was just the shudder from the towers.

Were they entering a new life? Would it be better than the last? He didn't know.

"They'll sing your praises," Rathven said. "If Shriek leads them back." She stared at him as if the enormity of events had finally found her.

Have I done what's best? Have I done the right thing or the wrong thing?

"They won't even remember my name, Rath."

"I will," she said.

An emotion rose up in him that he didn't think he deserved to feel.

Facing each other. Two survivors. Gliding through a dark tunnel, headed for the light.

* * *

Now Finch can see the frailty death has lent them. Now Finch can see the vulnerability. The way the light uses them in the same way it uses him . . . and looks out across the damaged face of Ambergris.

The wide expanse of the bay confronts their boat. A stiff, hot wind rising. The Spit just a trace of black smoke. The towers shambly and green to the left. Shuddering and quaking like something alive. Debris falling off of them into the water. On the right, the north shore, and the long arm of the HFZ. Agitated. Alive. A curving hand reaching out across the water toward the towers. A wave of orange-green-red spores. Already torn and jagged at the limits of its reach. Already fading back into itself.

From the towers, an ungodly roar and cacophony. Lines of light reach out from the tops of the towers into the city. Toward the blood-red mushroom stations. As if helping to hold them up. In front of the towers, the tiny shadows of rows of gray caps lined up on the bridge. As if in worship.

In that space between the towers, the gate—the door—has finally found what it was searching for.

A weak white disk in a porous pale sky, poor mimic of the sun beyond the towers. Framed in gray, gigantic living citadels rise in a swirl of glittering dust motes so tightly packed they can only be spores. Two, three hundred feet the citadels rise. Circular. Studded with tiny eyes for windows. A hundred curving causeways run between them. Rising from below, a thick forest of tendrils in constant, rippling motion. Waves of color washing across them, strobing from greens to reds to blues, and back again. Through this landscape, great beasts stride in perpetual gloom. Hunched over. Half-seen, half-heard. Cities of fungus rising from their backs.

But at the bottom of this scene, a tear or rip. Like a photograph with a flame burning through it in a rough triangle. Turning it to ash.

A green-gold door rising.

They watch from the boat as it lengthens, enlarges itself. Encroaches on the forest of tendrils. A whining sound. A kind of crackling and popping that hurts his ears. And no other sound out across the bay. Or across the city behind them. As if everyone holds their breath. Waiting for this new thing.

The background scene becomes glassy. Vague. Blurry.

The green-gold door stops growing.

The breath goes out of him, and then returns. As if he's been dead and now is coming back to life.

They come in numbers. In legions. Pouring through the door. Across the bridge, overrunning the gray cap positions like an unstoppable river, into the city. He can see them, toy soldiers, through the binoculars. A never-ending torrent running across the surface of the bay. Some wear strange clothes. Carry strange weapons that discharge violet light. Some with gas masks. Some encased in great armored suits of metal sinew and tendon. Others on horses. Some looking human. Others like Wyte at his worst. Some in motored vehicles. Others on foot. A few leading creatures he has never seen before.

The rending sound becomes louder. Vibrating in his ears. He is transfixed. She is transfixed. *People will ask him where he was on this day. He will say, "In a small boat in the bay. With a friend."*

The towers shake and shake but never fall. The men and women and things coming out from the door, their progress does not slacken. They keep spilling out, and as they do, the scene in the background becomes grayer and grayer. Like a smudge. The lines of force from the tops of the towers into the city begin to waver. Until one by one they erase themselves. Slowly. Then more quickly.

Waves now in the bay, like an aftershock. Smacking against the boat. He is holding her tight against the awful wonder of it. He is holding on to her like something familiar.

And still the rebels come, as the backdrop begins to fade. *Things* from the other side now touch that surface. Fall forward. Into the air. Their shapes that were in that other place graceful or translucent become crumpled and dark. Falling. Extinguished in the bay.

And still the rebels come. Transformed and normal. Through the green-gold door.

Something stirs in him. A hint of a feeling close to pride. Close to horror. Because he knows, and she knows, that the world has changed. And he helped change it.

It may not be better. It may be worse. But it will be different.

He's reached the end of being Finch. Of being Crossley. He's reached the end, and he has no idea who or what he will be next.

He sits in the rowboat next to her and watches the end and beginning of history.

Remembers it all.

Forgets it all.

ACKNOWLEDGMENTS

Four people read *Finch* in manuscript form and provided invaluable, often brilliant feedback. Thanks in particular for comments on pacing and logic by my wife Ann (twice, in rough draft and near-finished form), specific comments on character and situation by Tessa Kum, thoughts on Stark and the city itself by Howard Morhaim, and an analysis of and a methodology for sentence fragments (and much more) by Victoria Blake.

Thanks to Sonya Taaffe for Latin phrases. Thanks to John Coulthart for a genius-level cover and for gray cap symbols. Thanks to Dave Larsen for gun-related advice. Thanks to Matt Staggs for many kindnesses and his battery-like energy and creativity. Thanks to J. K. Stephens and Edward Duff for testing the novel's chronology. Thanks to Heidi Whitcomb and Rachel Miller for their proofing and design help.

Although I had the idea for this novel as early as 1998, it changed substantially as the result of trying to write an Ambergris story for John Klima's *Logorrhea* anthology in 2006, so thanks, John. Thanks also to the Turkey City Workshop, with whom I shared an early draft of the first fifty pages; the comments I received were crucial to determining my approach to the novel.

Thanks to all of those readers who followed me through *City of Saints & Madmen* and *Shriek: An Afterword* to this point. I truly appreciate each and every one of you.

ABOUT THE AUTHOR

Jeff VanderMeer is a forty-one-year-old, award-winning writer living in Tallahassee, Florida. Major works include the previous two standalone books in the Ambergris Cycle, *City of Saints & Madmen* and *Shriek: An Afterword,* as well as *Booklife: Strategies and Survival Tips for the 21st-Century Writer.* Recent and forthcoming books include the story collection *The Third Bear,* the nonfiction collection *Monstrous Creatures,* the humor book (with his wife Ann) *The Kosher Guide to Imaginary Animals,* and "The Situation," a graphic novel collaboration with the artist Eric Orchard. His work has also been adapted for short films by PlayStation Europe and others. VanderMeer writes book reviews for the *New York Times Book Review,* the *Washington Post Book World, The Believer,* and the *Barnes and Noble Review,* in addition to working as a columnist for Omnivoracious, the Amazon book blog. With his wife Ann, fiction editor of *Weird Tales,* he has edited a number of fiction anthologies as well as taught creative writing workshops all over the world. He is currently working on the definitive visual/textual overview of the steampunk subculture for Abrams Books. For more information on his work, visit www.jeffvandermeer.com.

ABOUT THE BOOK

In addition to *Finch,* two of Jeff VanderMeer's other novels are set in the Ambergris universe: *City of Saints & Madmen,* and *Shriek: An Afterword.* Although each of the Ambergris novels stands alone, together they form the complete "Ambergris Cycle," a vast 1,700-page story involving many of the same characters and themes, with *Finch* answering questions first posed in *City of Saints & Madmen* about the gray caps and about the nature of the city itself.

"I woke up one night from a vivid dream and the city was there in my head," Jeff VanderMeer says. "I immediately ran to the computer and typed the first several pages of the first story set in Ambergris. From there, I soon had this entire fantastical city opening up in my mind. It took fifteen years to finish all three novels. I never realized that that one moment of inspiration would lead to becoming a full-time fiction writer, or that it would consume so much of my life."

While remaining true to an overarching narrative about the history of Ambergris, each book has used the approach and style best suited to its characters and stories. The first Ambergris novel, *City of Saints & Madmen,* was a mosaic novel composed of multiple narratives that played with postmodern techniques, mixing formal experimentation with the tropes of weird, uncanny fiction. That first book used a stylized, baroque approach to language and was dedicated to the idea of book-as-artifact.

The second novel, *Shriek: An Afterword,* presented a sixty-year family chronicle through the eyes of a dysfunctional brother and sister, whose dueling voices formed the heart of the book. Although steeped in war, intrigue, and bizarre events, *Shriek* lay more in the realm of works by Vladimir Nabokov and Marcel Proust—dreamlike yet precise, chronicling the unhappy, the strange, the quirky.

Finch, by contrast, combines elements of noir, the thriller, spy stories, and fantasy, and in so doing gets to the true nitty-gritty of Ambergris. It's the first time readers have had a chance to explore the city—albeit during a time of occupation, crisis, and change—almost as if seeing what the main character sees by way of handheld camera.

Ambergris has become an iconic fantasy setting, with *City of Saints & Madmen* and *Shriek: An Afterword* translated into fifteen languages, making dozens of year's-best lists, and winning various awards, including the World Fantasy Award (for a novella from *City of Saints*) and awards in Finland and France. The books have resulted in musical and film collaborations with, among others, The Church and Murder by Death. Along with novels like Mark Danielewski's *House of Leaves* and China Miéville's *Perdido Street Station*, VanderMeer's Ambergris Cycle has redefined the possibilities of fantastical literature.

* * *

MURDER BY DEATH'S *FINCH* SOUNDTRACK

In a unique cross-pollination of media, the band Murder by Death has recorded a CD of music inspired by the novel *Finch*. This CD, which takes several scenes from *Finch* as the spark for extended songs, can be purchased via the band's website at www.murderbydeath.com and is also available with Underland's limited edition of the novel. VanderMeer listened to the entire Murder by Death back catalog while writing *Finch*, and it was a substantial influence on the novel's mood and tone.